Destiny Reborn

Karen Pugh and Linda Fagala
Writing as PF Karlin

PF KARLIN PUBLISHING
SUGAR LAND, TEXAS

ISBN: 978-0-9890247-3-0
Library of Congress Control Number: 2014958205

Destiny Reborn

By Karen Pugh…a.k.a. PF Karlin
Linda Fagala…a.k.a. PF Karllin

Copyright © 2015 by Karen Pugh and Linda Fagala
Writing as PF Karlin

All rights reserved. Except as permitted under the U.S. Copyright Act of 1976, no part of this publication may be reproduced, distributed, or transmitted in any form or by any means, electronic, mechanical, photocopying, recording, or stored in a database or retrieval system, or otherwise, without the prior written permission of the authors and/or their designated representatives or heirs. Any portion requested for use must be done so by contact via post mail to PF Karlin Publishing.

All photography used in the production of this book:
Copyright © 2015 by Linda Fagala and Karen Pugh.

Book cover design:
Copyright © 2015 by Linda Fagala and Karen Pugh.
Cover layout assistance by: Lane Simmons

If you are in possession of this book and it is without a cover, front or back, this book may have been stolen. And if stolen and/or reported as "Unsold or Destroyed" it may have been reported as such and that information stored in a data base.

Published by:

PF Karlin Publishing
Sugar Land, Texas

This is a work of fiction. Characters, places, and events portrayed in this book are either a product of the authors' imagination or used fictitiously, with the exception of certain towns and locations which were used to provide the reader with a sense of locale of the story line. Any similarity to actual places, events, or persons, living or dead, is coincidental and not intended by the authors.

ISBN: 978-0-9890247-3-0

Library of Congress Control Number: 2014958205

Printed in the United States of America

ACKNOWLEDGEMENTS

We owe so much to our families, friends, and fans for helping us muddle through to the completion of our second romance novel. Our intention was to end the love story of Belinda and Robert with this book. However, the encouragement we received has spurred us to write a third book, Fulfilling Destiny, in a series we now call the Kismet Collection. We have plans to add at least two more novels to the collection.

We extend a special "thank you" to our Beta Readers, **Joyce Combs, Jennifer Cordova, Lauren Millet-Costanza, Heather Combs,** and **Nancy Kaminsky** whose insights helped to improve our story.

As with Shattered Fate, the cover would not exist if it weren't for the computer wizardry of **Lane Simmons** and his ability to manipulate graphics like magic.

And a big "thank you" to **Brian Fagala,** who assisted us with the formatting and layout. Through his mentoring, we have improved our technical skills...a little.

Last but not least, many thanks to all of our readers, whose encouraging comments and reviews have been invaluable to us.

Destiny Reborn

CHAPTER 1

DARKNESS HOVERED EVERYWHERE and the silence…deafening.

Old memories of her car accident, nine months ago, flooded Belinda's mind that reminded her of the first time she had experienced this sinking feeling. She had fought for her life against the fogginess, but the darkness had won and dragged her into a coma.

Now she sensed herself lifting instead of sinking. She was awakening.

Her mind raced, suddenly filled with the remembrance of Robert's voice saying her name. She was at a New Year's party and just before the clock struck twelve midnight, a warm hand came to rest on her shoulder, causing her breath to hitch. In that split second, an all-too-familiar arousing stir ignited a memory. She recognized the touch as her Robert's, Robert Pennington, the man she'd dreamt of and married while in the deepest recesses of her coma.

The memory lingered—the last thing that happened before she fainted—the glimpse of a tall, attractive man who resembled her Robert. A warm sensation stirred deep in her stomach from the anticipation of what she just realized. Her pulse raced. The thought of finding Robert excited her, but it also scared her. She wondered if she could possibly be dreaming again. And if not, would he be like her Robert and want her?

As much as she prayed for this man to be him, it couldn't be because when she awoke from the coma six months later, everything she'd grown to cherish in her fantasy world vanished, including her beloved Robert.

Over the past months, she had suffered the stabbing pains of grief in her heart countless times, having to learn to live without him since he'd been only a figment of her imagination. Now, all that remained of him was the memory of a wonderful life her mind created so near to death.

Holding her breath, Belinda moved her fingers ever so lightly over the textured, patterned fabric at her side. The plush material felt nothing like the stiff, scratchy hospital bedding she remembered. She concentrated on the softness of the object beneath her head and imagined it could only be a goose down pillow.

She exhaled. *Thank God, I'm not in the hospital.*

Her palms moistened as she took deeper breaths. Her mind swirled, bouncing around, trying to make sense of what was happening....Had she just encountered a real version of Robert...*but how?*

***

"Belinda...Belinda." A soft voice dispersed the silence. "Belinda, can you hear me?" The voice grew louder. "Belinda, wake up." She recognized it as her best friend, Abbey Barnett.

She fought off the heaviness and tried to focus. A warm sensation encompassed her right hand, followed by an occasional pat on top. It comforted her. Raising her eyelids to slits, she glanced from side to side and found herself lying on what appeared to be a king-size poster bed in a low-lit room.

"She's waking up." Abbey's tone sounded bubbly. "Belinda?"

Turning her head toward the voice, Belinda opened her eyes. Abbey sat on the edge of the bed, a huge smile spread across her face.

At Abbey's side, Garrett stood peering down at her. "Belinda, you scared the hell out of us. Do you feel okay?"

"What happened? How did I get here?" She scanned the room and noticed the arrangement of the traditional, mahogany furniture, the ocean blue and gold color scheme, and the accessories. Her pulse sped up. They were shockingly similar to the furnishings in the Penningtons' master bedroom in her dreams.

"The last thing I remember is..." Belinda's gaze froze on a figure dressed in a black tuxedo at the foot of the bed. She trailed her eyes up the tall, lean body to his lips, his blue eyes, his dark hair, finally taking in his entire gorgeous face. A hitched breath caught in her throat.

My Robert?

This Robert's eyes had the same warm, hypnotic appearance as the ones Belinda remembered so fondly from her dreams. A rush of desire to embrace him shot through her causing a faint quiver. She wanted to reach out and touch him, but thought it might scare him away. He didn't know her and might think she belonged in a nut house. Belinda never took her gaze off him, half-afraid he'd vanish.

"You fainted." Abbey squeezed Belinda's hand.

She pulled it away and motioned with a wave for Abbey to come closer. "Do you know who he is?" Belinda nodded in Robert's direction.

Abbey hovered near her ear and whispered, "Yes. Robert Pendleton."

Pendleton? Pennington? How close they are!

"No, no. Did you ever meet him before tonight?" Belinda asked, voice slightly strained.

Abbey stiffened and leaned back. "No, tonight was the first time."

Belinda furrowed her brows as she glanced at Robert and then back at Abbey. "Robert Pendleton...and you've never met him before tonight?" In her dream, Abbey knew Robert. Now she needed clarification from her best friend to be sure she wasn't still dreaming.

"No, tonight's the first time. I swear." She covered her heart. "Let me introduce you to him." Abbey flipped her wrist pointing toward him. "Belinda, this is Robert Pen-dle-ton."

An army of jumping beans hopped around in the pit of Belinda's stomach while she forced a smile.

Abbey poked one of her fingers toward Belinda. "Robert, this is my best friend Belinda, Belinda Davies."

He maintained his straight posture, smiled and nodded. Robert showed no sign he had ever seen or met her before.

She maneuvered her elbows under her, propping herself up, to scrutinized him better. He stood with his thumbs hooked in his pants side pockets, pushing the jacket back.

She gave him the once over before breaking the silence. "You said my name. Do you know me?" The sound of her name flowing like silk from his lips and the exhilarating feeling of his touch had burned their way into her memory from their encounter as the New Year chimed in.

Scanning the other occupants in the room, Robert started with Garrett, and then Abbey and back to Belinda. His gaze slipped down to just below her wreath necklace. With a sudden shake of his head, he refocused on her face. "My mother told me."

Belinda peeped down at herself. She saw how much her position caused her breasts to bubble out of the bodice. After nudging Abbey to move back, she sat up on the edge of the bed.

"Abbey, would you two mind leaving the room for a few minutes? I need to talk to him. Alone."

This man standing in front of her didn't act like he knew her, and why would he? After all, she'd made him up in her head, but she wondered if he'd be willing to talk.

Abbey leaned in closer and whispered, "Is that him?"

Belinda shrugged. "I don't know. I just met him too."

Abbey rolled her eyes. "You know what I mean. Does he even look like him?"

Belinda paused, and then nodded.

Abbey backed away and let out a gasp. "Oh my God!"

A gentle knock followed by the opening of the bedroom door interrupted the conversation. The hosts of the party, whom Garrett had introduced to her before she fainted, entered the room.

"Oh good! You're awake." Sandra Pendleton, the woman Belinda recognized as Robert's mother, smiled at her. "You had us worried. Are you feeling alright?"

"Yes ma'am. I'm fine. Sorry I fainted. I hope I didn't cause any problems for your guests." She shuddered, imagining herself lying on the floor with everyone gawking at her. *How embarrassing!*

"Oh, no. Robert caught you and carried you in here before anyone even noticed something happened."

Relieved her fainting spell hadn't caused a scene, she kept it to herself that the shock of seeing Sandra's son had caused her to faint. She tilted her head at him. "Thank you…for catching me."

"My pleasure." One corner of Robert's mouth turned up.

"Honey, we're glad you're alright. If there is anything we can do, let us know." Mrs. Pendleton reached for her husband's arm.

Belinda nodded. "I will. Thank you."

Robert started to follow his parents out. Belinda called to him. "Robert, can I talk to you?"

With his back to her, he froze. He turned his head partially to the side and nodded.

Belinda directed her attention back to Abbey and Garrett. "I need to talk to him. Could you give us a few minutes alone?"

Abbey swooped down close to Belinda's ear. "You two acted like bunnies in your dream. Can I trust you with him?" She pulled back.

Belinda stared dumbfounded at her friend. *Does she think I'm going to hump his bones right here and now?* She grabbed Abbey's shoulder and pulled her close to whisper in her ear. "I only want to talk to him."

Abbey looked over her shoulder toward Robert and gave him the once over. Nodding her head, she stood. "Surrre." Abbey latched onto Garrett's forearm, led him out into the hall, and closed the door.

Robert Pendleton fought an irrational urge to run. At the same time, it took every ounce of control he had not to go to the blue-eyed beauty. Her long, golden brown hair glistened in the light. He wanted to entangle his fingers in it. To feel its softness.

The presence of others in the room had required a sense of decorum. Now he questioned if he could continue the control. The sensation he'd had when he touched her made him hot and full of desire. His heart had accelerated to the point he thought it would jump right out of his chest. He couldn't logically explain why she affected him this way. She was a stranger at his parent's party. She captivated him, but strangest of all, he sensed an unexpected connection.

Robert knew one thing—he wanted more of her. He wanted to reach out and stroke her beautiful, angelic face. He wanted to feel her full lips on his—to taste her. Aw shit…he wanted to strip her naked and take her.

His thoughts scared the crap out of him. He crossed his arms over his chest, tucking his hands under as they clenched into tight fists, his fingernails digging into his palms. Regretting his decision to be alone with her, he felt small beads of sweat form on his brow.

Leave! Leave the room now! Just go for the door and run! But his feet didn't move in that direction. Instead, he walked over to the satin-draped window. There he stood—staring out, confused and wondering what the hell he was doing.

Robert's cell vibrated in his jacket pocket but he ignored the call. He knew who it was and would call her back later.

Oh God! What is wrong with me? I can't, no, I shouldn't be having these thoughts—these feelings. For God's sake, I just got engaged tonight. I need to stay away—this woman could be big trouble for me. Only a couple of hours earlier, he'd asked Karen, the woman he'd been dating since July and with whom he thought he'd spend the rest of his life, to marry him. Now, he found himself wanting to bed a perfect stranger and knew if Belinda gave him any encouragement, he might not be able to stop.

Belinda gazed upon Robert's silhouette and a sense of longing swelled inside her to the point of pain. He reminded her in so many ways of the Robert from her dream. He ran one hand through his dark brown hair, the other planted firmly on his hip. The tuxedo hugged his form making his broad shoulders more than she could resist.

She rose from the bed, walked over and stood behind him. He didn't move and seemed oblivious to her close proximity. She couldn't refrain from touching him any longer. Her breath quickened as she raised her hands, hovering them over his shoulders for a few seconds. Slowly, she slid them down the back of his tuxedo-clad back, feeling the firmness of his muscles as he tensed under the gentleness of her touch. He lowered his arm, and, to her surprise, stood there allowing her exploration. Her breathing seemed to stop as her heartbeat sprinted. She slid her arms around his chest and hugged him while she laid her head against his back. Air rushed from his lungs with every breath he took. Inhaling deeply, she took in his masculine scent of musk with a hint of some spice, and sighed. Belinda tightened her arms attempting to experience every essence of this living, breathing version of her Dream Robert.

Robert closed his eyelids. He knew he'd lose his battle to stay away from her. Looking over his shoulder, he turned to face her.

She released her hold and reached up around his neck. Robert placed his arms around her waist, their eyes never faltering, until Belinda took a deep breath, closing hers. Tilting her head back, she exposed her neck and submitted.

Robert could hardly catch his breath, his mind a haze of overwhelming lust. He wanted her and his confusion didn't stop his next move. Cautiously, he bent down and placed one kiss on the soft, warm curve of her neck. A hot sensation surged through him, just like when he had touched her shoulder, except underneath his desire something else touched the deepest recesses of his soul. Something he'd never experienced before. The combination of his unexplained attraction and the new feeling compounded his longing. He tightened his grip, pulling her closer as he feathered kisses up her neck. His blood boiled with every gentle touch of his mouth against her flesh.

Soft moans escaped her lips with the first kiss. Her body tensed and arched while he skimmed his lips up her neck. The overpowering hunger for her shocked him.

Belinda gasped, remembering how Robert's touch had excited her in her dream. But she noticed a vast difference between her dream and the sensation she now experienced. The undeniable reality made it more powerful and ignited a strange new feeling that ran deep, touching her soul.

She entwined her fingers in his hair, adhering to him. What she wanted the most—his lips—she found. As they crushed their mouths together, a pleasurable electrifying tremble surged through her.

Belinda let him guide her backward toward the bed until her legs collided with the mattress, toppling them with Robert sprawled on top. Gripping her tighter around the waist, he helped her over the brocade comforter to the middle of the bed, their lips never breaking contact.

Her back arched as he placed soft kisses on each side of her mouth. Air rushed from her lungs and she wove her fingers through his thick hair. She pulled him close, not intending to stop him from doing whatever he wanted. The connection with the Robert in her dream heightened her senses, and the surge connecting her to the real-life version made her toes curl. She wanted to devour every inch of him.

Robert found himself responding wildly as their kisses became fast and feverish. Belinda parted her lips and he plunged his tongue in, exploring, and then caressing and twisting around hers. She locked her fingers in his hair, holding him close while he savored her taste. He groaned deep in his throat as their tongues danced around one another.

Robert pressed against her willing body and she reacted, molding herself to him. His sexual need for her blazed out of control as his body responded to her hip movements against him. Her moans excited him, pushing him nearly to the edge of losing all control. He reached for his jacket to slip it off, but the vibration from the phone snapped him back to reality. That brief moment gave him the reminder he needed to separate himself from this woman before he had them both stripped naked.

He drew back, abruptly ending the kiss. Out of breath, he pulled away and supported himself on his arms. His mind and body were fraught with desire and confusion as he peered down at the woman who lay beneath him. A stranger, and yet, he wanted her.

"I...I can't do this." He studied her for another brief moment before he sprang off the bed. He stuffed his hands into his pockets and paced back and forth, trying to control his desire to reach out for her—to touch her. To save his sanity, he needed to run from her as fast as he could, putting as much distance between them as possible.

"I can't do this." Robert hurried to the door and reached for the knob. Why did she have such a pull on him? He couldn't help but glance back.

Belinda sat up. She slid over to the edge of the bed and clenched the comforter with tightly balled fists. "Please, don't leave."

The sound of her distress incited a need to comfort her, to protect her. Unable to stop himself, he walked over, knelt in front of her, and spoke in a tender voice. "Angel, I can't now. I have to go."

She gasped and clutched her throat. Robert stiffened, stunned by her reaction and his own words ringing in his ears. *Why on earth did I just call her Angel?*

He stood and rushed back to the door. Bowing his head, Robert stared at the doorknob and spoke without thinking. "I'll get your number from Garrett and call you." He never looked at her again before leaving the room, closing the door behind him.

He couldn't believe how he had reacted. For a few brief moments he had an overwhelming impulse to make love to the woman he just met. His heartbeat quickened at the mere thought of what he'd experienced. Leaning his forehead against the door, he placed his hand on the doorknob and tightened his grip. Just a twist of his wrist would put him back in the arms of that sensual, willing creature.

But opening the door would make him a cheater and a liar. Hell, he'd just asked a wonderful woman to marry him and she deserved an honest man. He prided himself on his honesty, and knew he loved Karen, but now he was questioning himself.

It took every ounce of willpower not to go back into the room. He drew in a deep breath to gain control and then pulled it off the knob as if it seared his flesh. He felt his integrity being tested and wondered why in God's name he told her he'd call her. That would never happen. No, the safest thing for him would be to put distance between them as fast as he could.

He turned to leave just as Garrett and Abbey entered the hall.

Abbey stopped mid-stride and stiffened. "Is everything alright?"

"You should take her home. She seems tired." Robert briefly slowed his pace as he passed. "It was nice meeting you, Abbey. Goodnight. Goodnight, Garrett." Once out of the hallway, he increased his strides, not slowing again until he reached the back patio door.

***

Belinda gasped for air and could hardly control her breathing. She heard muffled voices coming from the hallway and assumed Robert and Garrett were talking. Then the voices went silent.

Seconds later the door opened. Belinda stared through tear-filled eyes at Abbey and Garrett as they entered. Abbey rushed over and sat next to her on the bed.

Garrett shifted from foot to foot before he inched his way toward the door. "I'll just go say good-bye to the Pendletons and get our things so we can leave."

After Garrett's departure, Abbey leaned back. Noticing Belinda's disheveled hair and dress, she asked, "So, what just happened?"

Belinda answered breathlessly, still dazed from her array of emotions and Robert's unexpected response. "I'd rather not talk about it now."

***

Robert ran out the back door to his car to avoid as many guests as possible. He didn't even take time to tell his parents of his departure.

He slid into the driver's seat and grasped the sides of his head. "What the hell is going on with me? With her?" He needed to get a grip on himself. Karen would be furious if she caught the slightest hint of what he'd just done.

Pressing the ignition button, he remembered the avoided calls and checked them. They were both from Karen, but he couldn't talk right now. He needed to get a better grip on his emotions. She knew his moods. When she traveled and they spoke on the phone, she could tell if something concerned him by the subtle changes in his voice. No, if they talked now, she would certainly know something bothered him. He needed the time the drive would give him. Besides, he had another problem. Having been gone so long, he'd missed what should've been his first and only New Year's kiss.

He headed back to the party at Karen's parents' house. Gripping the steering wheel, Robert struggled to keep his mind on driving. Questions filled his head. *What does this mean? Why now? Why couldn't I have met Belinda a few weeks ago before I decided to ask Karen to marry me?*

Robert's feelings for Karen were nothing like the passion he'd just experienced with Belinda. They had a comfortable relationship based on respect. The sex was good, really good, and she was there for him, willing and able whenever he wanted her. Yet what he sensed with Belinda was so different. Besides being lustful and hot, it seemed deeper. He had connected with her from the first time he touched the soft skin of her shoulder.

His arousal swelled just thinking about Belinda and he knew he needed more time to calm down. He couldn't walk into his future in-laws in his present physical and emotional state. So he took the next right off the beltway to drive the feeder road, which would take twice as long, and turned his thoughts to work. If anything could get his mind off his present condition that would.

He pulled into his future in-law's circular drive and saw Karen standing inside in front of the window. His heart grew heavy from guilt, watching her smiling face as she waved. Drawing air into his lungs, he made his first New Year's resolution—to forget about Belinda. He wasn't willing to hurt Karen. During the lowest point of his life, she stood by his side, and his loyalty lay with her.

As Robert walked into the house, Karen rushed over and threw her arms around his neck, planting a very sweet kiss on his lips. He pulled her tight, but it bore no resemblance to the heart-pounding emotions he experienced with Belinda. *Keep her out of your mind*, he reminded himself while he kissed Karen a bit longer, clearing his thoughts.

"That's your New Year's kiss you missed. What took you so long?" Karen looked upset and her voice confirmed it.

"Sorry, Baby. After talking with the client I went to see, I started talking to some other associates and lost track of the time." She accepted his excuse without a reaction. That meant he pulled off his deceit. He forced a smile and changed the subject, feeling guilty he just lied and Karen's kiss was his second for the New Year. The old year ended with an engagement to one woman. The New Year began with him passionately kissing a stranger. Now also feeling like a cheater, he pushed the thought out. "Let's get back to celebrating."

"Our engagement?" Karen's face lit up as she gave him a peck on the cheek.

"And that too." He gave her a squeeze, keeping up the ruse.

Robert offered Karen his arm. She latched onto it and rested her head against him, nuzzling her nose into his jacket. Her chest rose taking in a deep breath. She inhaled again. Pulling back from him, she furrowed her brow. "Is that perfume I smell?" Her nose wrinkled, sniffing again. "When did your mother start wearing Angel Scent?"

Caught off guard, Robert just spouted out the first thing that came to mind, and hoped it would satisfy her curiosity. "Oh, Mom said she'd like to have some. So I bought it for her." Karen lifted a brow, but didn't comment and led him into the party.

***

Belinda noticed the glances Garrett and Abbey kept flashing at each other as they drove her home. Their non-verbal communication made her feel guilty. She could tell they weren't sure what to say or even if they should say anything. Belinda appreciated that they didn't pry. Instead, she stared out the window, replaying her time with Robert. She lowered her eyelids and let the thrill grow inside as she began to fully realize she'd been in a passionate embrace with Robert—a real person who looked and felt even better than the Robert she fell in love with in a dream.

The car came to a stop in front of her home. Garrett jumped out and opened the back passenger door. Before Belinda climbed out, she reached over and placed her hand on Abbey's shoulder. "I'll call you tomorrow. We can talk then."

Abbey covered Belinda's with hers. "Belinda, he didn't hurt you did he?"

"No, no. We'll talk tomorrow."

After exiting the car, Belinda gave Garrett a quick kiss on the cheek. "Thank you." She knew he had done all he could to help in this damn uncomfortable situation.

Garrett glanced at the ground. "I won't leave until you get inside."

As Belinda made her way to the front door, she dreaded having to face her mother. She prayed Dora had gone to bed early, but expected that wouldn't happen. It wasn't in her mother's nature. Belinda knew she'd want all the details tonight. So, the light shining from the family room was not a good sign.

Belinda alternately balanced on each foot as she hooked a finger in the heel straps of her shoes to remove them. With both dangling from her fingers, she tiptoed as quietly as she could across the foyer to the stairs. She glanced into the only lit room. Her mom had fallen asleep on the couch. Relieved, she proceeded to the stairway in the darkened entry. Belinda started up the stairs hoping her luck would hold until she reached her room. Once behind the sanctuary of the closed door, she would be safe from her mother's "twenty questions," at least for the remainder of the night.

She took one stair at a time until an ill-placed footstep caused a loud squeak to free itself.

"Belinda, is that you?"

Crap! She froze and looked in the direction of the family room. "Yes, Mom. It's me. I didn't realize you were down there." She squinted and swallowed hard, praying.

Belinda watched Dora sit up on the edge of the couch and yawn. "Come here and tell me how the night went."

She knew the real meaning of the invitation was to divulge every detail. "Mom, not tonight, I'm exhausted. Can we talk over breakfast?" Belinda held her breath, waiting for her mother's reply, hoping!

"OOOkay….Good night, Honey."

Belinda let out a sigh of relief. "Good night, Mom."

She ran up the stairs to her room, shutting the door behind her. Feeling safe but tired, she prepared for bed and slid between the sheets. "Brrr." A shiver raced through her as her skin made contact with the cold fabric. She drew her knees up to her chest, yanked the covers up around her neck and prayed sleep would be fast and restful, but that didn't happen. Robert wouldn't let her find solace in her dreams.

CHAPTER 2

BELINDA'S NOSTRILS FLARED. Aromas of eggs, bacon, and coffee, filled the house, beckoning her to the kitchen. Expecting to smell pancakes shortly, she knew exactly what her mom had on her mind. Dora always used Belinda's favorite breakfast to get her out of bed so she could pump her for details. She buried her face in her pillow to block the wonderful smells, but her growling stomach wouldn't give her any peace until it had food. Rolling onto her back, she took a deep breath.

"Blast my mother!" she grumbled under her breath. Belinda wanted to lie in bed and run the events of last night through her head again. She now felt grateful everyone had encouraged her to go to the party. If she hadn't, she might never have found Robert.

A low, rolling rumble deep in her stomach seemed to go on forever as she picked up the scent of the pancakes added to the mix. "Blast my mother! Blast her!" she uttered in frustration. No longer able to resist the hunger pangs, Belinda pushed her thoughts of Robert aside. After a quick stop in the bathroom, she pranced downstairs to face her inquisitor. She loved her mom dearly, but her ability to rapidly fire questions annoyed Belinda. Dora was a pro when it came to prying for information.

Dora stood at the stove about to flip a pancake as she turned and glanced at Belinda. "Good morning, Honey. Did you sleep well?"

Belinda shrugged and grimaced, walking over to pour herself a cup of coffee. "Would you like one?" Her mother smiled and nodded. Belinda carried the cups to the table and slipped into a chair, braced for the onslaught of questions. Dora placed two plates of bacon, eggs, and stacks of Belinda's favorite food, pancakes, on the table and made herself comfortable, sitting across from her daughter. Belinda's mouth watered from the smell alone and she could only hope to get some of the food down before she had to fill her mother in about the eventful night.

"Where's Dad?" She poured syrup over her buttered pancakes.

"Oh, he went across the street to help Jack with his car. But I think it's just an excuse for him to stay awhile, and later have a few beers and watch football." She stopped slathering her pancakes with butter and shook her knife. "Those two haven't a clue what they're doing when it comes to cars." They both laughed.

"I agree. It's all for show and football," Belinda added.

Belinda cut the stack into pieces and took a bite. The temperature felt just right as the culinary mixture passed over her lips. Savoring each slow chew, she swirled the soft, syrupy delight with her tongue. At just the right moment, she swallowed. *This is heaven!*

Another stab filled the fork. About to indulge her taste buds, she hesitated. Belinda realized she could have some fun telling her mother about the party, right after a second trip to heaven. The pancakes went into her mouth and once swallowed, she planned to stop her mother cold with the bomb she was about to drop.

The two liked to banter. It had become their pastime that both practiced whenever the opportunity arose. Belinda loved that about her mother. Dora had a good sense of humor and made her laugh. She wondered how her mom would react to the information she had tucked up her sleeve. Either way, she knew this would be a very interesting conversation. She also knew not volunteering any information would drive Dora nuts. So she decided to make her mother work for it, and see how long it would take for the "rapid fire" of questions to begin.

Belinda managed to down several more bites and take a sip of coffee before the first question came.

"So, did you have fun last night?"

Belinda answered with a simple, "Yes," and continued eating. The pancakes were so tasty and hot, she savored her next bite.

"Were there lots of people there?"

"Yes." *Wait for it!*

"Was there lots of interesting food?"

"Yes." *Wait for it!*

"Did Abbey look nice?"

"Yeah." *Wait for it!*

"How did her dress look? Did she wear her hair up? Did Garrett have a tux on? How big was the house? Meet anyone interesting?"

Bingo! Rapid fire! Belinda smiled at her mother and sat back in her chair. "Slow down, Mom. I can only answer one question at a time." She stared at her mom and snickered, attempting to control her need to laugh. Dora stopped talking and snickered back at her daughter. Within seconds, the pair burst into laughter.

Her mom sat back in her chair. A huge smile spread cross her face. "If you would just give me some information like any polite human being engaging in a sensible conversation, I wouldn't have to ask so many questions!"

Belinda widened her eyes. She shook her head and giggled. As requested, she would engage in a sensible conversation and give her mother the information she desired, information that would shock her to the core.

***

Belinda began to compartmentalize her memories into three realities after waking from the coma. Everything she experienced before the real accident, which put her into the coma, fell within her "Old Reality." Her life with Robert took place in her "Dream Reality" during the coma. Anything she experienced after the shock of the dream accident that woke her up became tagged her "New Reality." When the need arose to explain something stored in her memory, she used these compartments and names.

Of the six other people who were aware of her realities, her psychologist knew the most details of her life with Dream Robert. Abbey came in second just a little ahead of Dora. Her father, Garrett, and the neurologist were on a need-to-know basis. However, Belinda's knowledge of Abbey told her Garrett probably knew more than he let on.

***

Belinda knew, as she wove her tale of the first social outing since her recovery, that Dora would soon connect the dots between Belinda's "Dream Reality" and her "New Reality," realizing the impact of the information her daughter shared. Belinda propped her elbows on the table, leaned in a bit closer, and began her story while her mother listened and ate.

"You know I wasn't real thrilled to go to this party, but I'm really glad I did. The house, it was huge—a Tuscan-style home on acreage. It wasn't situated at an angle on a corner but sat straight facing the street like the other houses. And the foyer. It was amazing. It was about twenty-five feet tall with this huge chandelier." She paused to see if her mother offered any signs of recognition.

Dora simply glanced at her and gave an encouraging nod while she ate.

So Belinda decided to describe more specific things that were in her "Dream Reality." "The most unusual aspect of the foyer was the horseshoe shaped stairway flanking the walls, and the two Bombay chests with huge, hand-blown, cobalt blue vases perched on top." Belinda made a slight sweeping motion to add drama to the mental scene she painted. She noticed her mother hesitate at the description of the vases.

Dora stopped sipping her coffee and peered up from her cup.

Leaning forward and closer, she continued. "You can imagine after seeing how opulent the house was, I was anxious to be introduced to the owners." Belinda stopped and took a bite of her cooling pancakes. She intentionally chewed slowly, watching her mother. Dora lifted her fork to her mouth about to take another bite. Belinda timed her next tidbit of information perfectly, blurting out, "Turns out, their names were Robert and Sandra Pendleton."

Dora stopped cold. Her mouth opened as she dropped her fork. The kitchen echoed with a high-pitched clang as it hit her plate.

Belinda put a smile across her face. Satisfaction warmed her, knowing she achieved her objective. Leaning over her plate, she just took another bite of food and reveled in her mother's reaction.

Finally, Dora took a deep breath. "Did you say Robert and Sandra Pendle-ton?"

Belinda nodded. "Oh yeah, and you'll never guess who else showed up. Robert, their son!"

Dora's eyes grew wide as her hand flew up to her mouth. For the first time in Belinda's life, Dora was rendered speechless. The long silence wasn't expected and it made Belinda uneasy. "Mom, are you okay?"

Dora crumpled her face as she clutched her daughter's hand. "Belinda, you've been through so much since the accident and waking up from the coma. I don't want to see you hurt anymore."

She knew what concerned her mother. Belinda was grieving the loss of a man she loved who didn't exist, but in her mind he was real, and so were her feelings for him.

Then there were the two accidents. Although she actually only had one accident, the one that had placed her in the coma, she had experienced two.

In her dream, a truck hit her, so two accidents were planted in her memory. The doctors explained the shock from the second accident, she had experienced in the dream, had awakened her mind.

The six-month coma had taken a toll on her. After she awoke, she couldn't even sit up by herself because of the diminished muscle mass. Belinda had worked so hard to accomplish what she had in the last three months. Finding someone who resembled her beloved Robert could upset her emotional well-being all over again.

Well into her grieving process, she had achieved a milestone by putting Robert to rest. Now this.

Tears welled in Dora's eyes. "Was it him?"

Watching her mother's expression fill with concern, Belinda began to lose her own composure. Belinda bent her head down in an attempt to hold back the threatening tears. She bit down on her lower lip, but to no avail, the droplets streamed down her cheeks. Looking up at her mother, she squeezed her hand as hard as she could, and nodded.

Dora took a deep breath. "Did he recognize you?"

Belinda cradled her head in her arms. Tears flowing freely, she rocked her head. "He didn't act like it."

She rested her cheek in the crook of her elbow. "But when he touched me, it was like I was back in the dream. I got that same electrified surge and I wanted him."

Dora's eyes widened. "He touched you?"

Belinda gave her mother an accounting of what happened, starting with experiencing the familiar feeling of Robert's touch, her fainting, regaining consciousness in the Pendletons' bedroom, and the introduction to Robert. Belinda started to describe the kiss she and Robert experienced, but thought it would be just too much information. She stopped talking and briefly lowered her head. "Then he left in a hurry. Mom, I'm so confused."

Dora picked up a napkin, gently wiped her daughter's moist face, and stroked her cheek. "When is your next session with your psychologist?"

"Next Monday."

"Belinda, do me a favor."

"Sure. What is it?"

"If Robert calls, don't see him until you have a chance to talk with Dr. Rosen."

"Why?"

"Sweetie, you've been through so much. You have to admit this is rather mind-blowing!" She rolled her eyes, exaggerating the point. "I don't want to see you hurt anymore. I don't know if I can watch you go through the emotional pain again, but whatever the outcome, you know I'm here for you. So is your dad." An impish smile crossed her face. "I'd sure like to be a ladybug on your shoulder when you break this news to the good doctor. Won't he be shocked to learn Robert isn't a figment of your imagination after all?"

Belinda smiled so big, crinkles formed at the outer corners of her eyes squeezing out one last drop. Wiping it away, she always knew her mother had her back, no matter what. She also knew her mother was right. This whole affair had been a lot to absorb, yet she couldn't wait to see the expression on Dr. Rosen's face. She looked at her mom and they both laughed through their tears.

CHAPTER 3

THEIR TALK ENDED about mid-morning, and after a quick kitchen clean up, Belinda dashed to her room and her electronic tablet.

Right after her hospital discharge, she had spent endless hours on the net trying to find out anything she could about Robert Pennington, but all her attempts led to dead ends. Now armed with his correct name, she plopped herself on the bed sitting cross-legged, staring at the glow of her tablet screen. She worked her fingers diligently typing "Robert P-E-N-D-L-E-T-O-N of Sugar Land Texas."

Within seconds, the life of the Pendleton family opened in front of her. She read the history of the founding of the Pendleton Financial Group of Houston, Texas, and found pictures and information on the fairytale wedding of Sandra and Robert Pendleton III. Tons of pictures…mostly of Robert Pendleton, IV, the son—baby pictures, pictures of him as a schoolboy that led up to his college years—were posted. In a recent article she read, Robert was named one of the most eligible bachelors in Texas.

Great! A ladies man in my "Dream Reality" and now one in my "New Reality."

Several hours passed and the strain on her vision began to tire her. Exhausted, the need for sleep engulfed her.

Belinda awoke from a restful nap about three p.m. and realized she didn't dream of Robert or at least she didn't remember it. In her "Dream Reality" she always dreamt of Robert. But in less than twenty-four hours, a real version of Robert had walked in and taken over her life, so it only made sense she would fantasize about him in her sleep. She actually hoped she could relive the excitement that raced through her under the spell of his touch from the night before. She felt cheated, as if something had been ripped from her, and didn't understand. Sensing a void, she became uneasy and that worried her.

Far too much had happened since Robert made his appearance. She knew she needed to talk to someone other than her mother. A dose of Abbey would do the trick. Besides, she promised her friend a phone call and knew Abbey would be more than willing to help. But she realized a phone call wouldn't be enough and needed a "girls' night in," a practice started when they were roommates in college. Strangely enough, they had kept it up even in Belinda's dream.

The only difference between the dream and reality seemed to be Belinda's dating experience. In her dream, she blew off Matt when she met and fell in love with Robert. In reality, she met Matt her sophomore year and dated him exclusively until they graduated. However, when he accepted a job in California after graduation, he didn't invite her along. That pissed her off. She thought they would get married. It seemed the only natural course to take. Instead, all she received was a "Have a good life" as he walked out of hers. Her only consolation was becoming the proud owner of his horse, Beau.

Thinking back over the whole incident, she had gotten the better end of the deal. Beau meant so much to her and riding him helped with her rehab. As far as she was concerned, Matt could stay in California. Good riddance!

"Hello." Abbey answered in her usual perky voice.

"Hey, you up for a sleepover?"

Abbey chuckled, "I hoped you'd call. You know I'm dying over here. I have to take care of a few things then I'll be right over."

"What, Garrett can't go a day without ravishing you?" Belinda teased.

"Belinda Davies, your mind's in the gutter!" She laughed heartily. "I'll be over in about an hour. What I have to do won't take too long."

Belinda started to make a comment about Garrett's stamina when Abbey chimed in, "Don't even go there. I'll see you in a few." The phone went dead. Belinda just smiled because Abbey knew her all too well.

Since her awakening, she and Abbey had spent several nights at her parents' home having sleepovers. Garrett had become accustomed to it, and Belinda really appreciated his patience. She figured he was as anxious as Abbey to find out the details of what took place behind the closed door of the Pendletons' master bedroom. If being without his wife was what it took, so be it.

Belinda had a genuine fondness for Mr. Garrett Barnett. He was strong, sensitive, smart, and handsome. When Abbey started dating him in college, Belinda had to admit her Green Monster reared its ugly head. She saw how Garrett treated Abbey and wished Matt had shown a small degree of the same kind of attentiveness to her. Through her sessions with Dr. Rosen, she figured out that she had based Robert's responses on Abbey and Garrett's relationship. On some level, she knew her relationship with Matt had fallen short in all aspects, so in her "Dream Reality" she filled the hollow space with a similar version of Garrett and named him Robert. Of course, Dream Robert was much better than Garrett in all aspects and from what she experienced the night before, the real Robert surpassed the imaginary.

Belinda hopped off her bed and strolled downstairs. "Mom, Abbey is coming over. What do we have to munch on?" she inquired, passing by her in the family room on her way to the kitchen. She noticed her mother reading her newest romance novel, <u>Shattered Fate</u>.

She glanced back and saw her mother mark the page with a bookmark before rising from the couch.

Belinda knew her mother would do anything to make Abbey feel welcome. Dora frequently referred to her as "a sparkling star" or "a breath of fresh air on a warm summer's day" because Abbey's personality could light up any room. She had also been there for Belinda during her recovery.

"What do you want me to fix?" Dora followed her daughter into the kitchen.

Belinda flaunted a big smile. "I love you, Mom." She planted a kiss on her mother's cheek. "What kind of wine do we have?"

"I think we have two bottles of zinfandel in the fridge. Go see."

Belinda sauntered to the refrigerator and opened it. "You're right." Two bottles sat in a shelf on the door.

So far, her day had been a seesaw of emotions and being around Abbey always made her feel better than good.

The ladies put the finishing touches on the snacks just as the doorbell rang one hour after Belinda hung up the phone with Abbey. Belinda flung open the door to find her pajama-clad friend toting an overnight bag and a bottle of wine, zinfandel of course.

Abbey had married Garrett in June of last year and worked as a schoolteacher until Belinda woke up. Without hesitation, she took a leave of absence to stay at her friend's side. The two had always been close, but the time they spent together after Belinda awoke bound them for life. Abbey became and would always be her best friend and sister.

So here she stood, Belinda's bubbly friend with striking green eyes and auburn hair. Belinda chuckled at the sight of her in hot pink, satin, boxer-cut shorts and matching camisole. "Have you no shame?! Get your butt in here!" She grabbed Abbey's forearm and tugged her into the house.

"What? They cover up the important stuff," she squeaked, big eyed as she grinned.

"What if you had an accident?" Belinda demanded.

"Then everyone would've gotten an eyeful, wouldn't they?" Abbey laughed as she swanked past swinging her hips. She dropped her tote bag on the tile floor near the steps. The loud thud echoed in the foyer.

"Or they'd think you're a hooker. I'm glad my dad's not home!"

Abbey spun around with her mouth agape. "Oh! I didn't think of that. If he saw me like this…I'd be so embarrassed." Her grimacing face slowly changed to a giggle. Belinda knew the giggle meant she felt silly being comfortable with the world seeing her in her alluring outfit, but Belinda's father was a different story.

"Well, you're safe. He's across the street watching football."

Abbey let out a sigh of relief, turning to face Belinda's mother as she entered the room. "Hi, Mrs. D. How are you?"

Dora just shook her head giving out a chuckle, eyeing Abbey from head to toe. "I'm fine, Sweetie. Happy New Year. Love the outfit." She hugged Abbey with all the tenderness a mother could give and then gave her a gentle kiss on the cheek.

Over the past few months, the two had become close while they stayed near Belinda during the recovery phase. Dora grew to think of Abbey as her second daughter and loved the girl's exuberant personality. She would always be a welcomed guest in the Davies household.

"You two go upstairs and I'll bring you some snacks."

In the bedroom, Belinda dug through her dresser for a comparable outfit to match Abbey's comfortable lounging attire. She pulled out a soft blue camisole and matching boxer shorts. Holding them up, she said, "I'll be right back." She slipped into the bathroom and emerged a few minutes later, ready to enjoy a girls' night in.

As Belinda walked out of the bathroom, Abbey dug around in her tote bag and pulled out a DVD. With a slight sashay to her walk, she waved the case. "I brought us a chick-flick to watch with that hunk Jonathan Morse in it." She placed it beside the TV before hopping on the bed with a bounce, landing on her stomach. Abbey bent her knees, and crossed her ankles as they swayed slowly side to side. Simultaneously, she positioned her elbows under her and propped her chin on her palms. She stared at Belinda and simply said, "Well?"

Fully aware her friend couldn't wait any longer, Belinda joined her on the bed and began to recount what took place behind the closed door at the party. She went into every sordid detail, especially the feelings of passion she experienced while they lay on the bed with Robert over her kissing her hard.

Reliving the events through her story stirred the emotions from the night before making her skin warm and tingly.

"I can't wait until he calls me. He told me he'd get my number from Garrett and I assumed he got it when I heard voices in the hall."

Abbey sat quietly. Finally she spoke. "Belinda, he never asked Garrett for your number. He just said you were tired and we should take you home."

Belinda scrunched her face into a frown and sat up straight. *How could he not want to see me again after what happened?*

Abbey piped in, grinning from ear to ear. "Although, that doesn't really mean anything. Robert is a VP of the company and has access to the employee files or he can ask Garrett at work for your number."

The explanation mollified Belinda until a horrible thought came into her head. *Or maybe he just thinks I'm nuts and wants nothing to do with me.*

His promise to call her was the bit of hope she had tucked deep into the recesses of her mind. It lingered, waiting for retrieval, but now it slowly melted away.

Self-doubt was second nature to her. A talent she had mentored most of her life, but with the help of Dr. Rosen, she had made great strides in the past few months. She felt her progress had weakened since Robert appeared, and became determined not to let that happen.

She'd worked hard to build up her self-esteem and no one, not even a person who looked like Robert, was going to make her throw it out the door. If he didn't call, fine. She would continue with her life plans. But tucked in the back of her mind, she prayed he would call.

Belinda scanned the room and settled on the DVD propped against the TV. Thinking now would be a good time to watch the movie, she retrieved it and popped it in. Maybe seeing someone else's "happily ever after" ending would put an end to her self-imposed pity party.

She plopped back on the bed and settled next to Abbey. "Guess what, Jonathan Morse was in my dream," she said, pointing the remote at the TV and punching some buttons. "In fact when you met him, you couldn't stay away from him." A twisted smile spread across Belinda's face. "Garrett wasn't a happy camper about it, either, because you crushed on him so bad."

Abbey balled up her fist and punched Belinda in the arm. "You never told me about Jonathan Morse being in it! Why did you dream about him?"

In an odd way, the jolt took Belinda's mind off her dilemma and she shrugged. "I don't know. Was I a fan of his before the accident?" she asked, trying to fill a gap in her memory.

Abbey cocked her head and flattened her lips. "No, not like me, but you knew who he was because I wouldn't let you forget. You know, we were flipping through a tabloid magazine before my bridal shower started. It was plastered full of photos of him."

"That could explain it. He is handsome. He'd be hard to forget." A can of worms had been opened, so Belinda decided to fill Abbey in on her relationship with the famous Mr. Jonathan Morse. She explained how he helped her survive during the time she spent away from Robert because of his cheating, and even gave her some of the intimate details, such as they were, between her and Jonathan to spice up the story.

CHAPTER 4

BELINDA PUSHED THE elevator button for the third floor. As the doors closed, she wondered how Dr. Rosen would react to the news she would soon divulge. Normally reserved, he'd answer her questions with another question, prompting her to explore her inner self. However, this time he wouldn't be able to manipulate the fact she'd met Robert.

Dr. Rosen's outer office was comfortably furnished. A worn leather couch flanked by two side tables with lamps filled one wall. The opposite wall featured two overstuffed wing-backed chairs with a table and lamp between them. The lamps let off a warm glow and were the only source of light. He didn't have a receptionist, using instead a light switch next to the inner door of the office. Patients arriving for their appointments would flip the switch. A dim red light above the door on the opposite side lit up alerting Dr. Rosen his next appointment had arrived. Any other patient in the room would exit the back door as their session ended. This simple, efficient system assured their privacy. Belinda flipped the switch, nestled herself into one of the overstuffed chairs and thumbed through a magazine, waiting for her turn.

Within a few minutes the inner door opened. "Hi, Belinda. I hope you're having a good new year so far." A disheveled Dr. Rosen stood at the door as he motioned for her to enter the room. His hair seemed a bit longer than their last meeting, but had its signature-uncombed appearance. His clothes, as usual, had a rumpled appearance and he had a five-o'clock-shadow despite the fact it was still morning. As she passed him, she recognized the familiar click as he flipped the switch, turning off the light above the door. They both made themselves comfortable in their usual seats facing each other.

He picked up his pad and pen as he rested back into his chair. "Well, where should we start?"

Instead of mincing her words like she did with her mother, Belinda used a more direct approach. "Remember the New Year's Eve party I told you I planned on attending? Well, I met Robert there." She leaned back in her chair to observe the doctor's reaction.

At first he said nothing, just sitting there as if trying to figure out a response. Finally, he asked, "What do you mean you met Robert?"

"I met a real version of Robert at the New Year's Eve party, but his last name is Pendleton." She just stared back. A smug feeling filled her knowing she had the upper hand.

Dr. Rosen cocked his head. "Belinda, please explain more."

Sighing, she rolled her eyes and proceeded to tell him what took place.

He jerked his head back. "His last name is Pendleton. That could explain why you didn't find anything about him in your search." He scowled before continuing. "This could complicate your recovery." She reassured him with a knowing nod. "So, where do you go from here?" he asked her.

Belinda stared into the room reviewing all the scenarios which could take place. The one she prayed for had Robert calling her, they'd hit it off, and both would ride off into the sunset to start their new life together, living happily ever after. In the other one, Robert didn't call because he thought she was crazy. That thought terrified her. Yet her practical logical side knew she had to live with those two possibilities.

She straightened in her chair and addressed the doctor. "I'll need a Plan A and a Plan B. In Plan A, I'll make room for Robert…if he calls. In plan B, I'll go on with my life as I've been planning…without him."

As the words passed her lips, she felt a tightening in her stomach that sent a shot of pain just below her ribs. She put her head down, taking in a few breaths. Going on without Robert wouldn't be the ending she hoped for, but it might be the likelier outcome and she'd have to learn to live with it.

She and the doctor talked more, exploring her feelings and the consequences to her recent experience. Glancing up, she saw the glow of the red light. Her session had ended.

"We can increase your sessions again if you need to," Dr. Rosen stated as he slowly stood and walked with her to the door.

Belinda knew it would take more than one session to solve anything, despite the fact she felt stronger than she had ever been in her life, both physically and emotionally. "We'll see how things go. Thank you." She exited the office, out the back door.

Belinda had a lot to think about on her drive home. She knew she couldn't put her plans on hold just because a person who resembled Robert suddenly came into her life. So she decided to continue living each day as if he didn't exist, but if by some quirk of fate he and she did form a relationship, she would alter her plans. For now, number one on the list would be shopping for a house. Next, finding a job. And lastly, starting to date. That last worried her the most!

CHAPTER 5

THE FIRST WEEK of February, Belinda began to implement her plan to move forward with her life by searching for a house of her own. She contacted a realtor who helped her find the perfect patio home for her lifestyle. It had an added benefit of being near the stables, Beau's home, and her parents' house. With everything her parents went through during her coma, she owed it to them to stay close.

To finalize her purchase, she needed to make a trip to see Garrett at the Pendleton Financial Group. He now managed her account. He had been there for Belinda during her complete ordeal and she loved him for that.

The financial position Belinda found herself in resulted directly from the real accident. The trucking firm acknowledged its responsibility and established a trust fund for her. The rather substantial fund would've paid for her medical needs for years. Fortunately, she woke up six months later and found herself quite well-off.

So, when Garrett interviewed for the job last November, she told him he could tell the interviewer he'd be bringing her as a client. The funds she received from the real accident gave Garrett a leg up over the other applicants and landed him the position. At the time, Belinda had no idea Garrett's new job would put her in close proximity to the real version of her beloved Robert.

Since their encounter at the New Year's Eve party, Belinda hadn't seen Robert or heard anything from him. The Robert of her "Dream Reality" would never have ignored her. Obviously, the Robert in her "New Reality" wanted little to do with her. This kinda pissed her off after the way he acted at the party. Fate seemed so cruel and painful, so she was grateful she still had her visits with her shrink. They helped to keep her grounded.

Belinda dreaded having to go up to the office to meet Garrett. He understood the cause of her apprehension and sought to reassure her, "I never even see the guy. The odds of you running into him are next to nil." This was the main reason she agreed to the meeting. She also knew Garrett could give her a better projection of her financial situation if he had everything he needed at his fingertips.

Belinda left home early enough to make her 1:30 appointment, making sure she had time to maneuver through the traffic and find parking. She headed for the office building located near the Galleria shopping mall. She hated driving to this area. The traffic was always so heavy, no matter the time of day.

Since the real accident, Belinda had trouble being in rush hour traffic alongside huge trucks. It made her extremely uncomfortable. She replaced her demolished vehicle with a small sport utility vehicle, which helped ease her fear some. The higher-riding Honda CR-V seemed to diminish the threatening nature of the big trucks.

But the scenario changed when a truck approached her from the rear. The sight of a big chrome grill coming at her caused her chest to tighten to the point she couldn't breathe. There was only one real accident that put her in a coma, but she experienced it twice. Dr. Rosen labeled her panic attacks Posttraumatic Stress Disorder, or as it's more popularly known, PTSD. He assured her the fear of large, bright shiny objects barreling down on her would diminish as she desensitized herself to highway driving. For now, Belinda avoided expressways and rush hour traffic, whenever possible, which didn't help with improving her desensitization.

After the appointment, Belinda planned to take advantage of her proximity to the Galleria since she very seldom traveled far from home. She wanted to do some power shopping. The mall housed every store imaginable in three huge buildings all connected by walkways. Belinda intended to shop in a few stores for a couple of hours. If everything went perfectly, she could even avoid rush hour traffic for her return trip to Sugar Land, some thirteen miles away.

Belinda arrived for the appointment a bit early, 12:45. She approached the reception desk and introduced herself.

"Oh, yes. Mr. Barnett told me to escort you to conference room B. If you would, please come this way." The receptionist rose from her seat and motioned for her to follow.

The office space, bright and very contemporary in design, looked rather impressive. Thick glass wall panels partitioned the space into offices, allowing natural sunlight to flow in unobstructed. Teak-covered columns served as supports for the glass. To warm the space, soft shades of blue and green graced the walls. The furniture appeared sleek and minimal. Large framed pictures hung strategically placed as focal points at the end of halls. By the appearance of the office, Garrett had done quite well for himself. The décor screamed "prosperity."

With lunchtime still in progress, the offices they passed as they wound their way down the halls stood empty. The quietness gave the space a serene feeling.

They stopped in front of a door labeled "B." "Here it is." The woman opened it and bade Belinda to make herself comfortable, and then offered her something to drink. Belinda shook her head and smiled. The receptionist pointed to the phone on the credenza. "If you change your mind, just dial extension two. I'll let Mr. Barnett know you're here as soon as he returns." She closed the door and left Belinda in a small but adequate room.

This space looked different—it lacked the glass used as a divider from the hall. A solid wall with a single door that had a full-length piece of frosted glass as an inset made it more private and less fishbowl-like. It made Belinda feel at ease and less intimidated. A table and chairs positioned in the center could seat up to six.

A second door led into an adjacent room. Being curious, Belinda peeked inside only to discover another conference room, but much bigger. Unlike the smaller room, this one consisted of mostly all glass. Floor to ceiling windows along the outer wall gave it a full view of Loop 610 and Memorial Park. The opposite wall, also glass, allowed anyone from the hall to look in. A large oval table and chairs that could seat up to twenty, sat in the center. At the far end of the room sat a counter with a coffee maker and an espresso machine.

Okay, what now? She had given herself the nickel tour of her temporary confines and glanced at her watch. Only three minutes had passed. Giving the smaller room a sweeping glance, she hoped to locate a magazine, nothing. She peered into the larger room and eyed one at the far end of the long table. Letting out a sigh, she took one step into the room just as laughter filled her ears from a group of young men entering from the hall at the far end. Without thinking, she stepped back and out of sight behind the wall. She thought about closing the door to give them privacy, but decided they could do it themselves. With nothing else to do, she walked to the large windows in the smaller room to watch the activity on the streets below.

***

The group of men gathered around the coffee bar, helping themselves to an expresso. They were all about the same age and resembled models in magazines, wearing tailored suits with ties in perfect order against their starched coordinated shirts. The conversation drifted from one subject to another as they seated themselves around the table.

Saji got their attention and started talking about an upcoming date he anticipated for the weekend. "This woman is something else. I have never seen a real female with such long legs. They come up to her neck." He motioned with his hand to make his point. "I can't wait until I wrap my hands around that. I'll let you know Monday if she's a genuine blonde."

Laughter ricocheted around the room, making light of the subject matter. Each man took a turn bragging about a recent conquest.

Finally, one of the members of the group directed his attention to a colleague who hadn't participated in the discussion. "What about you Robert? Tell us about the most beautiful girl you ever met."

Robert pushed back into the leather-covered chair and interlocked his fingers behind his neck while he searched his mind before he spoke. Recalling a vision he saw in his memory, a wisp of a smile formed across his face. "It was at college. I was cutting across the commons when I noticed her approaching." He paused, allowing the memory to flood his thoughts. "She was wearing a pair of the best-fitting jeans I ever saw." The vision in his mind made him smile again and his heart seemed to stop for a spilt second. He focused on the ceiling and inhaled, and then lowered his tone. "She had the sweetest smile and long, brown hair that glistened in the sunlight." The room fell silent, but he took no notice. "I was watching her and when she came within ten feet, that's when her big, blue eyes met mine. That was it for me…I was hers and I didn't even know who she was." He scanned the faces of his colleagues.

Saji leaned forward, resting his arms on the table. "Did you ever meet her?"

Silent and captivated by the memory, Robert just nodded, blocking out the other members of the group for a few seconds. The clearing of the throat of one of his colleagues grabbed his attention. He didn't move, but knew his momentary drift down memory lane would spur a discussion he didn't want to deal with. He already gave them too much information. Instead, he plotted a way out of his little dilemma. He slid a devilish grin across his mouth before he sat up to see the puzzled faces peering at him.

"Yeah. I married her," cunningly came out of his mouth.

Stunned, the group exchanged glances before refocusing on Robert.

His quick wit afforded him the ability to convince people of his sincerity. It made him successful at what he did for a living. Being part salesman and part confidant, he had a way of putting people at ease and they trusted him. He snapped back in a joking manner, "You fools! I've never been married. Go ask my father."

They all broke out in a hearty laugh. The group went on to other subjects of interest and none of them noticed Robert remained more reserved, still lost in the recall of a brown-haired beauty.

***

Belinda tapped her fingers on the windowsill. She formed a half curl on her mouth and huffed. The loud voices, with their somewhat appalling subject matter, begin to grate at her nerves. Now, closing the door seemed like a good idea. Giving the sill a pound with a closed fist, she walked toward it. About halfway there, Robert's voice floated into her ears. Although she wasn't prepared to see him, hearing his voice brought back memories of a time lost, and she welcomed the calm it showered over her. Her heart leapt.

Belinda backed against the wall next to the door and leaned in closer to the opening. Chewing on her lower lip, she listened to Robert. *Is he describing his girlfriend?* Whoever she may be, she obviously stole his heart. The peacefulness Belinda experienced from his voice shifted to one of sadness. Hearing enough, she closed the door and walked back to peer out the window, hating whomever he talked about.

***

Robert glanced toward the glass wall of the large conference room and noticed Garrett ambling along, seeming uncertain. He repeatedly took several steps and then paused, tapping the edge of the manila folder against his palm. Garrett stopped and scanned inside the glass enclosure. When their eyes met, Robert saw his brow furrow, a sign something bothered him.

Robert watched Garrett inhale a deep breath as he walked in on his colleagues. He headed straight for Robert, only giving the rest of the group a nod of recognition.

The young men began to empty out of the room. Robert remained seated a bit longer, sipping his drink. The last member of the group departed as Garrett reached Robert.

"I'm having a problem with this fund. Do you think you could help out?" Garrett flashed the folder in front of Robert.

"I'll see."

Garrett opened the folder and spread its contents on the table. The two discussed the possibilities.

Robert could tell Garrett didn't fully understand the complexities of this particular fund and offered his assistance. "Is your client coming in today?"

"She's here now," Garrett responded, tilting his head, "in the small conference room."

Robert cocked his wrist to check the time on his watch and suggested in his usual self-confident manner, "Would you like me to go over this with her? I could do it now. It won't take too long. I have plenty of time."

Garrett hesitated for a moment, tapping the papers with his index finger. "I think that might be a good idea, but I'll have to check with her first to see if she'd feel comfortable talking with you."

Comfortable with me? Robert's curiosity was piqued and he raised one brow, but quickly shook off the feeling and returned to his work mode. "Of course. Go find out."

"Thanks. I don't think I can give her the best advice about this fund. My client needs a good idea of her financial status. She's planning on paying cash for a house."

Garrett took a few steps in the direction of the small conference room and stopped. His reluctance confused Robert. Over the years, Robert learned to be a patient man. He would watch and wait, reading the body language of people with whom he interacted. If he gave them enough time and asked a few leading questions, almost everyone would open up and volunteer information.

"Ah...Robert, I think it's only fair I tell you who my client is." He shifted from foot to foot. "It's Belinda Davies."

Robert tightened his jaw. Rubbing the back of his neck, he gave the door to the adjacent room a quick glance and aimed a finger at it. "She's in there now?"

Garrett nodded. "Look, if there's someone else...."

Robert scrutinized the closed door. He could manage this in a professional manner just by keeping distance between them. "Go see if she'd mind." Garrett nodded, turned, and walked away.

His encounter with Belinda at the New Year's Eve party flashed through his mind. His throat suddenly thickened. *Did I just put my foot in my mouth?*

Belinda leaned against the sill, watching the traffic moving at a snail's pace on the 610 Loop. The muffled knock on the door drew her attention away from her thoughts of her perilous drive home. Garrett entered, closed the door behind him, and leaned against it. He slowly turned the corners of his mouth up into a smile. "Hi. Sorry you had to wait."

"It's okay. It wasn't that long."

Garrett walked over to the window where Belinda stood and explained the need to have an expert go over the different components of the fund. He told her, Robert Pendleton would do the honor of presenting the details.

"Belinda, I don't want to put you in an uncomfortable position. If you don't want to see him, I'll make some other arrangements."

Belinda listened to what Garrett had to say and thought it over. She took a deep breath. "No, I'm fine with that. I'll listen to Mr. Pendleton." It didn't seem right calling him Mr. Pendleton.

Garrett left and closed the door behind him. Belinda's anxiety level went into hyper-drive as she paced in front of the window, wringing her hands so hard she thought she would rub off the skin. This would be her first encounter with Robert since the party. The memory of him holding her made her heart flutter like the wings of a hummingbird.

She stopped, closed her eyes, and swallowed hard, remembering the vivid blue of his eyes and embracing the memory until a confident Robert followed by Garrett forced the door open. Wide eyed, she jumped and turned toward the noise. Her gaze rested on Robert's face. Though she thought she was prepared, seeing him made her more uncomfortable than she expected. It felt…foreign.

In her "Dream Reality," Robert always dressed well and so did this man. He sported a tailored gray suit, white shirt, and dark blue tie. The jacket hugged his broad shoulders and tapered at the waist. He looked as gorgeous as she remembered. It didn't feel right having to act as if she didn't know him, but she had no choice. With every nerve ending tingling at his closeness, Belinda stiffened and walked toward him.

She swallowed hard and cleared her throat to remove a lump. "Mr.

Pendleton, it's nice to see you again." He didn't step forward or extend a hand to shake as she assumed he would. He just stood there.

Robert knew he couldn't touch her. Just a hand on her shoulder at his parents' party had almost caused him to lose control. He had been all over her and didn't need that happening now. So, Robert decided to ignore the handshake.

"It's nice to see you again. Please, be seated." He pointed toward a chair at the table. He walked to the other side, taking a seat across from her, ensuring enough distance between them. Garrett sat at the head of the table between them.

"Garrett tells me you need a detailed explanation of this fund." Robert opened the folder and selected the needed papers. Maintaining his professional persona, he proceeded to review everything she needed to know about her financial position. During the presentation, he only glanced at her briefly to minimize the captivating effect of her phenomenal blue eyes.

While Belinda scanned some of the materials, he studied her for the first time since he entered the room. She looked so beautiful, more beautiful than he remembered—a natural beauty who wore very little makeup. Her long flowing hair framed her face. It seemed her eyelashes almost extended to the center of her cheeks. Her flawless skin enticed him to reach out and stroke it.

The impulse intensified when her lashes fluttered up. Busy fighting the desire to grab her, he couldn't say anything. To Robert's relief, he got a reprieve when Garrett interrupted, breaking the spell. He snapped his head in Garrett's direction.

"Robert, how much time do you have? I have one more fund I think you'd be able to explain better to Belinda than I would. Do you mind?"

"That would be fine." He held out his hand, fully expecting Garrett to give him the folder right then, but instead, Garrett excused himself from the room. Robert's mouth went dry. With the click of the door, he found himself alone with Belinda. He stared at the frosted glass inset to give himself a few seconds to think. He hoped she wouldn't bring up anything that occurred on New Year's Eve. Robert didn't quite understand what had happened and didn't want to try to explain himself. This wasn't the appropriate time or place. To avoid any further visual contact, he rose from his chair and ambled toward the pitcher of water and glasses arranged on the credenza. "Would you like one?" he asked Belinda in a cool controlled tone.

Belinda hitched her breath as she saw Garrett leave, and realized he had left her alone with Robert. Her mouth wet dry. Water might be a good idea. "Yes please."

She bowed her head to give herself a few seconds to get a grip. It didn't help. Her breathing became more difficult. She screamed inside, *Garrett, come back! I can't be alone with him!*

Her insides churned from the onslaught of confused emotions, wondering what he really thought of her. For all she knew, he thought she was a nut who needed to be locked up. She sat there staring down at the table. But when he walked behind her and stood at the credenza, she could almost feel the heat radiating off him like an electrical charge. She stiffened her back, screaming in her mind, *Garrett, please come back!*

What seemed like hours passed before Belinda got up the nerve to turn around and look up. Their gazes collided and both attempted to say something at the same time. He politely said, "Ladies first."

Belinda smiled and turned away. Seeing his handsome face threw all her senses out of alignment. His penetrating eyes just made her want to leap into his arms and kiss his luscious lips. Nibbling at the side of her lower lip, she cleared her mind, determined to ask the question gnawing at her. Planting her palms firmly on the table, she squared her shoulders. She wanted to ask him why he hadn't called and had no choice but to look at him again. Her mood became serious as she peered straight into his beautiful, blue eyes.

Parting her lips, Belinda managed to get out one syllable, "Ah." The sound of the door opening stole Robert's attention from her as he turned toward it. In that brief second, Garrett's untimely entrance deprived her of the opportunity for answers as he stepped back into the room.

Robert had the perfect excuse to leave, thanks to Garrett's return. He placed the glass of water in front of Belinda without looking at her, and then approached Garrett and took the folder. Glancing it over, he maintained his cool. "You know, I just remembered I need to get to an appointment. Sam can help you with your questions on this one as well as I can. I'll send him in." He didn't have another appointment—he just wanted out of the room as fast as his feet would take him.

Robert turned toward Belinda, making a half-assed gesture at politeness as he double-timed it for the door. "It was nice seeing you again."

Belinda lifted her tilted head, and squinted when she saw how eager Robert seemed to get away. "Same here. Thank you for all your help." Her voice resonated with a bit of sarcastic inflection mixed with disappointment that her chance for an answer had escaped.

"You're welcome," he called back, already out the door and heading down the hall.

***

The meeting with Sam and Garrett ended with Belinda feeling satisfied she had enough funds to live very well, possibly for the rest of her life. If she went back to teaching, even if only part time, she could stretch the money deep into retirement. She would have to be sensible on her vacations and with the cars she purchased, but she'd be taken care of monetarily.

For now, she would be buying a house and paying cash for it. She also decided to pay off her parents' mortgage. She knew they'd give her too many reasons to keep the money, but they deserved it and she wouldn't take "no" for an answer.

Belinda felt confident about her financial affairs, but she couldn't say the same about her emotional state. Seeing Robert had been harder than she imagined. She didn't understand why he wouldn't talk to her other than maybe he saw her as a nut job. For whatever reason, he made it clear he wanted little to do with her.

Belinda and Garrett walked to the elevator. She kissed him on the cheek, hugged him, and asked him to tell Abbey she'd call soon. A familiar ping preceded the opening of the steel doors. Garrett left as she entered. Belinda turned around to find Robert watching her through the glass wall of his office. For the past few hours, her emotions had been on a roller coaster ride. Seeing him again became more than she could handle. Tears welled up as she gazed into the depth of his soft, blue eyes. For a second she swore she saw him move toward her, but he stopped just as the elevator doors closed.

Alone, Belinda rested her head against the back wall. Never again did she want to experience being close to Robert and not be able to be with him. She rubbed away the tears before the doors opened.

On the way to her car, she passed by some of the reserved parking spaces and noticed a red BMW Roadster. It was the same make and model Robert drove in her "Dream Reality." She cautiously approached the space, half-afraid of what she might find. Belinda walked near enough to read the name on the plaque secured to the wall. Her muscles stiffened, paralyzed by what it said, **Mr. Robert Pendleton, IV.**

CHAPTER 6

BELINDA SAT IN her car for at least ten minutes after her encounter with Robert. As hard as she tried, her mind wouldn't let him go. Too many questions about the experience they shared at the New Year's Eve party needed answers.

She focused on the red roadster, leaning her head against the headrest. The muscles in her neck tightened and she rolled her head, attempting to relieve some of the tension. She took a deep breath and let her head tilt until the red roadster, a symbol of all her frustrations, came back into view.

"I'm acting like a fool." She gave the steering wheel a pop. She studied the situation as the familiar haunting questions raced through her mind. The only sensible conclusion was for her not to feel insecure or run from this version of Robert.

Belinda made a decision. From this day forward, she would no longer be a passive player. She wanted to know what happened on New Year's Eve and why he didn't call. Something didn't seem right. So, starting now, her mission would be to discover his motives.

She opened the glove box and pushed its contents around, fumbling for something suitable to write on. A fast food napkin would have to do. Pulling a pen from her purse, she wrote a note.

Robert,
Thank you for your help this afternoon. You took a difficult topic and made it easy for me to understand. I sincerely hope that if I have any further questions in the near future you would be willing to answer them.
Belinda

She snickered as she reread the note. Opening the door, she hopped out and strolled over to Robert's car.

She stopped at the front fender and scrutinized the windshield wiper. Rubbing her fingers against the rough texture of the napkin, she hesitated and grabbed her lower lip between her teeth as the same questions popped into her head. Tsking, she rolled her eyes. She lifted the wiper blade and tucked the note under it. "What the hell do I have to lose?" she mumbled under her breath.

She could tell Robert was attracted to her. Hell, his actions on New Year's Eve and the tension she just experienced in the conference room proved it. Now the ball was in his court and she had to see if he would volley it back.

As she walked past the car, she slid her fingers over the edge. She fondly remembered her first ride in the blue roadster, Robert owned in her dream.

For now, her memories would have to wait—she had some shopping to do. She straightened her back, lifted her head, and took confident steps toward her car, feeling just a bit proud of herself.

Belinda took off for the Galleria. The meeting ran longer than she expected and it had cut into her shopping time. If necessary, she'd have to stay longer than intended to avoid the sea of cars and trucks that would be waiting to intimidate her on the route home. For now, her mission would be to enjoy the rest of her evening by trying on some new clothes. Ones that might catch his attention.

Despite the fact the mall was only three blocks away—it took forty-five minutes to get to and find a parking space in the covered garage. She entered the Galleria having forgotten how much space it really occupied. The place hummed for a Thursday evening, full of business types bustling past to reach their destinations, getting in some shopping or meeting someone at one of the various restaurants.

Belinda proceeded to the first store on her mental list. It had been a long time since she enjoyed browsing and trying on clothes. When she woke up from the coma, it made no sense to buy anything new. Now, she had regained the weight she lost and her body shape looked better than ever before. The physical therapy, jogging, and riding Beau increased her muscle tone, giving her a suitable figure.

The plan to power shop quickly diminished as she walked from one store to the next. She lost track of time browsing through all the clothes on the racks.

During a brisk walk between stores, she glanced at her watch. It was 5:30 p.m. and she knew the drive home would be horrible due to the abundance of commuters congesting the highways. So she decided to stay and continue shopping, get something to eat, and then drive back to Sugar Land when the traffic died down. But first she needed to call her mother to inform her of the changed plans.

Belinda hadn't been going out much since she awoke and she knew her mother would be thrilled she was doing something other than sitting around the house.

Fumbling with her purse, she dug into it, feeling into its depths for the flat rectangular phone while she walked along. The sides of the bag annoyed her as they collapsed on themselves complicating her task. The pursuit became intense and determined. With her nose buried in the recesses of the purse's black hole, she hit what felt like a brick wall. The impact jolted the bag out of her hands. It hit the floor with a thud, but not before flipping over and depositing the contents around her feet.

Her mouth dropped open as she watched a tampon gracefully roll over and stop at the toe of a man's shoe. *Could it get more embarrassing?* Horrified, she immediately stooped down to scoop it up, praying the man didn't notice. Something hit the floor, burying itself into the mess. She glanced up in the direction from which the object fell to see Robert studying her. Her face went hot and her heart pounded.

Instinctively, and as a way to avoid further eye contact, Belinda began to retrieve the articles spread around the floor. Robert stooped down and helped shovel the contents back into their home. Neither of them spoke while they worked shoulder to shoulder.

Their last touch at the New Year's Eve party coupled with their reaction to each other had been electrifyingly passionate. Now curious, Belinda wanted to see what would happen with a gentle touch on his skin. She placed her hand across Robert's and hesitated, leaving it there to test her reaction. As passion stirred within her, she took a deep breath through her mouth and looked down. She glanced up and found Robert staring at her, his breathing a bit faster. His eyes intensified in a soft way as he studied her face, making her heart leap.

Abruptly, Robert pulled it out from under hers, breaking their bond. He reached into the scattered objects, retrieved his phone, and stood. He never offered to help her off the floor. He just turned and moved away, keeping his back to her the whole time.

After shoveling the rest of the stuff into her purse, Belinda stood and observed Robert, satisfied by his reaction to their touch, yet puzzled at his need to restrain himself. She took a step toward him, determined to ask him what just happened, but another male voice interrupted. Belinda turned toward the sound, recognizing the tall man as Colin. She hadn't noticed him standing a few feet away while she picked up her stuff.

Colin offered a warm, welcoming smile as he moved closer. "Hey, you're the girl from the Pendleton party. Belinda. Right?" He pointed at her before taking hold of her hand and shaking it a bit vigorously. "Remember me, I'm Colin Brockman. We shared a few dances. What happened to you? You just vanished. One minute you were there, the next POOF!" He made a bursting motion with his fingers.

Belinda remembered Colin well. He had paid attention to her exclusively at the party, until she made her disappearance in Robert's arms.

An attractive man at about 6'4", with sandy blonde hair, he had a good build and a nice personality to match.

Belinda gazed into his glacier blues and smiled in response to his friendly manner. "I didn't feel well, so I left early. I'm sorry I didn't get to say goodbye."

"Robert and I are on our way downstairs to the pub by the ice skating rink. We're meeting his girlfriend for drinks and dinner. If you don't have any plans, why don't you join us?"

Girlfriend?

Colin presented his proposal almost too eagerly, but Belinda couldn't believe her luck. Not only would she be able to be close to Robert, she would also have the chance to see his response to his…girlfriend?

"I would love to join you. I planned on getting something to eat and would enjoy having company rather than eating alone." Where they ate made no difference. "I'll just need to let my parents know I'll be late. They still worry about me. You know how parents can be," she said with a flip of her hair.

Belinda walked a few feet away from Colin to obtain some privacy. She hit the number two on the phone, her parents speed dial number. What she heard next surprised her. "Hello, Robert."

Belinda didn't know what to say. She hesitated and then blurted out, "Oh! I'm sorry. I think I have the wrong number."

"Who is this and how did you get Robert's phone?" The voice on the other end sounded upset.

Belinda read the display. It said Karen. She put the phone back to her ear. "Could you hold on a minute?" No reply came from the other end.

She walked over to Robert, who now stood in front of a store window. "Excuse me. I think we switched phones. You might want to take this." She reached out to give the phone to Robert. He placed his hand under hers so she could drop it. Belinda saw another opportunity to test his response to her.

She grabbed Robert's wrist and to her surprise, he tensed and twisted, attempting to pull away. With eyes slit, she tilted her head and studied his face. Lifting his chin, he widened his eyes slightly into a fixed glare as his breathing quickened. Her grip tightened with every twist. She knew he could get loose if he wanted, but his effort seemed feeble at best.

His eyes gradually softened and he stilled, melting her with his warm gaze. For a split second, time stopped and no one else existed.

What's happening? For heaven's sake, they were in the middle of a mall. She let out a huff and slapped the phone into his palm, letting go. But, the brief episode confirmed his attraction.

Robert turned away as soon as she released him. Reading the phone display, he saw Karen's name and realized he had Belinda's phone in his pocket. Robert had stopped to text Karen when Belinda slammed into his chest, causing him to juggle his cell and drop it into the mess scattered around his feet. At the time, he scanned the floor for it and chuckled to himself, seeing the small white cylindrical object stop at the tip of his shoe. How embarrassing, he thought, until the woman at his feet looked up at him and his heart skipped a beat.

Oh hell. The only thing he could do was help her pick up the crap. Everything would've been fine, but no, she had to go and grab his wrist. All he could think about was jumping her bones.

Taking a deep breath, he swiped his fingers through his hair. Now, he had to deal with Karen. Robert placed the phone to his ear and scrunched it with his shoulder to hold it in place. "Hello, Karen? Hang on a minute."

He pulled Belinda's phone out and peered at it, raising an eyebrow. It looked identical to his, down to the protective cover. Grasping it by the edge, he walked over to Colin and Belinda, and flicked it at her. He flattened his lips into a thin line and furrowed his brow. When she didn't take it fast enough, he narrowed his eyes and fixed them on hers, giving the phone one more hard flick to make his point.

Opening her hand, palm up under the phone, he dropped it in and gave her one last glare.

Robert walked far enough away from her and Colin to make sure they couldn't overhear his conversation. "Hey, Baby. Where are you?"

"Robert, who was that?" Karen sounded annoyed.

"She's one of my clients and our phones got switched accidently. They're exactly alike." To avoid too much explanation, Robert gave Karen just enough information. "She was up at the office."

"I'm in the parking lot. I'll meet you in front of the pub. Love you."

"I love you too. See you in a few."

Belinda and Colin chatted while Robert talked on the phone. Curious as to how serious their relationship might be, she asked, "How long have they been dating?"

"Let's see. Robert told me they reconnected last Fourth of July at the Pendletons' pool party."

"Reconnected?"

"Yeah. His dad's been taking care of her father's investments for years and they'd run into each other every now and then. She came with her parents to the party last year, and they seemed to hit it off, but they didn't really start seeing each other until late July."

Belinda thought over what Colin said and sized up Robert. She was still in the coma in August. She mentally went back to the timeline of her "Dream Reality." Robert was in summer school and spending time away from her with Erin. Belinda thought it strange the two names were so similar, Erin in the "Dream Reality" and Karen in her "New Reality." She brushed it off as a coincidence...for now.

Belinda watched Robert stare at his phone. She noticed a slight shift in his posture as he approached them. "Karen will meet us by the pub."

"Robert. I asked Belinda to join us for dinner. Okay?"

Robert showed no emotion Belinda could detect. In fact, he never even lifted his head. He just studied his phone in an indifferent manner. "Yeah. That's fine." He slipped his phone into his pocket, turned and started walking, leaving Belinda and Colin to pick up their pace to catch him.

The trio walked with Belinda between the two men, making it difficult for her to be this close to Robert, yet so far apart. She thought only of this man who knew nothing about her, determined to make the most of the night and discover all she could despite the news of a girlfriend.

Robert pointed toward a woman leaning against the rail of the ice skating rink. "There she is."

They approached and he gave her a tender kiss on the lips. He had to bend down to kiss Karen because of the difference in their height. She appeared to be about seven inches shorter than he was, with a nice build and short, layered, blonde hair that fluffed away from her face in a boyish style cut. Well-dressed in a suit with a form-fitting pencil skirt, she gave the impression of an extremely professional businesswoman. Although she found Karen very attractive, Belinda didn't quite see her and Robert together. They didn't seem to fit.

Placing her left hand on Robert's neck, Karen gave him a kiss. The massive diamond sitting on her ring finger nearly blinded Belinda. *Robert's engaged!*

Turning to Belinda, he introduced Karen. "Belinda this is my fiancée, Karen Mendelson. Karen this is Belinda Davies, the client I told you about." Belinda noticed a glint of concern on his face and decided to act as if she had just met him today.

Belinda hesitated, trying to recover from the announcement of the engagement. It wasn't until she noticed the questioning expression on Karen's face that she responded to the introduction. "Hi," Belinda said, trying to be as casual and polite as possible under the circumstances. "Is that an engagement ring?"

"Yes, he proposed on New Year's Eve a couple of hours before the stroke of midnight." Karen flashed it in front of Belinda. She glanced at Robert and smiled. He kept his head down, but slid a glance aside at her. "He wanted us to be engaged so we could start the year off together." She nestled close and rested against his chest. "He's so romantic."

Robert lifted his head. His eyes appeared soft and pleading. He glued them on Belinda's and shook his head ever so slightly. She understood his request and met his expectations by not mentioning their first passionate meeting.

All kinds of questions reeled through her mind. With a quick snort and a raised eyebrow, Belinda gave Robert a fleeting glance. *What kind of man becomes engaged then makes out passionately with another woman within a few hours? A player!* The engagement, however, did explain why Robert hadn't called and why he seemed so nervous after they kissed.

"The ring is beautiful. May I see it?"

Karen proudly posed her hand so Belinda could inspect the rock.

Belinda stepped in closer. "It's gorgeous. Did you help pick it out?"

"No. It was a total surprise." Karen's face seemed to be glowing. Suddenly she cocked her head. "What perfume are you wearing?"

Belinda wanted to cry, but needed to be polite. "Angel Scent."

She glanced up at Karen to see a frown form across her face.

Karen nodded and said warily, "I see. It seems to suit you."

A bit unnerved by Karen's tone and the news of the engagement, Belinda returned to pretending to study the beautifully mounted diamond, giving herself a few minutes to recover. "It's really beautiful." She straightened her posture and lifted her chin proudly, now pissed because Robert started to resemble an ass.

As Belinda started to walk past Robert, she took hold of Colin's arm and said loud enough for the group to hear, "You have good taste." Timing her next step perfectly, she bumped Robert and whispered, "Romeo."

CHAPTER 7

BELINDA WAITED FOR the group to sit around the table at the restaurant. Since the phone mix up, she hadn't had the chance to call her parents. She timed her next move well. "Excuse me." She stood. "I'll be right back." She grabbed her purse and flung it over her shoulder. Full of confidence, she turned and sashayed away from the table, exaggerating her hip movement as she walked. She knew she looked good in her jeans that hugged her ass and accentuated every curve, and her walk just made the view even more enjoyable for those who wished to observe. Most of the time she tried to play down her figure, but not tonight. To stoke a sense of jealousy in Robert, she wanted the whole damn place watching her, especially him. She noticed a few patrons' heads turn in her direction, so she amped up the swing of her hips to draw as much attention as possible.

Robert heard a whisper come out of Colin. "Oh. My. God!"

He studied his friend's face and watched Colin's mouth drop open. Following Colin's gaze, he turned his head toward whatever he was concentrating on—Belinda's perfect backside. He couldn't help but stare. He enjoyed watching the swing she put into every step and how her hips moved with the grace of a dancer. The jeans cradled her rear accentuating their upside down heart shape. He clenched his teeth and his jaw tightened. *What gives her the right to tempt me?*

The fantasy forming in his imagination, about caressing her ass, never had a chance. Karen punched him in the arm demanding his attention. Turning toward her, he saw a scowling face, but managed to distract her by throwing his arm around her shoulder and tugging her close. "I love you." He placed a kiss on her mouth. The softness of her lips gave him a familiar thrill. However, since the New Year's Eve party and the kiss he shared with

Belinda, he found himself making comparisons between the two women's kissing techniques. He enjoyed both, but Belinda luscious kisses beat Karen's. Her's radiated sensuality, and underneath, he sensed a connection, something he never experienced with Karen. The whole time he stayed lip-locked with Karen, he savored the image of Belinda.

After Belinda's head-turning walk out of their sight, the trio exchanged pleasantries about Karen's recent business trip. Colin acted like he was in heat with all the sideways glances he made in the direction Belinda had sashayed away and this annoyed Robert.

To prevent a repeat of Karen's negative reaction to his previous ogling, he kept his attention on Karen. Colin sat just inside of his peripheral vision, making it easy to watch for his reactions. Robert could tell from the smile on Colin's face, Belinda must be on her way back.

Like most men, Robert enjoyed the female form. So, he developed a subtle technique of quick glances. This allowed him the pleasure without staring when in the company of another female. In this case, he was far too attracted to Belinda and had difficulty controlling his compulsion. So instead, he opted to just watch Colin enjoy the view. However, over Colin's shoulder he noticed several tables of men turning their heads in the same direction. As he scanned around the restaurant, he noticed more men staring. He followed their gaze until he realized Colin wasn't the only one ogling Belinda. She had the whole damn restaurant watching her. He hated every one of those men drooling over her and fantasized punching each one to wipe the smirks off their faces. At that moment, his blood boiled.

Robert saw a smile settle across Belinda's face when Colin jumped up to pull a chair out for her. Seating herself, she stated, "Mission accomplished," and smiled sweetly at the group until she gazed at him. He watched her smile vanish.

Robert stared at Belinda. His clenched his jaw as the muscles around his eyes tensed. He was mad at her for her display, but knew he had no right. He needed to get a grip and calm down. *Remember your resolution,* rang through his mind. Hell, why did she bother him so much? He tossed back the rest of his drink and waved to the waiter to bring him a refill, taking his attention off her.

During dinner, the conversation at the table hit on a variety of subjects from sports to weather. Colin wasn't from Texas. He had moved here from Los Angeles late last fall and this would be his first summer in his new state.

They jokingly warned him about the heat, humidity, and the dangers of hurricanes.

Belinda noticed Robert's occasional glances while she ate and figured the only polite thing to do was return the flirt, of course with discretion. She realized her endeavor failed when she noticed Karen's miffed expression. Karen did and said nothing. She remained polite and unflustered.

The meal progressed with more conversation and laughter. Belinda was having a good time. Colin took every opportunity to flirt with her and it felt good having a male pay so much attention. Matt, who she had dated for four years in college, never gave her as much consideration.

She tried to be polite, but found it extremely difficult with Robert sitting across from her. His angry face had long faded away with a few drinks in him. He appeared more relaxed and seemed to be having fun.

At one point during the meal, Robert and Belinda reached for the saltshaker at the same time and his fingers wrapped around hers. Her eyes floated shut as the all-too-familiar sensual quiver ran up her spine. She became aware of his index finger gently stroking her skin until he slipped his hand away and turned back to Karen. The whole incident went unnoticed by the other two members of the party. What seemed to Belinda as minutes, took place in seconds.

Lost in her thoughts, she concentrated on her plate, cutting the steak. Now sure of Robert's attraction to her, the news of his engagement placed a different slant on the situation. Belinda knew she didn't have it in her to pursue Robert romantically as she planned. She never would allow herself to be "The Other Woman" at any cost.

The conversation suddenly turned to Belinda when Karen started asking questions. "Belinda, how do you know Robert and Colin?" Belinda replied with the appropriate answer giving a brief explanation of their financial connection.

Out of nowhere, Colin suddenly blurted out, "I met her at the Pendletons' New Year's Eve party."

Belinda gave a quick glance toward Robert. With his head down, she couldn't read his expression.

However, Karen's face clearly showed her interest piqued. Belinda needed to find a way to backpedal. "I was there with some friends. I didn't even make it to twelve midnight. I was under the weather and left early." She really stretched the truth, but it seemed to satisfy Karen.

"Oh, I see." Karen paused and seemed to study Belinda. Thankfully, she changed the subject. "What do you do for a living?"

At first, Belinda didn't know where to begin. She decided to answer as directly as possible. "Right now, nothing. I'm recovering from a car accident but my degree is in art education."

Karen zoned in on the accident. "How awful. What happened?"

"I was on my way home from a wedding shower last April when I was hit by a semi at the intersection of Highway Six and 59."

Belinda saw Robert's head swing her way, his brow furrowed. "When was your accident?"

"The first Sunday in April. Why?"

Robert tilted his head. "Was it about seven o'clock at night?"

Belinda nodded.

"A silver SUV? I couldn't figure out the make of the car."

Belinda nodded again.

"Wow!" Robert sat up straight as an arrow and shook his head. "I was sitting next to you at the light, waiting to turn left onto Highway Six. I was texting a friend. When the light turned green, I noticed the SUV moving in my peripheral vision. I looked up from putting my phone down and saw this semi fly through the intersection. It slammed into your car. The impact pushed the SUV into one of the pillars on the right. The semi ended up hitting one of the center pillars."

His face went pale. "If I hadn't hesitated because I was texting…"His voice seemed to crackle as he talked. "It could've been me dead or in a coma."

Karen gasped. Colin froze. Robert gave Belinda a penetrating gaze and for a second, they connected.

"I jumped out to see if I could do anything. All I saw was blood and hair, and realized, if the woman in the car was alive, I had no business moving her. So I called 911. The truck driver crawled out of his rig, but the woman…you. They had to use the "Jaws-of-Life" to cut you out. After I talked to the police, I sat in my car for about an hour. I couldn't do anything until they cleared the highway. I had a front row seat. From how the EMT's were handling you, I knew you were alive. It was as if everything moved in slow motion."

Belinda watched Robert, captivated by his story of her near demise.

When he finished, he gave her a strange look. "Are you okay?"

Belinda's thoughts ran rampant. *What if he'd been hit? What if he'd died? Oh, God. I wouldn't be sitting…we wouldn't be sitting here tonight. I never would have met him.*

She swallowed hard. "Yeah…it's just…this is the first time anyone has ever put into words what happened that night. I read the police reports, but it's different hearing it, especially from someone who could've also been hurt."

"When I saw them loading the stretcher into the ambulance, I said, 'God help whoever was in that car.'"

"Thank you. I guess He heard you."

Robert nodded and half smiled. He lowered his head and fiddled with his drink, rubbing a finger slowly up and down its side.

A hush fell over the people seated around the table. Robert's graphic description put a dent in the lite-hearted mood. Belinda didn't want anyone to pity her, so she attempted to make light of the situation. She waved as if to brush it off and readjusted herself to lean forward on the table. "Well, anyway, as a result of the collision, I spent six months in a coma. I woke up near the end of September."

Belinda noticed something. Robert didn't lift his head, but his finger stopped rubbing the side of the glass the second she gave her last explanation. This made Belinda curious.

"You were in a coma for six months? You don't even look like you were injured. Especially by the way you walk," Karen sneered, flashing a deceptive smile. "Do you remember anything after the accident?"

Belinda held her sight on Karen for an instant before she answered. "I remember some thoughts, maybe more like dreams." She glanced at Robert. He just sat there with his head down, not moving. "They expected me to die, but my doctor said my dreams kept me fighting for my life." Robert peered up with intense, steel blue eyes.

"What kind of dreams?" Karen cut her fish and took a bite.

Belinda diverted her attention back to Karen. "Things associated with the sounds I heard around me and the movements I felt." She didn't want to divulge the life she lived with Robert in her "Dream Reality" and Karen appeared satisfied with her brief explanation.

Karen picked up her glass and smirked. "You look pretty healthy."

"I was told it was because I was young and in pretty good shape before the accident—that's why I was able to recover so well. I also have my horse to thank. Besides having to do the physical labor of cleaning up after him, riding is a very good exercise to regain muscle tone and coordination."

Karen chimed in. "Robert is an excellent rider. He could've made the Olympic equestrian team when he was in college."

Belinda turned to Robert. "You ride?"

Robert opened his mouth to answer, but closed it as Karen butted in. "He loves his horse so much he still lives in his parents' guesthouse." A cackle arose while she stroked his arm.

Robert turned toward Karen and his response shocked Belinda. "I'm sure Belinda can understand that. She probably feels the same way about Beau."

Belinda sat up more erect. *He knows the name of my horse.* She knew she had never mentioned it, and where else would it have come up in a conversation?

Unable to let this go, she asked, "Robert, how do you know the name of my horse?"

Robert stiffened. "Garrett mentioned it at work."

Belinda studied him for a few seconds. His answer sounded reasonable, so she turned her attention back to Karen. "Do you ride, Karen?"

"OH, NO! I hate the filthy animals!"

As a polite gesture, she nodded as if she understood Karen's distaste of horses.

"Well, I'm glad you made it." Colin leaned in toward Karen, lifting his drink toward her as he emphasized his next statement. "And I *do* appreciate her walk." He sneered the whole time in Karen's direction before he turned back to Belinda. "If you hadn't made it, I would've missed out on getting to know you."

Belinda chuckled. "How could you have missed me? You never would've known I existed."

From across the table, she thought she heard Robert mumble something like, "But I would've." She decided to let it slide.

During a lull in the conversation, Belinda's mind drifted back to Robert's actions at the party, and to Karen's engagement ring. *Payback.* That's what she wanted. She would never mention his indiscretions in front of Karen, but she wanted to see Romeo squirm.

Belinda found the perfect time when Karen looked away, hailing a waiter. Acting as though she didn't see Robert glance her way, Belinda raked her index finger through the thick, creamy icing of her chocolate cake. She slipped her tongue out and slowly ran it over the icing, licking some off. To add sensual excitement, she plunged her finger into her mouth, puckering her lips around it, and rotated it back and forth to suck it clean. She slowly pulled it out and examined it. Finding a trace more chocolate, she flicked her tongue over the spot. Savoring the delicious taste, she closed her eyes and sucked in a deep breath as she ran her tongue around her lips, cleaning off every bit of icing. With a seductive glance, mouth slightly parted, she looked up through her lashes, ending the exhibition.

The expression on Robert's face spoke volumes as he seemed to force air into his lungs and shifted—clearly uncomfortable—from side to side. Satisfied, she thought, *another mission accomplished.* Belinda bowed her head and turned her attention back to the cake. Taking a bite, she acted like she had done nothing out of the ordinary.

Robert was caught off guard by Belinda's unexpected display of sensuality. That tongue. That mouth. He froze and his stomach knotted while he watched her erotic actions. Reaching for each side of his chair seat, he gripped it as tight as he could to control himself—to keep from leaping over the table and making a spectacle of himself. He wanted nothing more at the moment than to capture her tongue, her mouth and do...*STOP! Remember your resolution.* He couldn't believe she had the guts to pull something like that with Karen sitting beside him.

He glanced at Karen to make sure she wasn't watching. Thank goodness she was still in a deep conversation with the waiter she had waved down earlier over a menu item. With a ghost of a grin, he narrowed his eyes at Belinda and inconspicuously shook his head. He mouthed, *You're bad.* She just smirked and batted her lashes.

The waiter started clearing the dishes. Robert leaned in close against the table and asked Belinda where she parked. "I'm at the other end of the mall in the covered parking lot." Karen had parked right outside the restaurant. Colin had parked in the middle of the mall and Robert, to his surprise, had parked in the same lot as Belinda.

A discussion of how everyone would leave took a few minutes. The men wanted to make sure the ladies reached their vehicles safely. First, everyone would walk Karen to her car. Colin, Robert, and Belinda would proceed through the mall parting with Colin in the center. Finally, Robert would escort Belinda to the farthest parking lot.

Knowing he would be alone with Belinda tied his stomach in knots and he prayed Karen didn't notice his nervousness.

Robert escorted Karen to her Mini Cooper. Normally he would've been going home with her. However, she would be leaving early in the morning to catch a flight to Europe. She decided it wouldn't make sense for both of them to go without sleep.

"I'll call you when I get home."

"Okay." She smiled and stroked his cheek. "I love you and will miss you." She reached up to kiss him.

"I love you too." He opened the door. "Drive safely." Karen slid in. Robert pushed the door shut, stepped back, and waited.

Karen threw the gearshift into reverse and the car rolled backward. At full stop, she turned her gaze toward the mall door, and straight into Belinda's watchful stare. *Bitch!* She clutched the steering wheel tighter, turning her knuckles white. Ever since their engagement, Robert had seemed distracted.

The suspicious perfume scent detected on his jacket when he came back from his parents' party on New Year's Eve made her think there could be someone else, maybe Belinda, since she had attended. *Angel Scent?* His tightened jaw and tense shoulder muscles when they kissed goodbye told her something bothered him.

She prayed her fear was unfounded, but if he did stray, she would never know until after the fact because she traveled so much for her job. Still, when she was home, they spent every free minute together. *Angel Scent?* The more she dwelled on the possibility, the more it ate at her. Popping the car into drive, she drove past Robert and threw him a kiss, smiling broadly to disguise the tense muscles her suspicion created.

***

Belinda and Colin waited just inside in full view of the interaction between the couple in the parking lot. A wave of sadness came over Belinda as she witnessed how affectionately they responded to each other, but when Karen stared at her before driving off, the blood in her veins went cold.

"Belinda." She turned toward Colin, giving him her attention. "I'd really like to see you again. I planned to ask for your number at the party but waited too long and we know how that played out. Would you mind if I call you?"

Belinda turned back to the door and saw Robert walking in their direction. Saddened, she decided there would never be a Plan A. Robert wouldn't be part of her life because she could never be "the other woman." Karen seemed nice despite her death-ray stares and Belinda had no reason to hurt her by pursing Robert. Colin was a benefit. If she and Robert were destined to be apart in her "New Reality," then she would enjoy the company and affections of another man. Colin could provide this very nicely as Plan B. Turning back to Colin, she smiled and asked for his phone. She tapped in her number and gave it back without saying a word. With this small action, Plan B went into motion.

Just then, Robert came through the door and the trio proceeded to walk to their next destination, the center of the mall. Colin said his goodbyes to Robert and told him he would see him at work in the morning. He turned to Belinda and gave her a gentle kiss on the cheek. "I'll be in touch." She smiled and gave a nod.

Now alone, neither of them said anything while they walked—their pace deliberately slow, as if neither wanted this time together to end. Belinda had so many questions but she didn't know how to approach any of them without sounding like she was prying…or a lunatic. Finally, Robert broke the silence. "Where do you keep your horse?"

Belinda took a deep breath, glad he thought of something they could talk about. "The stables right next to your subdivision."

"The ones that share the trails around our house?"

"The very ones."

"I'm on those trails all the time. How come I've never seen you riding?"

"I don't know. I'm out there every day." She offered a more feasible explanation. "I ride in the morning, most likely when you're at work."

Silence filled the gap in the conversation until he spoke up. "Uh, thank you for your note."

A slight giggle escaped. "It was still on the windshield? I didn't know how else to say thank you. So I just left it."

He smiled at her and his deep blue gaze thrilled her soul. She couldn't help wondering if he knew what effect he cast on her.

The parking garage door came into view, meaning their time together would be over soon. Belinda wished with all her heart that she could hold Robert's hand as they walked. She constantly had to remind herself this wasn't the Robert of her "Dream Reality" and this one was engaged.

They reached the glass door that divided the mall from the parking lot. Just outside she saw a red BMW Roadster. Robert held the door open.

Belinda walked straight toward his car putting a bit of a sashay in her strut. She knew what she was doing. Just like the first time she saw Robert's car in her "Dream Reality," she slid her fingers as seductively as she could over the edge of it. She started with the back fender, moved across the door and then the front fender before turning on her heels to face Robert. "Nice red car."

Her heart almost jumped at the sight she saw when she turned on her heels toward him. He stood about five feet away from the rear of the car with his thumbs hooked in his pockets and his head slightly down, but she could tell he had watched her every move. The signature smile she loved so much grew across his face as he shook his head. She melted at the sight before commenting, "I once knew someone who owned a blue one."

"I prefer red over blue."

Suddenly his mood changed. He became more serious. She watched the softness fade. He straightened his posture as he lifted his head. "Where's your car?"

Belinda studied him. She wasn't sure what just took place, but she knew she wasn't going to find out.

"It's the silver CR-V in the next aisle." She started toward it. Robert followed at a respectable distance.

She unlocked her door. He reached around her and opened it. As she moved to get in, she came as close as she could to Robert. His short, hot breaths caressed her cheek as she turned toward him. Now inches from his mouth, she gazed at him and wished she could close the distance. Her lips tingled. "Thank you for tonight. You don't know how much this meant to me."

He stepped back while she settled into the seat. "Thank you for not saying anything to Karen about what happened at my parents' house."

Belinda didn't know how to respond. Her first instinct was to tell him it wasn't a mistake. They were meant to be together. She wanted to say it out loud, to hear him tell her he knew she was right. It took all her might just to nod as he closed the door. He waited for her to start the engine and back out before he went to his car.

Belinda repeatedly slammed a fist against the steering wheel as she drove toward home. Tears of frustration streamed down her cheeks.

Through her tears she yelled, "He's engaged!" hitting the steering wheel again.

A few blocks away from the freeway, Belinda realized she needed something to help relieve her tension. *Music!* That might do—soothing music. She reached over and punched the "on" button. Only it didn't help, but made matters worse. The words of "Forever in My Mind" floated from the speakers and filled her ears. More tears trailed down her cheeks as the song reminded her of a lost love—Dream Robert. Glorious memories of being in his arms dancing and singing the words to him, and the great times they spent together in her dream, filled her mind. Realization struck that that wouldn't happen with the real Robert.

Merging onto 610, Belinda forced herself to calm down. Driving on a highway still petrified her. She wiped the tears and gave a quick flash in the rearview mirror. She did the same to the driver side mirror to watch for merging traffic. Her grip on the steering wheel tightened as she cursed the car riding her tail. "For heaven's sake, just pass me up!"

She'd driven about five miles with the same car following close behind. The car appeared small, but in the dark and in the reflections of the oncoming headlights, she couldn't see the color or recognize the make, though the shape seemed familiar. She darted her eyes from the rearview mirror to the side mirror, catching a brief flash of color. *Red! It must be Robert.* He stayed with her all the way to the turnoff to her subdivision. After she made the corner, she glanced in the rearview mirror and saw his car drive straight past.

***

Robert found being around Belinda more difficult than he expected because of his conflicted emotions. He definitely felt attracted and enjoyed the kiss they'd shared way too much, but he was engaged and had to remember that.

When he opened the mall door at the parking lot, he'd had a hard time restraining himself as her scent lofted into his nose. He inhaled deeply, taking in what little of her he could. He had slowed his pace to put some distance between them. The space didn't help. When he looked up, her gorgeous sashaying hips were making their way to his car. Watching her fingers slide over the fender had made him wish he could just grab her and taste her full lips. As he watched in anticipation, her playful mannerisms had made him smile. That is until he opened his big mouth and killed the mood. What difference did his color preference make and why did she feel the need to get inches from his face when he opened her car door? Not that he minded, but being that close and not showing her any sign of affection wrenched his insides.

He raced through the yellow light and watched it turn red in the rearview mirror. Again, he focused on the CR-V a few cars ahead of him, knowing he had to be behind it before they reached the next light. If he didn't make the turn right after it, he would lose it. He swerved into the next lane and accelerated, passing the two cars that separated him from his target. Thankfully, the lead car slowed to make a right turn, giving him the space to switch lanes and fall in behind the Honda.

Robert let out a deep breath, relieved he was right where he wanted to be. Her safe arrival home was important to him, and following her seemed like the only way he could watch out for her without stepping over his own boundary line. He didn't want anything to happen to her. He knew he couldn't take that.

CHAPTER 8

BY THE LAST week of February, Plan B was in full swing because of Robert's engagement. Of course, Belinda wouldn't turn down an opportunity to be in close proximity to this version of Robert. If the occasion presented itself, she would enjoy his company while being ever so mindful of his plans to be married to someone else. Therefore, she had no choice but to follow her second plan for her future despite praying Plan A would've been well on its way at this point.

Belinda's closing on her purchased home was scheduled for the first week of March. She had mixed feelings about moving out of her parents' home because she loved living there. During Belinda's recovery phase, her mother and she had grown closer. She now had a relationship with her that was on an adult level. Dora still hovered when needed, but had become more supportive of Belinda's need to experience life on her own terms. Belinda knew she would miss having her mother available 24-7, but the time had come to spread her wings.

Unfortunately, Robert wouldn't be a crucial part of her life. Instead, Colin would be stepping in as a potential love interest. He called Belinda a week after the group had dinner at the pub in the Galleria. At first, Belinda put him off—giving him the excuse she was busy getting everything together for the closing. Though true to some extent, in reality she was scared. She hadn't had a real date since Matt dumped her almost a year and a half ago. For now, her relationship with Colin consisted of phone calls and texting. Belinda knew this would only go so far, so she decided to take the plunge. The next time Colin extended an invitation to go out, she'd accept.

Around six o'clock on Friday evening, Belinda sat in her room, lost in the pages of her recently acquired romance novel on her new electronic reader. She just finished reading a rather steamy chapter when her cell let out the quick beep informing her to check her text messages.

Colin: Busy???
She typed in her reply. Reading.
Colin: In your neighborhood. At a meeting.
Belinda took a deep breath before replying. She had a good idea of what would be coming next. She thought, *This is it. It's now or never.*
Belinda: Where are you?
Colin: Town square. Feel like dinner?
Belinda studied the phone for a few seconds and then typed in her response. OK!
Belinda waited for a reply. An answer didn't come as quickly as she expected. She wondered why it took him so long to respond. Finally....
Colin: Pick you up in 60 ☺
Belinda: How should I dress?
Colin: Comfortably. Nothing fancy. OK?
Belinda: I'll be ready
Colin: ☺☺☺☺☺☺ Is my excitement showing?!
Belinda: Yes! I have a date to get ready for. Bye!

Colin just stared at his phone with his mouth slightly open. He couldn't believe it. *She just accepted an invitation to dinner.* He made a fist pumping gesture followed by a muffled, "Yes!"

His client, Ben Taylor, walked back into the conference room to wind up the meeting as a sense of panic came over Colin. He really didn't know much about Sugar Land and the restaurants in the area. He wanted to make a good impression. Fortunately, his client lived there.

"Hey, Ben. If a guy wanted to impress a…let's say a very attractive lady he's been trying to go out with, where would he take her for a casual but nice dinner in this area?"

Colin, usually as steady as a rock, fought the jitters in his stomach. How funny, he thought, that a single female could bring a man to a state of such insecurity.

A broad smile came across Ben's face. "Well," he said. "I'd start with some wine at the wine bar across the street. Then have dinner at Sugar End. It's a casual, quiet place for good conversation. I'd finish off the night with ice cream or yogurt, eating it around the fountain in the square. If you're lucky there might be a band playing on the City Hall steps. If not, it's still a fun place to people watch."

Colin could feel a smile spread across his face. "Thanks Ben. That sounds perfect. Well I guess we're finished here, unless you have any other questions." He gathered up the folders in front of him and held them while he waited for Ben's response.

Ben shook his head and stood. Colin placed the folders in his briefcase. Standing up, he extended his hand to Ben. "Well as usual, it was nice seeing you again."

The men shook. Colin loosened his grip to release the shake when Ben tightened his grasp and took hold of Colin's upper arm. "You enjoy yourself tonight and good luck. I have a feeling this young lady is special."

Colin turned a corner of his mouth up. "She is."

He wasted no time walking to his car, an obsidian black metallic Mercedes Roadster, his pride and joy. After all, his new position as the VP of the company's planned Canadian branch afforded him the financial means. He opened the trunk and attempted to make himself more casual by removing his suit jacket. He carefully placed it in the trunk. The tie came next. Peering down at the jacket, he thought about it being February, and if the ground hog's prediction turned out to be right, spring wouldn't be here for six more weeks. So he decided to wear it in case the night air turned cooler. He closed the trunk and as he walked around to the driver's side, he unbuttoned the first two buttons of his shirt and slipped back into his jacket.

Once in the car, he flipped down the visor. As he exposed the mirror, the lights caused him to squint until his eyes adjusted to the brightness. He gave his hair a quick mussing. Satisfied, he retrieved a small plastic container from the console. Using his thumb, he flipped open the lid and popped a few breath mints in his mouth and crushed them between his teeth. He gave himself another once-over in the mirror and then pushed it shut. He had managed to kill only fifteen minutes.

He let out a sigh of frustration and placed his elbow on the door as he rubbed his chin. Waiting would drive him nuts. Patience wasn't his thing in situations like this. So he hit the start button and listened to the sound of the engine. It amplified off the concrete walls of the parking garage, setting his heart on fire almost as much as his thoughts of Belinda.

He attempted to drive very slowly to her house, but the sheer power of the car made it impossible. Then an idea came to him—he'd stop for flowers.

***

Belinda walked to her closet to select something to wear. She decided on a good pair of jeans, a white, long-sleeve, collared blouse, and a fitted blue blazer that ended just above her hips. A pair of black, three-inch pumps finished off the outfit. She decided to be dressed and ready before letting her parents know she'd be going out for the evening. She knew both would be shocked, but happy for her, especially her mother.

She stood in front of the full-length mirror making half-turns, wanting to be sure everything was in place. This would be her first date since before the accident. Her plans had changed, but life still had to go on. Feathers filled her throat and she prayed she wouldn't make a fool of herself. The dating scene had changed so much since her college years.

She gave herself one last once-over. "Well, it's now or never."

Belinda casually walked downstairs to the family room. "How do I look?" She twirled around.

Dora and James raised their heads from their reading materials. "Are you going out?" Dora asked.

"I accepted a date with Colin. We're going out to dinner."

Dora's expression softened as she looked at Belinda and then her husband. "Honey, we're so glad."

"I know. It's time." The room fell silent for a few uncomfortable seconds and Belinda's thoughts drifted to the memory of Robert until the chime of the doorbell broke the stillness. She shrugged. "Well, I guess this is it."

Belinda answered the door. There stood a handsome, tall, blonde-haired man with vivid blue eyes. Without saying a word, he presented her with a bouquet of assorted fresh-cut flowers he had hidden behind his back.

She smiled. "Thank you. They're lovely." Belinda placed the bouquet to her nose and took a deep breath. The scent should have encouraged thoughts of this sweet man's gesture, but it didn't. She thought, *they're not roses like "Dream Robert" gave me.*

She caught herself. If she allowed thoughts of Robert to invade her time with Colin, this poor man would never have a chance. Nor would she. So she kicked Robert out and vowed to give Colin the break he deserved. "Let me tell my parents I'm leaving and put these in some water." She disappeared, leaving the front door open. A few minutes later, she returned and closed it. "Okay, I'm ready. My mom said she'd take care of the flowers."

She walked beside Colin on the path to his car. He opened the passenger door. Belinda stopped momentarily to admire the convertible. "Nice!" Colin smiled as she slipped in. In the driver's seat, he seemed to puff out his chest while he backed out of the drive and accelerated, making the hum of the engine more exaggerated. Belinda chuckled silently. *Men!*

Colin took all the credit for Ben's suggestion of this well thought out date with this beautiful creature he'd been longing for since the first time he met her.

After the evening's events, they walked slowly down the street toward his car. Colin recalled her sashay at the Galleria and decided to let her stroll ahead of him so he could get another glimpse of her perfect derriere. He paused at a store window and pretended to be interested in the display, which gave her a few seconds' lead without putting too much distance between them. He glanced in her direction and enjoyed watching her walk away. When Belinda turned around and flipped her hair over her shoulder, flashing a huge smile of delight, his breath hitched. His ruse ended.

"Okay, bud!" she playfully warned as she pointed a finger at him, wagging it back and forth.

He thought his heart would drop at the sight and felt truly grateful she said yes to the date. Once he caught up, he almost put an arm around her but stopped for a second. He decided to take a chance and followed through. To his amazement, she not only let him, she snuggled closer. So he tightened his grip and enjoyed their walk.

Riding back to Belinda's house, they filled the time talking. Neither had given out too much personal information over the course of the evening. They conversed about the usual stuff a pair would talk about on a first date, mostly small talk.

The porch light was on and it shone brightly, marking the path to the door. She placed her key in the lock, gave it a twist, and then turned toward Colin. Even in heels, she only came up to his shoulders. "I had a really nice time. Thank you for inviting me."

"I enjoyed myself too. Thank you for saying yes, this time." Colin swallowed hard. He wondered if a kiss would be a nice touch or the premature end to what he deemed a perfect night. However, she didn't mind his arm around her when they walked, so he figured he'd go for it if the opportunity presented itself.

"I'm sorry. I'm just out of practice and was pretty nervous about dating again. The accident really took a good part of my life away from me." She bowed her head.

Colin inched closer. He gently raised her head with one finger placed under her chin. Extending his neck, he bent over to place a kiss on her delicious, full lips. At the same time, she rose on her tiptoes to maintain their contact.

The kiss could only be described as sweet. Not too long and no tongue, nevertheless it stirred Colin to the core. As they separated, he gazed down at Belinda with a faint smile on his face. To his surprise, she placed her arms around his neck as he lowered his to her waist. Their lips locked again. He pressed her to him and lifted her slightly. He brushed his teasing tongue across her warm lips. The action caused a pleasant reaction—Belinda parted hers. Colin noticed a twinge of heightened arousal and could've easily extended the kiss, but he knew not to prolong it past its prime. He didn't want to negate the wonderful night by expecting too much at the end. So he slowly steadied her on her feet and released her, much to his regret. Belinda's eyes remained closed as Colin placed her down. He scanned her face as he took in the softness of her features.

Belinda was amazed at how much she enjoyed the kiss. His lips were soft and he handled her very gently. She lowered her arms from his neck and opened her eyes. He gazed at her with a sweet smile on his face.

"Is this the first time you've been kissed since the accident?"

The warm sensation of blood rushed to her checks. She looked at the ground and fibbed. "It's the first time I've been kissed since I broke up with my old boyfriend."

"When did you break up with him?"

"Almost a year and a half ago." She quickly added, "Remember, almost a year of that was taken up by the accident."

He chuckled placing his arms around her waist again, tugging her close. "Well from what I just experienced, you're not that out of practice." He reached down and gave her a short playful kiss. "I think I'd better go. Thank you again for an enjoyable evening. I'll call you later."

Belinda nodded as she pulled back, opened the door, and stepped into the house. "Good night, Colin." She closed the door with a bump of her butt. Standing there for a second, she reviewed the night feeling pleased with herself. She had successfully gone on her first date and hadn't blown it. In fact, it was rather pleasant. The only thing that would've made it perfect would've been having the date with Robert.

"Belinda, come in here. I want to talk to you." Belinda giggled shaking her head as she walked into the family room to meet her inquisitor, her mother.

CHAPTER 9

BELINDA PICKED UP the pen and signed on every line tagged by a pink sticky arrow. The title company agent gathered the mortgage forms and thumbed through them. She smiled at Belinda and dangled a set of keys. "Congratulations! You're the proud owner of your own home."

"Thank you." Belinda wrapped her fingers around the keys as a slight flutter filled her chest.

Plan B seemed to be moving along nicely, but in her heart she still wished Plan A had won out. Colin and she had gone on several dates during the last few weeks. Ever the gentleman, he never pushed her for more than she was willing to give. She appreciated having him in her life, but he wasn't Robert. She constantly had to remind herself, her Robert didn't exist.

Walking out of the title company, she clutched the keys. The pointed teeth pressed into her palm. Tossing them into her bag, she decided to stop by her new home before going back to her parents' place.

Belinda didn't have far to drive down Highway Six. It only took about ten minutes to get to the entrance of her new neighborhood. The patio homes were at the front end. After a few turns, she pulled into the driveway.

Placing the key in the lock, she turned it slowly until she heard the click. A slight flutter arose in her heart as she pushed the door open about a foot. Heat blasted her before she ever took one step over the threshold. The AC had been off, but she didn't mind—this being her first time to walk in as the owner.

The flutter turned into a swarm of thoughts. *I'm a homeowner. Did I make the right decision? How will I be able to make this place meet my needs? Would it have been easier to continue living with my parents?*

"My parents?" flowed from her mouth in a whispered tone and stopped her from moving. Walking into this house would mark a new beginning. "Am I doing the right thing?" She stared at the door. Lifting her head, she let out a gust of air. "Well, I have to grow up sometime."

Belinda gripped the doorknob and pushed the door wide open. She inhaled deeply and stepped into the foyer. The odor of fresh paint overpowered her sense of smell and, mixed with the heat, made her gag.

"Great, now I'm going to throw up." She braced herself against the foyer wall, giving her stomach a few seconds to settle down. She cupped her hand over her nose and mouth. Taking a shallow breath, and another, she knew she would became accustomed to the smell, but the heat would limit how long she could stay.

Wanting to savor the short time, she forced herself to move on. Passing through the small entry, she stopped to study the long wall that led to the open-concept living, dining and kitchen area. "I'll put a hall table with two lamps, and a mirror above it right here." She flipped her hair over her shoulder and walked toward the great room putting a bounce in her step.

In the middle of the room, she stopped and fisted her hands on her hips. Here she could appreciate the new paint color. The light was brighter. As part of the purchase package, the seller completely repainted the place in the color Belinda picked—taupe beige. It added a warm tone. The neutral color would blend with any furniture choices.

A stone hit the pit of her stomach as she swung her head back and forth between the living and dining area. "I don't know what to do in here. The table in the foyer seemed easy compared to these two spaces." She shook her head. A bead of sweat ran down her temple, reminding her to move along. "I have a lot to think about." She wanted her home to reflect her personality and needed it to be somewhere she felt safe and comfortable.

Her mother planned on helping her put the place together, but Belinda questioned whether the two could pull it off. Making the wrong decisions on the size of the furniture pieces and the accessories concerned her. Belinda stopped and stood for a few seconds thinking. She allowed her mind to fill with too many doubts. A little of her past lack of self-confidence raised its ugly head. She scolded herself. "You're supposed to be enjoying this—not tormenting yourself."

Getting a hold, she walked through to the master bedroom. "I know I want a four-poster bed here with plush linens. Nothing too fussy. And floor length drapes." Spinning around, she walked to the other side of the room.

She covered her mouth and tapped a finger on her cheek, thinking for a second. "A nice long dresser with a lamp on this end and maybe a TV on the other." The flutter of excitement returned and she formed a smile.

Another bead of sweat trickled down and tickled her skin. She wiped the drop away and decided to leave. As she turned, the room slightly spun, making her wobble. Belinda braced herself against the doorjamb knowing she needed fresh air to escape the effects of the heat and fumes. She picked up her pace toward the front door, but stopped in the great room, giving the place one last look. "Mom and I will turn you into a home."

Her parents had told her she could stay with them as long as she wished. This gave her the luxury of taking her time with decorating the house to make it her home. Belinda paid cash for the place and could afford to wait with no pressure to move in until everything was ready.

Over the next few weeks, Belinda and her mother made multiple shopping trips. They purchased everything needed to stock a kitchen with all the basics. However, Belinda found herself questioning every decision, especially when it came to the style, color, and shape of the big pieces of furniture.

"Honey, just stick to neutrals for now. It'll be easy to add color with the accessories," her mother advised her. To some extent, Belinda knew her mother was right. She just couldn't decide what she wanted. She didn't want everything to be beige and browns. After all, she had an art degree, so putting a room together with scale and color shouldn't be too difficult. Nevertheless, it was. This was in 3D.

The Belinda from her "Old Reality" would have agonized over her situation to the point of hiding to avoid any unnecessary conflict. Not so with the new improved version. The new Belinda did the only thing a baffled art major would do—she took her indecision by the horns and decided to tackle her dilemma straight on. She browsed the library, bookstores, and magazines for ideas, and spent countless hours searching the web, setting out to teach herself about interior design. She became obsessed with the subject. Taking it one-step further, she placed all shopping trips for furniture on hold.

In her "Old Reality" right after graduation from college, Belinda lived in her own apartment. She didn't have much money, so she relied on hand-me-downs from her parents to furnish it. In fact, the apartment had less style than the room she shared with Abbey in college. It was an accumulation of mismatched belongings. The plan had been to replace things as she could afford it, but that never happened. The accident took care of her independent living.

Presented with the opportunity to design her space from scratch, Belinda wanted to do it right. So she poured over her collection of interior design books, studying the terms and the ins-and-outs of just how to design a room around a focal point. To her amazement, the subject didn't appear as foreign as she thought and her fears of failure diminished as she learned.

***

Two weeks ago, Belinda took possession of her home. Today would be the first time she would actually spend more than a few seconds running in and out to check something or drop off something.

She programmed the AC to a comfortable 76 degrees, and left, heading for an office supply store. By the time she would arrive back, the patio home would've aired out with no rush to leave early because of the heat.

Returning, she opened the door and a refreshing stream of cool air greeted her as a sense of calm embraced her. Today she could take her time studying her new environment.

Belinda placed the tools she needed for the task on the granite counter of the kitchen island. Armed with a thirty-foot tape measure, a pad of paper, and a pencil, she proceeded to measure the living room.

At the top of the first page she wrote, LIVING ROOM and then drew a sketch of the room below it. Belinda measured the first wall and transposed it to the corresponding wall of the sketch. Then she tackled the next one.

Two hours later, Belinda completed the first phase of her project. With every room of her new living space measured, a smile broke out across her face and a sense of satisfaction filled her.

When Belinda returned to her parent's home, she walked straight to the kitchen table and spread out the supplies. Her mother stood at the stove, busy cooking dinner. "Hi, Mom."

Dora walked up behind Belinda and looked over her shoulder. "What is all this?"

"I'm reproducing my floor plan. This way I can start buying furniture and know it'll fit."

"I don't understand."

"I just spent the last few hours measuring all the rooms. Now I'm going to transfer the measurements to this graph paper and make miniature versions of each room. Once I put it together, I'll have my house. Then when I see a piece of furniture I like, I'll measure it, make a graph paper version and place it in the room it belongs in on my floor plan. That way I'll know if it'll fit."

"Good idea. I'll leave you to your work. We can eat dinner in the dining room so your project won't be disturbed."

Belinda only stopped to eat. The digital display on the microwave read eleven o'clock when she put the last measurement on paper. Her eyes hurt from the strain of counting the squares of the graph paper. As she rubbed them, she could hear the monologue from a host of one of the late late night shows and hoped her mom hadn't dozed off.

"Mom."

"Yeah."

"Can you come in here? I'm finished."

Dora walked in and stood next to her daughter, reviewing her masterpiece.

"Well, what do you think?" Belinda asked.

"I think this will help you get your place furnished." Dora nudged her shoulder. "You know, Belinda, if you bought a bed and some stools for the kitchen island, you could move in. Living there might make it easier to figure out what you want. Not that there is a rush for you to move out. You know your dad and I will miss you."

Belinda didn't say anything. She just nodded.

Dora nudged her on the arm. "We could make a trip to go see Jim McIngvale tomorrow."

"Who?"

"You know 'Mattress Mack' the owner of Gallery Furniture."

The next day the pair piled into Belinda's CR-V and drove to the showroom located on I-45 North. Given Belinda's dislike for freeway driving, she wanted a place where she could pick out everything she needed, kind of a one-stop shopping retail chain. Gallery Furniture would fit the bill.

On one of her internet searches of the store's inventory, she found a contemporary, mahogany, four-poster bed. The two walked straight to the bedroom section.

Locating the bed, Belinda first took pictures of it from all angles with her cell phone. Next, she pulled a tape measure from her purse. "Here." She handed the tip of the tape to her mother and the two obtained the height, width, and length of the bed in no time.

After obtaining all the needed ordering numbers, the two left to hunt for stools for the kitchen island. Belinda stopped and turned to give the bed one more look from a distance, when the matching dresser caught her attention. She studied it for a moment and decided she liked it too. Turning toward her mother, she pointed at it. "Mom, let's measure the dresser as well. I think it will fit my needs."

The bar stools acquisition came easier than Belinda anticipated. She found three wrought iron ones she liked right off the bat. Walking to the main desk, the women passed by some artwork. Belinda stopped to study a forest scene. "Mom, how do you think this would work in the living room?"

Dora stood beside her daughter and studied the painting. "It looks similar to one you did in college. Why don't you use your own pictures?"

"Mine?"

"Yes, yours. I saved them. They're stored in the closet of the guest room. Look'em over before you buy anything. I think I'd rather see your originals on the walls than this stuff. We can pull them out later this week."

Art teachers were required to take a variety of art classes in college, but did that translate into her being able to paint? *How creative was I? Did I have any talent?* After waking from the coma, Belinda had no desire to pick up a brush and place it on canvas. In fact, it seemed she had difficulty with anything creative. What most disturbed her, though, was she didn't remember any of her paintings. Giving the forest scene one last look, she turned to follow her mother.

The next stop was the main desk to ask questions about ordering over the phone and delivery. Belinda didn't want to place the order until she knew the pieces would fit. She'd make her paper furniture templates, and if everything fit, she'd call in the order, saving her a tormenting drive on the freeway.

Jim McIngvale seemed more than willing to help her. He patiently answered all her questions and made all the arrangements to deliver her purchases once she confirmed them.

"I can have everything delivered and set up this evening if you'd like." Same day delivery was a unique feature of Jim's business and he had built a furniture empire around it.

At first, Belinda had almost jumped at the chance to spend her first night in her own place. But, a hint of sadness in her mother's face made her decide that the next day would do fine. "No, I'll wait until tomorrow."

***

As the delivery truck pulled away, Belinda stood in her bedroom admiring her new bed and matching dresser. The makeshift floor plan idea had worked and the bed didn't overpower the master bedroom.

Scanning around the room, she imagined the finished product once the curtains softened the space. She drifted her fingers over the foot of the mattress, now covered in soft Egyptian cotton sheets. She moved her hand up the cool, firm mahogany bedpost and stroked it up and down, allowing her mind to wander where it shouldn't go.

Gripping the post, she spun around and flopped backward, landing in the middle of the bed. She shut her eyes and clenched the sheet as she visualized Robert and herself in the throes of passion, like the numerous times that took place in her dreams. Her breathing quickened and her back arched, remembering the heat of Robert's flesh against hers. She only allowed herself to enjoy a brief visit to this smoldering memory before she came to her senses.

Belinda opened her eyes and stared up at the ceiling, her heart now heavy with sadness. What occurred in her dream would never happen with the real Robert and she needed to stop dwelling on the fact they'd never be together. Taking a deep breath, Belinda rocked her head to clear the thoughts and get her mind back on track. She sat up and reminded herself, *Move on with your life.*

Now with the furniture delivered, she couldn't think of one reason not to move in. Belinda had purchased everything she needed to make the place functional, and living there might help her finish furnishing it like her mother had suggested. She would talk with her parents and plan to move in over the weekend. Maybe Colin would be willing to help as well.

***

Belinda watched Colin sitting on the floor with pieces of wood scattered around him, attempting to assemble the two side tables she had purchased at a huge box store. In front of him on the floor lay the tiny tool that came packaged with the instructions and an open bag of hardware. He held the instruction sheet in one hand while the other repeatedly swiped through his blonde hair. Belinda giggled at the flurry of sounds coming from him. "Uh. Gosh! What the heck? WWWhat the…?"

Belinda just finished unpacking the last box of clothes. "Those instructions getting to you?"

Without looking up, he thrust the sheet of paper at her. "Here, you try."

She took the instructions and gave them a quick scan. Studying the mess on the floor, she furrowed her brow and knew the construction process might be a little more difficult than she had anticipated. The paper floated to the floor when she released it. "Hmmm. I'll be right back. I think this is going to require some wine."

About ten minutes later she returned with a small but well stocked toolbox, a cookie sheet with two wine glasses and an open bottle of wine balanced on it. An empty cupcake tin shared the cookie sheet.

Colin scrunched his nose. "Are you going to bake something?"

Laughing, she carefully placed her possessions on the floor in front of her before sitting beside him. "This should help." First, she poured them each a glass of wine and motioned for him to join her in a silent toast, and then they drank. Placing the glasses aside she said, "Watch and learn."

She picked up the opened hardware bag and separated everything into the cupcake tin. Next, the wooden pieces were categorized in neat piles. Looking over her organized, disassembled side table, she extended her hand toward Colin. "Instructions please." He firmly placed the rumpled paper in her palm. Taking one step at a time, the two worked to assemble the first table.

Two hours passed before the second table found its new home next to the bed. A crystal ball lamp sat atop each table. A soft glow of light emanated through the white shades. Belinda walked over and turned off the overhead light. The mood of the room changed—it softened.

Belinda joined Colin at the foot of the bed to admire their handiwork. She could now picture the room as she had imagined it. When finished, it would be a tranquil, comfortable room—her sanctuary from the world.

She smiled up at him. "Thank you for your help."

"Umm, you're the one who got it organized."

Colin wondered if he'd ever be invited into her bed. They had been on several dates together and he had been more than willing to help her out when she needed it. Their relationship seemed very comfortable in most aspects, but when it came to intimacy, she held back. They had kissed and her kisses sent him through the roof, but she wouldn't go any further. Taking the relationship to the next level was all he could think about when the kissing got really hot. Belinda was a sweet, gorgeous, sexy, intelligent woman and he was a healthy male filled with raging hormones.

He decided to ask a question that would either get him kicked out or open up an invitation. "Do you think the bed is long enough for me?" He kept his eyes straight ahead and waited for her response.

Not saying a word, she turned and walked out of the room. Colin lowered his chin to his chest. He was going to be kicked out. "Belinda! I didn't mean anything by that." He backpedaled as he turned and followed her down the hall into the kitchen. "Belinda, please?"

Belinda picked up another breathing bottle of wine and two clean wine glasses. "Okay, sit. We need to talk." He did as she asked. She poured the wine and joined Colin at the island. After taking a deep breath, she began. "Colin, I really like you—"

He finished the statement with, "But I'm not—"

Belinda placed her finger over his mouth, stopping him from speaking. "Let me finish." He nodded and she removed it. "I really like you. I liked you from the first time we met at the Pendleton party. You're everything I could ask for if I was going to become romantic with a man."

Feeling her face flash warm, she lowered her head, hoping he wouldn't notice, and paused for a few moments. "The accident, well I'm just not ready." She gazed into his glacier blue eyes and wished she could tell him the complete truth—the truth which included Robert. For now, the partial story would have to do.

Searching for the words, she did the best she could to explain what rattled around in her brain. "There's a lot I remember, but I still have gaps. My friends and family have helped me fill in lots of the empty spaces because they experienced those memories with me, but there are still areas of my life I can't remember. Bits and pieces are just gone—like experiences with people I don't see anymore. For example, there are parts of my relationship with Matt, my old boyfriend, I may never get back. I spent three years with him and remember very little of what we did when we were together.

"Since the accident, I've experienced episodes. I'll be in a restaurant or a store that triggers a memory. Everything starts revolving around me and I'm just standing in the middle of this blur. Then as the spinning slows down, details come into focus and fall into place like a puzzle. When it stops, I have a piece of my memory back. It's very confusing and it takes me a few minutes to process what happened. This has been happening more frequently lately.

"My psychologist doesn't think it would be a good idea for me to be emotionally attached to anyone while I'm still having these experiences and I agree with him."

Colin's heart squeezed from the sad, lost look on Belinda's face, making him appreciate how much she had really been through since she woke up. Her round, soft eyes, glazed with tears gave him a wrenching feeling.

He reached over and wrapped his arms around her. Warmth radiated from her and she felt so good. He wished he could expect more but knew that was impossible. Colin didn't say anything. He tried to put himself in her place and wondered how he would feel if he couldn't remember anything about this magnificent creature in his arms. He pulled away and released her, placing his hands on hers to let her know he felt empathetic to her situation and to encourage her to continue. "What can I do?"

"Be my friend. I promise you'll be the first to know if I can take our relationship further." She hesitated and briefly lowered her head. "I'll also understand if you need to move on."

Her sad look killed him inside, melting him until he became putty. He had no alternative but to give her what she asked. He would hang in there, praying she would decide to take their relationship to the next level, and possibly beyond. "Okay. Friends it is."

After pulling her closer, he held her head to his chest. They stayed locked in the embrace until Colin scanned around the empty living and dining room. "What are you planning on doing with these rooms?"

Belinda swiveled the stool seat around to survey the space in question. "I have no idea."

"Why don't you ask Mrs. Pendleton for some ideas? She's an interior designer. Tell her I told you to call." He gave her a gentle squeeze. "Remember Robert? That's his mom, and since he and I are best friends, I'm sure she'd be glad to help you out."

With her back to Colin, he couldn't see her surprised reaction to the information. She almost dismissed the notion. Then she thought, *Why not?* Robert would never be a part of her life. Anyway, why should she live her life around anything that does or does not involve him? Robert made his decision, now she had to make hers according to what was best for her. If asking Robert's mother for help was good for her, then Mrs. Pendleton would be asked. So she nodded and said, "That just might be a good idea."

CHAPTER 10

THE CELL PHONE sat on the kitchen counter. Belinda just stared at it. She hadn't discussed the conversation she had with Colin about Sandra Pendleton with anyone, especially her mother. She figured she'd call first and then fill her mother in on her plan to consult an interior designer. After all if it didn't pan out, why say anything to inflate potential emotions over the idea?

Belinda sighed and picked up the phone, punching in the numbers to the Crescent Oaks Interior Design Company.

"Hello. Sandra Pendleton. May I help you?"

Belinda held her breath, unable to respond immediately. She wasn't expecting Mrs. Pendleton to answer. "Um. Uh. Yes. Hello. I don't know if you remember me. I'm Belinda Davies, the girl who fainted at your New Year's Eve party." She tapped her fist on the counter for starting the conversation that way.

"Oh, yes. How are you?"

"Very well, thank you." Belinda's words faltered. Her mouth went dry and her stomach flip-flopped as she squeezed the phone a bit tighter. She was talking to the mother of Robert Pendleton, the man of her dreams. "The reason I'm calling…well, I need some help. I just purchased a home and…well, I don't have any furniture for my great room and I don't know where to start."

A giggle came through the phone. "Oh, I fully understand. Is this your first place?"

"Yes, my first purchased one. Colin Brockman suggested I call you. He said you might be able to help me out."

"You know Colin? He's such a sweet man."

"He's a friend." Belinda added, "A dear friend."

"Well, I'll have to see it. Are you free anytime today?"

Belinda's mind did a quick balancing act. *Can this actually be happening this fast?* "I'm free all day. Just give me a time."

The two hashed out the details. As Belinda disconnected the call, butterflies stirred in the recesses of her stomach. Mrs. Sandra Pendleton, Robert Pendleton's mother would be at her home at one o'clock.

As the clock on the kitchen wall neared the appointed time, Belinda's frayed nerves made her nearly pass out. She paced the room, wringing her hands. The excited butterflies in her stomach reached tornado status and wouldn't let her calm down.

She opened the refrigerator door and wrapped her fingers around the neck of a bottle of wine. About to pull it off the shelf, she hesitated and decided against it. She wanted to make a good impression on Mrs. Pendleton and alcohol on her breath could be a hindrance.

Belinda walked laps around the island, easing the tension in her mind, until the chime from the doorbell interrupted. Glancing at the clock that read 12:55, she bit her lower lip to ward off another wave of queasiness. Steadying herself with her hip, Belinda rested against the counter top while she told herself to breathe. A gush of air filled her lungs. "I can do this," she said softly to herself. Another chime from the doorbell shattered the air, startling her. She drew in another deep breath and then headed for the door.

As she reached for the doorknob, memories of her "Dream Reality" mother-in-law overwhelmed her mind. She couldn't help wondering if the woman on the other side of the door would be similar. Belinda felt a bond to the Sandra in her dreams. Would the bond enter into this reality?

About to turn the knob, she experienced a strange sensation—something she had never encountered before. She sensed her life would never be the same. Belinda took a second to shake off the feeling and placed a broad smile across her face as she opened the door.

On the doorstep stood Sandra, dressed in a pair of black slacks, a simple white tee, and layers of gold chains around her neck. Her hair was perfectly styled in a short pageboy and her makeup complemented her look. She appeared comfortable yet professional. "Good afternoon, Belinda," she said as she extended her hand.

A warm, peaceful sensation waved over Belinda as she returned Sandra's greeting. She stood there bewildered, staring at Sandra, but didn't release the handshake, acutely aware of her body relaxing.

Sandra tightened her grip. A familiar wave of emotion stirred deep inside her. She realized this young woman standing in front of her was someone with a gentle and kind soul. Sandra prided herself on recognizing what she referred to as "pure souls," people who were not vindictive or had an agenda. They were just honest, good people who wanted to do the right thing and Miss Davies fit that description.

She smiled and placed her other hand over Belinda's. "Shall we go in to see your home?" She didn't give Belinda a chance to respond—she just walked in. Stepping aside, Belinda opened the door wider. Sandra made her way to the great room before she turned on her heels toward Belinda. "This is a very nice floor plan. I love how open it is. Miss Davies, what would you like my help with?"

The simple question opened the floodgates to Belinda's ideas, or lack of them. She showed Sandra what she'd accomplished in the bedroom. Back in the kitchen, with some encouragement from Sandra, Belinda displayed her paper floor plan of her home. "I'm just not sure where to go from here. I want to make sure I choose the right scale furniture for these two rooms." Belinda pointed to the empty living and dining rooms.

"Well, from what I can see, you have a very good start. The bedroom furniture fits the size and dimension of the space. You did some of the work I would've done by measuring all the rooms. This will save some time and money. I can transfer your measurements into my computer program. Then we can look at these rooms in 3D when we fill them up with virtual furniture and accessories. I have my laptop with me. If you'd like we can plug in some numbers and see what we can do."

Belinda formed a hint of a curled smile. The tension she harbored minutes before opening the door dissolved. "I'd love that. Would you like some wine while you work?"

The two sat at the kitchen island talking and sipping wine while Sandra entered the measurements into the program. During the course of the conversation, Belinda told Sandra about her accident and the coma, minus the details of her dream life with Sandra's son. The subject of Robert did however come up several times after Belinda described her impromptu dinner at the Galleria with Robert, Karen, and Colin.

Pursing her lips, Sandra didn't seem to hold back her displeasure for Karen. "She isn't what I'd call daughter-in-law material and I don't really appreciate that they're engaged. I tolerate her and she does the same to me.

Oh, she's nice enough but…" She trailed off her statement before she looked up from the computer. She stared at Belinda with a serious expression. "He needs someone like you."

Belinda's mouth dropped open, not exactly sure how to respond, so she didn't. She noticed Sandra became more somber.

"He needs someone who is kind and would love him for who he is. For the past year or so, he has seemed so lost. He tells us he's fine, but his father and I have noticed a change."

Flashing Belinda an embarrassed glance, Sandra didn't say anything else for a few seconds. "I don't know why I brought that up to you. It's not like me to be so open with my personal life to someone I've just met. I'm sorry." Like a light bulb that turned on, Sandra lit up and a huge smile spread across her face. She patted Belinda's forearm and scrunched her nose slightly. "Shall we get back to work?"

She could see the concern Sandra had over Robert's life choices, but knew that subject had ended, at least for now. With a smile, Belinda lifted her wine glass to Sandra. Sandra returned the gesture as the two toasted and took a sip. Belinda felt a connection to this elegant, soft-spoken woman and knew she liked her.

At six o'clock, the two women finished playing with the multiple configurations of the rooms, thanks to the three-dimensional planning program. Now the subject of cost became the priority for Belinda. She really liked Sandra and wanted her help, but she knew it wouldn't come cheap. Her mood became more somber. "I really appreciate you working me in today. I know you can help me. Now I need to know what your services will cost."

"Well, I charge one hundred and fifty dollars an hour."

Belinda quickly did the math and realized she just racked up a bill of seven hundred and fifty dollars. She wasn't quite sure how to respond and figured the deer-in-the-headlights expression gave her away as she held her breath.

Sandra studied Belinda and realized she wasn't breathing. She placed a hand over the shocked girl's before continuing. "Today is free. This was a consultation. I admit it was a little longer than I usually spend on my first meeting, but I was enjoying myself so." She laughed as she noticed Belinda release a sigh and relax.

"So, now we have to decide where to go from here. There are two ways we can do this. I can do everything for you. I'll do the shopping, make sure all the deliveries come on time, organize any needed contractors, and then I'll put the rooms together for you. All you have to do is sit back and enjoy your new home. That's the very expensive route. The more affordable path is using me as just a consultant. This means you do all the work and I'll help you with sensible but tasteful decisions." Sandra liked Belinda and knew she'd be more than a consultant to this young lady. She knew they would become friends.

Belinda thought over her options and chose the last one. She had money, but she needed to be careful to make it last. Besides, she liked the idea of doing everything. Time wasn't an issue and her mother loved running around with her. The thought of her mother finally getting the chance to help make purchases for the patio home made her laugh to herself. Dora's frustration over her daughter's indecision would be relieved.

***

Sandra drove home trying to figure out what she could put together for dinner. Her husband usually arrived home first, followed by her son about an hour and a half later. To make things easier, she referred to her husband as Rob instead of Robert, and called her son Robert.

Rob was pretty laid back about her cooking times. Although she tried to have something ready every night, he understood her career would occasionally interfere with their meals. Most times she tried to warn him, but today she forgot all about calling because she enjoyed her visit with Belinda.

As Sandra walked through the back door of her home, she saw her husband in the kitchen. He stood at the sink with an apron on, washing lettuce. "Hi, Doll." He winked. "I figured I'd get a start on salads. I hope that's in the plan."

Her husband Rob, the President and CEO of his own financial firm, never ceased to amaze her how down to earth and comfortable he seemed in the kitchen. It also reminded her why she found him so attractive. Despite his years, he had maintained a good physique, and looked distinguished with his salt and pepper hair. The apron only added to his sex appeal. She loved a man who knew his way around the kitchen and her husband was well suited for the task. "There's no plan, so salads are a good start." She wrapped her arms around him and rested her cheek against his back. "Is Robert home?"

"Yeah. He's out there doing whatever he does these days." Concern came through in his tone.

To an observer in the outside world, Robert functioned very well. But in the confines of his dwelling, the scenario changed. About a year ago, he began to isolate himself. He managed to complete a normal workday, but once at home, he retreated to his bed—sleeping every chance he got. His parents knew the signs of depression and attempted to seek help for him. Nothing they suggested seemed to sway him. He wasn't a danger to himself or others, and he refused any psychiatric intervention. So they did the only thing they could do within their power—be there for him. Then he suddenly emerged from his hibernation period and began to engage in more activities. He seemed to be on a path to recovery, but his parents knew he wasn't the same. Something seemed missing when he began living again, but he would never tell them what caused the change. To both his parents a piece of their son had died during those months of solitude.

Around the same time, Karen came into Robert's life. Neither parent approved of her. In their hearts, they knew she wasn't right for him, but she helped draw him out and for that, they were grateful. He started acting more like the Robert they were fighting to find again, so they kept their thoughts about his love interest to themselves. They hoped he would discover how ill-suited Karen was for him on his own before they finalized their marriage.

Sandra understood Rob's comment all too well. "Will he be joining us for dinner?" She tightened her arms around Rob and he leaned into her, but never stopped his salad prep.

"He told me to call him when you came home."

Sandra stretched on her tiptoes to kiss her husband on the back of the neck and gave him a final hug. She reached for the house phone and called handset #2. "Hi, Sweetie. I just walked in. Dad started salads and…" She opened the freezer door and rummaged around for something fast to finish off dinner. "How does salads, Dijon chicken and mashed potatoes sound?"

"That sounds fine. I'm hungry."

"Good. Start walking over. You can set the table." She put the phone down and turned toward Rob. "He sounds good today." A soft smile grew on her face.

"Karen must be out of town again. He always sounds better when she's not around."

"Rob, behave yourself. I want to enjoy our dinner." Sandra gave her husband a gentle punch to the arm as the back door opened.

"Robert." A smile swept across her face at the sight of her only child walking through the door. She approached him and wrapped her fingers around his biceps. She gave him a kiss on his check. "Have a good day?"

"Yeah, not bad."

"Good. Tell me about it while we're eating. Dinner won't take long to prepare." She winked at him. "Please set the table." She returned to the stove to start cooking.

All the dinnerware sat on the table arranged with a man's touch. Sandra shook her head as she placed the food on the counter for everyone to serve themselves. "Thank you Robert for helping."

The family wasted no time filling their plates. They sat around the table, ready to enjoy their time together. Rob started to recount his busy day and then Robert took his turn. The course of the conversation shifted when Rob started a discussion about current news events. It sparked opposite opinions from both men. Sandra knew Rob loved these heated discussions with his son. In the past year, they were few and far between, so Rob took every opportunity he could to keep things interesting.

Ten minutes into the political posturing of the two most important men in her life, Sandra reached her tolerance level and interjected an explanation of her day. "I had a meeting with Belinda Davies. She called and asked if I could help her with her new home." She turned toward her husband. "Honey, you remember, she's the very attractive girl who fainted at the New Year's Eve party."

"Oh yes. Is she alright?"

"She's fine and I spent the entire afternoon with her. In fact, the meeting with her is why dinner is so late tonight."

She focused all her attention on Rob and didn't even notice Robert's reaction. When she did glance over at her son, he looked like he'd seen a ghost. He appeared physically paler and just stared at his plate.

"Robert, are you okay?"

He panned from his mother to his father. "I'm fine. I was just thinking about something. I'm sorry. What were you saying about Ms. Davies?" His voice sounded cold and curt.

Sandra's gaze drifted to her husband. Rob sat still. His brows pinched together as he focused all his attention back to his son.

An unsettling feeling came over Sandra as she turned back to watch Robert. "You sure you're okay?" This time she put more force behind her words. His expression made her uneasy.

"Yeah, why wouldn't I be? Go on with your story."

She studied him, but knew it would be futile to press him, so she continued her description of a very delightful afternoon. "I really like this woman. She's bright, funny, and a very warm person. I'm excited about working with her."

Robert listened to his mother and maintained eye contact, but had to fight not to lose his concentration. He didn't want any attention directed toward him to ruin his enjoyable evening meal with his parents, but he wasn't very pleased with his mother's subject matter at the moment. He let out a sigh of relief when the conversation moved to another topic.

***

Belinda drove to her parents' house, the minute Sandra left, to tell her mother about her plans to move forward by using Sandra's decorating help.

"Mom I don't see how working with Sandra will be a problem. In fact, I think it will be fun. She just happens to be Robert's mother."

She knew Dora didn't see it that way and her mother's countenance told her so. "You know how I feel about this version of Robert interfering with you going on with your life. I don't want to see you get hurt."

"He's not interfering. I'm just working with his mother. What are the chances I'd actually run into him? She'll be acting as my consultant. I won't even see her that much."

With pursed lips, Dora sat back in her chair. Her chin dropped to her chest as she folded her arms across it. She glared up from across the table.

***

Dora agreed to her daughter's arrangement to meet Sandra at a local restaurant for breakfast. There, the trio would talk over the plans for Belinda's decorating scheme. She remained skeptical about the idea, but if it meant Belinda could move forward with her decisions to complete her home, she would be willing to support her daughter.

Dora opened the door to the restaurant and found her breakfast partners in a deep discussion. She was pleasantly surprised to see Belinda so animated in the way she freely expressed herself using the terms she learned from reading all those interior design books. To Dora's delight, her daughter looked happier than she'd been in months. Maybe this wasn't as bad an idea as she originally thought.

She approached the table with little notice from the two women who were concentrating the computer screen. "I'm sorry I'm late." She pulled out a chair and sat down to the pleasant smiling faces focusing their full attention on her.

"Hi, Mom." Belinda wasted no time with the introductions. "We waited for you."

Belinda handed a menu to her mother. After a few minutes, Dora placed it on the table. "Are you ready," Belinda asked. Dora nodded. Belinda waved to their waitress, signaling they were ready to order. Dora and Sandra placed theirs orders first. Belinda finished with, "I'll have coffee and a blueberry bagel with cream cheese." Belinda looked at Sandra. "I love blueberry bagels with cream cheese."

A smile grew across Sandra's face and she nodded. What she said next floored Belinda. "So does my son, Robert. In fact, he'd have that for breakfast everyday if he could."

The Robert from her "Dream Reality" loved blueberry bagels with cream cheese. In her dream, the couple ate this combination of doughy perfection as often as they could. This had to be just another coincidence, so Belinda brushed it off.

The breakfast meeting went better than Belinda could hope. Dora and Sandra hit it off and before Belinda could say or do anything, the two were in a deep discussion over furniture for the living room. Belinda sat back and watched them talk. The memory of a breakfast with their parents the morning after her marriage to Robert in her "Dream Reality" floated back. Watching the two women talk reminded her of the meeting where the two started planning a wedding reception that never took place. Just like then, the women were completely at ease with each other.

Several hours passed as the three enjoyed each other's company. Sandra glanced at her watch. "Oh my! I've lost track of time again. I have to leave. I have another appointment." She gathered up her belongings spread over the table. "Dora, it was very nice to meet you and I look forward to seeing you again." Sandra excused herself and left.

"I told you she was really nice." Belinda scowled at her mother.

"Okay, I'll admit I like her too. Now should we go make a visit to 'Mattress Mack'? Then you can come home for dinner and look over your paintings."

***

The two raced upstairs to the guest room. Belinda swung open the door. To her amusement, the closet contained all sizes and shapes of canvases leaning up against the walls. They started pulling them out and spread them all around for a better view in the well-lit sunny room, propping them against anything that would hold the artwork upright.

"Sweetie, I'm going to go downstairs to start dinner. You stay here."

A soft thud from the bedroom door closing went unnoticed by Belinda. She stood in the center of the room and glanced from one picture to the next.

The room started to spin, slowly at first, and then faster and faster as memory after memory piled atop each other. Just when she thought her brain would go into overload, the spinning stopped. She fell to her knees and grabbed the sides of her head as she squeezed her eyes shut. Her head throbbed. Her breathing accelerated.

After a few minutes, the pain lessened and her breathing slowed. She opened her eyes and stood. Picking up one painting at a time, she studied each one, remembering what she'd been doing when she painted it. Each one held its own memories, some very pleasant and some not. She arranged the pictures in order of her timeline of life—from the first one she completed in college to the last one just before the accident. Once organized, she sat on the floor and reminisced.

***

Belinda's mom suggested she take the paintings she wanted home. She also encouraged Belinda to take all her art supplies with her. The unfurnished back bedroom of the patio home would be perfect for painting. The sunlight filtered in most of the day so Belinda could easily turn it into a studio.

After dinner, Dora helped her daughter load up the car. On the drive home, Belinda thought about one of her paintings that drew her in more than the others. It was something she painted back during a happier time in her college career, but more so it reminded her of her time with Robert during the coma.

Belinda hauled the paintings to the back bedroom and stacked them upright against the wall. She selected the forest scene and held it out in front of her. She studied it. "Not half bad," she muttered under her breath. "Not half bad and better than the stuff I've been looking at to buy. Hmm. Maybe I do have an artist hiding in me."

Walking into the living room, she propped it against the neediest wall. She paced in front of it, studying it. The colors complemented the room, but somehow it seemed incomplete. She decided to leave the painting leaning against the wall and take another look with the light of day.

About to flip the light switch off in the living room, she took one more glance. "Yep. Definitely needs something." With one flip of her finger, the room plunged into darkness.

***

Belinda padded into the kitchen. Her hair flopped everywhere as she brushed it off her face. Mornings were her favorite time of the day. It was quiet and the world seemed at peace with itself as it awoke under the morning sun.

The first planned item on today's agenda was a quick stop to tend to Beau's needs. Afterward, she'd come home to change before meeting her mother for lunch.

Reaching for her mug, she popped a k-cup in and brewed it. Inhaling the aroma of fresh brewed coffee tantalized her olfactory nerves at any time of the day, but not like the first cup. That first jolt of caffeine coursing through her veins every morning was her only real vice and she thoroughly enjoyed it.

Armed with the mug of coffee, she started to walk back to the bedroom. She stopped to give the painting against the far wall a quick glance and began to take a sip of the piping hot drink. Before her lips touched the rim, a thought flew into her mind. Abandoning the cup on the kitchen counter, she grabbed the painting and hurried down the hall to the back bedroom. There in the light of the morning, she unpacked the supplies, set up the easel, and started painting.

She took several steps backward rubbing her chin while she studied her finished piece. The melodic tune of the cell phone from the pocket of her boxer shorts sliced her concentration. Without checking the caller ID, she answered, "Hello."

"Sweetie, are you okay?"

She heard the concern in her mother's voice. "Yeah. I'm fine. Why?"

"I've been waiting for you for almost thirty minutes."

"What time is it?"

"One o'clock. We were supposed to meet for lunch."

She opened her mouth to answer, but stopped when she realized she hadn't even taken off her pajamas. She ran her tongue around the inside of her mouth—or brushed her teeth. A strand of hair took that precise moment to fall in front of her nose. A quick burst of air from the side of her mouth blew it back into place. "I'm sorry. I started painting and lost all track of time."

She paused for her mother's response. Nothing.

"Mom. This is all your fault."

"Mine?"

"Yeah. You're the one who told me to start painting again."

A small chuckle came over the phone. "Well, are you satisfied with your work?"

"Surprisingly, yes I am."

CHAPTER 11

THE SUN SHONE through the trees on this magnificent Saturday morning. Belinda planned to ride Beau. The animal and his needs had been pushed aside and only given an hour or so daily because she had been busy the past few weeks with the decorating of her home. Today, she would lavish her beloved horse with attention. He'd be washed, brushed, ridden, and well fed.

First on the agenda—a long-awaited ride. Belinda's inattention to Beau had also reduced any chance of running into Robert while he rode his horse on the same trails. It was now the middle of April and despite working with Robert's mother, Belinda hadn't seen him since the accidental encounter at the Galleria in January. What she had learned about Robert came from her conversations with Sandra, whose favorite subject was her son. So seeing Robert was the last thing on her mind as she mounted up and set off on her ride.

Beau's steady gait made Belinda think far too much. The back and forth motion of the horse worked its magic on her mind causing it to wander, placing her in a daydream state. She became so preoccupied in her meditative trance it took a few second for her to comprehend who rode toward her—a man riding a chocolate brown thoroughbred. As he came closer, she realized it was Robert. Her heart stopped and she couldn't breathe.

The trail gave her nowhere else to ride but ahead. She could turn and run, but that would serve no constructive purpose. So she straightened her back, tightened up on the reins and headed directly into harm's way.

"Belinda?" Robert said as he approached, stopping his horse alongside.

A lump rose and stuck in her throat, making her voice quaver. "Hi, Robert. I'm surprised to see you out here."

Robert looked around at the trees, attempting to disguise his uneasiness. Nervous pangs in his gut always erupted around this woman, but he took control of his emotions. Belinda was no different from anyone else he talked to and decided to treat this situation the same as a casual business meeting. He was comfortable with meeting new people and could act that way through any circumstance.

Going into his professional persona, he flashed his signature smile as he turned back toward her. "I just got back into town. I haven't ridden for some time and this morning…" He scanned the sky and trees, and sucked in a deep, slow breath of fresh air, filling his lungs. He exhaled as slowly as he inhaled, allowing his shoulders to drop. Repositioning himself in the saddle, he refocused on her. "It was just too perfect to waste."

Belinda studied his face when he glanced away. His smile brought back all the wonderful memories of her life with Dream Robert. Closing her eyes, she plunged herself into a full-blown fantasy. She pictured herself jumping from Beau into the arms of her love, planting a hot, long kiss on his tempting lips, tasting him as her tongue explored every inch of his mouth. She imagined electricity surging through her as the embrace led to their love making before they rode off into the morning sun, forever in love. Letting out a gentle sigh, she found herself becoming aroused.

Robert watched Belinda, intrigued by her expression. Her mouth was slightly open—breathing a bit irregular. Flowing waves of hair caressed her face as the wind blew ever so lightly lifting a few strands. At that moment, she was the sexiest woman he had ever laid eyes on. He watched her as she relaxed, lost in a world of her own. His mind wandered as he thought how she would feel lying next to him…naked. He knew he wanted her. With a harsh surge of reality, he regained control because that would never happen. He had more integrity than that and he would follow through with his promise to marry Karen. Without disturbing her, Robert just enjoyed watching for a few more seconds before he spoke.

"Belinda, are you alright?"

Belinda popped her eyes open when she realized how crazy she must have appeared. As she squirmed against the leather of the saddle, it enhanced the sexual feeling, a residual from her fantasy. *Why is this happening now?* She flushed from embarrassment. With the instinct to cover it, she dropped her chin to her chest allowing her hair to fall and shield her hot cheeks. She needed her wits about her and all she was doing was making a fool of herself. "I'm fine," she said, keeping her head down too flustered to look at him.

Slowly, she lifted her head. A smile grew across his face as he chuckled at her. He seemed comfortable and more like the gorgeous, loving Robert from her "Dream Reality." His expression made her relax as she diverted the conversation from her to the thoroughbred. "Your horse is beautiful. What's his name?"

"It's Scout."

She saw him beam while he gently stroked the horse's neck. It seemed to lean into his touch. She giggled. The name didn't seem to fit. "You named that magnificent animal Scout?"

"His full name is Crossed Arrows Apache Indian Scout."

"Oh! I see. Scout it is." She looked the animal over. "Do you prefer to ride with an English saddle?"

"That's what I learned on and it seems to fit Scout better than a Western. I see you ride Western."

"Yeah. I've never ridden with an English saddle. Is it hard?"

"I don't think so." His face lit up. "Would you like me to show you sometime?"

Belinda didn't even hesitate. "Yes, I'd like that. When?" When the words came out of her mouth, she realized it was too late.

Robert hadn't put much thought into offering to help her ride using an English saddle. He just said it before he could corral the impulse.

"I have to go out of town again in two weeks for work. This week I have to play catch up. How about I call you when I get back?" Feeling more confident, he felt it would be easy to put distance between them, correcting his lack of judgment. He knew she saw Colin on a regular basis because she was all Colin could talk about. Belinda this and Belinda that. Sometimes all he wanted to do was punch him in the mouth to get him to shut up. Then another part of him wanted to hear everything his friend had to say about this beautiful woman, but he had his loyalties and would not breach those either. So he made it clear he was aware Colin was a part of her life.

"Maybe Colin could join us." He cocked his head and waited for her reaction.

Belinda snapped her gaze to him. Not knowing his motives, she responded, "That might be nice, and what about Karen?" She heard the curtness in her voice.

"She might join the three of us afterward. Remember, she isn't fond of horses. Well, I'd better be going. It was nice seeing you again."

He didn't say another word. The tightened reins made Scout lift his head and straighten his ears. Robert's weight shifted. Scout moved forward putting distance between them, then broke into a canter.

Belinda turned and watched Scout's tail swish, ending the chance encounter. She didn't leave immediately, but just watched Robert ride away. No one she had ever known caused her to experience such an array of emotions, especially not someone who was such an arrogant SOB. She saw red watching him move further away and huffed. With a gentle kick to his sides, she rode in the opposite direction.

The rest of the day she spent as planned. After the ride, she let Beau out to pasture while she mucked the stall and lined it with fresh straw. A bath and a good brushing came next. To dry his coat, she let him loose to run in the late afternoon sun. The sun glistened off him as he bucked and galloped through the tall grass, obviously pleased he was freed from the torment of the water hose.

The sight warmed Belinda's heart because she loved the horse. That is until he lay down and rolled on his back, flailing his legs above him, destroying all her hard work.

"Oh Beau! You crazy horse." After pulling a few of his favorite tasty morsels from her pocket, she stretched out her palm, presenting the treat. "Hey Beau, carrots?" The dusty animal ambled straight for her. As he munched, she attached the lead. "Look at you. You're a mess."

Belinda walked toward the stable with her horse in tow, and then safely secured him in his box stall. "See you tomorrow fellow." After giving him a good rubbing behind the ear, Belinda left to get ready for her date with Colin.

She would have to work hard on pushing thoughts of Robert out of her mind. Even though he angered her, he crept in all day. The repetitive work involved with taking care of Beau, allowed him to take over her fantasies while she completed her chores. She knew it was her love for the dream Robert she felt, but the real Robert could be just as charming. Those occasional glimpses of charm gave her the small amount of hope she clung to. Although, in her heart, she knew it would never lead to anything.

***

The doorbell rang. Colin was right on time as usual. Belinda opened the door and there stood her tall, handsome date for the evening who she hadn't seen for the past week. He stepped in and swept her off her feet, planting a big kiss. She responded and the pair remained locked in their embrace as the kiss grew more passionate. "Boy, if I didn't know better I'd say someone missed me." Colin smiled down at her with his glacier blue eyes. He pulled her closer and placed a soft kiss on the top of her head.

She tightened her hug around him as she snuggled against his chest. She did miss him. He wasn't Robert but he did care about her and for that, she loved him. "How was the trip?"

He leaned over and sniffed at her hair. "You smell so good….The trip was fine. I'll tell you all about it, but now, I just want you in my arms." She chuckled. He picked her up and swung her around as he found her lips.

Still in an embrace with their lips locked, Colin carried Belinda into the kitchen. He put her down and gave her a quick, tight squeeze. Seeing a breathing bottle of wine sitting on the counter, he curled up the corners of his mouth into a big smile. "Great! Wine! Join me." He approached the cabernet, and poured two glasses. "This traveling back and forth is getting to me. I'm here this week then gone again the next."

Just after the first of the year, the Pendleton Financial Group started planning their Canadian branch opening. Colin would manage it as vice president. While the office was in the initial stages, he remained stateside and worked out of the Houston office with occasional trips to our northern neighbor. Recently he informed Belinda his traveling would increase. For now, he would be making trips between the United States and Canada, but he warned her at some point he'd be moving.

Belinda had been spending more time with Colin. When he wasn't traveling, he'd been there to help with anything she needed to assemble her new living room and dining room. The weeks he was around, the couple spent at least three evenings together. They would go to a movie and dinner or Belinda would cook for a night in. Despite spending so much time together, she hadn't let their physical relationship progress any further than snuggling on the couch with heavy making out. Belinda was very aware Colin wanted more, and a few times she came very close to inviting him into her bedroom. But something inside her stopped her from committing. Still, she knew she'd have to make a decision very soon or risk losing him.

If Colin moved she would miss his companionship, but it would make it easier for her. She wouldn't have to worry about taking their relationship to the next level. Belinda knew her indecision could result in the loss of a perfectly wonderful man, and the opportunity for a potential marriage proposal. Often she thought her inability to take the romance with Matt further was the major reason why that relationship ended. Now she found herself once again in a similar situation. The one difference between the two was that Colin informed her of what the future may hold for him. Matt never afforded her that courtesy—he just left.

These dilemmas were the main topic of her weekly session with Dr. Rosen. He seemed very pleased with her progress and her ability to form a relationship with a man whose name wasn't Robert. However, no matter how hard she tried to move on with Colin, Robert or her memory of him, crept in.

"You'll release yourself when the time is right. You've been able to make so many positive decisions in the past few months. If Colin is who you decide to be with, your decision will come." Dr. Rosen always encouraged her. For now, she would just continue on the present course. Colin was a good friend whom she enjoyed spending time.

Dinner and a movie were on the schedule. Belinda enjoyed her evening with Colin, as usual. When he escorted her back home, she invited him in. He sat on the couch as she filled wine glasses and then joined him. The conversation dropped off as Colin sat with his arm around her neck, fiddling with a strand of her hair between his fingers. She leaned her head back against his arm and sipped the wine. The wine and physical labor of caring for Beau earlier in the day relaxed her.

"This place has really come together. It's real comfortable," Colin said, lifting his glass. "Hat's off to the decorator."

They clicked glasses and took a sip. Belinda took pride in what she had accomplished in such a short time. "And to my helper," she added, making a reference to Colin's assistance. Raising her glass to him, the rims touched, followed by a drink.

The living and dining rooms were comfortable with elegant touches done on a woman's conservative budget. The ceiling to floor faux silk curtains that graced the windows consisted of two different sets. The top champagne color was too short, so Dora added the sea foam green to the bottom to extend the length. Complementary throw pillows made of the left over curtain fabric, graced the couch. The bigger pieces maintained the more neutral tones, while the color splashes of teal, chocolate, and soft green accessories added the needed color. Their placement made the eye travel from one area of color to the next, giving both rooms a cohesive feel of luxury.

"There's going to be a cocktail party at the Wilson Hotel in the Galleria two weeks from today to celebrate the official opening of the Canadian branch. Ah'd be honored, Ms. Belinda, if you'd accompany me as mah date."

Belinda laughed at Colin's attempt at a faux-southern accent. "It would be mah pleasure sir," she said, batting her eyelashes.

Colin's desire for her began to grow to more than he could take. He placed his wine glass on the coffee table, and then did the same with Belinda's. Placing his fingers under her chin, he kissed her full lips. She placed her arms around his neck. As he leaned back, she draped herself across his lap, and fast, short kisses passed between them.

It didn't take long for the kissing to escalate into full-blown passion on his part. Colin felt a growing need for her as he roamed his hands over her back and then slipped them under her top. He relished the feel of the warm, soft flesh under his fingertips as he slid them across her back. Moving north, he released the latch of her bra. Her breasts relaxed from their restraint against his chest. This excited him as his need for her grew, pressing against her hip. Reaching around, he found and cupped her more than ample, firm breast. His breathing became more irregular—their kisses now deep and hard. She stopped him momentarily while she repositioned herself and straddled him.

Her sultry stare gave him no indication she had any plan to stop him. Their breathing became heavy. His heart pounding, he moved his hands across the skin of her firm back toward her neck, pulling her close. Now he could feel her heart hammering in her chest.

She seemed willing to continue so Colin took a big chance. Picking her up, he cradled her in his arms and walked toward the hall that led to the bedroom.

At the threshold, Belinda stiffened and screamed, "Colin put me down!"

Colin stopped cold, closed his eyes, took a deep breath, and set her on her feet. He stood there studying Belinda. She cast her gaze to the ground and wouldn't even look at him.

He sighed. "I think I should go." Belinda said nothing, but kept her head down. Colin hugged her and gave her a kiss on the forehead. "I'll call you." His heart ached as he turned and walked out.

Outside, he quickened his pace to his car. He wondered how much longer she would continue with the roadblocks and how long he would be willing to put up with them. He was a patient man, but his patience was wearing very thin. He slammed the car door and drove off squealing the tires, hoping the power of his car would help relieve his sexual frustration. When he got home, a cool shower took care of the rest.

Belinda found tonight's date particularly hard. Robert, on Scout, came along in her mind, taking her attention away from Colin. She found herself fighting to keep focused.

She had decided tonight would be the first time Colin would be invited to spend the night in her bed. She allowed herself to feel the sexual excitement Colin ignited within her. In the heated last moments of the evening, when Colin picked her up, the name Robert almost slipped softly past her lips. Thankfully, she caught herself before she reached the point of no return. At that moment, she felt she was deceiving Colin and knew she had to stop.

CHAPTER 12

THE CREAM COLORED, strapless, silk dress with a matching Bolero jacket that her mom had bought her when she lay in the coma, was pulled from the closet. It was identical to the one she had worn when she married Dream Robert. She hung it on the back of the closet door as she carefully ran her fingertips down the front, experiencing a faint moment of melancholy over the lost love. The memory of Dream Robert would always be with her, but she was learning to let him go. So tonight, she would put the dress on and attend a party. A black clutch, three-inch black heels, and a simple strand of pearls with matching earrings rounded out the outfit.

After their last date, Belinda wasn't sure how Colin would respond. As promised he called, but his busy work schedule didn't allow him to come over during the week. It was probably for the best. It gave them both some needed space.

The ride to the Wilson Hotel was pleasant. In fact, Colin was his usual attentive self and acted as if nothing had happened the weekend before.

They entered the grand foyer of the hotel. Mr. and Mrs. Pendleton stood in front of one of the doors to the main ballroom, greeting their guests. Sandra saw Belinda and approached her with outstretched arms. "I'm so pleased you could come. How did everything you picked out fit in the niches?"

"I took your advice and made those changes you suggested. Everything balanced nicely."

"Remember my husband, Robert Pendleton?" Sandra reached for his arm. "It's Belinda."

He turned his attention from Colin and reached for Belinda's hand. "It's nice to see you again. I take it you're doing well."

As he took hold of it, Belinda noticed a subtle shift in his demeanor. His smile disappeared while he studied hers. "It's nice to see you again sir."

A faint smile returned. "Please enjoy yourself. I'm glad you were able to join us."

The couple entered the dimly lit ballroom to the sound of a familiar perky voice. "Belinda, come over here." Abbey stood from her chair and waved. "We saved some seats for you." They walked toward the table situated about halfway down the side of the dance floor to join her best friend.

The smile she wore deteriorated when Garrett stood exposing Robert, who sat beside him. She expected to see him here. After all, his father was the President and CEO and Robert was a VP. She just didn't think she would have to sit at the same table.

It amazed her that the feelings she experienced with the dream Robert didn't transfer to the real Robert. The initial excitement for this one seemed to diminish with every encounter. For now, she would be pleasant. She took a seat directly across the table from him and gave him a nod of recognition. His stare felt cold and intentional when he didn't acknowledge her in return. Her tolerance of his manipulative behavior grew thinner with each meeting.

Abbey leaned into her friend. "Does it bother you being this close to him?" Belinda glared. "That bad, huh!"

She turned her chair toward Abbey. "You have no idea. He's such a jerk."

Abbey lifted her brows and with a slow upward motion of her mouth, a full-blown smile appeared. She swung her chair around and yanked it closer. Belinda knew Abbey's detail antenna had risen. The two were deep in conversation as the party accelerated into full swing around them.

Music blared as the laughter of the participants filled the room. Colin switched into work mode, and excused himself from Belinda's side. She didn't mind while Abbey and she caught up, visiting. Garrett found himself in much the same position, so the two men went to work conversing with their clients.

Colin's new position required him to be on top of all the functioning aspects of the Toronto office. This also meant knowing who the clients were, the names of their children, the wife's name, and any other aspect of the client's life which made them feel they had a friend in Colin. He was good at his job, and schmoozing came easy as he worked the room.

Robert had the luxury of hanging back tonight. Of course, he would be expected to engage in some client promotion, but not as much as Colin. The party's focus was on the potential Canadian investors. For once, he wasn't in the spotlight and could afford a little relaxation.

"Robert, I have a big favor to ask." Robert focused on his friend. "I'll be able to give Belinda some attention tonight, but I'm going to be pretty busy. Do you think you can fill in for me since Karen couldn't make it? Just ask her to dance a few times," Colin asked.

Robert didn't know why, but he agreed to help.

Well, I just shot my evening to hell. Robert never changed his facial expression. How could Colin be asking this of him? Pairing Belinda with him would be like mixing oil and vinegar or rubbing salt on his wounds.

"Thanks, dude. I owe you." Colin walked away to do the gentlemanly thing by inviting his date to dance.

He walked over to the open bar and requested a scotch on the rocks. Downing it in a few gulps, he signaled the bartender for a refill. The ice cubes clinked against the side of the glass with every rotation of his hand. He knew she didn't see him sitting at the table when she walked into the party. The slight widening of her eyes told him so. Breaking the gaze, she fidgeted with her purse and focused on Abbey.

Time had seemed to slow as he watched her walk across the floor. She appeared to float with each step. The light reflected off every lock of hair and cast a glow that framed her features. Her hips moved seductively from side to side. The dress she wore caused his heart to race and his breath to cease. When she sat down across from him, he found himself staring at her in that dress.

The cool glass touched his lower lip. The vision of Belinda in that dress lingered. He tilted his head back, downed the scotch, and slammed the glass on the bar, getting the bartender's attention. The bartender motioned for a refill. Robert nodded and waited. With his glass filled, he walked back to the empty table.

He wasn't alone long. Shortly, Abbey sat down. Colin soon followed, escorting Belinda to her seat. He excused himself the minute she made herself comfortable. She shot Robert a glare, and then turned her attention to Abbey. The music started up again. Robert just sat and watched Belinda talk to her friend while he sipped his scotch. When the next song started, he noticed her glance toward Colin, now in deep conversation with one of his newer clients. Garrett seemed to come out of nowhere to sweep his wife off her feet. On the dance floor, they held each other close to the romantic music.

Belinda flashed a half-smile toward Robert as she reached for her wine glass. Robert looked down and took a deep breath. Standing, he walked around behind Belinda and whispered in her ear, "Would you dance with me?"

Belinda's heart stopped and she almost forgot to breathe when she heard his soft, masculine voice she loved so much. Memories flooded her mind causing her eyes to moisten. She closed them for a moment and let her hair fall to the side of her face, shielding her expression from him. She needed a second, and then with all the grace she had put into practice over the years, she flung her hair over her shoulder and flashed a seductive smile. "I'd love to."

He took her by the arm and she thought she would die. Immediately, his simple touch started to drive her nuts, but she controlled herself as he led her to the dance floor. She fully expected him to keep her at arm's length during the slow dance. To the contrary, the opposite happened. Robert placed his arm around her waist and pulled her close. Their eyes connected and what happened next shocked and amazed her. He slowly reached up to the side of her head and gently pulled it against his chest. He tightened his grip around her waist pressing her as close as he could. With one graceful step, the couple began to float as one around the dance floor to the tune of her favorite song, "Forever in My Mind."

With her cheek pressed against his chest, she could hear each beat of his heart. She closed her eyes and filled her mind with the Robert she loved from her dream and how this one gave her only a small glimmer of that love, but for how long? Her dislike for the real Robert dwindled as she lavished being held in his arms.

When the music stopped, neither of them moved. Afraid to look up, she listened to every rhythmic rub-dub, rub-dub beat. Robert didn't let go. He stroked her hair and placed a tender kiss on the top of her head, which caused her to nuzzle into his chest. The band started to play another slow song and the couple resumed their graceful association with the dance floor.

Sandra watched the interaction between her son and Belinda. She reached over and patted her husband's arm to get his attention. She pointed in the direction of the dancing couple.

Rob glanced at his wife. He followed her finger to watch Belinda and his son move across the dance floor.

"What do you think of that?" She studied her loving spouse.

"I haven't seen him that peaceful in months."

"Those two belong together and you know it. Karen is all wrong for him." Sandra never hesitated to let Rob know her thoughts on the subject of Karen.

"Sandra, you can't interfere." He warned her.

"I'm not going to interfere. We're going to just give them a slight push."

"You keep me out of your plan."

Sandra turned toward her husband. "You know you have to be a part of this. You know that deep in your bones. You felt it when you shook her hand. I know you did." She poked his chest. "I saw your expression change. You know she's the one for him."

Rob studied his wife's face. "We'll talk about it later."

***

"May I have this dance?" The couple separated from their tender embrace when Colin joined them. Robert bowed and took his leave, returning to the table.

Colin took Belinda in his arms. "Well, have you been enjoying yourself?"

Belinda felt the stir of butterflies which stood as a reminder that she enjoyed the closeness to Robert. She wondered how much Colin saw of their intimate dance. "I'm having a nice time."

"Good. I've been so preoccupied with my clients." He gently stroked her cheek. "I'm sorry I'm not paying that much attention to you."

"That's okay. I understand." The thought of Colin still being upset from the last time they were together crossed her mind, but she dismissed the idea as fast as it entered. This man didn't have a spiteful bone in his body. That single character trait set him apart from the real Robert. She found Colin to be consistent and sincere, something Robert never showed.

Nevertheless, the memory of her life with the dream Robert and her present brief encounters with the real version sent every fiber of her being into turmoil. Robert's tender touch caused her senses to react, compounding her confusion, despite all the attempts she had made to distance herself from her feelings about her dream life.

At the end of the dance, Colin escorted her back to the table, setting the pattern for the night. Abbey and she would visit, she'd have a few very close almost too intimate dances with Robert, Colin would make the occasional appearance, and the cycle would start all over. To complicate the strangeness of the night, Colin became far too busy to notice Robert's advances toward his date.

Toward the evenings end, Belinda said goodbye to Abbey and her husband. She found herself alone at the table and propped her chin on an open palm. At the far end of the room, she noticed Rob, Colin, and Robert talking. Their different expressions interested her and she tried to imagine what could bring on such an intense discussion. When the conversation wrapped up, Colin and Robert approached the table. Now, more intrigued, she waited to hear what else this strange evening had to offer. Colin seated himself beside her, and this time, Robert sat next to him. Colin scooted his chair back so she could clearly see Robert. She realized he adjusted it so Robert could be included in their conversation.

"I'm going to have to stay for a meeting with one of my clients who has to fly back to Toronto early in the morning. Mr. Pendleton is also staying. Robert has agreed to drive you and his mother home, if that's alright with you."

Belinda bit her lower lip and stared at Robert, wondering what else this strange evening could bring. Her gaze wandered back to Colin. Knowing how important advancing his career was to him, she placed her hand on his. "That'll be fine."

He smiled back and kissed her on the cheek. "Thank you. I have to go but I'll call. Robert said he can leave whenever you and his mother are ready." He stood and left, leaving Belinda alone at the table with Robert.

Belinda reached for her wine glass, trying to give herself something to do. Sitting alone with Robert made her feel awkward. She shifted in her seat when a warm hand rested on her shoulder. Seeing Sandra's smiling face gave her the diversion she needed.

"I'll be ready to go home soon. It's getting late and most of the guests have left, leaving me only a few more obligatory "goodbyes" and "thank yous." Sandra winked.

Belinda had watched Sandra earlier working the room, playing her role as the corporate wife. She was a strong, confident woman with a good head for business, and Belinda admired her.

"Why don't you two dance while I finish up?" Sandra panned between them before she left.

Robert looked at Belinda and extended his hand. She took it and he led her to the dance floor.

The lights dimmed even more, as this would be the last dance of the night. Belinda's heart raced as Robert, not saying a word, peered into her eyes and pulled her close. With one arm around her waist, he clasped her hand in his between them. She placed her other one around his neck, and as she felt him lean back into it, he inhaled deeply. Widening her eyes, she watched him breathe deeper.

They began to move across the dance floor as if suspended in air. She found herself transported to a time when she knew the deepest love she'd ever experienced, and she didn't want it to end.

The music faded away but the couple continued to dance. In the background, the M.C. thanked everyone for attending. The lights brightened and the trance broke. Belinda blinked and her heart sank returning her to reality. "Thank you."

He smiled, and then scanned the room, but didn't release her. "My mother is waiting at the door. Looks like she's ready to leave." He looked down at Belinda. She stood there, staring at him. A faint smile swept across his face. "Are you ready to go?"

"Mm-hmm," came out of her mouth as they stepped apart. He escorted her to the table to retrieve her bag. She was glad Abbey and Garret left earlier, sparing her from having to explain herself to her friends. She had enough difficulty trying to make sense of the evening.

Belinda saw Sandra gather up her belongings and walk to the exit. Her smile grew wider with each step they made toward her.

"Robert, here's the keys to your dad's car." From her finger dangled a ring of keys.

Sandra claimed the back, leaving Belinda to sit up front. The traffic was light so the ride home only took about twenty minutes. However, this was the longest twenty minutes of Belinda's life in the quiet car.

The silence broke when Belinda gave Robert directions to her house. When the car stopped in front, Sandra wasted no time. "Robert, be a gentleman and walk Belinda to the door."

Her words grated at Robert. *What the hell did she think I would do? Just open the door and dump her out?* He had every intention of making sure she was safe behind the confines of her door before he sped off into the night. Robert turned slowly in the direction of his mother. She wore a familiar broad smile on her face. Her expression brought on a sudden twinge of concern. He realized his mother was up to something, he just didn't know what.

He exited the car and walked over to open Belinda's door. Sandra said goodbye while he waited. With the pleasantries completed, he walked Belinda to the small porch.

Sandra opened the door of the car to move to the front seat. She gave a discrete glance in the direction of the couple as they faded into the dark recess. Sandra was pleased. She knew they belonged together and the rest of the mess known as Karen would work herself out of her son's life in time. With her confidence renewed, Sandra slipped into the car and closed the door, her smile even broader.

Robert bent down and picked up Belinda's house keys that she had dropped, fumbling to open her front door. He stopped and studied the metal, red rose key chain attached to it before placing it in the lock. He opened the door to a crack, and then turned and stood, blocking her from entering the house. He placed his hands on either side of her head. Slowly, he moved closer until he found her lips. He wasn't sure why he was kissing her, all he knew was he wanted to and she wasn't stopping him. Continuing the kiss, he maneuvered Belinda back into a darker region of the porch, away from the possible peering eyes of his mother. He now wished he'd taken his mother home first.

The coolness of the brick against Belinda's back momentarily shocked her. Not minding the situation, she wrapped her arms around Robert's back, and lost herself in the softness of his lips. He began to kiss her with more fervor as both their respirations deepened. His hands went to her back, tugging her close, and hers moved up around his neck. Entwining her fingers in his hair, she pulled him as close as she could. His hands roamed her back finding her rear. Cupping each cheek, he squeezed sending a thrill through her. She rolled her head to the side. Robert brushed kisses down her neck as he ran a hand up the bare skin of her thigh. Gasping, she pulled him closer, the heat of his body penetrating the sheer fabric of the dress. Belinda had the feeling that, unlike their first encounter, Robert didn't intend to stop his advances. His hands roamed her body, heightening her longing for him. He touched her with the familiarity of a love she once knew.

A hushed pleading whisper escaped her lips before she could think about the ramifications of her words. "Robert, don't do this, then leave." In that instant, the passion diffused.

With a type of sadness, Robert gazed into her eyes. His breath became fast and short. He contorted his mouth and reached for her hands, releasing them from around his neck and exhaled. "You'd better go in."

She sneered and clenched her fists. "No! You tell me what's going on. You're not doing this to me again. And what about Karen?" With each mounting second of frustration, she dug her fingernails deeper into her palms.

Robert stepped back from her. "I don't know....I mean....I don't know....I can't." He let out a breath. "Please go in."

Belinda didn't want to make a scene with Sandra sitting at the curb. She glared at him while he just stood there offering her nothing to explain his actions. She wasn't something he could just toy with when the mood struck him. The first kiss was a mistake. This one had put her very close to fitting the role of the other woman.

"I hate you for this." With open palms, she hit him squarely on the shoulders. The force caused him to stumble back. In a huff, she pushed her way past him as she ran into the house, slamming the door behind her, and locking it.

Belinda stood with her back to the door. She heard a car door close and the car drive away. Crying, she slumped to the floor, wondering why Robert acted this way. He had to know how much it hurt. The feeling of guilt overpowered her. Karen never did anything to her, but when Robert tenderly touched her, she lost all sense of right from wrong. Because he insisted on toying with her emotions, hate crept into her heart where only love once harbored.

***

Robert kept repeating in his mind, *remember the resolution, remember the resolution.* He questioned himself and his motives. Feeling guilty as hell, he slipped into the driver seat without glancing at his mother. To his relief, they didn't talk on the way home. He pulled the sedan into the garage of the Tuscan mansion. As the garage door closed, Sandra waited in the car until Robert came around to help her out. He was raised to be a gentleman, but now he felt like a cheater.

"Are you alright?" she took hold of her son's arm.

"I'm fine. I'm just exhausted. I plan to sleep in tomorrow, so I'll see you in the afternoon. Would you like to take the horses out in the evening?"

"Yes, I think I'd like that. I'll see if your father wants to come along." She crossed in front of him and walked toward the door.

Robert reached for her arm and kissed her on the cheek. "Mom, I love you."

Sandra smiled and patted him on the arm. "I know. I'll see you tomorrow. Sleep well."

Robert waited for his mother to lock the door behind her before he left through the side entrance, closest to the guesthouse. Normally he would take his time, but tonight he sprinted across the lawn to reach his front door. As he ran, he loosened his tie and pulled off his jacket. Once inside, he rushed straight for the bedroom.

Though small, the place provided him everything he needed, all an expensive apartment in the financial district offered. At his insistence, he paid his parents rent to offset any expenses like electricity and food. An added benefit to this arrangement was being close to Scout and the outside space. He preferred living in the solitude his parents' twenty-five acre estate provided. He'd never been the urban-jungle type.

In the bedroom, his thoughts of Belinda accelerated. He had managed to shove her into the recesses of his mind during the drive home with his mother sitting next to him. However, now alone, she came flooding back.

The little voice in his head screamed, *remember your resolution.*

He thought he had prepared himself and could handle seeing Belinda Davies tonight, but when she came floating across the floor in that dress...he could feel his resolve melting.

Holding her, smelling her, feeling her warm body pressed against his when they danced proved move than he could resist. He relived the taste of her luscious lips as he remembered the feelings that stirred deep inside him when they kissed. That strange connection he experienced with her drove him nuts. She was a narcotic to him and he knew he must go cold turkey. He needed to stay away and, most of all, there could not be any type of physical contact. With one touch, he turns into a moth and becomes so attracted to her flame that he can't help but fly into it, making him vulnerable. After what he put his parents through last summer, he needed to be careful not to make any mistakes.

Remember the resolution! What did he think he was doing anyway?

For God's sake, she was Colin's girlfriend and he was engaged. It wasn't as if either he or Belinda were free agents able to do whatever. There were two other innocent people involved in this little foursome, even though they were in the dark about the indiscretions.

His boxers were the last piece of clothing to hit the floor. He looked down at himself and sighed over the distress a little one percent of his body could cause him. Rolling his eyes, he snatched a towel off the chair before hitting the shower.

The tepid water rolled over his head and down his body. He braced himself against the cool tile, letting the water work its magic. About forty-five minutes later, he emerged from the bathroom wrapped in a towel tied around his waist.

Robert picked up his clothes. He hung his jacket in the closet and caught the scent of Belinda's perfume, Angel Scent. "Damn, damn her." He couldn't win could he?

He slammed the closet door, ripped off the towel and crawled into bed, pulling the sheet up to his chest. The only problem, he wasn't alone. Belinda crawled in with him and occupied his mind. Her scent lingered in his memory making his mind run rampant with images of her, and the sensations he experienced when they touched. A slight movement of the sheet drew his attention and he saw a teepee rising in his nether regions. "Oh God. Get her out of my head," he groaned as he threw his arm over his face, rocking his head from side to side. *Remember the resolution! Remember the resolution! Remember the resolution!*

CHAPTER 13

DR. ROSEN STROKED his five o'clock stubble. "We have to discuss your need to put yourself in these situations."

"What do you mean my need? Was I supposed to walk home? I had no choice!" Belinda raised her voice in an angry tone.

He stopped stoking his beard and gave her a questioning look.

"Okay. I could've stopped the kiss," she said in a huff as she crossed her arms and sat back in her chair. "But I didn't want to." She looked down at the floor, twisting her mouth. She found herself in a love-hate relationship with a man she had no right to want.

In future sessions, they would continue to explore how Belinda could protect herself against the emotional upheaval Robert caused. Slowly, she began to recognize the differences between her Dream Robert and the real Robert. The real person wasn't as confident as her dream man. The real one also had problems with expressing himself and ran whenever she confronted him. In short, he possessed more flaws that made him very different from the dream version.

As far as the real Robert was concerned, she wasn't even sure she liked him. Yes, there was that irresistible sensual connection they experienced. The sexual tension when they were together was so thick you could cut it with a knife, but he was engaged to Karen, and that may have been a blessing in disguise. His involvement with another woman kept him away from her and this allowed her the time to heal and separate.

What to do about Colin posed another dilemma. She loved being around him. Although his job took him to Toronto during the workweek, they talked daily. Over the weekends, they spent as much time together as they could. Belinda knew it would be just a matter of time before she needed to make a decision. Colin would be moving. She knew he'd been putting his relocation off as long as he could, but more and more, the demands of his job were up north. His relocation would have to take place soon. With that came the possibility of a marriage proposal or a very sad good-bye. Belinda wasn't sure how she would react to either.

Eight months had passed since she awoke from her coma. It was now May. Spring was in full swing and with every passing day, the sorrow she felt from the loss of her love and husband in her "Dream Reality" weakened. She was managing to grieve and grow emotionally stronger to take on the world and Robert Pendleton.

Her memory also was healing. Flashes or pictures appeared in her mind when she was in a familiar place—sometimes a whole scenario. Once the incident finished, a piece of her life unfolded.

She even made a few trips back to the college she attended in East Texas. The time she had spent with Matt gave her the most trouble with reconstructing her past. No one could help her piece together their relationship because no one witnessed their private times together. Her only memories of Matt came from the recounting of what others told her.

Being on the school grounds in places she and Matt had frequented, helped her with some of the missing parts. She figured out that she had settled for someone who wasn't right for her, and just accepted how he treated her because of her lack of self-confidence.

Her memories of Matt made her thankful he left. The idea of being married with three children, no career, and in a loveless marriage haunted her. So, the only sensible thing was to neatly pack him away in her past and in California. She neither knew nor cared about him anymore.

An added benefit of going back to the campus was saying goodbye to her beloved Dream Robert. With every visit she made, a piece of him slipped away as a pleasant memory she would always cherish. The grieving process was following a healthy path. Although he never existed, her emotions told her he did and she needed to go through the steps of grieving as if she had lost a real person. As she let go of the dream Robert, she found herself experiencing more of her own life.

Belinda found she now had a lot of spare time. Colin kept himself busy with work and traveling. The decorating of her house was almost complete. Sandra was very busy with new clients and her time with Belinda decreased.

So she found herself moving into the next phase of her plan—job hunting. It was the right time of the year if she planned to pursue a possible teaching position.

She called Abbey for help and to get her view of the idea.

"I think it's a great idea. But do you want to work fulltime?"

"I'm not sure. I could sub. Then I could work as much as I wanted."

"That doesn't pay much."

"I know but it's something to think about. See what you can find out. I think it would be fun working together fulltime or even if I just subbed," Belinda said. The two friends continued to talk about their daily lives when the subject of Colin came up.

"Do you think he'll ask you to go with him when he moves?"

"I don't know....I'm not even sure moving to Canada would be something I'd consider. Maybe I'll go visit and see how things go." She paused. "Oh Abbey, I don't even know if he wants me. We both seem to avoid the subject, but I know I'll miss him."

Abbey hesitated. "What about Robert?"

Belinda laughed under her breath. "Which one?"

"You know which one."

She let out a big sigh. "He's engaged, and other than those marvelous kisses we experienced, he doesn't seem interested in me. He's acting like a man who's getting married."

"Unless you count those two *marvelous* kisses, both of which, may I remind you, happened when he was an engaged man," Abbey told her.

Belinda rolled her eyes at the phone and changed the subject.

***

Sandra placed a cup of hot coffee on the table in front of her husband. She took a seat and puffed out her lower lip.

Rob looked at her from over his cup while he sipped. "Okay, bumper lip, you have my attention."

Her lips flattened into a smile before she started to explain. "Well, you know my business is growing. So, I think it's time I hired someone to help me."

"And this involves me how? You run your business as you see fit." He took another sip of coffee.

"I want to hire Belinda Davies and I want you to move her horse to our stables," she revealed, with batting lashes and teeth flashing.

Rob, now in mid-swallow nearly choked. He sputtered out, "What!?"

Sandra offered her distressed spouse no comfort. She knew he would survive, but now she held his undivided attention. "You know Robert and Belinda belong together. You saw how they acted at the party, and if it wasn't for the tentacles Karen has wrapped around him, I'd be calling Belinda my daughter-in-law."

Rob raised his eyebrow at his wife of thirty-five years. "I can't believe what I'm about to say and I hope I don't live to regret this." He gave his index finger a slight wave in the air. "So, I'm supposed to just horse-nap the animal and relocate him to our stable in the depths of the night?"

"No, silly." Sandra swatted Rob's upper arm. "Let me see if I can get her to work with me. Robert will be leaving for three weeks in seven days. That would be a great time for her to start. If she agrees to help me, we'll invite her to stay for dinner and to take a late ride with us. Then you can suggest she bed down her horse in the empty stall because it would be easier…due to the late hour and all. After a few times of doing that…you just insist she leave the horse here all the time, for convenience and safety's sake. After all, you wouldn't want your future daughter-in-law riding around in the woods after dark."

Rob gave his wife a sharp glance.

"Then in three weeks when Robert gets back, she'll be practically living with us at least three days a week."

Hovering over his now cooling cup of coffee, Rob shook his head. "Alright, but what if your plan backfires?"

"I'll worry about that later." Sandra stood and sashayed toward the sink, exaggerating her hip swing. Looking over her shoulder she said, "Today, I need to hire me some help."

***

Around eleven o'clock the phone rang at Belinda's home. "Hello."

"Belinda, its Sandra. Are you free for a late lunch?"

"What time were you thinking?" She couldn't fathom asking such a stupid question—like she had anything better to do. She didn't care what time Sandra wanted to eat lunch. It would give her something to do. She always enjoyed Sandra's company and frankly missed seeing her.

"How about I pick you up about one?"

"I'll be looking forward to it. Sandra, may I ask why you want to see me?"

"I just miss your beautiful smile and need a dose of Belinda."

Belinda chuckled, "I'll be ready."

Sandra didn't see her as a client any longer, especially after she saw her son's reaction to this delightful young lady. Belinda seemed so different from her intended daughter-in-law, Karen. When Robert first started dating Karen, they seemed well matched. She came from a well-off family, was educated, and had chosen a good career path. At first, the two showered affection on each other like most couples who are in a new relationship. Then something changed after the New Year's Eve party, the night of the engagement.

After that night, Karen became more possessive. She wanted to know where Robert was every minute. She called him frequently to check up on him.

Before the engagement, Karen came over to the Pendletons' for dinner, and just to visit. Sandra gave her a chance back then, when Karen seemed pleasant and fun to be around. Even that changed. She stopped visiting altogether. With her absence, Robert also left, spending more time at his fiancée's apartment. The only time Sandra could see her son was when Karen left town.

Sandra also noticed a shift in Robert's mood. When he was around Karen, he was quiet, almost reclusive. However, Karen traveled a great deal, which meant Robert stayed home during her absences. At those times, Sandra was able to enjoy her son as the loving person she knew him to be.

Her greatest fear was that Karen would prevent Robert from seeing her after they were married. She already kept him away. Sandra could imagine it would only get worse after Robert made the biggest mistake of his life by marrying her. The way she saw it, it was up to her to prevent that marriage to save her son. If her plan worked, Belinda would be the one she would welcome into the family instead of Karen.

***

Belinda's imagination ran out of control while she paced and bit her lower lip. "What could Sandra possibly what to talk about?" The chime of the doorbell rang precisely at one o'clock.

"Hi, Sandra. Nice to see you again. Come in." Belinda opened the door wider to allow her visitor to enter.

Sandra walked into the open concept rooms and peered around. "You made more changes. They look great." She smiled from ear to ear.

"Thanks. I still haven't done anything with the extra two bedrooms.

Sometimes I think buying a three bedroom house didn't make much sense for me."

Sandra raised her finger and shook it. "Always think resale. Having those bedrooms will help this house sell better than a one or two bedroom house. You never know when you might decide to sell, so always be prepared." She flipped her wrist toward the front door. "Shall we go? I'm hungry."

***

Once their orders were placed, Sandra explained the reason for her invitation. Belinda listened with intensity to the proposal set before her. The idea intrigued her. This would put her on a whole new career path, but there were a few obstacles she'd have to consider. The main one carried the name of Robert.

"Are you sure I can do something like this? I'm not an interior designer."

Sandra smiled. "Not yet, but look what you've done in the past few months. You taught yourself the program I use to design rooms. You've grasped the concepts of what makes a room work…I have faith in you and you have the background, being an art major and all."

Belinda thought for a second. She rapidly went through all the reasons why she should take Sandra's offer. Then she reviewed the reasons not to. Robert was the only one on that list. For her, he didn't seem important enough to stand in the way of making a decision that would be good for her. So in that split second, she looked at Sandra and gave her a nod.

Sandra spread a smile across her face, pleased with herself. She leaned back in her chair. Like magic, the first step of her plan fell into place to make Belinda her daughter-in-law.

CHAPTER 14

EARLY MONDAY MORNING the CR-V pulled in front of the Tuscan-style house located on Crescent Oak Circle, home of the office of Crescent Oak Interior Design Company. Sandra opened the door, inviting Belinda into the kitchen to talk and have a cup of coffee. She followed Sandra through the all-too-familiar rooms she hadn't seen since the New Year's Eve party. Being in the house made her feel queasy, and knowing she could run into Robert didn't help. She wondered if she was making a mistake.

"How do you take your coffee?" Sandra walked over to the kitchen counter.

"With cream and sugar."

Sandra pointed toward the table. "Go have a seat and I'll bring everything over so you can fix it yourself."

Belinda walked to the large oval table nestled at the end of the room in front of a huge bay window. From that vantage point, the barn was visible and she could see the horse's heads bobbing in and out of their stalls. As Sandra approached, Belinda asked, "How many horses do you own?"

Sandra placed the tray with the coffee down. "Three. We each have one, but there are six stalls. We use one as a tack room, one for feed, and one is empty." She motioned for Belinda to sit. "We'll go out later to meet them if you like."

Belinda lit up her face. "I'd like that. I have a horse and keep him at the stables on the other side of the woods. His name is Beau."

"Really? When you come back on Wednesday, why don't you plan to stay for dinner? Then afterward, we can go for a ride. Rob can run you over in the car to get Beau."

"Will Robert be joining us?" Belinda reached for her cup from the tray.

"No. He's in Canada for three weeks. He'll be working for the first two then he and Karen are going on vacation for a week. So your partners will just be Rob and I."

With relief sweeping over her, Belinda let out a slight sigh. Robert wouldn't be an issue and, for the next three weeks, she could concentrate on learning her new job. "I think that sounds like a plan. I'll bring some riding clothes with me."

"Bring a swimsuit as well. I like to take a dip afterward and sit in the hot tub. It's really relaxing. We can have some wine and talk."

Sandra had just set the stage for part two of her plan. Now she had to make sure Rob did his bit. If he did, the scheme would come together without a hitch. That is, if Robert allowed his attraction to Belinda to take hold, the final step in Sandra's plot. Then sometime in the near future, when Robert and Belinda decide to formalize their relationship with marriage, Sandra and Rob would explain their motives. By that time, the happy couple would be able to understand the reason for her meddling and they would forgive them.

While the women sipped coffee, Sandra explained the reasons for her need to hire someone to help with the design business, as well as the expected responsibilities. "I won't expect you to do anything you don't feel comfortable doing, and if I give you too much to do, you need to tell me to back off."

Belinda grinned. She really liked Sandra and felt very at ease around her. She didn't feel pressured, and related to Sandra more as a friend than as her new boss. The two laid out who would do what, and how to cover all the aspects of the job.

"I have a few errands to run this morning. Would you feel comfortable answering the phone while I'm gone?" Sandra leaned back in her chair. "Just tell everyone I'm out and take their number. I'll call them when I get back."

"Sure. I think I can manage that. Just show me to the phone."

"I can do better than that. I'll show you the office and your desk." Sandra motioned for Belinda to follow her. She led Belinda up the back stairs in the kitchen to an ample-sized room located at the back of the house. It was nicely decorated and had hardwood bookshelves lining two sides. The shelves were heavy with books of sample fabrics, window coverings, flooring, and anything else an interior designer might need to appoint a well laid out room. At the far end of the office were large windows facing the barn and pasture, the pool area, and the guesthouse. An overstuffed sofa sat in the middle of the room facing the windows, dividing it in two. On the opposite wall from the windows sat a large, French Country style, barn table Sandra used as a desk.

Sandra walked Belinda to a desk facing one of the windows. "I hope this will be alright." She gave her new assistant a brief tour of the office. "I have to go, but while I'm gone, feel free to explore so you'll know where things are. If you want anything from the kitchen, help yourself. I'll be back before lunch. If it's alright with you I'll pick up some sandwiches." Sandra walked to the door and turned back before walking out. "We can eat lunch by the pool." She waited for Belinda's approval, smiled, and closed the door as she left.

Now alone, Belinda glanced around the room trying to figure out where she should start. Her desk! She sat down in the ergonomically correct rolling chair. Testing out the positions, she found the best one. She probed in the drawers and located everything she could possibly need to perform her job efficiently. On the desk sat a brand new state-of-the-art laptop. As she looked over the desk, she realized it was new as well. It appeared Sandra spared no expense trying to make sure it met her assistant's needs.

She rubbed her fingertips over the top of the desk and then placed her elbow on the shiny surface. She rested her head in her hand as she took in her new work surroundings. Gradually, she drifted her eyes to the scene just outside the window above the desk. The guesthouse, Robert's residence, came into full view just beyond the pool. She wouldn't be able to avoid watching him come and go if he were to arrive home while she sat there working. Now she wasn't sure about its placement and scanned the room for somewhere else to move it. After her analysis of the room, she decided the arrangement met a very specific need and moving the desk wouldn't be an option. She relaxed her back as she supported her chin with her palm and tapped her fingers on the hard surface, which filled her ears with a muffled drumming beat. A snort huffed out her nose.

Unable to fix her immediate problem, she pushed her chair away from the desk and swiveled around to observe the room. "What else can I poke around in?"

A group of pictures hanging on one of the walls caught her attention. As she approached, she thought to herself they looked like pages out of a magazine that had been matted, and framed. Each frame hung uniformly spaced from the next in perfect rows. Standing in front of the arrangement, she hitched her breath. The pages were from a magazine article showcasing the Pendletons' house. One exhibited the front hall with the Bombay chests, cobalt blue vases, and the horseshoe shaped staircase. Another was of the dining room. In the picture of the family room, Sandra and Robert Pendleton sat on the leather couch near the massive fireplace. Robert posed behind them with his arms crossed on the back of the couch. She ran her fingers over the smooth glass that covered his face. "Robert."

Sandra's right hand was draped over Rob's knee. On her ring finger, she wore a three-stone diamond ring, an exact duplicate of the one Robert gave her when they became engaged in her "Dream Reality." She slid her fingertips down the glass. "My ring."

Belinda darted her eyes to the lower right corner to see the publishing date. It was dated a month before she fell into a coma. She must have seen this magazine before the accident and plugged the memory into her dream. She became excited knowing another piece of her memory puzzle was solved. The only thing she couldn't figure out was how she knew what drawer the wine bottle opener was in on New Year's Eve.

Continuing to scan from one photo to the next, she soon realized each one represented a part of the house she used in her dream. The lowest and last picture was of Rob standing in the kitchen with his back to the camera. He had his left hand on the neck of a wine bottle resting on the counter, and his right one hovered over a drawer at his side, holding a bottle opener. The very one Belinda had retrieved it from at the party. She let out a sigh of relief and mumbled under her breath, "Dr. Rosen will have a field day with this."

Belinda spent the next hour or so answering the few calls that came in. The rest of the time she poked around the office, which she enjoyed.

She sat at her new desk playing around with the design program on her computer as Sandra walked in. "How did it go?"

"I think I did okay. There were a few calls. Nothing earth shattering."

Sandra chuckled. "I'm glad. Lunch is downstairs. I'll get to the calls after we eat."

The women gathered the items necessary to eat lunch. They proceeded to take a leisurely hour under the covered porch overlooking the sparkling clear water of the pool and waterfall.

The gentle trickle of the water cascading down the rocks made Belinda relax. She could become accustomed to this very quickly, and wondered how long the honeymoon phase would last. However, this job was different and her new boss was unlike any she'd ever had before.

***

Wednesday morning, Belinda found herself excited to dress for work. The job not only gave her something to do, but she liked the new direction her career path could take. Sandra had filled her in on the ins and outs of the design profession and what it would take to become a certified designer. It appeared Belinda was well on her way because of her chosen academic field. So, with some experience and a few more courses, Belinda could apply for the title of Interior Designer.

The day proceeded with Belinda making herself useful as Sandra's new assistant. Sandra did a great job of mentoring her new employee and juggling her present clients. Belinda was amazed by Sandra's ability to multi-task and keep her cool at the same time. On Friday, Belinda would accompany Sandra on a new build project of a 7,000 square-foot home. Sandra wanted her to see how the design process worked from the ground up.

At four o'clock sharp, Sandra walked over to the phone and placed it on Do Not Disturb. "Did you bring your riding clothes and swimsuit?"

"Yes ma'am."

"Okay, go change and meet me downstairs. You can earn your keep by helping me with dinner. Rob will be home in about thirty minutes. One of the perks of being the boss, he gets to leave before rush hour when he's not in a meeting."

Belinda met Sandra in the kitchen and pitched in. She stood at the table facing toward the kitchen, about to set it. Rob walked in with his glasses perched down toward the tip of his nose, shuffling through a handful of envelopes and didn't seem to notice her. He put the mail down on the counter and wrapped his arms around the waist of his wife who stood at the kitchen island. He nuzzled into her neck and kissed her ever so gently. Sandra seemed to soften as she leaned into her husband in response to his loving gesture. The two were engrossed in their moment.

Belinda tried to keep her head down, but the compulsion to watch the CEO of a major corporation in such an intimate embrace with his wife proved too strong. She saw something very familiar. Sandra responded to her husband the same way Belinda and Robert had in her dream.

Rob started to become more intimate as his left hand began to move north on Sandra's torso, clearly targeting her breast. Just before he made contact, Sandra spoke. "Honey, we have company. Belinda is joining us for dinner. Remember?"

He stopped moving. With his nose buried in her neck, he looked up from under his brow at Belinda standing at the kitchen table. Belinda gave him a quick restrained wave. It seemed uncanny how much they acted like Dream Robert and her, and how much he resembled both Roberts.

Rob let out a short snort and gave his wife one last kiss, whispering, "Later."

She smiled. "I hope so."

He released her and acknowledged Belinda. "It's nice to see you again. I'm glad you could join us." He started backing out of the room. "I'm going to go change." His voice became fainter halfway across the family room. "I'll be back to help."

Sandra gave Belinda an impish smile. "We may be getting older, but we're not dead." The statement broke the tension and Belinda let out a small giggle. "Go ahead and laugh. It was funny!" The two women laughed harder. Belinda finished setting the table while Sandra continued her work.

Rob didn't take long to return dressed in jeans and a t-shirt. For someone in his fifties, he had a nice physique that matched his slight ruggedness. He looked as if he would be just as comfortable running a ranch as he was running his company.

"Well, what's left to do or did I time it right and get lucky?"

Sandra glanced at him. "You always try to get out of helping me."

"And most of the time I'm successful." He received a smack from the corner of a towel Sandra held. They both gave each other a playful smile before Rob grabbed her and planted a kiss on her lips. "Now what can I do."

"Make the salad."

With the ease of a chef, he went into action collecting everything he needed.

"I can help cut up vegetables." Belinda sat down on one of the stools at the island.

Rob completed his gathering and set up shop alongside his wife. He handed Belinda a knife, cutting board, and a cucumber. He then turned to get something else.

Sandra had her back to her husband and never lifted her head. "Rob, here." She held out a cutting knife to him. He turned around, took it without saying a word, and returned to the counter to finish his task.

Belinda found the interchange she witnessed intriguing. It appeared Sandra read his mind.

Sandra timed dinner to take longer than usual. As planned, Rob drove Belinda to the stables to saddle up Beau. Sandra and he would come with their horses to meet her.

Rob returned to his barn to find Sandra sitting atop her horse waiting. She had saddled his horse, Billy and held the reins. "Remember what you're doing tonight." She jutted the reins toward him. "I did my part with a late dinner."

"How could I forget?" he mumbled back at her. He sighed, took the reins from his wife, and checked his cinch before mounting.

The trio met up and took a relaxing ride that lasted until after dusk. Their ride ended back at the Pendletons' barn.

Sandra dismounted and held Mouse's reins. She waited to make sure Rob remembered his part of the plan. Rob dismounted and started to lead Billy toward the barn. Sandra cleared her throat and caught Rob's attention. She tilted her head toward Belinda as she turned to lead her horse into the barn. The exchange she heard, met with her approval.

Belinda stayed mounted and wasn't looking forward to riding the dark trail back to the stable. She wished they would've gotten an earlier start, but she'd had such an enjoyable evening. "I'll ride Beau back. Rob would you mind picking me up so I can come get my car?"

"Belinda, Sandra tells me the two of you were planning on sitting in the hot tub. Since it's so late, why don't you leave Beau here for the night? We have that empty stall."

Belinda thought about the proposition for a few minutes. It made sense, so she agreed.

With the horses bedded down, the hot tub came next on the agenda with a relaxing glass of wine to round off the night. The three sat and genuinely seemed to enjoy each other's company. Belinda learned more about her new boss and husband. In return, they were learning about her. Belinda felt a bond with them and knew she liked them. They were not stuffy like she imagined someone in their position would be. Both of them were down-to-earth kind of folks who made her feel welcome and wanted.

At ten o'clock, Belinda sat in her car for the ride home. All she could think about was the hours of discussion the evening would spur on with Dr. Rosen, Abbey and her mother.

***

Sandra and Rob were in a tender embrace while lying in bed. She rested her head on his chest and he stroked her hair. "Are you happy now?" He gave her a soft kiss.

She looked up at him with a hint of a smile. "You did well. Now all you have to do is convince her to move Beau here permanently. Then phase two will be complete."

Rob huffed, but knew her prying was the right thing to do.

CHAPTER 15

EARLY THE NEXT morning, Belinda called Sandra to find out when she could come by to pick up Beau. It wasn't one of her scheduled workdays and she didn't want Beau to overextend his stay.

"Oh, Belinda, I hope you don't mind. I'm going to be gone all day, so I fed Beau and turned him out with the other horses. He seems to get along with them just fine."

"Thank you, but I don't want to take advantage of your generosity."

Sandra let out a small laugh. "We don't mind at all. In fact, since we're planning to ride again tomorrow night, why not just leave him where he is? It would be easier for you."

"That'll work for me. Anything he eats can be deducted from my pay."

"Oh! Don't you worry about that. If you want, you can come over earlier and help me feed the horses before work."

"I'd be glad to. I would've done the same thing at the stables anyway." Belinda knew the plan made more sense than moving Beau back and forth.

"Good. I'll have some coffee on. See you tomorrow morning. Say around seven."

"I'll see you then, and thank you, Sandra."

"You're welcome, darling. See you in the morning."

***

As scheduled, Belinda arrived at the Pendleton estate at seven a.m. sharp. Dressed in jeans, a white t-shirt, and boots, she exited her car carrying her work clothes. Today would be busy. She would help with the horses and then clean up and be ready to go on her first off-site visit. Her job would be to take notes while Sandra walked around making decisions with the owner of the home. When they came back, Belinda would write up the report and

Sandra would complete the layout. On Monday afternoon, they would review the presentation with the owner.

Belinda's heart took flight, mixed with a healthy dose of nerves. She wanted to make a good impression and hoped she wouldn't mess up.

The day went as planned and the women worked well together. Belinda completed her end of the presentation by four p.m. Sandra sat at her computer working on the design program when Belinda approached her.

"I have the report finished. Do you want to go over it? I'd like to know what I did wrong."

Sandra stopped working and frowned at Belinda. "What you did *wrong*? Darling, we don't do wrong here. We do 'room-for-improvement.'" She grinned making air quotes. "Give it to me and make yourself comfortable." She pointed to the overstuffed chair by her desk.

Sandra read making slight facial gestures with each flip of a page until a broad smile came across her face. She passed it back to Belinda. "You're a fast learner. The report is perfect. There'll be no changes."

She glanced at the clock and proclaimed with one finger on the Do Not Disturb button, "Quittin' time. I'm going to change and I'll see you downstairs."

Belinda bounced down the back stairs into the kitchen to find Rob and Sandra in a passionate kiss. Neither of them heard or noticed her until she cleared her throat.

They turned their heads in her direction at the same time. Rob's lips pursed and he let out a sigh. "I'm going to change. See you two in a minute."

Belinda bit the corner of her lip and apologized for the intrusion. Sandra reassured her she did nothing intrusive at all. She warned Belinda it was something she might need to get used to if she was going to be hanging around the Pendleton household. Sandra explained, she and Rob were still madly in love and couldn't get enough of each other. Belinda thought *how unusual* and envied them for their passion.

She had managed to complete her first full week of employment with the Crescent Oaks Interior Design Company. Over the past week, she'd learned a lot from her new boss as she became more familiar with the couple she knew as her in-laws in a past memory. In her dream, she had limited contact with the Penningtons. What she knew about them came from a chance encounter with a magazine article she had read before the accident.

Now she had the opportunity to learn what they were really like. She found it fascinating that the two people from the article, who lived a life she could only dream of, actually had invited her into their lives.

The evening ended with a relaxing soak in the hot tub. Rob strutted out of the house with three glasses of wine. Belinda's heart jumped when she noticed his silhouette walking toward her. In the dimness of the pool lights, he appeared younger. He resembled Robert. He sat on the edge of the tub and handed each woman a glass. "Belinda, Sandra tells me your first week went well."

Belinda wasn't sure where the conversation would lead, but she responded with, "I'm very pleased with it." She glanced at Sandra who gave her a nod confirming her statement.

"So it looks like you'll be coming back next week?"

Now she was confused, but his question piqued her interest. "What are you asking me? I'd like to come back next week, if that's okay."

Rob's mouth opened and a blank look swept across his face. "No, no. That's not what I meant. Look, I'll just come out and ask. Since you'll be spending at least three days a week here...Sandra and I thought it would be easier if you permanently kept Beau in our barn. There I said it." He gave a nod, seeming pleased with himself.

Belinda thought Rob seemed uncomfortable by the way he presented the question. It was unexpected from this otherwise confident businessman. She hesitated and gave his proposal some thought, and said, "It makes sense, but there would have to be some ground rules."

Rob looked at his wife, and then turned back to Belinda. "Go on."

"I'll rent the stall from you and pay for his food."

Rob smiled. "Young lady, you have a deal."

Sandra sank back against the lounge seat of the hot tub. The water rose to her neck as she rested her head back to see the night sky. Watching the lights from a distant plane pass overhead, she felt confident phase three of her plan would only be a few weeks away. By the time Robert returned, Belinda would practically be family.

***

Karen and Robert sat next to each other, each in their own comfortable lounge chair in the clubroom of the airline. They were on their way back to Houston, waiting for their flight in the Toronto Airport. Karen paged through a bridal magazine and Robert sat watching the planes on the tarmac.

Karen studied the center page that featured a gorgeous dress by a top designer. It was breathtaking and she knew it would be out of her price range. Excited, she called, "Robert." He didn't move. She again repeated, in a slightly higher voice, "Robert." Again, no indication he even heard her. Out of frustration, she let the magazine fall to her lap.

This wasn't the first time he seemed preoccupied on their trip. Something was bothering him. She noticed a shift in his mood about a week after their engagement. The first time, whatever distracted him only lasted a few days. In February, another short episode occurred. However, over the past several weeks, it never seemed to stop and she had hoped being together in a five-star hotel on Lake Louise would spark their romance. She didn't seem to have any problem keeping his attention when she pranced around half-naked. It was when Robert sat quietly that he seemed more distant and that scared her the most. She thought about asking him what was going on, but didn't want to nag.

She touched his arm. "Robert."

He turned toward her as she lifted the picture of the exquisite dress.

***

Belinda began to think of Sandra and Rob as extended family. Their warm and comfortable manner made it easy for her to forget they were Robert's parents. Her workdays centered around her office duties, the care of her horse, and socializing with the Pendletons after hours.

On Friday, about three o'clock in the afternoon, Belinda changed out of her work clothes and left for the barn. Sandra and Rob would fix dinner by themselves while she worked on grooming the horses.

Armed with her iPod, she inserted her ear buds. She started listening to some of her favorite songs as she led Beau from his stall and tethered him to a post. As she brushed him, she moved to the rhythm of the music. Slowly at first, but as the rhythm of the music intensified, so did her movements.

***

Robert pulled into the driveway for the first time in three weeks from his business slash vacation trip and noticed a strange car in the circle drive as he drove past to the guesthouse. After unloading his luggage, he walked across to the main house and located his mom in the kitchen working on supper. "Sure smells good. I'm starving." He took in a deep breath of the mouthwatering scent and could feel the saliva building in his mouth. "Pot roast?"

She shot him a glance over her shoulder and smiled. "Thanks. You're right and it'll be ready in about half an hour. I'm finishing the gravy and potatoes. Glad you're back. How was your trip?" Robert walked over to his mom and gave her a kiss on the cheek. Her smile widened.

"Good to be home. I think the business trip was successful. We now have some new clients. The vacation was okay. By the way, who does the car in the driveway belong to?" He snatched a tomato out of the salad and popped it in his mouth.

His mom pointed toward the kitchen window at the stables. "Belinda."

Robert inquired in a gruff voice still chewing the tomato. "What's she doing here?"

"Grooming her horse."

Robert walked to the kitchen table and supported himself on his knuckles to peer out the window. "What's Beau doing here?"

"She's boarding him here. Belinda now works for me part-time. She's a really sweet, young lady." She stopped her chore and looked at her son as he glared at her.

With a jerk of his head, he turned back to the window.

"Robert, be a dear and go ask her to come in and clean up."

Robert could feel himself flush as his heart rate sped up from his low boiling rage. "Why!?"

"Because she's staying for dinner and I need her to set the table." She paused. "In fact the two of you can set it together. Now go on."

Robert's mouth dropped open as he stared at his mother, not intending to take her on at this point. He was tired and hungry. All he wanted was to eat and go to sleep. So he did as she requested and set off for the barn.

Sandra stopped cooking and walked over to the island where she had a clear view of her son walking, hands clinched into fists. Smiling, she realized the third phase of her plan was about to begin. She changed her position, taking a better vantage point behind the kitchen table, close enough to see into the barn without being noticed.

***

Robert approached the barn not really sure what he would do when he reached Belinda. She managed to stick in his head and hide there like a little mouse waiting to be given the chance to scurry around. For the past three weeks, she was all he thought about, even when he was with Karen. The way Belinda felt, the softness of her skin, how she moved, how she laughed.

She had packed her bags and moved right into his mind, refusing to leave. His biggest fear was breaking down and giving in to his impulses, because around her, he seemed to have very little control.

When he reached the barn, he was determined to keep his resolution no matter what. There would be no physical contact of any sort. He would just pass on his mother's message and leave. At the doorway, he stopped, paralyzed by the sound and sight presented before him.

As he watched her, Belinda appeared to float as though she danced with an invisible partner—her arms positioned as if around some one's neck. Earbuds in place, she sang, "Dear love, my only sweet true love." Her voice filled his ears like the voice of an angel. He couldn't remember hearing anyone sing so sweetly.

His balled fists relaxed open and the tension in his shoulders vanished as he gazed at her for a few minutes—spellbound. Intensely drawn to her, he walked over to Belinda and stepped into her arms, taking hold of her, throwing his resolution aside.

Her eyes shot open and she froze with her hands suspended up in front of her shoulders. Inches away, he could smell her perfume mixed with the distinctive smell of horse. He filled his nostrils and rubbed his palms against her's until their fingers laced. In slow motion, he guided her arms around his neck. He removed one of her earbuds and inserted it into his ear. "Don't stop." He tugged her to his chest. She tightened her grip as he glided her around the dirt floor.

***

Sandra heard Rob arrive home and walk into the kitchen flipping through the mail. She stood behind the table with her arms crossed over her chest still viewing her son and hopefully future daughter-in-law through the window. "Honey, come look at this," she called to her husband.

He stopped shuffling through the envelopes. "What?"

"Look in the stable. See them dancing. See how they're looking at each other. She's his soul mate." She wrapped her arm around Rob's waist and snuggled into his side.

"I know you're right. Now let's see if those two can take it to the next step. Sandra, you're part is done. Now it's up to them."

Sandra nestled into her husband's arm and let out a sigh. "Okay, but is it alright if I give them a little nudge now and then? You know, just to keep them on track."

He gave her a squeeze. "You're so bad! That's why I love you. Just don't push too much."

"I promise." The couple turned back toward the window to watch what else might unfold.

***

Belinda waited for Robert to release his hold when the song ended, and then shoved him away.

He stumbled backward a few steps. "I'm sorry. I guess I shouldn't have done that."

Belinda's miffed level rose. What made him think he could just walk in and out of her emotions? "You bet you shouldn't have done that!" she snapped back at him. Yanking the earbud out of his ear, she turned away to finish brushing Beau.

"Mom sent me out here to ask you to come in. I understand you're joining us for dinner."

Belinda stopped grooming the horse and glared at him. "Tell her I'll be right there."

Not saying another word, he turned to walk back to the house.

Scout stuck his head out of his stall just as Robert started to walk past. Belinda watched him smile as he stroked Scout's nose and then rubbed behind his ear. She could hardly believe what she heard. A soft cooing sound came from Robert the closer he moved toward the horse. Scout's ear was level with Robert's mouth as he continued to make the soothing sound. He stood next to the animal for several seconds and then looked over his shoulder at Belinda and walked out.

Her heart melted watching his response to Scout. That was the sweetest thing she had ever seen. Belinda threw her arms over Beau's back and rested against the horse, mumbling, "That SOB. How could he be so mean one minute and so absolutely adorable the next?" Beau swung his head back and nibbled at her. She inhaled and untied Beau to lead him into his stall.

***

Belinda scoped out the occupants in the kitchen when she opened the door. Sandra stood at the island working and Robert sat on one of the stools across from her. He turned toward her. His smug expression threw her off guard but she recovered quickly. "Sandra, I'll be right down. I'm going to go clean up," she said strolling past Robert. Giving him a sideways glance, she walked up the stairs.

"Don't take too long. I need you and Robert to set the table."

Belinda made it halfway up the stairs when she heard Sandra's request. "Shit!" came spontaneously out of her mouth, under her breath.

Minutes later, a spruced up Belinda bounced down the stairs. She purposely walked toward Robert. As she strutted past, she elbowed him squarely in the ribs. Maybe a bit of pain would convey the message she was angry. She turned toward Sandra and could see Robert watching her through squinted eyes. She ignored him. "Sandra, what table should I set?"

"I think the one under the patio cover, dear. Robert will help you."

Belinda took a tray from the center lower cabinet and placed all the needed dinnerware on it. After picking it up, she marched toward Robert and placed the tray on the island. She shoved it at him and glared. "I'll get the door." With a flip of her hair, she turned and walked away. The soft pat of a shoe tapping resonated while she stood by the open door with her arms crossed.

Reaching for the tray, he heard a very sweet muffled voice come from the direction of his mother. "Robert, play nice." He sighed and looked at her with a raised eyebrow, trying to figure out just what in the heck had he gotten himself into. It felt like a setup, but he wasn't sure. All he knew was his mother was up to something. He gave her a scowl before turning toward the other woman he found himself pitted against.

Alone on the patio, no one spoke. Robert placed the tray on the cart across from the table and Belinda proceeded to arrange the placemats. He picked up the plates, attempting to help as instructed, but approached with caution.

Wrapping her fingers around the edges of the smooth ceramic dinnerware, she tried to take them away from him. "I'll do this. I don't need your help."

Increasing his grip, he firmly stated, "No. We'll do this together."

They both stood there, hands clutching the plates, in a non-verbal tug of war. Belinda gritted her teeth as she tightened her grip around the stack. Robert responded by tightening his. After all, he was the stronger of the two and would win this battle. The sound of plate grinding against plate caused both to loosen up.

Belinda rolled her eyes and let out a loud sigh. "Whatever." She released her hold as a low-pitched tone of the top plate cracking, sliced through the air.

Robert gasped. "Oh shit! This is Mom's good stuff."

Belinda flapped her hands in front of her. "What can we do? Can you sneak in and get another one?"

Robert nodded and started for the door just as Sandra opened it for Rob, who carried another tray with the food for the evening meal. Robert swung around to look at Belinda and abandoned his quest. She searched for a place to stash the broken plate. Under the nearest patio chair cushion made a perfect spot. She quickly stood, trying to act as if nothing happened.

Sandra looked at Robert and Belinda. Robert stared back, just as Belinda clutched her wrist behind her and looked at her feet. If she didn't know better, the pair acted like two little kids who just got caught doing something naughty. She knew what his expression meant. It was his, "I'm sorry. I didn't mean to do it," face. Sandra looked at the stack of plates now sitting on the table. She counted three. "Where's the fourth plate?"

The pair shot repeated glances at each other and his parents. Belinda pursed her lips. Several seconds passed before Robert finally spoke up. "Ah, there's been a slight accident."

Sandra crossed her arms, watching the interactions between the two naughty children.

"Go on. Show her."

Belinda reached under the cushion and pulled out the two halves of the plate.

Sandra slowly panned from Robert to Belinda. She scrunched her nose and shook her head. "I just bought those. I guess I'll go buy a few more before the sale runs out. I only paid a buck apiece for them."

Mouth agape, Belinda glared at Robert. "I thought these were her good stuff."

"I'm a guy. What do I know about dishes?"

They stood there in a stare down like two gunfighters about to have a shootout. Never taking his gaze off her, he formed a crooked smile. Belinda gave him a wary stare and pushed out her lower lip, letting out a huff. A smile broke out across her face. She pulled out her chair and made herself comfortable. "You know it's all his fault." She pointed her thumb in Robert's direction.

"No it wasn't!" His scoff seemed exaggerated. He took his seat beside her.

Belinda snapped her head back to Robert. With an impish grin, she nodded. "Yes it was. It's always the guy's fault. Don't you know that? So just apologize."

A muffled giggle from Sandra and a throaty chuckle from Rob distracted her, but she didn't take her glare off him. "Well. Go on. Apologize."

He exhaled and snickered out, "I'm sorry."

Belinda shielded her mouth and leaned into Sandra as if she needed to tell her something in confidence. Of course, she didn't lower her voice. "It really wasn't entirely his fault, but we'll let him take the blame."

She heard a snorty laugh come from Robert. He apparently had taken a swig of his drink and found her antics comical enough to almost choke. Rob's perturbed expression indicated that he didn't see the humor in the incident. He was busy mopping the droplets that had flown across the table off his face with his napkin.

Belinda and Sandra busted out in gut wrenching laughter. Rob and Robert followed and the interaction broke the tension.

As bowls of food passed around the table, the foursome's laughter fell into a relaxed conversation.

Robert and Belinda ended the evening in the hot tub, drinking wine, alone. Sandra and Rob decided they needed their rest.

CHAPTER 16

FOR THE NEXT week, with Karen in town, Robert spent his time away from home. Belinda found herself in the midst of helping Sandra plan the Pendletons' annual Fourth of July Party. This year's event was expected to be bigger than usual because the fourth fell on a Saturday, allowing for more out-of-town guests.

The phone started ringing the minute Belinda came in the front door. She grabbed her coffee from the kitchen counter and headed straight for the office. Sandra was already hard at work pouring over some plans for one of her design projects, ignoring the invasive noise from the phone. She barely noticed as Belinda rushed to her desk to answer it.

"Good morning. Crescent Oaks Interior Design.

"Could I please speak with Sandra?"

"I'm sorry, she's not available. May I take a message?"

"Ask her to call Mrs. Kaminski about the fabric samples she requested last week."

"Alright, I'll let her know. Could I have your number?"

"She has it."

"I'll give her your message as soon as she comes in. Have a nice day."

Sandra looked up over the rims of her glasses with a faint smile. "Thank you." Belinda acknowledged her with a nod, but had no time to respond as she answered another call. She figured this would be the work pace for the next couple of weeks. Sandra worked nonstop, wearing two hats: interior designer and event planner.

She hired someone to manage the preparations, but because of her need for perfection when it came to her parties, she micro-managed until the scheduled date. The day of the party, the event would become the responsibility of the hired party planner, so Sandra could enjoy her family, friends, and guests.

About mid-morning, the phone calls died down. Belinda watched Sandra lean back in her chair, stretch her arms, and rotate her head with her eyes closed. "Do you think you could give me more of your time for the next few weeks? I'm going to be pretty busy for a while."

"How much time would you need?"

"I'll take every day, but if you can't, I'll take whatever you can spare."

"Are you talking about weekends as well?"

Sandra tightened her lips, causing them to form a thin line and nodded. "But only if you can."

Belinda studied her. She was grateful she worked with Sandra and loved her job. Sandra and Rob had been so generous and she felt this would be a way to give something back to show she appreciated them. "I have some appointments I'll need to go to and a week from this Saturday we both need to be off." Sandra raised her head from the back of the chair and tilted it toward Belinda. "I'm planning a small housewarming dinner and I expect you and Rob to attend."

Sandra grinned. "Go ahead and put it on my calendar. You can plan on us being there." Sandra no sooner finished her last word when the phone rang again, causing their brief break to end.

The remainder of the week was as hectic as Monday. Belinda, as promised, increased her hours at work and was now fulltime plus. However, when Friday rolled around, she had a date. Colin was back in town. At five o'clock sharp, Belinda stood and announced she was leaving. "Sandra. Why don't you shut off the computer and go enjoy the night with Rob. I'm sure he misses you."

"I'm sure he does too," she agreed. "I miss him."

Belinda walked over and stood behind Sandra, placing her hands on her shoulders. She bent down and whispered, "So stop working and go enjoy your husband. We can pick up with this in the morning."

Sandra took off her glasses and rubbed her eyes. "What are you and Colin planning for the evening?"

"I have no clue. I'm letting him take care of those plans."

"Well, go have fun," Sandra encouraged as Belinda left the room.

Sandra watched her protégée vanish into the hall. She had to be patient. She loved Colin like a son, but she felt confident their relationship would fade away. Belinda didn't talk about him like most young women in love. She had a fondness for him, but Sandra knew Belinda wasn't in love with him. So when Colin would make his final move to Canada in a few weeks, Sandra knew Belinda wouldn't be following him.

Sandra rose from her desk and went downstairs to find Rob sitting on the sofa with his feet propped up. She plopped down beside him and snuggled into his chest. He placed his arm around her shoulders and gave her a squeeze. "Finished for the night?"

"Mm-hmm."

"You hungry? I can make you a sandwich or a salad."

"I'd like a sandwich. I'll come with you. You know, watching you slaving in the kitchen always turns me on."

He smiled.

***

Robert pulled out of the airport-parking garage after escorting Karen to the security check. She left on one of her two week trips to Europe.

As he entered the Beltway 8 toll road, making his way back to Sugar Land, he experienced a sense of excitement at the possibility that Belinda would still be at his parents.

An irrepressible urge grew in his loins the closer he came to the house. As he turned into the drive, his heart sank—her car wasn't there.

***

Sandra sat at the counter watching the food preparation taking place before her. Rob had such a knack for the dramatic and could even transform sandwich making into an art form. She turned when she heard the back door open as Robert walked in.

"Hi, Sweetie. Did you get Karen to the airport alright?"

Robert nodded as he approached the counter observing his father's handiwork. "Is there enough for another one of those?" He picked at the sandwich fixings. "Mom, where's your adopted daughter?" He popped a slice of roast beef into his mouth.

Sandra and Rob both chuckled at his statement. "Out with my adopted son, Colin."

He contorted his face as he felt a twinge of jealousy. "Isn't that incest?"

***

Saturday morning the workload centered on design projects because both women planned to take Sunday off. Colin would be leaving again for

Canada and Belinda felt the need to see him. Sandra wanted time to sleep late and be with Rob. Come Monday morning, the party planning would be on the front burner again.

Belinda worked hard on her computer. Her eyes grew tired from staring at the screen all morning. Closing them, she took a deep breath and rested her head in her palm. Slowly, she lifted her lids and looked out the window. Catching movement out of the corner of her eye, she focused her vision on the guesthouse. Robert stood with a hose, spraying down his beamer. She watched him as he moved from one side of the car to the next. Taking the soapy sponge from the bucket, he began to rub down the hood.

By ten a.m., the sunny morning quickly raised the temperature to around ninety degrees. He hadn't worked too long before he threw the sponge in the bucket and stopped to peel off his t-shirt. Using it, he wiped the sweat from his brow. She watched him look up at the second story window of his mother's office. He stared at her with a devilish smile. In slow motion, he rubbed the sweat from his chest with the t-shirt. His gaze never faltered.

Belinda gasped a bit too loud, now observing more intently.

"Are you alright over there?" Sandra asked.

Belinda turned slightly toward Sandra, but never took her eyes off Robert. "I'm fine. Just taking a moment."

Robert again walked from side to side and front to back rinsing the car. He paused and used the hose to douse himself. Her breathing increased and she squirmed in her seat as she watched the water ripple down his well-formed chest and arms causing his skin to glisten in the sun. She parted her lips. She concentrated on every movement he made.

Once finished, he walked in the direction of the main house only wearing a pair of cut-offs and flip-flops. He approached the pool and began to unbutton his jeans. Never breaking stride, he reached for the zipper next. Belinda stared in anticipation of what he was about to do. When he reached the edge of the pool, he stopped with his thumbs in the waistband. The shoes were kicked off. Just before pulling down the cut-offs, he looked up and stared at Belinda. Her heart stopped as she held her breath, realizing she had nowhere to hide.

He tilted his head, and then raised one corner of his mouth, giving her a sultry half-smile. Not taking his eyes off her, he stripped off his cut-offs and exposed a pair of the snuggest excuse for male swimwear she had ever seen that left very little to the imagination. When he straightened up, she realized he was as excited as she was. Robert gave her one last look before diving into the water.

Instantly, Belinda stood from her desk, gasping a breath. "I need something to drink. Do you want anything?"

"No, I'm fine." Sandra watched her as she left the room and smiled to herself. Earlier that morning, she had intentionally pulled up all the blinds knowing Robert always washed his car every Saturday morning when he was home, followed by a quick dip in the pool. Sandra gave her the excuse she was in the mood for more light and from the way she had watched Belinda squirm, she knew her son had putting on a good show. Whether Robert knew it or not, he played into her plan.

***

Bright and early on Monday, Belinda pulled into the Pendleton driveway and caught a glimpse of Beau grazing. The way his coat glistened in the morning sun and his methodical movements distracted her. She realized she had never painted a portrait of him and decided to snap a few pictures after she parked the car.

Her gaze drifted back to the road. The sight of a red roadster coming straight for her scared the crap out of her. She jerked the steering wheel to swerve into the circular drive to avoid hitting Robert.

He didn't attempt to give up any portion of his side of the driveway or slow down. The only acknowledgement of recognition he offered was an adjustment of his sunglasses as he passed.

The roadster slowed at the end of the drive, turned and faded out of view. "What an arrogant ass," she muttered, parking the car in the usual spot. As she reached for her phone to take the pictures, it pinged a text alert. It was from Robert and she wondered how long he'd had her number.

> Robert: You drive like an old woman.
> Belinda: Old man!
> Robert: Who me?????
> Belinda: Are you driving and texting?
> Robert: At stop sign. You concerned?

Belinda hesitated. She wasn't sure how to answer and then responded: Yes!

She waited for a few seconds, expecting a response, but none came.

Opening the door, she hopped out, walked over to the fence that surrounded the pasture, and adjusted her aim. Beau lazily grazed until she stepped on a twig that sent a crisp snap through the air. He raised his head and looked back at her. She smiled and snapped away.

At the car, she placed the phone in her purse and gathered up her belongings, which included a complete dinner she had made for the evening meal.

Belinda walked into the kitchen balancing freshly made lasagna, salad fixings, and garlic bread.

Sandra sat at the kitchen table watching the juggling act. "What's all that?"

"Dinner for tonight."

"Dinner?"

"Yep. I decided I needed to contribute to the food supply around here. So from now on, every Monday I provide dinner." Completing her task of putting the food neatly away in the chill of the refrigerator, she poured a cup of coffee and joined Sandra at the table. Belinda slipped into a chair, making herself comfortable.

"You don't—"

Belinda held up a hand stopping Sandra from finishing her statement. "Yes I do. This is one of my ground rules. It's right up there with the Beau rules. Okay?"

Sandra nodded and pressed no further.

It would be another grueling workday. They ate lunch at their desks as they caught up with the design end of the business in between the Fourth of July party planning. It seemed the day would never end, and by five o'clock Sandra threw her hands up. "Stop working. We're going to go eat your wonderful dinner, and then relax by the pool with some adult beverages."

The invitation to quit was all Belinda needed to shut down the computer. She was more than ready.

After turning on the oven, she placed the lasagna in to warm. Sandra volunteered to make the salads while Belinda took a short break to go visit her horse.

Armed with Beau's usual treat, she walked to the barn. "Hey Beau, carrots." She held out the morsels as the horse poked his head from his stall to retrieve them.

Belinda stroked Beau's nose, lost in her thoughts, when she felt the grip of arms around her waist and a simultaneous whisper in her ear. "Did you enjoy the view Saturday morning?" the intruder said, nuzzling her hair. He was gentle and she instinctively softened, molding herself to the strong chest pressing against her back. At that moment, she would've let go and given herself to him if he gave her any further encouragement. Against her hip, she felt a recognizable vibration of a phone followed by the sudden release from his arms.

His reaction to his phone reminded her of his engagement. She whirled around toward Robert and poked a finger in his chest. "What do you want? And what do you think you're doing?" She felt her face run hot and her muscles tense as she clenched her fists.

Not at all apologetic for his actions, he seemed confident and arrogant as usual. "I just asked you a question."

Now, even more indignant with him, she shoved him away. "Do you always just come up behind women you barely know and wrap your arms around them like that to ask them a question?" He didn't answer. "Robert, you can be such an ass."

"Yeah. I've heard that from people on occasion," he said with a smirk. "Mom sent me out to tell you the lasagna is ready to come out of the oven."

Belinda huffed past shaking her head, but he still intrigued her. This Robert was more complicated and challenging. When she realized he was keeping an even pace behind her, she stepped up the game and put more sassy in her sashay to give him something to watch.

Robert dropped back and followed behind her across the yard. Now and then she glanced over her shoulder. Apparently, her hips swaying side to side brought a lopsided smile to his face. It appeared he enjoyed her tease, but she reminded herself, he was taken.

***

Well into the meal, Robert commented, "Mom, this is great lasagna. Is it a new recipe?"

"No, I didn't make it. Belinda did."

With a heaping helping of the Italian cuisine on his fork, Robert lifted it to Belinda. "My compliments to the chef," and then mumbled, "My Baby Sister can cook, too."

Belinda took notice of Robert's comment, and scrunched up her nose before mouthing, *Baby Sister?*

Robert shoved the lasagna into his mouth and ignored her.

***

For the next few days, the pace didn't let up. During work hours, the phone calls never stopped. Sandra attended meetings with the party planner, and multiple clients, but always managed to mix in some down time.

Belinda most cherished the time spent away from the office with the Pendletons. As soon as she and Sandra left the second floor and entered the kitchen, the mood changed drastically. The Pendleton family worked hard but when it came time to relax, they put as much effort into unwinding.

A pattern had formed. After each dinner, the Pendletons would invite Belinda to take a ride on the trails, sit in the hot tub, swim, or watch a movie. All of which, of course, had Robert in attendance. Although she knew he was off limits sexually because of their involvement with other people, she found it stimulating and dangerously tempting being so close. Belinda no longer saw him as the Robert of her dreams. He was very different and she embraced him for who he was, not who she remembered.

Saturday arrived and Belinda would only be putting in a few hours so she could finish her preparations for the planned housewarming. Everyone invited planned to attend. It would be a small, but comfortable group.

Dora and James arrived early to help. After their hello's, Belinda's dad firmly planted himself in front of the TV with the remote, surfing for any sports-related show. Both women agreed this was the best help he could give them—he was out of their way.

Since the increase in Belinda's work hours, she and her mom had little time to spend together. They talked frequently via phone, which kept her mother in the loop about the relationship she was forming with the Pendletons, including Robert. Dora never hesitated to remind Belinda of her concern. Fully aware her mom didn't want to see her hurt again, Belinda always reassured her she'd be careful.

The women busied themselves in the kitchen arranging the appetizers and eating utensils on the island. It would be a simple meal of barbeque chicken, her mom's world-class potato salad, baked beans, and tossed salad. Dora surprised Belinda with dessert, a homemade apple pie, and ice cream to be served on the side.

"Did everyone respond to your invitation?"

"Yep! Abbey of course said yes right off the bat, just like you and dad. Sandra confirmed again just before I left work this morning. I'll be the 'fifth wheel' in the group since Colin is out of town."

The doorbell rang as Belinda arranged the chicken on a platter, getting it ready for the grill. She looked at her mom. "Can you get that for me?"

"Sure."

Abbey and Garrett arrived with Zinfandel and a housewarming present. Immediately the energy level increased as Abbey acted her usual perky self. "Wha'cha doin' in here?" She rested her chin on Belinda's shoulder.

"Getting the chicken ready for the grill." Belinda leaned her head into Abbey's. "I'm so glad to see you. Where's Garrett?"

"With your father." The two giggled.

Dora opened a bottle and began filling glasses. The chime of a doorbell alerted them to the arrival of the last guests.

"I got it." Belinda turned the corner into the foyer to answer the front door.

She took a second to fluff her hair and planted a radiant smile on her face before she opened it. "Sandra and Rob, I'm so glad you could...." Sandra stepped aside to reveal a third person—Robert. Belinda let out a shallow sigh.

From her reaction, Robert must have realized he wasn't expected because he gave the back of his mother's head a wary look. With suspicion in his voice he asked, "Mom, was I invited?"

Sandra turned slowly around and patted Robert's arm. "Not exactly, dear." Turning to address Belinda, she asked with a sweet smile, "You don't mind that we brought Robert, do you? He would've been all alone tonight."

Belinda took a deep breath, let it out, and faked a smile. She knew Sandra and Rob had been purposely leaving her and Robert alone together in the past week. One night the pair excused themselves about forty-five minutes into a movie. On another evening, Rob suddenly started yawning in the hot tub and got out to go to bed, with Sandra following shortly after.

Belinda looked at Robert. He shrugged and shook his head. Belinda cast an eye over the small group and snickered. "No, I don't mind. There's plenty of food." Stepping aside, she let the new arrivals in.

Robert's expression flattened and she saw him inhale, seeming relieved. Entering, he paused and muttered, "Sorry."

"Really, it's alright. I'm glad you're here." She closed the door and followed him into the living room.

To Belinda's delight, the dinner party seemed to be going very well. The women talked and laughed and, of course, the men gathered around the

TV watching one of the basketball playoffs, hootin' and hollerin', except for Robert. He made an occasional visit to the men's side of the house, but most of the time he actually helped, taking on the role as host.

Robert grabbed the chicken off the counter. "This ready for the grill?"

Before Belinda could answer, he strode out the door, his steps wide and determined. All she could do was to make sure he had what he needed to barbeque. She picked up the tray and followed him out.

"Okay, have you ever done this before?"

Robert opened his mouth, jerked his head back, and tsked. "Yeah! I do a fair job with a grill. Ye woman of little faith," he said, snapping the tongs inches from her nose.

"I was just checking. I've never seen you cook before."

He studied her for a second. "Just because I don't cook doesn't mean I can't." He turned back to his undertaking.

"Excuse me. What did you say?" His statement had a familiar ring. Dream Robert had once said the exact same thing.

"What?" He raised his shoulders. "Mom and Dad have taught me a few things. I can manage in the kitchen if I need to, but I have Mom." He looked over at Belinda and raised his brows several times. "They also didn't raise a fool. Mom likes to spoil me and I let her. It makes her feel good."

Belinda scoffed and then scrutinized this man grilling away in front of her. Earlier in the kitchen, the two had worked side by side on the preparation of the meal. They had waltzed around each other in a synchronized rhythm. It seemed so natural having him in her home. It was as if he belonged there.

Dinner was a great success. Everyone sat around the table socializing and laughing. Robert's chicken was a hit. It was moist and flavorful, smothered in his tangy red concoction, and blended with the rest of the meal perfectly. Belinda found herself glancing at him frequently while the group ate. A few times their eyes met, sending a wave of excitement through her. She'd looked away quickly, hoping no one else at the table noticed.

After dinner, Robert stayed true to form, assisting Belinda with clearing and putting away the food before he returned to the guests, now gathered on the covered patio. He made sure everyone's glasses never went dry for the remainder of the evening.

Around two a.m., Abbey and Garrett left first. Sandra and Dora were saying their goodbyes to each other when Sandra scanned the kitchen.

"There's still a lot of cleanup to do. It will be three before she's finished." Just about then, Robert walked past his mother. "Robert, why don't you stay and help Belinda finish up around here?" She didn't give him a chance to answer before she honed in on Dora, not taking a breath. "Could you drop us home?"

Belinda caught Dora's look of concern. In a soft voice, she assured her, "I'll be alright."

Once everyone left, they went to work clearing the mess. She finished by wiping off the counter.

Robert retrieved his wine glass from the island and wandered into the living room. In the quiet, this was the first time he'd had a chance to admire Belinda's and Sandra's handiwork. "You did a good job on this place."

"Thank you."

He placed his drink on the coffee table. "I'll be right back." He made his way down the hall and was about to turn into the restroom when he glanced to his left and noticed one of the posts of Belinda's bed. He checked to see if she was still in the kitchen before he stopped at the threshold to the master bedroom. Observing the plush linens, he experienced a wave of jealousy as he wondered how many times Colin had been entwined with her in the throes of passion. He shut his eyes and clenched his teeth as he pictured Belinda straddling Colin, his roaming hands finding the sensitive regions of her body. He envisioned her with head thrown back and mouth agape as she embraced the thrill of searching for her heighten pleasure, moaning. Now, with ragged breathing and the awareness that his arousal was in full effect, Robert fell against the doorjamb just as his phone gave off a vibration. Ignoring it, he backed away and proceeded to his original destination.

Robert walked into the great room after his prolonged stay in the restroom. Belinda sat waiting on the couch. "More wine?" She raised the bottle to refill his glass as he walked toward her.

"No, I'd better not."

He walked past her and stood in front of the painting hanging on the far wall above the credenza. He leaned in closer. "I noticed this earlier, but didn't have a chance to really get a good look. Fine brush strokes." He started with the upper left corner and moved around the painted canvas, observing the forest scene with a path that led into it. At the lower left corner, he stopped and looked at the head and neck of a horse entering the picture, heading toward the trees. On the neck of the horse lay a dainty female hand. He straightened and studied the upper right-hand section, appearing to examine every detail of the entrance to the woods where a small silhouette of a man stood. "Interesting painting." He looked at the lower right corner where he saw the signature, Belinda, written in script. He whipped around toward her. "You painted this?"

"Yeah. I started it before the accident and finished it recently."

More solemn, he turned back and ran a finger over two angel wings used as the dot over the "I" in the name. "Angel wings. Nice touch." Still studying, he read the title, "Remembering...." He just stood there with his back to Belinda for a few seconds, before saying, "I need to go."

Belinda walked him to the door and opened it, standing partially behind it with her shoulder pressed against the edge. "Thank you for all your help tonight." She glanced at the ground with a shy smile and then looked up through her lashes at him. "I...liked it."

Robert turned and grabbed the edge of the door, and then peered down at her. Neither of them moved.

He bent forward and kissed her on the forehead. "Good night," was all he said, before turning to stroll away.

Walking to the car, Robert almost turned around and went back. He knew if he did, Belinda would willingly be with him. It was written all over her face. The time he had spent with her over the past two weeks compounded his dilemma. He liked being around her and found himself fantasizing about her every chance he had. She dwelt in his thoughts constantly. His only problem was what to do about Colin and Karen. Neither Belinda nor Colin had said anything about her moving to Canada, so he wondered how strong their bond was, but couldn't bring himself to ask Colin what his intentions were. He knew his relationship with Karen was slowly deteriorating because of his preoccupation with Belinda. Yet he didn't know how to end it with Karen.

He stopped and took a moment, turning back in the direction of the front door, the only thing between him and the woman he knew he was falling madly in love with. All he had to do was knock and she would be his. He unlocked the door of the car, got in, and drove off, ignoring the umpteenth incoming call from Karen.

CHAPTER 17

ROBERT AWOKE JUST as the sunlight peeked through the window, thinking about the night before. He wondered why it felt so natural being there helping her—as though their minds and bodies were communicating—and so comfortable being around her. He had never experienced anything like this with another woman. Their actions reminded him of his parents—how they floated around one another in an effortless manner, not talking, but knowing what each other needed. He was glad to be alone so he could think this through.

Just then, his phone rang. He knew he couldn't ignore it again. "Hi, Karen."

***

The irritating ringing of the phone awoke Belinda. Fumbling for it on the nightstand, she answered in a low groggy voice. "Hello."

"Belinda, are you still asleep? It's almost eleven." Perky Abbey's voice chimed in on the other end.

She yawned. "Oh, hi. I didn't get to sleep until after four."

"What time did Robert leave?"

Belinda thought for a second. "Oh, he's still here." Knowing she'd jerked Abbey's chain, she had trouble keeping from laughing out loud.

Dead silence emanated from the other end of the phone—a first for Abbey in the history of their relationship. After a few seconds, a very quiet voice spoke up. "Should we hang up?"

Belinda couldn't contain herself any longer and let out a soft giggle that grew into a robust low laugh.

"He's not there is he?"

Belinda answered through short spurts of muffled laughter. "No."

"You bitch. Okay, what time did he leave?"

Belinda got up and fixed herself a cup of coffee while she filled Abbey in on all the minuscule and titillating details of what took place after she and Garrett left. She made herself comfortable on the couch because she knew this would take more than a few minutes.

"So you're telling me you're falling for this guy?"

"Ah, maybe. I...guess so. He's really nice."

"And engaged may I remind you," Abbey warned.

"Yeah, there's that little problem."

"What about Colin?"

"I think when he moves, my situation will just go away."

"Well, you just be careful. I and a few other people don't want to see you hurt."

The conversation lasted for another hour before Abbey hung up, citing grocery shopping and maybe a movie on the Barnett household agenda.

She got up and walked to the kitchen to put her cup in the sink. On her way back to the bedroom, the painting that had so interested Robert caught her attention. She stood before it, giving it a long steady look as she remembered a life that was becoming more and more a distant memory. Hearing her bed calling, she continued to her room and crawled back in to dream.

Belinda was disappointed that Robert hadn't attempted to touch her again in a romantic way since his surprise embrace in the barn. During the remainder of the week, before Karen returned, he kept his distance. Belinda missed the physical contact—the bits of it she'd experienced. Instead, their friendship matured.

Frequently, Rob and Sandra declined to accompany the two on the trails or they were encouraged to sit around the pool while the older Pendletons retreated to their bedroom. No matter what excuse his parent's gave, it became more apparent to Belinda they were trying to push Robert and her together. Belinda didn't mind and would accept all the encouragement they wanted to give. She enjoyed being around Robert and found it oddly pleasant. He was funny and smart, and also very kind and gentle. The only major flaw she saw with him was his relationship with Karen, and that was something she had no control over.

To Belinda, Robert seemed less restrained when it came to being around her. She couldn't quite figure out what had changed. For now, she enjoyed his company and took every moment she could steal from Karen. However, a thought nagged at her. Was she becoming "the other woman?"

The week went by quickly. Karen had planned to return on Saturday morning, taking Robert away for however long she remained in town. The prospect of not having access to him didn't please Belinda, but knowing he would be at home in the evenings, during Karen's absences, made her workday more exciting.

Texting became part of their routine. Robert started when he turned off Highway 6 and would give her a blow-by-blow account of just how far he was from the house. When he drove into view, he parked the car and sent the final text. Like magic, he emerged and looked straight at her, sporting his signature smile. It always made her melt.

***

Thursday night, jealousy crept in as she imagined Karen and Robert together making love. She tossed and turned because her mind wouldn't release her from the visions she kept replaying—awake or in a deep sleep.

Belinda imagined Robert placing a caressing hand on either side of Karen's head. Her breaths intensifying with every one of his soft kisses molding to her lips. His hands exploring her body as they retreated to a reclining position on her bed. Robert on top moving in a steady lurching motion as his breath quickened. Him looking down at her with softened eyes just before….

***

On Friday, the day before Karen's arrival home, Belinda managed to keep herself in a miserable state. She felt worn down by the conflict between her dreams of them in the throes of lovemaking and the knowledge that Karen's presence would keep Robert away.

The plan for this evening included a mix of some serious hot tub time and wine. Of course, she fully expected Sandra and Rob to bow out of the activities, leaving her alone with Robert. After tonight, there would be nothing until Karen flew off again on her broom. Belinda couldn't wait.

Dinner was late and, as expected, Sandra and Rob retreated to their room afterward, leaving kitchen duty to Belinda and Robert. He cleared the table while she filled the dishwasher.

Placing the last plate on the counter, Robert leaned against it and watched her. She was the most graceful and beautiful woman he'd ever met. He enjoyed how she made the simple task of rinsing dishes seem like performing a ballet. He could just stand there and be with her all night. "I'm going to miss this."

"What?" She huffed at him before she relented. "I will too." After drying her hands, she folded the dishtowel and laid it on the counter. "I'll go get my suit on and meet you outside."

He ran to his place as fast as he could. Stripping off his clothes, he left them where they fell on the floor and pulled on his trunks. Robert rushed to make it to the hot tub first. He hurriedly set the mood by dimming the lights and lighting candles placed strategically around the hot tub to increase the ambience. With his objective complete, he stepped into the bubbling water, positioning himself so he could watch Belinda come out of the house. He liked the way the light played off her skin, giving her an alluring glow, and knew he would never tire of that vision.

Belinda walked out in a teal, one-piece suit carrying a bottle of wine and two glasses. The dim light caused her to stop and take notice of the subdued surrounding. Their eyes locked as she tilted her head and exaggerated her walk, swinging her hips as she sashayed toward him. The closer she came, the broader the smile stretched across his face.

The bubbling warm water felt good and relaxing, washing away the tensions of the week. As they sipped wine, they talked and laughed at each other's stories of things that happened during their hectic daily schedules.

Robert was captivated by Belinda's display of emotions—her sparkling eyes danced as her body moved and hands gracefully gestured. Her cute giggle touched his heart. At one point when she tossed her head back in laughter exposing her slender neck, it was all he could do to control his urge to envelop her in his arms. He imagined skimming feathery kisses up the appealing flesh, across her delicate jaw, and then to her beckoning mouth—tasting her sweet lips and savoring every precious second.

Noticing he appeared lost in the moment, Belinda stopped and interrupted his fantasy. Cocking her head, she smiled. "What are you thinking about? You have this...look on your face."

He just made a half grin with his enticing lips. "Oh, nothing. Just enjoying the evening."

While Robert talked, Belinda remembered how much she enjoyed listening to Dream Robert for hours all cuddled up in his warm, secure arms, and imagined doing the same with this one. Robert's voice and actions made her comfortable—like she'd known him forever.

Focusing on his mouth, she recalled their last passionate kiss—his warm, moist, soft lips pressed hard against hers and how he made her feel all tingly and hot inside. Belinda ran her tongue over her lips, moistening them, and then bit her lower one. Oh, how she wished she could inch over closer, if only to brush against his arm to feel the stir within. But that would be asking for trouble. Instead, she wrapped her fingers over the edge of the seat, gripping it tight for control. She didn't know if she'd be able to restrain her desires to feel her desperate mouth against his—tongues tasting, teasing— and to have his strong arms wrapped around her pressing their warm, excited bodies together.

***

Missing Robert was the excuse Karen gave herself as to why she decided to come home a day early. But deep down, a nagging feeling hovered in her mind that something wasn't quite right between the two of them. Ever since he came back to her New Year's party, he'd been acting differently. She knew it wasn't her imagination. He seemed to be less affectionate and she often caught him staring off into space, lost in his thoughts. Now, he wasn't taking all her calls. More and more often, most of them were going to voice mail and not returned. He'd excuse them with "I was busy" or "I forgot."

Karen made her first call on the plane after landing, and then in the airport, and again when she arrived home, but got the usual—"leave a message." Wanting to be with him, she decided to surprise him at his place. She thought having a glass of wine and a nice relaxing evening smooching and cuddling in the hot tub might be just what the doctor ordered. To get him in the mood, she decided to wear her new sexy bikini and cover-up.

After pulling into the Pendletons' circular drive, she parked her car, then primped in the rearview mirror—making sure her make-up and hair were perfect. Walking toward the back to Robert's residence, she noticed a strange car parked next to his in the driveway. The hair on the back of her neck stood up. "I knew it. He's up to something," she mumbled to herself.

She snapped her head in the direction of the pool when she heard a female voice and Robert talking and laughing. Karen wondered for one second if she'd made a mistake by coming over. Another female laugh filled her ears and she clenched her fists, digging nails into the skin of her palms. Her breathing shortened with every exchange of laughter.

At first, her strides were wide. They slowed the more the romantic setting of the pool area came into sight. The flicker of candles seemed to be concentrated around the hot tub. She made sure she stayed in the shadow until she was ready to reveal herself.

Bushes alongside the house obstructed her view, but she could hear plenty. The soft cooing laughter and the high pitched ping of glass being set on the stone deck around the tub told her what was going on.

The familiar voice saying Robert's name made her blood boil. "Belinda, you bitch. He's my fiancé and I'm not letting go of him," she mumbled. She splayed her fingers and concentrated on her breathing. Karen began to force herself to calm down. Dropping her arms to her sides, she shook them to further relax, as a prizefighter would who was preparing to go into the ring. Taking one last deep breath, she stepped onto the pool deck and removed her cover-up, dragging it along hooked on one finger.

Belinda came into view first with her head tossed back in laughter over something Robert just said. Karen drew in slow, steady breaths. She narrowed her eyes. "Bitch," she muttered. She could only see the back of Robert, but his laughter indicated a huge smile. Taking a few deep breaths, she walked within their sight and asked, "What's going on?"

Robert jerked his head around. "Nothing. Just visiting." His smile vanished.

Standing over him, Karen knelt down in front of him to give him a better view of her latest purchase, three hot pink patches of fabric held together with a few strings. "Mind if I join you?"

"Ah, no. Not at all. What are you doing back early? I thought you were coming home tomorrow." His voice cracked.

"I missed you," but she also thought, *I needed to check up on you.* "I thought we might have a romantic evening relaxing in this tub." Karen shifted her weight, resting on her hip and propping herself on one elbow so she could reach Robert's lips easier. Lacing her fingers in his hair, she pulled him close enough to her bustline, attempting to divert all his attention. She planted her lips and pushed her tongue into his mouth. After a few seconds she withdrew, pleased Robert never attempted to break their contact.

She slid into the hot tub and sat on Robert's lap. Before wrapping her arms around his neck, she gave Belinda a discreet warning glare. In one fluid motion, she planted another passionate kiss on his mouth.

Belinda could feel her blood boil at the scene unfolding in front of her. Her mouth fell open. She couldn't believe the nerve of this woman barging in unannounced, unexpected, and acting this way. How dare Karen come over, looking like that, ruining her evening with Robert? This was supposed to be her time to enjoy his company. She thought about yanking Karen off Robert, but sadness crept in. It occurred to her she had no right to think that. After all, he was engaged to Karen and technically taken.

In the middle of the kiss, Robert glanced up at Belinda. He ended Karen's advance and asked her, "Wouldn't you be more comfortable sitting beside me?"

Karen shook her head. "No. I'm very comfortable right here." She kissed his cheek.

Not wanting to cause a problem, Belinda stood and announced, "It's getting late. I'd better be heading home." Giving a sliver of a smile at them, she automatically, without thinking, said, "Have a good evening," and climbed out.

Belinda turned back and watched Karen reposition herself, straddling him, as she emphasized, "Oh, we will." Running her hands up of his neck, she plunged her lips to his, not giving Robert a chance to say good night.

Wishing those last four words hadn't emerged from her mouth, Belinda cringed as she hurried toward the house. Seeing Karen in that skimpy excuse for a bathing suit made her imagination ran wild—their lips crushed together in long passionate kisses, hands groping each other's body, out-of-control emotions and reactions….She shook her head to clear the disturbing thoughts as angry tears began to well.

"You leaving so soon?"

The unexpected sound of Sandra's voice made her jump when she entered the house. "He has company," she sighed.

"What?" Sandra walked to the window and peered out. "What's she doing here? She wasn't supposed to get back 'til tomorrow." Sandra sounded exasperated by the sight of Karen.

"She said she missed him." Belinda kept her eyes down, attempting to hold back the moisture welling in them. "I'm dripping wet and need to get changed." Tears started flowing as she turned, running up the stairs.

Sandra stood at the bottom of the stairs and watched Belinda walk out of view. She didn't know if she should go after her or leave things alone, but one thing she knew for sure, Belinda had feelings for Robert. So she decided her son needed another gentle push. She could see how close they had grown in the past few weeks and had watched how Robert blended so well with Belinda during the dinner party.

Storming into the bedroom, she sped past Rob reading in bed. She saw him look up over the rim of his glasses, but she was on a mission. She quickly changed into her swimsuit before turning to leave the bedroom. "I'm going to be in the hot tub."

Rob raised a brow. "Aren't our kids in there?"

Sandra stopped at the foot of the bed and gave him a cold stare. "No, Karen is!"

"Oh, okay. Well, have fun," he said, before he repositioned his glasses and returned to his book.

Drink in hand, Sandra opened the door and in stealth mode, walked onto the patio. The drone of the bubbles helped feed into her silent approach. Neither Robert nor Karen noticed. At the edge of the tub, she hesitated, and then stepped in. She seated herself until the water covered her up to her shoulders. Quietly she sat, glaring for a few seconds, until she saw wandering fingers go for the string ties on Karen's back. That was it—she cleared her throat.

Robert opened his eyes slightly and saw his mother glaring him from across the steamy water. Her expression flashed from perturbed to devilish. Without hesitation, he grabbed Karen around the waist and jerked her off his lap, flinging her onto the seat next to him.

"What did you do that for?" Karen shouted, before she noticed Sandra sitting across from her with an impish grin plastered across her face. "Sandra," she proclaimed, appearing surprised and embarrassed.

"Why hello, Karen. We didn't expect you back until tomorrow. I'm sure you don't mind if I join you?"

"No, not at all." Karen scrunched her nose.

Sandra thought the shadows, caused by the flickering candle light, gave Karen the appearance of a demon.

***

Belinda changed in the dark office. She deliberately didn't turn on the lights so she could peek down at the hot tub from the window above her desk without being seen. She covered her mouth trying to restrain her laughter as she watched the scene below.

Sandra stepped into the tub unnoticed by the other two occupants. Robert's reaction to his mother's presence was priceless and put Belinda in stitches. She laughed so hard she had to support herself against the desk. She mumbled, "You go, girl."

***

The trio sat in silence. Karen nudged Robert. He figured she wanted to leave, but he didn't attempt to move. He sat with his arms stretched out resting on the edge of the hot tub, giving his body time to recover.

He rolled his head back and to the side. Out of the corner of his eye, he detected movement by the cars. Fortunately, Karen's gaze stayed fixed on his mother. He adjusted to improve his view and saw Belinda standing by her car. She swiped her cheek with the back of her hand, and then disappeared as she slipped into the driver's seat and left. A twinge of pain pierced his sinking heart because he wished she was still beside him. He told Karen, "I'm ready to go."

After hopping out, he offered Karen his hand as he gave his mother a sideways smile. "Good night."

Sandra flashed a smirk. "Good night."

Once at Robert's place, behind a secured door, Karen continued her pursuit. Determined to have his full attention, she took him by the hand and walked backward in a sultry, seductive way. She moved her fingers around to her back releasing the ties on the bikini—first the top fell and next the bottom. With the calves of her legs against the bed, she laid down inviting him to join her by pulling him to her.

Karen knew Robert was a healthy male who wouldn't refuse what she offered.

Her breathing became fast and hard as he kissed her neck and mouth with feverish zeal. She wrapped her legs around Robert, encouraging him. They began a rhythmic dance that took him to another place. With his mouth next to Karen's ear, he moaned, "Belinda."

CHAPTER 18

KAREN SAT AT the table with a cup of steaming coffee, fiddling with the two-carat solitaire engagement ring on her finger. It was early and Robert lay fast asleep in the next room. Because of what had happened the night before, she now knew she wasn't crazy. Robert confirmed that when he called her Belinda just before the climax of their lovemaking. What made it worse, he seemed unaware he'd even whispered Belinda's name. Taking a sip of coffee, she contemplated just what she should do about the bothersome other woman. Belinda had infringed on her territory and she'd have to be stopped. Karen needed a plan.

A shuffle up the hall toward the kitchen told Karen her fiancé was up. He walked in bare chested and clad in a pair of loose fitting jogging pants.

"Hi, Sweetie. You're up early." He bent to give her a kiss on the cheek and then went to make himself a cup of coffee. Popping a cup into the coffee maker, he hit the brew button.

Karen watched his gaze follow the CR-V drive past the window. She recognized it as her nemesis' vehicle. Her blood started a slow simmer. Karen clenched her jaw, but was too much of a lady to start a rant. Instead, she decided to utilize the only weapon readily available, her body.

She rose from her chair and approached her man with the stealth of a cat. In one fluid motion, she clutched the end of the t-shirt, lifting it over her head and tossing it on the floor, exposing her naked form.

Karen stood behind Robert. He was too busy watching out the window to notice. She never faltered. Rubbing her bare breast against his back, she softly ran her hands around his hips slipping her fingers under the waistband to just below his navel, lingering, teasing there for a few moments before pushing his pants down lower. Robert's breath hitched and his muscles tensed. Slowly she trailed her hands up his chest while she brushed kisses over his shoulder and up his neck. His body came alive. He turned and wrapped his arms around her, lifting her off her feet, and then tugged their bodies tight together.

Aroused, Karen slid her hands around and up his neck into his hair, and then threw her legs around his torso and jerked her hips against him as she crushed her lips to his.

He staggered back against the counter. Enthusiastically, he rotated around, pressing her to the cool granite counter. With their mouths pressed together, she caressed and teased his tongue with hers. Her breathing became ragged, igniting the passion inside her until she put him in the place of no return.

Karen felt more confident. She had kept Robert rather busy all morning. Now, he seemed to have only her on his mind.

Around noon, the couple left the guesthouse and walked arm in arm to the main house. Karen felt more confident. She kept Robert rather busy all morning. He seemed to have only her on his mind. Of course, this would be tested as they entered the kitchen.

Robert held the door open. Karen sported a broad smile and jaunty air as she walked in. Sandra and Belinda sat at the table eating lunch. Robert's smile faded when he saw his mother and Belinda. Sandra looked at him warily, Belinda with suspicion, and Karen with adoration. He glanced from one woman to the next feeling like a sacrificial lamb that just stepped into a pride of lionesses, searching for their next meal, him.

Karen turned to address them. "Good afternoon, ladies."

Belinda and Sandra's briefly exchanged glances. Sandra responded, "Good afternoon. Would you like something to eat?"

Robert chimed in, "We can manage ourselves, but thanks, Mom." He led Karen to the opposite end of the kitchen.

Belinda had her back to the pair, but could hear all the sick attempts at flirtation Karen tossed at Robert. The bad part, he flirted back. Belinda rolled her eyes at Sandra, who let out a giggle.

Once they finished preparing their meals, they joined them at the table. Robert sat across from his mother just out of Belinda's line of sight. She was very aware of what he and Karen had been up to all morning and the images gave her a queasy, sick feeling. Her heart palpitated. Feeling her blood pressure rise, she knew she had no right to be angry. Robert wasn't her fiancé, although he should be. She watched Karen from across the table and she returned the stares. Both were so polite to each other it made her nauseated. They were in a battle for the same man and they were drawing mental lines with their glares, daring each other.

At this point, Karen knew she had the upper hand. She was sleeping with him. It became very clear that she had made progress by the way he responded in Belinda's presence. She had to maintain the momentum. Her next move would be absolute genius.

"Sandra, I'll be home this week and part of next week. I know it'll be nuts around here because of the party. I'd like to help out if you could use me." She reached over and took hold of Robert's hand, and then produced a half smile directed at Belinda.

"I think that would be a splendid idea," Sandra responded immediately.

Belinda swallowed a piece of bread and almost choked when she heard Sandra's answer. She didn't want Karen around, but had no say in the matter. She was an employee and as she saw it, low man, or in this case low woman, on the totem pole. So she kept her thoughts to herself and cast glares at Karen while she finished her meal.

The tension between Karen and Belinda became so thick a knife couldn't cut it. Robert saw the reality of the situation. Here were two very different women that held his attraction. One he was engaged to. He knew he could have his way with her anytime he pleased and she was very inventive. He liked that about her, but realized something else seemed missing—the closeness he'd seen and felt between his parents throughout the years wasn't there. Although Karen and he had a great sex life, he realized he didn't love her.

His thoughts turned to Belinda. Oh, sweet Belinda. She was such a beautiful, gentle creature who left him breathless with a single touch of her soft skin. And when they kissed...his world turned upside down. In the past few weeks, he had grown closer and more comfortable around her in a natural way—as though he were home. Their movements around one another reminded him of his parents, which brought a smile to his face. When he was with her, he felt a missing part of him fall into place. She was an intelligent woman with a good sense of humor and someone he now considered more than a friend.

He knew he was more in love with Belinda than Karen, but didn't know how to break off the engagement. Biding his time, Robert hoped somehow he'd make the right move when the situation arose. For now, he felt stuck in the middle of a catfight that he secretly rather enjoyed. But being intimate with Karen started to give him a sense of guilt, like he was cheating on Belinda.

Right after lunch, Karen and Robert slipped back to the guesthouse and weren't seen again for the remainder of the weekend.

***

Belinda reported for work on Monday. Robert's and Karen's cars were gone. She accepted her fate for now and would bide her time. Karen would be leaving town again soon. Once Karen left, Belinda planned to take a big leap of faith and reveal her feelings to Robert. She knew she would be taking the risk of becoming "the other woman." If he didn't reciprocate, she would not only need many hours of therapy time with Dr. Rosen, she could be putting her job in jeopardy as well, but she would take the chance. She knew she loved him.

The workweek began with a roar as workmen, housekeepers, landscapers, chefs and tent builders swarmed the estate. To an outsider, it would've appeared as pure chaos, but right in the middle and at the helm stood Sandra. She was the conductor of her own symphony with every point of her finger. Belinda was amazed, admiring the grace with which she managed every detail, and wondering if Rob knew how much he should appreciate his wife for her efforts.

Belinda's main responsibility became manning the phone and fielding the calls. When something came in that needed Sandra's immediate attention, Belinda would place the call on hold and text Sandra's cell. Sandra would then text back a response or take the call. The system worked flawlessly and allowed the uninterrupted party orchestration to continue.

Belinda watched Robert arrive home around four o'clock. She fully expected Karen to follow shortly. That never happened. At five p.m., Belinda switched the office line to "Do Not Disturb" and went to the kitchen. The caterers had prepared plates of food before they left for the day. Sandra, Rob, and Robert gathered in the kitchen, each taking one. Karen was nowhere in sight. This puzzled Belinda, but she picked up the last plate and joined the trio at the table.

Sandra wasted no time in laying out the plans for the rest of the week after work hours. "I'm going to have Karen running around this week after work, picking up the things we'll need for the party. In fact, that's exactly what she's doing now, so she won't be joining us for dinner. I suspect she'll be busy shopping until the stores close. You two will clean out the barn." She pointed a finger at Robert and Belinda before continuing. "In the past, Robert had the job all by himself." She smiled at him. "So having you help him will be an added plus." Sandra locked her eyes on Belinda's. Belinda stared back mesmerized. She was positive she heard Sandra tell her to enjoy the time with Robert, but Sandra wasn't moving her lips. A chill ran through Belinda. Offering a quick smile, Sandra turned away and the feeling vanished.

Not sure what she just experienced, Belinda answered, "Okay."

"Good, now finish eating. The barn needs lots of attention."

Robert and Belinda walked to the barn in silence. Grateful for the unexpected time, she felt in her heart she should say something, but how do you tell a man you love him without seeming like a complete fool. So she decided to keep it to herself. When they reached the entrance, Robert explained the task. "We have to clear everything out and hose down the place."

"What do you mean, hose it down?"

"Just that. When I was doing this by myself, I'd start with the tack room. Clear it out, then hose it down. Then I'd oil all the leather and clean all the metal. The next day I'd put everything back after the inside of the room was dry. Then I'd start out here, one stall at a time, until I was done. The outside is the last part."

Belinda dropped her mouth opened as she scanned the barn. "That's a lot of work for one person."

"It usually took me two weeks of work after I'd get home in the evenings. I was wondering when Mom was going to tell me to get started. I guess she figured with the two of us on it, a week would be enough."

"Well, you seem to have a plan, so where do you want the tack once it's hauled out." Belinda scrutinized the area, hands on hips.

Robert's face lit up. He bowed at the waist and stretched out his arm to his side. "This way my lady, please follow me." Belinda giggled and curtsied back before she followed him.

The pair worked for an hour without saying a word until they'd emptied the room and all the equine equipment lay strewn over the remainder of the barn. Robert disappeared outside leaving Belinda waiting in the doorway of the small but adequate tack room. When he returned, he held a water hose ready to discharge a force strong enough to remove a year's worth of dust and grime. "You better get out of the way. This can get messy." He stepped in front of her, turning the hose on full blast and started spraying.

Belinda backed away and sat on a hay bale just outside the room. A fine mist filtered out of the doorway. It felt good and, because she had worked up a sweat, it cooled her down. While he held the hose, his t-shirt absorbed the overspray making it cling to his hard body. She surveyed every ripple of his back muscles as he worked his way around the room. Although she wouldn't have minded seeing his smooth, taut, muscled chest glistening from the water dripping off, she prayed he wouldn't take the t-shirt off. That would be just a bit more than she wanted to handle right now.

His back was still toward her when he turned the hose on himself. Belinda's breath hitched. She fought the impulse to jump up and join him. She imagined rubbing her hands across his broad shoulders, but instead she controlled herself by grabbing the wires of the hay bale. When he turned off the water, he rubbed his hands over his face and through his hair, sending excess droplets flying through the air. He looked over at her and flashed an enormous smile. "Ready for phase two?"

She held her breath and nodded.

With saddle soap cans and rags, the two worked on every piece of leather they could find. Belinda buffed the last saddle. During a period of deep thought, before she could stop, "Why are you with her?" escaped her mouth. She stopped working and slowly lifted her head to watch him.

He ceased polishing the bridle, but didn't raise his head. He responded with a hint of uncertainty to his voice. "I love her?" He offered no other explanation as he went back to work.

"Oh." Realizing her question put him in an awkward position, she changed the subject. "Will you be glad when the party is over?" She could see Robert's body relax as he shot a glance her way.

Robert was glad for a different question not connected to his relationship with a woman he wasn't in love with. He didn't have an acceptable answer for her because he was trying to figure that one out himself. He concentrated on the bridle. "Yeah, but it's not that bad. This year there's more planning because we'll have more guests. As for the barn cleaning, it would have to be done anyway."

Belinda didn't have a chance to respond before the devil herself walked in.

"Robert! There you are. Are you almost finished?" Karen headed right for him. Standing in front of him, she entwined her fingers in his hair and held him so he looked up at her. She started to bend down to kiss him, but he dropped the bridle and grabbed her wrists to make her release his hair, and then stood.

"We can finish this tomorrow. It's getting late," he said to Belinda.

"You go on. I want to finish up here," Belinda answered in a sharp tone, not wanting to keep him from the clutches of the woman he loved. He seemed a tad anxious to leave and she didn't want to stand in his way.

"Will you be alright?"

Belinda's stare snagged Robert's. "Of course I will." In a huff, she picked up her rag, put her head down, and returned to cleaning the saddle, applying the saddle soap with more zeal than she intended. Belinda gave a quick glance toward the door and saw Karen shoot a glare over her shoulder with a smug smile. Belinda threw her rag across the floor almost panting from her chest tightening with rage. "That bitch!"

The next day, Belinda had time to think in between the phone calls. She slumped over her desk. The smooth eraser tip hit her lip as she flicked a pencil between her fingers. The way she saw it, she could be mad at Robert or she could make the most of her time with him. He was engaged but not married, and until he slipped a ring on Karen's finger, she still had a chance. As far as she knew, a wedding date hadn't been set either. So for the next week, she'd be as pleasant as she could until Karen showed up in the evening to steal him away, leaving Belinda with nothing but her green-eyed monster to keep her company.

***

Friday evening, Sandra turned everything over to the party planner—her job finished. She sat on the patio enjoying the serenity. All the people who had blustered around all week were gone. On Saturday morning, she planned to retreat to the privacy of her bedroom where she'd have her meals delivered while she relaxed, reading until time to get ready to receive her guests.

She heard the French door open and hoped it was Belinda. She hadn't thanked her for all her hard work, but hadn't seen her for the past three hours. She wondered if Belinda left without saying goodbye.

"Excuse me, Sandra. Is there anything else I can do before I leave?"

Sandra never opened her eyes while she lay on the lounge chair. "Yes, bring out two glasses of wine and come join me."

Belinda did as requested. Sandra heard the clatter of the glasses as Belinda placed them on the table between the chairs. Sandra let out a sigh. "Sit down and make yourself comfortable. I'm glad this week is over." She reached over and squeezed Belinda's forearm. "Thanks for all your help."

"You're welcome. I'm glad I was useful."

"You two did a great job on the barn. I was out there this morning. I don't know why, but sooner or later, most of our guests end up taking a walk through there. It never fails." Sandra placed a sliver of a smile across her face as she released her grip. "Where's my glass? I'm in need of an adult beverage."

CHAPTER 19

BELINDA HURRIED, TRYING on several outfit combinations. She hadn't given it much thought because she'd been so busy the past week. Nothing she tried on seemed to have the "wow" factor she hoped for. Although she would be attending the party with Colin, it was Robert she really wanted to impress. Clothes lay strewn about her bedroom. Fine beads of sweat formed on her brow. Looking at the clock, she calculated how much time she had left before Colin would arrive. Three hours. She scurried into the kitchen and dragged her purse off the counter along with her keys. Slamming the door of her car shut, she drove to the mall.

Belinda returned satisfied she had found the perfect outfit. One hour remained for her to do everything needed for the date. So she hurried, feeling guilty all her efforts weren't meant for the man who'd be accompanying her.

The doorbell rang as she put the finishing touches on her ponytail. Flinging the door open, she immediately knew she had accomplished her goal by Colin's expression. The outfit worked its magic. He stood there with a huge smile, giving her the once-over from her head to her toes. "You look fantastic."

"Thank you. I'm glad you like it." Pressed for time, she grabbed her purse off the table in the hall and walked straight for the door. As she passed by Colin, she gave him a short kiss. "We better hurry or we might be late."

Robert patrolled the pool area, greeting the guests as they entered. Karen hadn't arrived yet but would join him at his side when she did. She was still in his guesthouse, dressing and running late, as usual. He had just finished welcoming one of the new arrivals when he saw Colin walk around and open the door of his car. He thought he would die when he saw a beige and black patent leather, four inch platform-clad foot emerge. Then the other appeared on the ground. When Belinda stood, he held his breath. She wore a skimpy camisole. The skirt came to mid-thigh, which exaggerated the length of her legs in those heels. With her tanned skin, she looked so damn sexy. She wore her hair up in a ponytail that swayed back and forth keeping rhythm to the bounce of every step she took.

Still captivated by the sight, Robert heard someone clear his throat. He glanced to his side and saw one of his clients grinning from ear to ear.

Taking hold of Robert's forearm, he pulled close and whispered, "I'd be staring myself if my wife wasn't with me, but all I can do is sneak a peek, not to get her mad." Tilting his head in Belinda's direction, he said, "That one's a looker."

Had I been that obvious? He would have to watch himself. "Yes she is," Robert said. The two men discreetly snuck a peek in Belinda's direction before the introduction of the wife took place.

Robert tried with all his might not to let what he felt be noticed by his best friend as the couple approached. Up to now, he had done nothing other than kiss the girl his friend was dating, but that offense seemed bad enough. He swore after the last time, he would never cross that line again because of his friendship with Colin. He had managed to respect that boundary despite growing closer to Belinda over the past several weeks. But because of the way she looked tonight, he was on the verge of losing his fight. He could only study her with fleeting glances, when he really wanted to stare at her, watching her every move.

Robert jerked from the guy-like slap on his back.

"Hey. How've you been?" Colin scanned the guests at the party. "We've got a lot of catching up to do tonight. I'll catch you later." He tugged Belinda along as he passed Robert.

Robert agreed with a nod. "Yeah, see ya later when things calm down." He nervously turned to Belinda. "You look fantastic, Baby Sister."

In a whispered tone so Colin couldn't hear, she said, "Thank you. Kind of you to say so. I'm glad I'm appealing to you." She glanced over her shoulder with a bright, sexy smile causing Robert to stiffen until her smile faded, watching something behind him.

He turned to see what caused the change in her expression as Karen planted a kiss on his lips. She threw her arms around his neck and held on tight, almost smothering him. He maneuvered them around so he could look over her shoulder to see Belinda, whose teeth seemed clenched as her eyes narrowed. With a sudden jerk of her head, she turned away making her ponytail flick.

Colin was enjoying himself conversing with his clients with Belinda by his side. She was a real asset and he lavished in the attention she received by her mere grace and beauty. The move north to Toronto would be taking place in the upcoming week. On Wednesday, the truck would arrive to pack up his apartment and on Thursday, he'd take off on the drive over the US/Canadian border, alone. As he watched her graceful movements, he wished she'd be coming along. Colin hadn't brought up a future together because he never thought it a possibility. Whenever he discussed the impending relocation, he would watch for possible clues. He prayed for them, but they never came. It seemed his lot was to be her friend and he reluctantly accepted that.

Karen noticed the occasional looks Belinda and Robert shot in each other's direction. They'd stay locked in their gaze longer than they should. It became very clear to Karen that Belinda planned to distract her man. She wasn't about to let that happen. Her objective for the evening—keep Robert occupied and clear of Belinda.

Up until now, Karen had successfully kept him distracted and out of Belinda's reach. Glancing around the food tent, Karen scanned for any signs of her and spotted her standing near the pool. She needed a powder room break. Feeling confident Belinda was preoccupied, she excused herself and walked toward the guesthouse, which would take less time to reach than the main house.

Belinda felt her stomach erupt in a rumble that vibrated clear through her. She reached for Colin's arm. "I'm hungry. Let's go eat."

"Do you mind going ahead? I'll catch up with you. I'd like to finish this conversation."

Giving him a kiss on the cheek, she turned and left for the buffet under the massive tent.

It was nicely laid out with a variety of grilled and smoked meats prepared by Rob, his crowning glory and contribution to the evening. The way he put it, "Well, it's not a barbecue if you don't barbecue." He had spent the week at the grill or smoker. The savory meat-scented smoke had floated into the house, filling it with the most mouthwatering scents.

The memory of the weeklong taunting smells led Belinda straight to the buffet line. With every step closer, she heard her stomach growl as the aromas that filled the air became stronger.

All the waiters were dressed as cowboys with crisp, white shirts, jeans, boots, and belt buckles the size of Texas. Black hats sat atop their heads. The wooden picnic tables displayed red and white checkered tablecloths. Salt, pepper, tabasco sauce, knives, forks, and spoons filled empty six-pack beer cartons placed in the middle of each table. On either side, rolls of paper towels stood like little sentries.

As she walked away from the buffet with her plate of Rob's masterful cooking, she saw Robert sitting alone. Searching around for Karen, who was nowhere around, Belinda headed toward him. "May I join you?"

He jumped to his feet and swung around. "Please do."

They both sat, with her sitting across from him. "Where's Karen?" Belinda picked up a rib and bit down, tearing free a chunk of the savory meat. Her mouth filled with a burst of tangy barbeque sauce.

"She went to the guesthouse," he said, eyeing her plate full of food.

"You hungry. I have plenty. Help yourself." She shoved the plate toward him.

"I don't mind if I do. Thanks." He grabbed a rib and joined her.

She took a fork out of the carton, filled it with potato salad, and then offered it to Robert. He reached for the fork, but Belinda pulled it back, wagging her finger at him. "Open your mouth." He did as she instructed and she placed the tangy concoction on his tongue. With sheer delight, he watched her every move.

"What are you looking at?" Her voice was low and seductive.

"You."

"Aren't you worried your fiancée will come back and catch you with me?"

"Why do you have to be such a downer?"

"Me?! I'm not the one who's engaged here."

"Can we change the subject?"

"I would but I don't think we'd have time," Belinda said as she jutted her chin toward her nemesis walking toward them.

Robert didn't bother to turn around. "Karen's on her way over here?"

"Yep." Belinda stared at him just before tearing another chunk of meat off the rib bone.

Belinda watched her approach. Karen didn't look happy, stiffening and clenching her hands at her side. Belinda suspected she saw her feed Robert. She would swear her eyes glowed red. Halfway to the table, Karen stopped, took a deep breath, and unclenched her fist. Continuing on, she reached Robert and stood behind him, placing her hands on his shoulders. She glared at Belinda, bent down, and kissed him on the cheek. "Here you are, Darling." She stood, still glaring. "Belinda, how nice to see you."

Belinda wanted to puke, but responded with equal insincerity. "Thank you. Same here."

"Darling, don't you think we should go talk to more of the guests." She never stopped staring at Belinda or seemed to care that Robert was hungry.

Robert appeared to visibly tense when Karen addressed him. She wondered if Karen's antics had started to annoy him. Belinda half believed she still might have a real chance here.

He stood to leave. With Karen still eyeing her, Belinda smugly said, "You two enjoy your evening now." Then she winked at Karen as she chomped down on the last bit of meat left on the bone.

***

Karen watched for Belinda. *Just who does she think she is?* Her tolerance level had reached its peak and she planned to make it clear. She wanted Belinda to stay away from Robert. After all, she was just an employee.

She spotted her walking across the lawn toward the pool and seemed to be searching for someone.

"It better not be Robert," Karen mumbled to herself through clenched teeth.

Timing would be critical. She made sure Robert remained busy enough so she could slip away to confront Belinda. He was engaged in a financial discussion with someone. She walked toward Belinda, who now stood alongside the pool. Karen approached and grabbed her forearm, giving it a shake. "You stay away from him. Do you understand?"

Belinda couldn't believe she would actually stoop so low as to touch her in a threatening manner in public. Turning to confront Karen, she could feel the anger inside reaching its capacity. Why she didn't lash out at her she'd never know. All she did was look down at her arm where Karen held it and, in a controlled voice, she demanded, "Let go of my arm."

"Or else, what?"

Belinda narrowed her eyes and kept them fixed on Karen. "Or else you won't have a fiancé when you come back next time, because he'll be mine."

She watched Karen's face contort in the passing seconds as she felt a palm shove against her chest. A shriek escaped Belinda as she fell backward into the pool. The sting of cold water engulfed her. From under the water, she heard a muffled scream. "You bitch!"

Belinda bobbed up to the surface, gasping for air and treading water. She recognized Robert's voice next to her in the pool ask, "Are you alright?"

She wiped the water from her face and snorted. "You're all wet."

"Are you alright?" he again asked.

"Yes, I think so." In an instant, she felt his arms wrap around her, lifting her to the side of the pool. He hopped out, picked her up, and marched toward the house.

Belinda felt a burning sensation on her calf and reached for her leg as Sandra rushed to their side carrying a towel.

"Oh, you're hurt." Sandra dabbed at the wound where blood streamed down Belinda's wet leg. "Robert put her down on the lounge chair." She gave the wound a few more pats. "It doesn't look too bad. I don't think you'll need stitches. Come inside so we can get this bandaged."

Robert turned to Karen and glared at her. She grabbed his arm as she attempted to explain, but he wouldn't listen. "What the hell were you thinking?" Scrutinized her grip, he jerked his arm free. He walked away, leaving her standing there alone, as the other guests stared. He took a few seconds to scan the immediate area for Colin, but couldn't find him, so he went to the house to check on Belinda.

Robert entered the back door and saw Sandra walking through the great room toward him. "Is she alright?" He could hear the concern in his voice and realized he'd never shown that with Karen.

"Sweetie, she'll be fine. It's only a minor cut. I cleaned and dressed it. She'll be out in a minute." Sandra gave him a gentle pat on the cheek before leaving.

He had turned and started for the master bedroom when he saw Belinda walk into the great room. Her clothes were still wet and the camisole clung a bit too much.

In the dark room, they met halfway, just in front of a fifteen-foot arched window. She was barefooted and holding wet shoes, making her a good bit shorter as she looked up into his eyes.

"Are you okay?"

"Yes. Your mother took good care of me."

The first explosion from the fireworks display startled them. They chuckled and turned to see a red starburst through the top of the window. The room glowed red as the burst dissipated to ash. Another one went off with an explosion of white, blue, and red in the night sky.

Robert stood so close she could feel the heat radiate from his body. Turning, she peered up at him, her heart about to leap out of her chest. Her breathing became irregular. If he kissed her, she'd be his for the taking, letting him have whatever he wanted. The pair stood mesmerized by each other, silhouetted against the backdrop of starbursts on the back lawn.

He bent down moving closer to her lips. She rose ever so slightly to reach his. His quick puffs of breath warmed her cheek. Millimeters away from making contact, she heard a voice ring out from behind them.

"*Robert*, I want to go home *now!*"

He pulled back. His face appeared emotionless. Without a word, he turned, leaving her standing there to watch him walk out with Karen.

Belinda ran upstairs to her office window. She knew she could see them walk to the guesthouse. Scanning the lawn, she spotted them. They didn't appear to be talking to each other. When they stopped next to Robert's car, the discussion seemed to explode. After several angry gestures from each of them, Robert threw his hands in the air as Karen turned and stomped into the guesthouse. Minutes later, she emerged with a suitcase and shoved it at him. She yanked the car door open and crawled in.

The noise from the slamming trunk caused Belinda to watch him. With his fists clenched, he walked to the driver's side and stood. He rested his forearms on the roof and fiddled with his keys. Seconds later, he opened the door, dropped in and sped off.

Belinda didn't understand the significance of what she had just witnessed, but she did know she had a date to find, and she wanted to leave.

CHAPTER 20

AS PLANNED AND on time as usual, Colin rang the doorbell to Belinda's patio home at ten a. m. Her heart filled with heaviness and periodic waves of sadness. The feeling that she never gave him a real chance, hovered in her mind and nagged at her like a toothache, at times settling down, but always lingering in the recesses, ready to spring. The subject of Colin even entered into every session with Dr. Rosen. She also talked about it with Abbey, who usually helped center her into seeing the practical side. It didn't help. She couldn't stop wondering if she would be making a mistake by letting him walk out of her life.

This would be one of the last times she'd be with him before he moved to Canada later in the week. They planned on a farewell, so to speak, dinner on Tuesday evening, after which miles would separate them.

Today he'd be coming over for a light breakfast. Then they would go to visit Beau and take care of all four horses' needs. After that, the day would be free for whatever met their fancy.

"Good morning, my fair lady." Colin presented Belinda with a bouquet of fresh flowers as she opened the door. In the months he'd been seeing her, not once did he ever buy roses, something she was glad about. It wouldn't have felt right if Colin had given her roses. Something would've been missing.

"Oh, thank you. They're lovely." She turned to walk into the kitchen, leaving Colin to attend to the door. The table was set and ready for a nice light meal. Belinda reached for a vase from the cabinet, filled it with water, and arranged the flowers. Colin sat on one of the stools across from her, watching.

The breakfast conversation centered on superficial talk about his new place, his office, and how he liked Canada so far. Once they cleared the table, they left for the Pendletons' and the horses.

Colin turned into the drive of the Pendleton estate, and Belinda immediately noticed the red Beamer parked in its usual spot. She thought it odd and wondered why Robert wasn't with Karen.

Driving to the barn took a little maneuvering. The tent still stood on the back lawn. It would be broken down early Monday morning. Except for it and the tables and chairs stacked underneath it, no one would've ever known a party had been held at the house the night before.

Parking the car next to the barn, Colin and Belinda went to greet Beau. He stuck his head out of the stall in anticipation of his treat, as he always did when he heard the car pull up. "Hey, Beau. You want a carrot?" After he took her offering, Belinda stroked his neck and cooed softly to the animal. She gave Colin the extras and asked him to give the other three horses a carrot.

He flashed Belinda a grin. "You want me to put my hand near their mouths. They have huge teeth that could chomp down on me." He shook the bag of carrots in the direction of the horses and rubbed his free hand through his hair.

She snorted and then laughed. "Come on, I'll show you." Giving the first carrot to Scout, she instructed, "Hold your palm open with your fingers flat and out of the way." The horse took his treat without a problem. "Now you give some to the other two."

Colin did as she asked. After Mouse gobbled down her tidbit, Colin counted his fingers and wiggled them at Belinda, a broad smile plastered across his face. "All there."

Taking care of the animals wouldn't take too long because the stalls had been cleaned for the party. The horses just needed turning out, their nightly deposits picked up, feedbags filled, and fresh water supplied. About an hour and a-half's worth of work, if Belinda estimated it right. "Have any idea what you want to do after we're done here?"

Not sure, he placed his chin on his fist to think. "I know I'd like to go say goodbye to Sandra." Just about the time the words came out of his mouth, Sandra appeared at the barn entrance.

"Well, good morning, you two." She walked over to Colin and placed her arm in his, locking at the elbows. "Are you all ready for your move?"

"Everything is arranged. I leave Thursday."

She patted his arm. "I'll miss you. You know that."

He gazed down at her and swung his other arm around her shoulder, pulling her close. "I'll miss you too." They remained in their embrace for a few moments with Colin swaying back and forth ever so gently.

Sandra gave him one last hug. "Will you two be interested in eating any lunch? It'll be a repeat of last night's menu." She turned to Belinda, and then to Colin, waiting for an answer.

Belinda rubbed her stomach. "We just ate breakfast."

"Well then, how about a swim in the pool after you're finished here? You can cool off and work up an appetite at the same time."

Belinda glanced at Colin, feeling him out. He shrugged. "Sounds good to me. I never turn down a swim or invite to eat."

"Then it's settled. We'll see you at the house in a little while."

Sandra turned to walk out when Robert walked in. Her surprised expression told Belinda that Robert wasn't expected. She greeted her son with a kiss on the cheek and said, "Good morning, Sweetie," and then turned to leave.

"Hi, Mom." He gave her a kiss back before addressing Belinda and Colin. "You two need some help."

After last night, Robert needed a diversion to get his mind off Karen. The drive to her house had ended up being the worst forty-five minutes of his life. She never said a word on the road, but when she got into the apartment, all hell broke loose, accusing him and Belinda of every type of sordid sexual diversions. She called Belinda names even he would've been too embarrassed to repeat.

During Karen's rant, Robert experienced bouts of stomach knotting. It felt like his neck and face were engulfed in flames. He couldn't feel his arms or legs. At work, he handled conflict with confidence. It followed a pattern he could predict. Karen's outburst gave a new meaning to the art of fighting. She came across as irrational. Robert said little to defend himself and that seemed to enrage her more. So when she threw the engagement ring at him and told him to pack up, he got out of there as fast as possible.

"Here, Robert, you can finish cleaning out this stall." Colin gladly offered Robert his pitchfork. "I'm not into picking up large animal waste."

Robert grinned and grabbed it. "Here give me that thing." He began to finished off what Colin had struggled to start.

While he worked, he glanced in Belinda's direction, watching her as unobtrusively as possible, making sure Colin didn't notice. Her graceful movement drove him nuts. Every time he saw her or stood near her, his insides went into a raging war. He wanted to touch her, hold her, caress her hair, take her full, warm, luscious lower lip in his mouth and nibble, but he couldn't because of Colin. For now, he was doomed to watch but not touch. He would wait and see what played out between his friends. Colin's move could very well be the downfall of their relationship. Robert would be there waiting with open arms if that were the case. Belinda would need little encouragement because he knew she was attracted to him. Her past responses confirmed it.

The trio laughed, mostly making fun of Colin, who constructed a lounge chair out of several bales of hay. He sat there, legs stretched out, gnawing on a piece of hay, looking as comfortable as if he were watching TV.

Robert returned to the barn after dumping out the last wheelbarrow. Wiping his brow with his forearm, he asked, "You two up for a ride?" He turned to Belinda. "Do you still want to try riding English? You can ride Scout. I'll ride Beau and Colin can ride Billy."

Colin shot up from his relaxed lounging position. "You want me on one of those things. Dude, I'm from LA. The biggest thing I've ever seen with four legs is a Great Dane."

Robert thought for a brief second. "Okay, I'll ride Billy and you take Beau. He's a really good horse to ride, and easy. He'll do everything for you." He glanced at Belinda and hoped she'd back him up after his suggestion.

With a look of recognition, she chimed in, "He is easy to ride, and Robert is right. He would be perfect for you."

Colin looked at them before he reluctantly agreed. "I just hope I live through it and don't regret this decision." He glanced over his shoulder in the direction of the pool. "The pool is looking real good about now."

Robert snickered at Colin. "We'll all go swimming after the ride. Trust me, you'll enjoy the pool more after you get off the hot trails."

Colin jerked back. "Dude, I don't do sweaty. I do cool and comfortable, but for you and this little lady, I'll make an exception. Lead me to my steed." He made a sweeping gesture with his right arm as he brought it in front of him and bowed.

Robert shook his head and Belinda giggled. Colin had a flare for the dramatic and Robert liked that about his friend. Robert saw himself as reserved most of the time, and Colin's pendulum swung on the opposite end. He possessed a clownish side Robert appreciated. In short, Colin made him laugh.

With the horses saddled, Robert informed his mother of the change in plans. The trio would go swimming and eat after the ride.

Robert walked over to adjust Belinda's stirrups. "Now, he can be high strung, so make sure you don't let him get away with anything. Keep a tight rein on him. Once he tires, he'll calm down. Usually takes about twenty minutes. I'll keep up with you on Billy and when Scout slows down, I'll give you more instructions." Helping her place her foot back in the stirrup, he grabbed her calf and gave it a squeeze. He looked up at her, totally in love with what he saw—her perfect features framed by supple strands of golden brown hair and striking, penetrating blue eyes. They fixed their eyes on one another's for a second before Belinda turned away. "Are you ready," he asked. She nodded and stared straight ahead.

He turned his attention to Colin. "Okay, up you go." He gave him blow-by-blow instructions on how to mount a horse. Despite his height, Colin couldn't quite swing his leg over Beau's back. Robert led the horse to a hay bale.

"Stand on the bale." Robert pointed to it. Colin hesitated and then walked over and stood on it as instructed. Colin's hips were now level with Beau's back. "Get on." Robert held the reins so the horse stayed in position. Colin placed his foot in the stirrup, hoisted his long leg over Beau's back, and landed in the saddle. Robert shook his head.

"What?" Colin made an exaggerated movement inspecting each side of the horse. "Hey, where's the brakes on this thing?"

Robert heard a muffled giggle come from behind him. He shrugged. "Belinda, you're not helping."

"I can't help it. Beau looks so small with Colin on him." She giggled again.

Robert backhanded Colin's calf. "Pay attention. This is how you stop." He showed him how to hold the reins, but most of all, how to pull back by applying the right pressure. "If the ride gets too bumpy, grab onto this." Robert took hold of the horn. "It'll help keep you in the saddle. I'll help if you have any questions or get yourself in trouble."

Robert mounted Billy. "We all set?" With nods from the others, he tightened up on the reins and pointed Scout in the direction of the trails.

Scout acted just as Robert had predicted and, thank heaven, so did Beau. Colin had no trouble keeping up with the pace Scout set. About twenty minutes into the ride, Scout settled down into a nice, easy walk. The friends rode three abreast. "Hey, this isn't as bad as I thought. In fact, I'm sorta enjoying this," Colin stated.

About fifteen minutes later, Robert figured Scout was calm enough to give Belinda her first lesson on an English saddle.

"Colin, can you hold Beau back while Belinda and I go ahead. I'd like to let her get a better feel for the saddle."

"Sure. I think I can handle that."

Robert and Belinda rode up the trail about fifty feet in a fast walk. He began to post and explain to her what he was doing. Belinda tried. With very little effort, she began to move with the horse. The two sped up the pace to a canter. Robert nearly gasped out loud, but he managed to suppress it. He couldn't stop himself from glancing at her. Strands of hair glowed from the sunlight bouncing off. She made little purring sounds that transformed into muffled giggles of delight with every upward hesitation of her posting movement. Her cheeks lifted from the broad smile she hosted. At that moment, Robert knew he had found love.

Colin just let Beau amble along and do his thing. He sat back in the saddle, relaxed, and watched Belinda's graceful movements. He liked the way she held the reins and how she moved in the saddle. Wishing things had worked out differently between them, he instinctively knew his hope would never become reality. So for now, he would enjoy what little time he had left and avoid any unpleasant subjects or actions that might ruin the day. He wanted it to be as perfect as possible and prayed she would visit him after the relocation.

Colin fully intended to follow along at a slower pace, but Beau had a different idea. Once the distance between Beau and the other horses widened, he helped himself to the smorgasbord of grasses along the trail. Head bent down, he tore at the grass and wouldn't move. Colin tried pulling back on the reins. With the shake of his muscular neck, Beau just ignored him. He talked in soft tones to encourage the horse to move—nothing. So he gave in and would let the animal eat his fill until one of his fellow riders decided to come back and rescue him.

Robert shifted in the saddle to turn around, fearing they were getting too far away from Colin. He saw him just sitting on his mount with his arms crossed over his chest, and couldn't keep from laughing. He signaled for Belinda to stop Scout, and pointed his thumb for her to check behind him. She saw what caused Robert's laughter and joined in with a hearty outburst at the comical scene. "Think we should go back and help him?" Robert asked.

"Seems like the right thing to do."

As they approached Colin, he sneered, "Nice of you to come back for me." He still had his arms crossed over his chest.

Robert went up ahead of Belinda. She stopped far enough away, giving Robert the room he needed to persuade Beau. Robert and Colin were deep in a discussion when Robert noticed Colin's eyes widened.

Hearing the commotion behind and Belinda scream, he swung Billy around to see Scout rearing up. Her legs and arms flailed in the air just before she hit the ground. Without thinking, he leapt over Billy's head—running to her side. He dropped to his knees and held her down by her shoulder to prevent her from getting up. Frantically, he roamed his free hand over her body searching for any signs of an injury. "Angel, are you okay?"

"Honey…I think I am."

"Lie still. Now lift your right leg." She did as asked. "Any pain?" She shook her head. He instructed her to move her left one, and then her arms. He checked her head. "Did you hit your head?"

Belinda reached for Robert's wrist and grasped it. "I think I'm okay." She looked deep into his eyes as he stopped his examination and stared back. "I'm going to get up now. Help me?"

He leaned back on his heels, and then stood and stretched out his hand to assist her. Once she stood, he again asked as he helped brush the dust from her clothes, "Angel, are you sure you're okay?"

Belinda took hold of his arm to steady herself and repeated, "Honey…I'm fine."

Robert held her close by her waist, and she wrapped her arms around his neck. "You scared the hell outta me. Don't you ever do that again. Do you hear me?"

"I couldn't help it. A rabbit ran across the trail. The next thing I knew…I was on the ground."

Colin was glad Robert moved as quickly as he did. He knew he would've been useless. While Robert tended to Belinda, Colin safely dismounted and managed to gather the horses together. His back was to them, but he heard how they talked to each other. His stiffened the more he heard. He turned and approached the pair who were embraced in each other's arms. He stood right behind Robert. "Excuse me!"

Belinda gasped when she saw Colin. They released their embrace. Robert spun around.

"Can you explain to me why you two were wrapped around each other? And why she's calling you 'Honey' and you're calling her 'Angel'?" He frowned at Belinda. "Have you been seeing him when I'm out of town?"

She approached Colin. "No! It's nothing like that."

Robert made similar statements from behind her.

Belinda stood halfway between them when Colin put up his hand. "I'm out of here." He mounted Beau and rode off, not quite knowing what he was doing or where he would go. He just knew he wanted away from them.

She stopped and turned back to Robert. "I have to go after him."

He nodded. "Take Billy. He's easier to handle."

It didn't take long for her to reach Colin. They rode along for a few seconds, not saying anything. She glanced at him and could see the signs of her betrayal all over his face. Knowing she needed to make him listen, she broke the silence. "Colin, we need to talk."

He shot her a hard stare. "Why, what's there to talk about?"

"I haven't been completely honest with you."

Again, he gave her a hard, cold stare. "That's pretty obvious…isn't it?"

"No, it's not what you think. The barn I used to keep Beau in is right over there. Come with me so I can explain." She took hold of his wrist and gave it a tug.

His eyes softened, and he nodded. "Okay."

The coupled secured the horses and walked inside the barn. They straddled a hay bale facing each other.

Colin said nothing. Belinda took a deep breath. "Brace yourself. This is a lot to take in." She started in with her story where she met, fell in love with, and married Robert in her coma. She explained how they split up because he had difficulty staying away from other girls. Then she explained their love was so strong, they reunited only to be torn apart when she came out of the coma. As she realized it had all been a dream, she feared she had lost him forever.

He looked puzzled. "You met Robert in your coma?"

"That's only half of it." With an explanation of what took place at the

New Year's Eve party, minus the whole kissing and bed incident, she finished and leaned back studying him. "After the New Year's Eve party I didn't think I'd ever see the real Robert again, but things kept happening and we kept crossing paths. Sometimes months passed, and then there he was. The first time I saw him was when I went to talk to Garrett at the office. Then again, later that evening, when we accidently met at the Galleria."

"So when did you start seeing him?"

Belinda dropped her mouth open. Appalled by his question, she felt her brow furrow. "I have *never* starting seeing him. He's engaged and I was with you. I wouldn't do something like that to you or Karen."

"Okay then, what was that I just witnessed between the two of you?"

Staring off at the floor, Belinda couldn't answer the question with a logical response. She looked back at Colin. "I don't know. In the coma, he called me 'Angel' and I called him 'Honey'. I can't explain what happened on the trail. This Robert is not the same as my dream Robert. He's different in a lot of ways." Pointing in the direction where they left Robert, she said, "And that Robert has no way of knowing I dreamt about him in the coma because I've never told him. The first time he met me was on New Year's Eve." Belinda wrapped Colin's hand with her fingers. "You're now the eighth person who knows anything about this stuff." Tears started running down her cheeks. "I'm sorry I didn't tell you, but you have to admit it all sounds rather nuts."

Colin studied Belinda's pitiful face and couldn't be mad at her. Besides, he believed her, as crazy as it sounded. He reached over, put his arm around her neck, and pulled her to his shoulder, cradling her close. Wrapping his other arm around her, he held her close. "Well, you're kinda nuts anyway."

Giving him a love punch to the back gave him a non-verbal response he didn't expect.

He held her for a few seconds figuring he should in turn be honest as well. Knowing his timing might be off and this could end badly, he took a leap of faith and went for it. Swallowing hard, he asked, "If I had asked you to marry me, would you have agreed?"

Colin heard her take a deep breath, which she didn't let out until she pulled away from him. She took her lower lip between her teeth. Taking another breath, she answered his question.

"There was a good chance a few months ago I would've said yes, or at least given the proposal some real thought. Back then, I felt there'd never be anything between Robert and me, and I figured I needed and deserved a life. You're a good man who I know cares about me." She reached for his hand and gave it a squeeze. "You know I love you."

His heart jumped knowing the other shoe was about to drop so, he finished her statement. "But you're not in love with me." He lifted her chin. "You're in love with Robert, aren't you?"

Tears streamed down as she nodded.

Disappointment tugged at him, but he knew there had to be a reason she never committed. Now the truth came out, and if he had to lose her to someone, Robert would've been his first choice. From what he witnessed on the trail, he knew Robert had the same feelings for her.

Belinda sniffled. "Okay, that's enough crying," he told her. She reached up and brushed the tears from her face. "What are you going to do? You have to get Karen out of the picture."

"I know. I was planning to tell him how I felt the week after you left. She's leaving again and I decided it would be now or never."

He smiled. "Let me know how it works out." He moved his eyebrows rapidly up and down several times.

Belinda punched his arm and giggled. "I'll never kiss and tell."

"Okay then, I'll just ask Robert," he said jumping to his feet.

Forming an 'O' with her mouth, she frowned at Colin. "You wouldn't dare." She stood.

A raised eyebrow followed as a half-smile crossed his face. "Oh wouldn't I." He pulled her closer resting her cheek against his chest. Feeling her warmth as she softened in his arms, he kissed her and stroked her soft hair, most likely for the last time. God, he would miss being with her.

When they arrived back at the Pendletons', Robert's car was gone. They stabled the horses and went into the house to change. After swimming, they joined Rob and Sandra for lunch. Robert never came home the whole time they visited with his parents.

***

Monday morning, at the Pendleton Financial Group, Colin arrived to a surprise breakfast planned by the secretarial staff. The affair lasted about an hour. He was both disappointed and hurt his friend Robert never showed up.

Walking into his office, he started to pack up. Colin noticed Robert sitting at his desk shuffling through some papers. He knew Robert saw him. How could he not through all the glass walls? Placing the last item in the box, he made one final sweep of the office. He would miss this place. With a sigh, he lifted his packed belongs and headed for Robert's office. He walked in unannounced and placed the edge of the box on his desk.

"Hey, Bud. Are we still on for our last round of golf tomorrow afternoon?"

Robert looked up, doing a double take. "You're not mad at me about what happened?"

Surprised by the question, Colin asked, "Should I be? Is there something going on between the two of you?"

"Absolutely not. We're just friends."

"Well then, what's the problem?"

Robert's face lit up as he stood and shook his friend's hand. "You know, my mom is going to be depressed over you leaving."

"Yeah, I know. She couldn't stop doting over me at lunch on Sunday."

Sliding his fingers partially into his pockets, Robert looked down at the floor. "Yeah...I just thought it would be better if I made myself scarce. Sorry about breakfast, too."

"It's okay. We're cool. Now you owe me a fishing trip. I hear there's some good spots just due north of my new digs. So, golf tomorrow as planned?" Colin asked, lifting the box. At the door, he stopped and looked back. "I'm going to miss you. You know that."

Robert nodded. "Golf tomorrow as planned."

CHAPTER 21

AS SCHEDULED, COLIN and Robert met Tuesday afternoon at the country club for their last round of golf before Colin's move to Canada. A cool, gentle breeze sent billowy clouds drifting across the big, blue sky blocking the hot sun, making it a perfect day. Colin drove the cart out to the first tee. With the guys occasionally chatting and concentrating on their swings, the game progressed at a normal pace through the first five holes. Robert started in rare form, but on the sixth he became more distracted causing his swing to veer slightly to the left.

They were about to finish off the front nine when Colin gave his friend a sympathetic look. "Is there something going on? You don't seem to have your head in the game." He poked Robert in the ribs. "Where are you?"

"Oh sorry." Robert frowned. "Yeah….Ah….Karen…we broke up after the party."

Colin rarely had a mean thought, but the only thing that came to his mind was *Karen problem solved*. However, social graces demanded he offer a sympathetic ear. "Do you want to talk about it?"

Robert jumped out of the cart and selected his club. "Hold on for a minute while I take my shot." He approached the ball. Colin watched him peer down the fairway. He stepped back, positioning himself and set the club before taking a practice swing. Colin admired Robert's form and his ability to follow through. Robert took a step forward, addressed the ball, and clobbered it.

"Colin. Eyes!" They watched it land and roll a few feet beyond the hole. "Yes!" Robert exclaimed, pumping his fist. Placing the nine iron back in his bag, he jumped into the cart and Colin started to drive across the fairway toward his ball.

Colin gave Robert a quick glance. "Well?"

Robert puckered his lips before starting. "Hmmm. Okay, the relationship started going south after the first of the year. I just didn't know how to get out of it. Now it's done and I'm grateful."

The cart jerked to a stop. Colin jumped out and selected the eight iron, and then addressed his ball. "Maybe I should let you go on being distracted so I'll have a better chance at winning." He looked up at Robert and grinned, and then turned his attention to his game. After taking a solid swing, he followed it, watching it land and roll about a foot from the hole. "Okay, talk. What are friends for?" he said, plopping into the driver's seat.

Robert started fiddling with his glove. "Where do I start?"

"I have a few cold ones in the cooler. Let's sink these and go park under a tree for a break," Colin said, pointing as he drove toward the green. "I have something I need to talk to you about and I guess this is as good a time as any."

Picking up their golf balls and replacing the pin, they hopped into the cart and drove toward the tree line. Colin selected a spot and turned the cart facing the fairway of the tenth hole, toward the setting sun. The course had a quiet and peaceful ambience for a normally busy afternoon. Colin reached into the cooler, pulled out a beer, and tossed it to Robert. As he fished for another can, the ice chilled his hand, biting his skin. Droplets streamed down as he rubbed the can across his brow and the back of his neck. The sound of the top popping followed by the hiss reminded him of how much he enjoyed a cold beer with his good friend and hoped this wouldn't be the last.

After taking that first satisfying gulp, Robert looked at Colin. "Okay, you had something to say."

Robert's statement caught Colin in mid-mouthful. He swallowed and wiped his mouth with the back of his hand. "You know, I've really enjoyed dating Belinda, but she just isn't…totally into me. Sunday evening after we left you, we went to the barn where she used to keep Beau and she finally confided in me. Do you remember at the Galleria, her telling us that while she was in a coma she had dreams?"

"Yeah. Why?"

"Belinda told me she met a guy after she woke up, but the strange part is, she said she dreamt about this guy while in her coma."

Colin noticed Robert tensed slightly and furrowed his brow as he stared at him. "So? People dream about other people all the time."

"The strangest part about this dream is she didn't just dream about him once. She dreamt a life with him."

Robert sat quietly and took a gulp of his beer. "Okay, and?"

"Here's the weirdest part. I know the guy she dreamt about."

"Colin just say what you have to say," Robert insisted, his tone now irritated.

Colin raised an eyebrow and half grinned at Robert. "She dreamt about you, dude." He poked him in the arm with his elbow.

Robert did a double take. "Me?"

"Yep. I've noticed how she looks at you and the way the two of you act around each other. She's never looked at me that way. Not only did she dream about you, she told me you two were drawn to one another by some special connection, fell in love, and got married."

"We got married?" Robert paused and twisted his mouth while his brow ridged. "I'm sorry. I'll admit I'm attracted to her, but I promise you we haven't been seeing each other. I swear."

"Yep. That's what she told me too. Don't worry. I believe the both of you." Colin took another drink of his beer.

"You have to admit, she is beautiful." He lifted his can toward Colin.

"Yeah, I'll give you that," Colin said, tapping the edge of Robert's can with his.

The two stared straight ahead over the golf course and raised their beers, taking a gulp.

Robert broke the moment of silence. "Look Colin, I have my loyalties and I would never interfere with you and her. I just want you to know that." He finished his statement with a firm slicing motion of his hand.

Colin chose to take a more laid-back approach. He knew he wasn't winning the prize, so there was no need for him to sweat it anymore.

"Thanks for the consideration, but I'm leaving and she's not going with me. She won't even consider it. I'll never be more than just a friend to her." He formed a funny grin. "That is unless something happens to you. Then maybe…" White teeth flashed, followed by a muffled chuckle emphasizing the humor he saw in his comment.

"What do you mean me?" Robert raised a brow dubiously at Colin.

"Dude, she dreamt about you when she didn't even know who you were. That says something. Right?"

Robert didn't respond.

Silence fell over the two until Colin chimed back up. "So, as I see it, you're two single people who need to talk." He took another swig of the beer. "We're supposed to go out tonight, but I'm going to cancel. You go over there instead and try to get her to open up and fill you in on the dream. I have confidence you two will work this out."

Robert hesitated, watching the horizon. "It's your last night. Don't cancel on her. I can talk to her after you leave."

"No, I insist," Colin said, giving him a stern look. "It's settled. You're getting your ass over there tonight."

Colin leaned back in his seat, slouching, and propped his foot on the console of the cart. "So we're good here?"

"We're good."

"I've lost interest in this game." Colin reached back into the cooler, pulled out another can, and offered it to Robert. "Let's call it quits and just enjoy these beers. Okay?"

"Fine with me."

***

Belinda had completed all her errands and chores early so she'd have plenty of time to prepare for her date with Colin. She looked forward to going out with him one last time. He'd always be a friend who would occupy a little corner of her heart, and she would miss him.

She had just finished showering when her cell rang. She hurriedly threw on her thigh length, nylon robe, and bunny slippers and then ran for her phone. The caller i.d. gave away the identity of the person on the other end so she answered in an upbeat tone. "Hi, Colin."

In a raspy voice, he responded, "Hey, Belinda. I have some bad news. I'm sorry, but I have to cancel our date." Cough....Cough. "I feel like I'm coming down sick and I don't want to expose you to it."

"Oh...okay. So will I get to see you before you leave?

He hesitated. "How about breakfast on Thursday before I drive out?"

"You have a date. I hope you get to feeling better soon."

"Thanks. I do too. Have a good evening. Bye." Cough....Cough.

"Bye."

Belinda let out a huff, rested her phone on the table, and tapped the case. She'd been looking forward to her date all day. She would miss him and wished things between them could've worked out differently. "Oh well. Such is life. I guess I'm back in the dating scene," she muttered.

She returned to the bathroom to comb out her wet hair. She decided to just stay in her robe and bunnies. They were comfortable, and sitting around the house didn't require being dressed. She finished and walked into the kitchen, grabbing a soda and a bag of cookies, and then went to the living room. She seated herself with her legs curled up next to her on the couch and surfed the TV channels, searching for something interesting to fill her long, boring night—maybe a romantic comedy?

***

Robert finally got up the courage about eight p.m. to go over to Belinda's place. He had gone over what to say a hundred times in his head and found himself running the scenarios through his mind again.

About to turn down her street, he had a thought. Instead, he made a U-turn and pulled into the grocery store parking lot at the entrance of her subdivision. He purchased a single red rose.

He raised his fist, poised to knock on a door, but stopped just before it made contact. "Is this a good idea?" Robert mumbled. Pressing his lips together in a slight grimace, he lowered his hand. He turned around, and walked halfway to the driveway. Stopping, he turned toward the house and stood contemplating his situation. He took a deep breath and, with determination in his steps, walked back to the door. This time, without hesitation, he knocked and took a few steps back to lean against the cool brick of the alcove. Fiddling with the rose, he began to wonder if he should've called first.

The unexpected rap on the door surprised Belinda. *Who could that be at this time of night?* She hurried over to peer out the peephole. Her heart skipped a beat and she let out a gasp at the sight of Robert. Plastering her back against the door, she threw her hand over her mouth. She turned back to the peephole and studied the lean, t-shirt and jean clad man standing on her porch. "What in the world is he doing here?" she whispered. Then she noticed the rose. Her brows knitted together. *Why a red rose?*

Clutching the silky fabric of her robe tight, she thought about running to put on a tee and shorts but decided he might leave before she returned. She grasped a bigger chunk of fabric making the robe even tighter. She opened the door just enough so only her head poked out, shielding the rest of herself behind it.

"Robert? What are you doing here?" Her heart raced as she studied him propped casually against the brick.

He didn't answer, but stared at her for a few seconds before he smiled and said, "I'll explain. Do you mind if I come in?" He held the rose out in front of him and stepped toward her, putting it within reach. "I brought a peace offering."

At first she hesitated, and then took it and sniffed the petals as she stepped back, allowing him to enter. He closed the door and leaned back against it, not saying anything. He just studied her.

Words finally passed his lips. "I came to…" His statement trailed off as he looked down at her feet. "Bunny slippers? Really?" he snickered, glancing back at her.

After letting out a huff, she defended her choice of casual footwear. "They're comfortable."

Her favorite compelling smile grew across his mouth and his crystal blue eyes became lustful as they traced down her body and back to her face. "Nice robe too."

The conversation started to sound very familiar. It reminded her of the first time Robert kissed her in her dream. Enthralled by his presence and gift, she had let go of the robe until his comment compelled her to look down at herself. Exposing a little too much, she grabbed and wrapped it tighter around her form as she crossed her arms over her chest to keep it in place. He made her feel uncomfortable. Slowly she looked up at him through her lashes. Her heart accelerated and her breathing became faster. She watched his features change. They appeared to become full of determination.

He took a step toward her. She took one back. He hesitated, tilting his head. She watched him raise a brow. His facial expression changed as he took a few steps closer. A few feet away, he stopped and studied her before he rushed at her, closing the gap. He wrapped his arms around her waist. She went limp as his hand moved up her back. He lifted her off her feet and found her lips, kissing her hard.

A surge of electricity shot up her spine, inducing every inch of her to quiver. She wasn't about to protest. Instead, she jumped, encircling his hips with her legs and locking her arms around his neck. She knotted her fingers in his thick hair—adhering to his magnificent physique. Belinda's whole body screamed for him to make love to her, but she kept silent and kissed him right back with all the pent-up need she had kept controlled for far too long. All Belinda could think about was rocking his world.

Sliding one hand down from her waist to her ass, he kept her airborne and clinging to him. The hand on her back trailed up, locking into her hair. He plunged his tongue between her parted lips, searching.

Feeling his muscles tense excited her and she threw her head back. Short puffs of warm breath brushed her skin as his lips kissed every inch of her jaw and neck, while he edged them into the living area.

She felt him bump into a chair causing him to lose his balance and stumble. They clung to each other as they landed on the couch with him on top of her. Longer, hard kisses prevailed after short, sweet ones slid up her neck, across her jawline, and back to her awaiting lips, inducing sighs and moans of arousal.

He abruptly stopped and with his lustful, hypnotic, clear blue eyes, he gazed into hers and breathlessly whispered, "I want you. I want you so bad." Heart hammering, she sucked in air. Robert grabbed her up into his arms and carried her toward the bedroom. He hesitated at the door and his expression became serious. "I just came to talk but...I didn't plan for this to happen...I didn't bring—"

Belinda placed her finger over his lips. "Don't worry, we're covered." She winked. "I'm on the pill and I have condoms in the nightstand."

Nodding, he let out a sigh as a half-smile swept across his lips. He wasted no time carrying her to the bed.

He reached behind his neck and yanked his t-shirt forward over his head. Belinda gasped at the sight of his taut chest muscles. He untied her robe and slid it off. It slipped down around her feet, leaving her standing naked. A wide grin appeared as his passionate gaze scanned down her body.

Belinda traced the rippled muscles of his abdomen down to his buckle. She gave it a tug causing him to stumble toward her. He seized her hands, pulling them up about his neck, and lifted her onto her tiptoes. Robert secured his arms around her waist and squeezed their bodies tight together. Feeling his warmth, she let out a loud sigh and said, "You feel so good." In one quick fluid movement, he scooped up Belinda and laid her in bed, and then sat on the edge. His soft, sensual lips and warm, gentle hands roamed her entire body setting her reactions into motion. In a matter of seconds, his clothes were off. He knelt above her and pointed to the nightstand drawer.

She nodded.

With the speed and grace of a gazelle, he was ready and laid partially over her.

She trembled with sexual desire. As her lips found his, their limbs entangled, and pressed heat against heat. She relinquished control, letting her body respond to his. Neither spoke—only their bodies communicated.

He slid on top, settling between her legs. Her breathing accelerated in anticipation as she waited for the pain. With the first thrust, she tensed throwing her head back against the mattress and moaned. She grabbed at the smooth sheet taking fistfuls. Robert stopped. She relaxed, seeing him peer down at her. A gentle placement of her hands on his ass accompanied by the downward pressure encouraged him to continue. He thrust again.

This time Belinda arched her back, molding to him, and moaned with pleasure. Digging her nails into his flesh, she encouraged him again and again until they rhythmically moved as one. She closed her eyes tight as sparks of light flashed against the back of her lids. Every nerve ending in her came alive. About to reach her peak, she dug her nails deeper into his flesh and cried out, "Robert." She felt him stiffen as he made a final thrust, followed by a rocking motion that sent waves of ecstasy through every inch of her body. Then he relaxed. Panting, with beads of sweat trickling down his chest, Robert rolled over onto his back and lay quietly.

For the first time since Robert appeared at her door, Belinda began to contemplate the evening's events. She couldn't believe what had just happened, but didn't have the nerve to question his actions. She wanted to relish his body as long as she could, so she rolled on her side and snuggled against his warmth, curling over him. He wrapped his arms around her and tightened his grip, offering no explanation as he nuzzled her hair. Belinda reveled in his embrace as the pair fell asleep.

Belinda awoke in the dark to the exciting thrill of Robert's touch as his fingers gently rubbed circles on her stomach. At first, she thought she imagined the events of a few hours ago. Now more awake, she became aware of Robert's hand wandering over her stomach. His tantalizing touch sent a zingy charge up her spine making her back arch. Robert's ragged breaths increased in response to her movement. Seconds later, his lips moved across her cheek. Belinda tilted her head up as she reached over cupping his cheek to direct his lips to hers. Robert came alive rolling over on top of her. In united euphoria, they made mind blowing, passionate love.

A slight back and forth motion awakened Belinda from her peaceful sleep. A lazy yawn floated over her lips while she stretched and focused on Robert. He sat on the edge of the bed. Bent over, his back to her, he rummaged through the pile of clothes they had discarded in their haste to reach the bed. *Is he trying to sneak out?* No discussion took place about why he even came over. Not to mention how he ravished her without a word. She loved his advances and had waited too long, so she wasn't about to let him out of her sight without a decent explanation.

"Where do you think you're goin', mister?"

Half leaning off the bed, very naked, Robert jerked his head toward Belinda and flashed his signature smile. "Good morning, Angel. I do have a job to get to."

Belinda scowled as her mouth dropped open. *Is he jacking me around again?* Her back went straight. *How dare he come over and make love to me.* Then it struck her, why did he call her Angel? The whole scenario seemed peculiar and she needed questions answered. She had to figure out a way to keep him with her.

Seduction! Turning over and reaching for her phone on the bedside table, she stretched and the sheet slid down exposing the upper half of her torso.

Robert took notice and stopped rummaging for his clothes.

She had his full attention. Belinda sat up, pressed a number on her cell, and never stopped looking at Robert. He stared intently back at her as she put her plan into play, leaving a message for her employer. "Sandra, this is Belinda." She paused as she moved her eyes down his rippled chest muscles. Her gaze continued downward to below his waist as she finished her message. "Something's come up and I won't be in today." She disconnected the call and held out her cell toward him.

Robert beamed. His breathing quickened. Smiling from ear to ear, he gathered his jeans from the floor and retrieved his cell. "I'll use mine."

He used speed dial and waited for a response. "Gail, how heavy is my day?...Okay, great!...I need you to reschedule those appointments for later in the week and let my dad know I won't be in today. Tell him I'll talk to him later, but I'm alright." He disconnected the call, turned off the phone, and placed it on the nightstand.

With slow intentional movements, Robert crawled over the bed and straddled her. Placing his mouth close to hers, he gently ran the tip of his tongue over her soft lips, and then pressed their lips together as his tongue slipped in to caress hers. She responded, throwing her arms around his neck, pulling him to her, carrying on their lovemaking from the night before.

Around ten a.m., Belinda awoke from round three. In sheer bliss, she looked calmly at a sleeping Robert. He was as handsome as she remembered from her dream and she couldn't believe he was really lying beside her. She lightly ran her fingers over his chest to convince herself he was real. She felt the all-too-familiar arousing stir and was satisfied, *but why is he here? What changed that brought him to my door?* She had too many questions, but for now, she was content to take in his essence.

As Belinda traced her finger over his lips, Robert's blue eyes flickered open and he reached for her hand, gently kissing her palm.

"Good morning again, Angel," he said, smiling. "I need a shower. You interested?" With a devilish grin, he leapt out of bed and extended his hand. She knew that look. It only meant one thing and she was game. Forty-five minutes later, they walked out of the bathroom.

Wrapped in a towel, Belinda rummaged through a drawer for something comfortable to put on. A camisole and shorts fit the bill.

Still clad in just a towel, and rubbing his hair with another, Robert walked over and stopped at the side of the bed. He looked down at something.

Belinda strolled over to see what caught his attention. There on the sheets she saw a blood stain, a remnant of her first sexual encounter. Robert shot a glance at her with a questioning, concerned look. Slowly he approached her, and then tenderly placed his arms around her waist and kissed the top of her head. "You were a virgin?"

Belinda nodded.

In a soft voice he asked, "Are you okay with this?"

Again, Belinda nodded and looked up at him. She could tell something was on his mind. "Why?"

"I was just wondering why you're on birth control pills and have condoms. I'm just a little confused. I thought you and Colin…"

Belinda glanced away and lightly bit her lower lip, not knowing if she should answer him truthfully. After a few seconds of thought, she decided lying would get her nowhere and blurted out, "I started on the pill the week after the New Year's Eve party." She looked into his eyes. "I never slept with Colin or anyone. I've been waiting for you."

Robert caught his breath and studied her intently. He tugged her to him and hugged her tight, kissing the top of her head again, not sure how to sort out the emotions he felt at the moment. To gain some time to think, he broke the mood. "I don't know about you, but I'm starving. How about you start breakfast and I'll take care of the bed. Where's your clean sheets?" He managed to place a huge grin on his face, hiding his confusion, as he let her go.

Belinda picked up her clothes and went into the bathroom. A few seconds later, she tossed the sheets on the bed and returned to the bathroom. He assumed to take care of a few things in private.

Emerging dressed and with her hair in a ponytail, she asked, "Blueberry bagels, coffee and OJ okay?"

Robert, now dressed only in his jeans, worked on making the bed. "I love blueberry bagels!"

Belinda gave him a nod. "Blueberry bagels, coffee and OJ it is." She padded to the kitchen.

Walking through the living room, she noticed the rose she'd dropped on the credenza behind the couch. It was the farthest thing from her mind after Robert's advances. Now she could appreciate it for its beauty. She picked it up and held it under her nose, taking a deep breath thinking, *why a red rose?* She walked into the kitchen, found a suitable vase and placed the rose in it, and then set her new possession in the center of the table.

Belinda busied herself making orange juice and toasting bagels. Robert entered the kitchen with an armful of sheets. "Where do you want these?" She scrunched up her nose and pointed with the knife to the door at the end of the kitchen. Robert obliged, completing his task. "How about if I make the coffee?"

She nodded and asked softly, "Please wash your hands first." Robert let out a laugh while he walked over to the sink, again obliging her before taking on his new chore.

Robert put the OJ and freshly made coffee on the table, and then sat down to wait for Belinda. She followed shortly and placed his bagel in front of him. It was lightly toasted and spread with cream cheese.

"It looks perfect." He took a bite and nodded. "It's perfect. I couldn't have done it better if I made it myself. My compliments to the chef."

Taking another bite, Robert knew he owed her an explanation of why he chose to invade her home in the manner he did. "Pull your chair next to mine." He tightened his jaw, something that happened when his anxiety level rose. He shifted in his seat to face her and encouraged her to do the same. Taking her hands in his, he said, "Angel, we have a lot to talk about."

CHAPTER 22

"ROBERT, WHY DO you call me Angel?"

He took a deep breath and slowly exhaled, rubbing his thumbs over the top of her hands. "What I have to say may sound a little crazy and I can't explain how this happened or why. Just bear with me." Raising his head, he studied her. She tightened her lips and nodded.

"A year ago last April, after witnessing your car wreck, I went to bed and had a dream about a woman riding a chestnut horse on a college campus. I was walking with some friends across the commons when the horse reared up in front of me and her eyes met mine. From that moment on, I was hooked and in love."

An audible gasp escaped Belinda. She threw her hand up to cover her mouth. He watched her for a second, and continued his story. "Night after night I found myself in the same dream. I lived a life with this woman. We even got married. Everything seemed great until sometime in July, she left because she saw me kissing my study partner in my blue BMW Roadster. Her name was Erin."

"Robert." Belinda's voice quavered.

"Before you say anything, let me finish." Taking hold of her hand again, he pressed on.

"I fell madly in love with this woman and did everything I could to be with her. I'd come home right from work night after night and jump into bed so I could be in the dream. My parents thought I was depressed and did everything they could to help me. They even tried to get me to see a psychiatrist, but I refused.

"By July the dream had become more important to me than reality. I knew I would go nuts if I didn't do something. That's when I started dating

Karen. I would stay awake more and the funny part is the dream reflected my absence.

"In the dream, the woman moved to Atlanta about the same time I started up with Karen. My life with my dream girl turned into phone calls and texts, but after weeks of talking, she agreed to meet me for one night in September. We reconnected and decided we would work at our marriage and live as husband and wife. After that dream, they suddenly stopped and she was gone.

"Then around November, I had another dream about her. It picked up the morning after we spent the reconciliation night together. I found a note telling me she had to run an errand and she'd be back soon. I decided to go buy our favorite breakfast of bagels and coffee. As I pulled up to the bakery, I saw her pulling into the intersection where a semi seemed to come out of nowhere and broadsided her. I thought my life would end right there. I ran to her and cradled her in my arms. Blood was everywhere. That was the last time I ever dreamt about her." He swallowed hard.... "I thought you died."

Tears welled and his chest tightened from the pain of the memory of the grief. Belinda reached up and stroked his cheek.

"When Mom called New Year's Eve and told me there was a young lady by the name of Belinda asking about me, my heart froze. I asked her to describe you and knew immediately who you were. I rushed home. Mom pointed you out, but the minute I spotted you, I knew you were the Belinda of my dreams. What surprised me the most was when I touched you. It was the same experience as in the dreams—an arousal of all my senses, but more intense. I felt an immediate connection to you. Up to now, I've been afraid to say anything out of fear. I thought you'd think I was crazy. To tell the truth, I felt crazy and wasn't sure if you were the same sweet, caring person I dreamt about."

Giving her hands a slight squeeze, he finished with "Pretty nuts. Huh?"

He watched Belinda for signs of acceptance. Her pupils constantly widened and narrowed, her mouth slightly parted, taking in short steady breaths. Occasionally her head moved from side to side.

She reached for his face and cupped his cheek. He grabbed her wrist and placed tiny kisses in her palm. Tears streamed down her cheeks. "Robert, I love you," floated over her lips in the tone of an angel.

Robert's soul took flight. Her words validated he wasn't insane and she understood even though he gave her no indication he knew about her dream.

There would be time to answer all their questions and compare. They would have a lifetime. This he knew for certain.

"I love you too, Angel."

A tear stained face looked back at him, corners turning up to form a sweet smile.

Leaving the cold bagels and coffee abandoned on the table, they retreated to the bed to continue their conversation. Belinda lay curled up in his arms as they talked.

"Robert, what you just told me about your dreams....Well, as strange as this sounds…I…I…I dreamt about you in my coma and it sounds like it was at the same time you were dreaming about me." She repositioned herself so she could see him.

"I know."

"You know?" She rolled onto her side and propped herself on her elbow. "How did you know I had the same dream?"

"Colin and I played golf yesterday and he told me. That's why I came over here. He told me if I didn't straighten this out with you, he'd kick my ass. My plan was to just talk, but when I saw you in that robe and those bunnies…the memory of our first kiss in our dream…I couldn't control myself."

She giggled. "You saw all that?" She bit her lip. "Robert, how could that have happened?"

He shook his head. "I don't know. What I do know is I found you and I don't want to let you go." He stroked her cheek. "That's only if you want to stay."

Her eyes moistened, wetting her lashes. "I'm right where I always wanted to be."

A faint sniffle escaped her nose. Robert chuckled, wiping each eye with his thumb. "No more crying. Agreed?" She nodded and nestled her body against his chest.

He gazed at the ceiling. "You asked me why I called you Angel. As I see it there are two reasons why. First, the night of the New Year's party when I saw you, I felt I was seeing an angel. I thought you died in our dream, but there you were—alive and real." He paused and gave her a tug, bringing her closer. "I was devastated after the dreams stopped. I mourned for you—for a person I'd never met."

"I've also spent many an hour working through the grief I experienced when I found out you didn't exist—that you were only a figment of my imagination and my life with you was only a dream. I wished I hadn't come out of the coma so I could've stayed with you."

Robert winced, rubbing his hand up and down her upper arm. "Don't say that. Us. Being here now wouldn't be happening if you hadn't."

"So, what is the second reason?"

"Because I called you Angel in our dream. You were sent to me from heaven." He took hold of her hand and kissed it.

"Robert. Why didn't you say or do something to change the outcome of our dream?"

"I couldn't. I tried a few times, but nothing happened. It was like I was a character in a movie. I got to experience everything, but had no control over what happened. I was just along for the ride."

"You mean you really felt everything."

"Angel, it was as real as you being here with me now." He exhaled. "How did it feel to you?"

"Oh very, very real." She rolled over on her stomach to face him. "But you're here now…" Belinda touched the skin on his chest and he tensed. "What does it feel like when I touch you?" She continued toying with his skin. His lids narrowed and his breathing became shallow.

He took a deep breath and searched his mind for the words. "Like my body is about to explode. It's like every nerve ending is on fire and you are the only thing that will put out the fire. But there's something else. When I'm around you I don't feel alone. I feel like I'm home." He looked into her eyes. "Does that make sense?"

She nodded. "Perfect sense. When you touch me…it's like a jolt of electricity shoots through me….It's the most sensual feeling you can ever imagine. And when I'm around you, I feel like my life is…complete."

Slowly, Belinda danced her fingers across his stomach and down to the button of his jeans. He swallowed hard, sucking in air as he watched her finger playfully circle the button over and over again. Very artfully, she freed it from the buttonhole. A zipping sound followed, opening the fly. She slipped her hand down the front of his pants. His body tensed and a groan arose from deep in his throat, exciting her. She hopped onto her knees, grabbed the waistband of his jeans, and tugged. He reached for her camisole and pulled it off, throwing it across the room. Her shorts sailed through the air next. He finished taking off his jeans and she straddled him.

Breaths short and fast, Belinda peered down at Robert. "But this, you, they're so much better than in our dream." She kneaded her fingers into his chest. He reached for her and rolled on top, positioning himself to begin their lovemaking.

***

Belinda fluttered her eyelids open in the morning to find Robert propped on his elbow, watching her. Her heart filled with the joy of knowing he was beside her—that is until the thought of Karen came crashing in like one of the semi's, hitting her all over again. She couldn't return his gaze. *Had she turned into the other woman?*

"Belinda, what's wrong?"

She pulled the covers up around her, wringing the smooth sheets with her balled fists. "What about Karen?"

"Oh." He rolled onto his back, placing his locked fingers behind his neck. "We broke up. I guess I started acting differently after the New Year's Eve party. She could tell there was something going on between the two of us when she saw us in the hot tub and in my parent's great room on the Fourth of July. Karen packed everything she had at my place before I drove her home after the party. When we got to her's, she threw a trash bag at me and told me to pack up. Then she tossed me out on my ass."

Almost afraid of Robert's response, she asked, "Any regrets?" Air stopped filling her lungs while she waited for the answer.

"Nope. Not a one. I'm glad it's over and I'm right where I wanna be."

Air passed in and out of her nostrils. She could breathe again. Not only was he a free agent, she hadn't infringed on another woman's territory, and to top it off, he loved her.

"When we were in the hot tub, I imagined you holding me. I remembered how safe and wanted I felt when you held me in our dream."

He shot back up on his elbow, rocking the bed as he adjusted his position. "I remember how much I enjoyed holding you. How affectionate you were." He ran his fingers gently down her cheek and bushed his lips over her forehead.

"I was so mad when Karen showed up. I wanted to yank her away from—"

Robert interrupted, "Like you did to Lora."

Belinda jerked her head toward him and smiled. "Yeah. Just like Lora. I hated her too."

Robert raised his eyebrows. "I can still feel the sting from the slap you gave me the second time you caught me with her."

"You deserved it. Ah, I mean he deserved it."

"I know." His tone lowered and his fingers lightly touched her cheek. "I'll never do that to you. I'm not him. I'm different from that Robert."

Belinda parted her lips. She could see the sadness on his face. Her fingers reached to gently stroke the side of it and comb through his hair. "I know you are. I figured that out several months ago and I like this version of Robert much better." Her cheeks flashed hot. "Besides, hands down, you're a far better lover."

He shook his head and raised the corners on his mouth, lifting his cheeks. "I like this version of you better, too." Robert brushed his fingers over her breast, causing her breath to hitch. "Oh yeah." He nodded. "Much better."

Giving Belinda the once-over, he slid a smug smile across his face that turned devilish. "Besides. It's not every day a guy gets to take a girl's virginity twice." His brow lifted and his mouth thinned.

Her cheeks flushed from the blood rushing to flood them. Palm open, she let Robert have it on the shoulder. "Robert, you bad boy."

He rolled on his back, laughing. "That's me." As quickly as he started laughing, he stopped and sat up in bed. "I need another shower." With one jump, he stood at the side of the bed. He tilted his head as he bent in closer, scooping her up. "And you're coming with me."

Belinda threw her arms about his neck, feeling herself go airborne. A stir of butterflies danced in her stomach. She threw her head back and remembered their dream.

CHAPTER 23

AT FOUR O'CLOCK in the afternoon, Robert and Belinda left for the Pendleton residence in his car. The horses needed their attention and the couple owed an explanation to his parents, who also happened to be their employers. Robert pulled into the driveway and after parking next to the guesthouse, the pair strolled arm in arm across the back lawn.

"I think we should go in and see Mom first. I'm assuming we'll be eating here tonight."

Belinda looked at him, her brow knitted. "I haven't eaten all day thanks to you." She gave him a gentle slap on the chest.

He snorted under his breath. "Well, we have been pretty busy. But I don't recall you protesting, unless I misinterpreted all that moaning…" A sharp poke in his rib cage reminded him his comment wasn't appreciated. However, the little chuckle from his partner told him she could see some humor in it. They made a heading correction toward the back door of the house.

"Mom!" Robert called out. There was no answer. He looked at the clock on the kitchen wall. "She must be in the office." He started upstairs with Belinda in tow. At the door of the office, he stepped aside and motioned for her to go in first. Her slow, faint smile told him she understood his reasoning.

Taking a step, she entered the office. Robert positioned himself outside the door so he could see his mother, but she couldn't see him. He knew seeing Belinda with him would delight her. After all, his parents weren't very subtle in their attempts to encourage his deeper association with her.

"Sandra."

Sandra stood bent over her desk, supporting herself on her elbows, concentrating on the plans spread out in front of her. It took a second for her to turn in Belinda's direction.

"Hi. What are you doing here?"

"I came to take care of the horses." No sooner had the words come out of Belinda's mouth than Robert appeared beside her, slipping one arm around her waist.

Sandra stood. She panned between them, stopping on Robert's face.

He gave Belinda a slight tug, pulling her closer. He never broke eye contact with his mother until he bent down and placed a kiss on Belinda's forehead. Looking back at his mother, he waited for a reaction.

Sandra didn't speak, but sported a broad smile of dazzling teeth. He hadn't seen a smile like that on her in years.

She stepped toward them and took one of each of their hands in hers. "This sure took the two of you long enough." She placed a kiss on Belinda's cheek and then Robert's.

"And this goof wouldn't take a hint no matter what I did or said." She stretched up on her tiptoes to ruffle his hair. "Bend down here. You've gotten too tall."

Robert rolled his eyes and bent his knees. "Yeah. Well I'm disappointed in you. You knew I wouldn't do anything as long as I was engaged. Nice try though." He winked at her.

"Belinda and I will be staying for dinner. We're going to take care of the horses, and then we'll come back in and help. Okay?"

"That'll be fine. But don't rush." She turned back toward her work and picked up a page from the plans strewn across the desk. "Dinner won't be until around seven. Your dad had a late meeting."

"Good. That'll give us time to clean up as well. See you later."

"There's a bag of baby carrots in the vegetable bin."

Robert grabbed Belinda's hand and raced down the stairs, stopping at the refrigerator for the carrots. At the back door, he swung her around, slamming her into his chest. He wrapped her in his arms and kissed her on her full, warm lips. He loved the contours of her back, her warm soft form pressing against his. His breath became more ragged as his mind filled with images of how her soft, naked body felt against his chest. He slid his hands into her hair and it excited him. She responded, kissing him back. He was about to suggest they go to the guesthouse when he felt a pair of palms push against his chest.

"Robert, we'll never get anything done if we keep this up." Belinda continued pushing, putting an arm's length between them.

He let out a huff. "Okay. You're right." He opened the door and let her pass, but inhaled as deeply as he could, drawing in her scent.

Belinda agreed to play water boy while Robert cleaned the stalls. She busied herself filling the trough outside. He came out of the barn with the last wheelbarrow of horse excrement mixed with wet straw. A distinctive sweet smell that screamed horse and one she was particularly fond of.

She watched Robert's arm muscles tense and relax with every maneuver of the wheelbarrow. His sweat-soaked tee clung to his chest and his well-developed biceps glistened in the sun. She continued enjoying the view until he vanished around the side of the barn *en route* to the compost pile.

The squeaking of the front wheel alerted Belinda he was on his way back. She listened. Timing would be critical. She planted her feet to give her a broader stance and took aim with the hose, positioning herself at the right angle waiting for Robert to come around the barn corner. The squeak grew louder and louder. She waited. The wheel entered her line of vision first. Next came the bucket of the wheelbarrow and finally Robert. She let him have it, soaking him with a steady stream of cold stinging water.

"That's for starving me all day. I ate some of the carrots just so I could survive."

The wheelbarrow went flying onto its side. Robert jumped over it and landed on his feet. He stopped. His face sinister, he balled his fists, lowered his head and tucked a shoulder, charging straight for Belinda. She screamed, spinning on her heels, and took off running. She had a small lead, so she turned back and blasted him again, momentarily slowing him down.

His hands flew up to his face, attempting to protect himself as he dodged from side to side. He reached down and grabbed the hose, giving it a yank. The nozzle flew through the air, landing a few feet from him.

Belinda watched him juggle it until he had a firm grip. The coil of hose by the faucet made her realize she stood in the danger zone. She made a half-turn as the bite of the forceful stream hit her side. She lifted her leg and arms, screaming, "Robert!" It didn't help. The stream kept coming. He grabbed her forearm and she started to flail her arms wildly.

During the process of her self-preservation, she saw the hose dislodge and fall on the ground. The two continued to struggle. Laughter mixed with Belinda's squeals the whole time.

She twisted and wrenched to get out of his grip. The heel of her boot landed in a puddle of slippery goo, and her leg slipped out from under her. In a fraction of a second, she hit the ground with a thud, lying flat on her back. The muddy water soaked through her t-shirt, chilling her skin. It oozed into her hair and down around the waist of her jeans.

She turned to her side attempting to get up, but Robert jumped on top, straddling and pinning her down at the wrists. His voice turned sinister. "Where do you think you're going?"

"Robert let me up. I'm all wet."

"And I'm not?!"

They stared at each other. A steady spray of water continued to settle under her, soaking her even more, but she didn't care. The allure of his face captivated her.

"Do you remember?...From our dream," he asked.

Twisting from side to side, she struggled under his weight. "Yeah, and the only thing missing is your cockroach frat brothers." She snickered, giving up her fight and lay quietly, studying his eyes. They had a glint she had never seen before in her dream Robert. He looked damn sexy and she wanted him.

"I think I need another shower." He sprang to his feet and offered to help her up.

"Boy, the thought of sex sure gets you moving."

He snorted and winked, his voice low and sexy. "Anything that gets you out of your clothes is music to me."

She clamped onto his forearm and, before she knew it, she bounced to her feet, plastered against Robert. The expansion of his pupils told her he had one thing on his mind—her in the shower with him, something she knew she'd enjoy about now. "Your right. I think I need a shower too."

A soft breeze rustled through the trees, giving Belinda a sudden shiver. "You getting cold?" She nodded. "Let me pull in the hose and turn off the water. Start walking back, I'll catch up."

Belinda started across the back lawn toward the guesthouse and noticed Sandra standing on the patio, waving. "You're a mess."

"Thanks, Sandra."

"Here take these. I know the tee will fit. The shorts might be a little big, but I think they'll be comfortable and *dry*."

She smiled at Sandra as Robert came up from behind and wrapped his warm arms around her waist, resting his chin on her shoulder. His breathing was fast and shallow from his short jaunt. Belinda felt his hot breath on her neck.

"We're going to take a shower. When we're done, we'll come in and help with dinner," he told his mother, clasping onto Belinda's hand and moving toward the guesthouse. "She needs to get out of these wet clothes."

Belinda turned back to Sandra and waved. "Thank you."

"You're welcome. You have about an hour and a-half to do whatever."

Belinda dropped her mouth open and jerked her head toward Robert. She caught him in mid-wince.

He lowered his head and shook it. "I can't believe my *mother* just said that."

***

Robert and Belinda entered the house through the back door. Sandra stood at the stove stirring something in a pot. The table had plates arranged on placemats with glasses and flatware fixed in the artistic way Sandra did everything. The aroma of pork chops filled the air.

"What can we do to help?" Robert stuck his finger into the bowl of pudding sitting on the counter.

"Get out of there!" Sandra squealed. "You're not three years old anymore. Go watch some TV. I've got this under control. Your dad's not far and should be here soon. I'm making pork chops, mashed potatoes, steamed green beans, a salad, and bread pudding for dessert. Okay?"

"I love your pork chops." He walked behind Sandra and kissed her cheek to distract her. Timing his next move, he poked his finger back into the creamy confection. "We'll be in there." He pointed his pudding-laden finger toward the family room before popping it into his mouth and sucking it clean.

"Robert!" Sandra swatted at him, but missed. "I hope you have clean hands."

He scoffed at her and took Belinda's hand. She waved and shrugged at Sandra as she passed.

The couple settled on the couch. Belinda curled up under Robert's arm while he surfed the channels. "News okay?"

"That's fine." She paused. "What day is it?"

"Wednesday. Why?"

"Where's my phone. I have to call Colin. I have a breakfast date planned with him in the morning." She patted at the nonexistent pockets of the shorts. "Oh, I remember. I left it on your nightstand."

Robert shifted and pulled his from his back pocket. "Here use mine."

Belinda settled back against Robert's side and scrolled through his contacts. "Any girls in here I should know about?"

"Nope, just Karen and you already know about her."

She tapped Colin's picture and waited. "Hi, Colin. It's Belinda."

"You're on Robert's phone?"

"Yeah." She chuckled under her breath.

"So does that mean you're together?"

"I guess you can say that."

"In bed?"

"Behave yourself. Besides, it's none of your business."

"Wait a minute. Who sent him over to your place? Ingrate."

"Okay, we can talk about it over breakfast. By the way, thank you." Belinda glanced at Robert. His mouth twisted and brow knitted. Still concentrating on Robert's strained expression, she asked Colin, "Are we still on in the morning?"

"You're welcome. Yeah, how about we meet at Billie Boys off the Southwest Freeway?"

"Okay, see you then."

"Belinda."

"Yeah."

"Bring that sorry-ass boyfriend of yours along. I'd like to get his take on the two of you." She heard a faint chuckle under his breath.

"Colin!" She snorted. "I'll ask. See you in the morning."

Robert's mouth appeared less contorted when Belinda turned and handed him the phone. "So it sounds like you'll be going to breakfast with him in the morning."

"Yep and he told me to bring your sorry-ass with me."

Robert glared at her.

Belinda postured in a defensive manner. "His words, not mine. So do you want to come?"

He raised a brow. "You know I always want to do that."

Belinda caught the double meaning of her words. She didn't say anything for a few seconds, and then blurted out, "Robert Pendleton that is *not* what I meant." She glanced into the kitchen then back at him. "Well, do you want to *accompany* Colin and me to breakfast?" Her sarcastic words were well pronounced in a whispered tone, so Sandra wouldn't overhear her.

Robert grinned and pulled her close. "Yes, I'll go with you, but afterward be prepared." A sudden jab to the ribs made him wince.

***

Around seven o'clock the door from the garage opened. Glasses perched on the bridge of his nose, Rob thumbed through a stack of envelopes he picked out of the mailbox. Robert and Belinda watched as he slowly walked past the couch. He glanced up momentarily and shot out, "Hi, Robert. Hi, Belinda."

About to take another step, he stopped and turned toward the couple seated on the leather sofa staring at him. Looking at them from over his glasses, he studied their close proximity to each other.

"Hi, Dad." Robert peered at his father, confident his arm around Belinda caused his father's sudden state of shock. Rob didn't say a word to him, but his mouth spread into a slow smile. He turned his gaze toward the kitchen.

Robert repositioned himself to see his mother propped against the kitchen table with her arms crossed in front of her. Her head lifted and a wide smile grew across her face as she studied her husband.

Rob moved toward Sandra. In a fluid motion, he raised his hand as hers met his, making a smacking sound as they high-fived each other. He kept walking and disappeared into the hallway that led into the master bedroom. Sandra returned to the stove.

Robert settled back on the couch beside Belinda.

"What was all that?" Belinda asked.

"My mother's way of telling my father all her meddling in our affairs paid off. What I don't understand is how she talked him into helping her."

***

Robert watched his parents all through dinner. They acted as if he and Belinda had always been a couple. The conversation flowed and the laughter came naturally. The part that puzzled him the most was his father's participation in his mother's plot.

Robert grew up with his mother's meddling. He became accustomed to her attempting to tilt the outcome of his life to what she thought would be best for him. When he was younger, he objected to her sticking her nose where it wasn't wanted. As he grew older, he could see she only interfered when his decisions could've placed him on the wrong path. He learned to appreciate her parenting technique because when he followed it, things usually turned out better for him.

His father stayed on the other end of the spectrum. He guided Robert, but in a much different way. They had man-to-man talks, as Rob liked to call them. Through those talks, Robert learned things about his father. This is why his cooperation in Sandra's meddling didn't seem to fit Rob's personality. All of Robert's life, his father drew a line when it came to his mother's plotting. He tolerated it, but stayed clear.

Robert scrutinized his mother and wondered, what was different this time?

"Belinda." Sandra crossed her arms in front of her on the table. "You worked so hard helping me with the party, I think you deserve some time off."

Robert studied his mother. *She's meddling again.* He sat back wondering what she would say next.

"Why don't you take the rest of the week off and come in on Monday."

Robert watched her give his father a gentle squeeze on the arm.

Rob had just filled his spoon with some bread pudding and shoved it into his mouth. He swung his head toward her. "What?" spewed out.

Sandra raised a brow and jutted her chin toward Belinda and him.

He swallowed and wiped his mouth with the napkin. Stammering, Rob blurted out, "Robert why don't you do the same. I'll cover for you and have Gail rearrange your schedule." He sat back and winked at Sandra. She reached over and stroked his cheek.

Robert looked at Belinda who watched the interaction, seemingly as confused as he was. Neither had responded to his parents' comments, but the decision seemed final. They had the rest of the week off.

CHAPTER 24

ROBERT SCANNED THE restaurant and found Colin seated at a window booth. Colin stood as they approached and gave Belinda a big bear hug, swinging her from side to side. He leaned down to give her a kiss, but stopped. Flashing Robert a quick glance, he chuckled as his gaze returned to Belinda. His eyes looked like they concentrated on her luscious lips. "I guess those are off limits now."

Belinda huffed, "Not to you." She pulled him close and planted an adequate but respectful kiss on his mouth.

Robert waited for them to separate before he stepped forward and offered Colin his hand. He knew the situation between Colin and Belinda. He also knew he was the third wheel at this breakfast.

"Hey, Colin."

The handshake Colin gave Robert had a hearty quality. Colin nodded and gestured toward the table for everyone to sit. "I had the waitress bring a pot of coffee." He scooted to the middle of the bench seat. Fiddling with his napkin, he unfolded it and spread it across his lap, and then shot a fleeting glance at the couple sitting across from him. He wasted no time getting to the point.

"Sooo, what's up in your world?" He made an exaggerated movement by folding his hands in front of him on the table and glanced between them. He waited for a few seconds.

Robert wouldn't be the first one to open his mouth. Nope he had more sense than that and suspected he would be on the couch for at least a week. He waited. Belinda said nothing and just sat there.

"Oh, for heaven's sakes. So are you or aren't you? And don't tell me you're just friends." A stern look flashed toward Belinda.

"Are we or are we not what?" spat Belinda, with a hint of irritation.

Colin moved closer to her. "Are-you-or-are-you-not-a-couple?"

Continuing to keep his mouth shut, Robert wanted to hear how Belinda would answer. He had a good idea, but his curiosity was still piqued.

Belinda blinked her lashes, and then bit her lower lip. "We're more than friends and might be working on being a...Colin, it's only been one day and I don't know what this is." She pointed wildly between Robert and herself. "What we are?"

She seemed frustrated by the question. Robert patted her arm. "It's okay, Angel." He gave Colin a cold stare. "He's just messing with you and seeing if he can bait me as well. It's what he always does." Robert made a circular motion with his hand in Colin's direction. "Ignore the evil tall, blonde man sitting across from you."

A grin slid across Colin's face as he pointed a wagging finger at Belinda. "I'll accept your answer because it tells me what I wanted to know. So Miss Davies, by my calculations, you two have been waiting for the go ahead for some time. Well, now you have it." He pushed himself back against the backrest of the booth. "I also know the two of you are my best friends. I just want to see the both of you happy. Do you understand?"

Belinda reached across the table and spread her fingers over Colin's hand. "I understand clearly and thank you."

He winked.

Robert spoke up as Colin filled coffee cups. "The other day when you told me about Belinda's dream...." He pursed his lips and then made a small up and down motion with his head. "I didn't tell you the whole story."

Colin stopped pouring and looked up at Robert. "Okay, you grabbed my attention. What did you leave out?"

Robert placed his arm around Belinda. She turned toward him and gave him a nod, telling him to go on.

"I didn't tell you I was dreaming about Belinda when she was in her coma. As far as we can tell, I was actually in her dream."

Colin squinted and his mouth opened as he tilted his head with signs of confusion written all over his face. "Let me get this straight. Are you telling me you had the same dream?"

"Yeah. At the same time, but it was more than that. I actually experienced the dream. Feelings, smells...just as if I was awake. I walked around in the dream as if it were real."

Colin stiffened, sitting up straighter. "How does that happen?"

Belinda took a sip of coffee before she chimed in. "We can't explain it, but he was there. From what we have been able to figure out, his dreaming started the night I fell into the coma and ended when I woke up. When I saw him at the New Year's Eve party, I thought I was going nuts. I didn't know he recognized me. After all, logically he would have no way of knowing who I was." She turned toward Robert. "But I was so attracted to him and when we kissed in his parents' master bedroom, I knew he was the man I fell in love with during those six months in the coma."

Holding up his hand, Colin asked, "Whoa! Hold up. You kissed?"

She turned toward Colin, biting her lower lip. Robert focused on her mouth and watched her nibble the way she did during every one of their chance encounters. He loved it, and it made him want to bite her tempting lip too. Over the past months, all he did was watch and want. Now he could and would nibble away at will, but later.

"I didn't tell you everything Tuesday night. It didn't seem like a good thing to do at the time."

"So tell me now."

She proceeded to fill him in with the rest of the master bedroom drama she had selectively omitting when they talked in the barn. Colin listened intently, mouth open and looking befuddled.

"The night at the Galleria, when I found out Robert was engaged, I had no choice but to make plans to go on with my life. That's why I gave you my number and later agreed to go out with you. Colin. The night we almost ended up in my bedroom—"

"Ah. This might not be the best time to go into that." With knitted brows, he shot Robert a glance.

The waitress appeared at the edge of the table, shifting the attention to her. "Are you ready to order?"

Colin exhaled and scrambled for his menu.

As soon as the waitress left, Belinda wasted no time getting back into her explanation. "Colin."

Mid sip of coffee, he gazed at her under his brows. "You're going to insist on finishing your story?"

"Yes I am. It's important to me you understand what was going on between you and me....Why I couldn't make a commitment to you."

"Sweetie, I think I figured it out and you don't owe me anything."

Colin extended a finger in Robert's direction. "This goof over here got in the way and that's okay. We'll just blame everything on him."

"I don't think that's fair," Robert piped up. "First of all, it was her dream. I had nothing to do with it."

Colin scoffed at him. "From what she just said, it sounds like you enjoyed it as much as she did."

"I may have enjoyed it, but I also thought I was going crazy." He shifted in his seat. "That's something I never want to go through again."

Belinda swung around and cooed, "Robert." She reached for him, and he kissed her palm, exhaling.

"Look guys. I understand. There's no hard feelings here, but I have to admit your story is rather strange. You should talk to someone who can explain this to you."

"I have an appointment with Dr. Rosen this afternoon. Robert's going with me. I can't wait to see his face when he meets Robert, but we're also going to ask him for some help. It's got us stumped."

***

Robert pushed his plate away, poured himself another cup of coffee, and then offered his two companions the same. Glancing at Colin, he asked, "When do you leave for Canada?"

Colin propped himself with his back to the window and stretched his long legs out on the booth seat. "As soon as we're finished here. I plan on driving as long as I can today, but I'm taking my time. I've never seen much of the country north of here and figured I'd take some time sightseeing on the way – the St Louis Arch, Sears Tower, Starved Rock State Park, etc., etc." He sipped his coffee. "I expect you to come up to go fishing next summer." He shook a finger at Robert. "I hear the black flies are rather friendly at that time of the year."

Robert sucked in a short laugh. "Bet they're nothing like the roaches down here."

"I'll give you that one. I don't think a black fly can grab the can of raid from you and spray you with it." Tapping the tabletop, he swung his legs from his reclining position. "Well, I'd better get going or I'll only get as far as Dallas today." He looked at his friends. "You know, I'm going to miss you two."

Robert and Belinda escorted Colin to his car. "I guess this is it."

"You'll be back every now and then for a meeting with your Houston counterparts. I'll try to talk my dad into giving you a reprieve from the frozen north this winter, so you don't freeze."

"You've got a deal," Colin said before engaging in a brisk handshake. The corners of his mouth turned up. He spread out his arms and approached Belinda. "As for you young lady…" He engulfed her as he held her close, giving her a firm squeeze. Slightly pulling away, he cocked his head and said in a serious tone, "You know I love you."

Belinda let out a gasp. "I hope like a sister."

His mouth contorted. "No, I think a little more than that." He pulled her close again to kiss the top of her forehead and then stroked her hair. He gave Robert a stare as he raised his eyebrows up and down swiftly.

Robert peered back at Colin, but knew it was his way of goading him. He and Colin were good friends and he had nothing to worry about even if Colin knew more about Belinda than he cared for him to know.

"I want to take a selfie of the three of us by your car." Belinda retrieved her phone from her purse. The trio posed and she snapped the picture. "Let me look at it to make sure it's okay." She showed it to her companions. Colin was headless and Robert lost half of his.

Robert figured her smaller stature made it impossible for her to achieve the right angle. Colin took the phone and retook the picture.

"Let me see." Belinda's nose scrunched up. "We are three intelligent people. You'd think we could figure this out." She held the phone so the men could see it. Only the top half of Belinda's face showed. "Colin, you're too tall. Robert you try." She shoved the phone toward him. A slight scurry followed as the trio jockeyed into position.

"Everyone say cheese." Robert heard the telltale click and scrutinized the picture. A smile grew across his face. He thought it captured each person's essence. Colin, with his causal self-confident stance, Belinda, perky and beautiful, sporting her faint smile that made him wish he could just kiss those lips now, and him…reserved as ever. He held it out for the other to see. "Good"

Colin threw a thumb up.

Belinda, all smiles, replied, "We're good."

Colin closed the door to his car, started the engine, and placed it in gear.

"I'll send you the picture. Call us tonight and let us know where you are. If you don't…" Belinda shook her finger at him. "I'll send the cops after you."

"Okay, Mom. Well, you two take care and remember to name the first boy after me." One of his shit-eating grins slithered across his lips just before he broke out into a laugh. Robert opened his mouth to spit out a rhetorical comment, but Colin drove off waving out the window. He turned out of the parking lot onto the frontage road that would lead him to US Highway 59 and north to his new home.

CHAPTER 25

"WELL, WE HAVE a few hours before your appointment with the fine doctor. What should we do?" Robert hoped she'd agree to go to her place and crawl back in bed with him, but knew there would be a slim-to-none chance of that happening. He realized, at some point, the lustful need he felt would die down as they settled into a more normal routine. His practical side told him to plan on a lifetime of settling with her.

He wanted to enjoy the excitement as long as he could because he had waited and imagined it for months. Now his fantasy came in the form of a living, breathing human female. Not only did this woman excite the hell out of him, he loved everything about her. The way she tilted her head when she seemed puzzled, her breathy giggles, the sparkle in her eyes, her nose, her hair, her lower lip, and the list never ended. He would have four uninterrupted days of exploration with her and couldn't wait.

"We're close to Memorial Park and it's a beautiful day. Let's go for a walk and talk more about our dream. Compare. Kind of plan what we will tell Dr. Rosen." Belinda slid into the front seat of the Beamer as he held the door open.

"I like that idea. Top up or down?"

Belinda retrieved a scrunchy from her pocket and pulled her hair into a ponytail. "Definitely down."

Robert warmed just looking at her. God he loved this woman. He started the car, retracted the roof, and drove toward Memorial Park.

***

Belinda flipped the switch in Dr. Rosen's office, alerting him his next client had arrived. She took a seat next to Robert on the couch and wrapped her arm through his. They had talked exclusively about the dream and made comparisons on their three-hour stroll in the park. They found they could explain away a good portion of the events either as a past memory of an experience she had or something she just filled in the blanks with, something she liked. Neither of them could come up with a reasonable explanation of how Robert managed to have the same dream.

The door to the inner office opened. Dr. Rosen opened his mouth as if he was about to greet Belinda in his usual manner, but hesitated instead.

Belinda rose. "Hello, Dr. Rosen."

The doctor didn't reply. He just stood in the doorway, with a blank stare on his face. Belinda led Robert past the doctor into the inner office, not saying a word. She pointed to one of the two upholstered chairs that faced a single similar one across a wooden coffee table.

Robert wiggled around in the seat and clutched the armrests. He leaned back and glanced around the room, and then started bouncing the heel of his right foot. He shot Belinda a faint grin.

Belinda nestled without the theatrics and reached for Robert's hand. "Are you okay?"

"Yeah. Yeah. I'm fine." He readjusted himself in his chair.

Belinda smiled and leaned in closer. "It'll be alright. He doesn't bite."

Dr. Rosen took his time joining them. Belinda watched him study his client and her guest. He rubbed the stubble on his chin until he stopped behind the chair he eventually would settle into. "Belinda, may I ask what's going on?"

Belinda smiled at him. "I'd like you to meet Robert Pendleton."

Robert stood to shake the doctor's hand. "I'm glad to meet you, sir." He waited until Dr. Rosen moved from behind the chair and took his hand.

"Nice to meet you as well."

Robert backed up and sat down. This time he leaned forward with his arms resting on his legs. He addressed the doctor, "You've been the topic of several of our conversations. Belinda tells me you've been very helpful with her recovery. Thank you for that."

Dr. Rosen found his way to his seat and picked up his pad of paper and a pencil from the coffee table. "Thank you for the compliments. Now Belinda, would you please tell me what's going on?"

Belinda looked at Robert. "Go ahead," he encouraged.

Swallowing hard, she began. "We thought it would be a good idea if Robert came to see you with me. I hope you don't mind." The doctor didn't respond but motioned with his finger for her to continue. "As you can see, our relationship has changed." Belinda bounced forward in her seat. "We're in love…we love each other." She glanced over at Robert with a half-smile and then she turned back toward the doctor.

"When did this happen?" Dr. Rosen supported his chin, resting it in his palm with one of his fingers rubbing over his cheek.

"Tuesday evening," Belinda answered, her voice almost mouse-like.

The finger stopped moving. He took a deep breath and leaned forward. "Okay. Before we go any further, you understand I can't discuss anything about you in front of Robert because of privacy issues."

Belinda panned from the doctor to Robert and back. "I didn't think about that. But we have to talk to you about something. It's important."

"Very well. Robert, would you be willing to participate?"

"Yeah. Sure."

"Belinda, do I have your permission to discuss your case with Robert if needed?"

"Of course."

He went over to his desk, rummaged through the mess and pulled out some papers, spilling half of one stack on the floor. He placed several forms on two clipboards, and then stepped over the pile on his way back to the pair. "I'll need these papers signed before we can continue." He gave a clipboard to each of them.

Belinda started reading her forms. She looked at Robert, who leafed through his forms. "I think I have yours." He handed his clipboard over and she did the same.

Once they returned the papers, the doctor resumed his position in his chair, elbow on the armrest as his hand supported his head with a finger cupped over his mouth, rubbing his upper lip. "So…you think you're in love. Belinda, what changed since our last meeting?"

The floodgates opened as Belinda recapped the story of Robert's break up, Colin's departure, and how he encouraged Robert to go to her house. She told him they had spent the last several nights together.

"You seem to be moving very fast, and that concerns me. Robert, how do you feel about all this?"

"I agree, sir. This might seem fast to an outsider, not that you're an outsider…I mean." He flopped back into the chair. "Look. I've never done anything like this before, and I'm not sure what you expect."

"I expect you to talk to me. Tell me how you feel so we can explore what needs to be understood." Dr. Rosen continued to rub his upper lip.

Belinda saw Robert sit straight up in his chair. He glanced at her. "Can I tell him?" She nodded.

"I know Belinda has told you all about our lives together in *our* dream." When Robert emphasized *our*, Dr. Rosen raised an eyebrow.

"Ah. I see you noticed when I said *our* dream. You see, it seems I was in Belinda's dream, and experienced it at the same time. We've talked about it and compared notes. I can remember details and feelings about her just like she can about me. Now I know there are several things she has been able to explain. Things like how she plugged my parents' house into the dream. What we don't understand is how I experienced her dream. That's where we need your help."

Dr. Rosen sat back in his chair and tapped his fingers on the armrest. Belinda suspected he was trying to process what Robert had just said. "I don't know. You're telling me you experienced the same dream Belinda had about you?"

"Yes. Right down to smells, tastes, what we had for dinner, and how wonderful she felt."

"And I experienced the same. When Robert came over on Tuesday, we didn't even really talk to each other. He saw me in my robe and bunny slippers, just like in our dream, picked me up, and that was it. I can't explain this, but it's like I've always known him." She turned toward Robert. "Like we belong together."

Dr. Rosen studied the couple, making Belinda feel awkward. She had learned to read his non-verbal signals over the past year, but this seemed different. He appeared dumfounded. Several seconds passed.

"Well, what do you think?" Belinda asked.

Dr. Rosen threw his hands up in front of him, barely hanging on to his pencil and flopped back against the chair. "I don't know. This is a new one on me."

"We were hoping you could help us figure out how this happened," Robert said.

The doctor twisted his mouth several times. He shot his index finger in the air. "I might have something." He jumped out of his seat and walked over to a bookshelf. He started scanning the titles using his finger as a pointer. He came to one title and tapped the spine. "No." Starting up again, he stepped sideways moving down the bookshelves spanning one wall of the room. Stopping, he pulled a book from the shelf and thumbed through it.

Belinda's heart sputtered. *Will he be able to explain what happened?* She watched as he snapped the book closed and returned it to the shelf.

"I'm sorry. I thought there might be something in that last book, but no." He thumbed toward the bookshelf. "I'll ask around and do some research to see if any of my colleagues know or have heard about anything like this before." He returned to his seat. "Everyone's brain maintains in their memories everything they have ever done or seen. Some people are very good at recalling those memories, while others have a harder time. Obviously, in Belinda's deepened sleep, she accessed the memories hidden in *her* mind."

He looked at Robert. "The mind is complex and full of areas still not understood. I have no way to explain how you ended up experiencing the same dream. What if this can't be explained? This might just have to be accepted. How would you two feel about that? Robert, you go first."

"I don't think it would really matter. The way I look at it, that's six months more I got to know her."

"But is she the same person as in the…your dream?"

"Pretty much. There's differences. She's more confident than the Belinda in the dream. This one has no trouble telling me what's on her mind. She stands her ground."

"Belinda, what about you? Is it important you find out how this happened?" the doctor asked.

Belinda smiled at Robert before addressing the question. "No, I don't think it really matters. We talked about Dream Robert in my other sessions, but this Robert is better. In the time we spent together the last few weeks, I've learned he's sensitive and more grounded. He loves his parents. He's an honest man and he loves his horse." Belinda cooed at him. "Who can't love a man who loves his horse, but he has his faults."

"Faults?" Robert spat out.

Belinda swung her head in Robert's direction. "Stop it. You're not perfect and neither am I. But we're real and that's what's important."

Dr. Rosen interrupted. "Robert, what happened to your dream when Belinda woke up?"

Belinda watched Robert's face go white. He focused on the doctor. "I thought she died and that's why it ended."

"And how are you doing now? Do you feel like you've worked through the grief?"

"I don't know."

Belinda noticed the glare of the red light above the door. Their hour was up.

Dr. Rosen picked up his appointment book from the coffee table. "Your time is up. We'll have to continue this at our next session. Are you alright with that?" The pair nodded.

"How about I continue to see Belinda on Thursdays as scheduled? On Wednesdays around four, I'll see the two of you together." He looked up waiting for their answer.

"I can do that," Robert agreed.

"So can I."

"Robert, if you feel like you would like some sessions without Belinda present, I can set some time aside for you. I'll let you decide."

Robert nodded as he pushed out of the chair. Belinda and Dr. Rosen followed. Robert extended his hand once again to the doctor. "Thank you. I'm finding this very interesting."

Dr. Rosen shook Robert's hand, and then gestured toward the back door.

***

"So what do you think?" Belinda asked as they walked toward the car.

"Interesting."

"He has helped me a lot, Robert. Give it a chance."

"I will. Who knows, he might be able to tighten a few of my loose screws."

"So what do we do with the rest of our time off?"

Robert rubbed his chin and twisted his mouth. "How about the company beach house in Galveston?"

Belinda grew a smile a mile wide. "Perfect, but I have to call my mom and Abbey tonight. They'd never forgive me if I didn't fill them in. Especially Abbey."

"You can call the on the drive down."

"That works."

CHAPTER 26

BRIGHT AND EARLY Friday morning, Robert and Belinda hopped into the roadster with the top down and drove south toward Surfside Beach near Freeport, Texas. They would spend the next two nights in the corporate luxury beachfront house, doing whatever met their fancy.

On the drive down, Belinda occupied herself with the calls she needed to make, alerting all concerned parties of the situation that developed between her and Robert. She had found herself too busy the night before between giving attention to Robert and packing for the trip. She knew she wouldn't have been able to give her mother or Abbey the time they deserved. Dora came first and as usual, Belinda knew this phone call would be less complicated. She filled her in on the details of what transpired, again with an edit, giving just enough information to satisfy her.

"Yes, Mom. That's right. Robert and I are on our way to Galveston Island."

"That sounds like fun. What are you going to do?"

"I don't know. I guess whatever we want. We're staying in Robert's company's beach house."

"Belinda, are you sure this is a good idea?"

Her mother had nothing to be concerned about. It was Robert. "I'll be fine."

She studied Robert while he concentrated on his driving, looking all hot and sexy, in his white t-shirt, jeans and designer sunglasses. Flip-flops completed the outfit. His elbow rested on the door as he slouched back in the seat with his hand flopped over the steering wheel, his head bobbing to the tune blaring from the radio.

"You call us if you need a ride home or anything."

Belinda filled her lungs and let out a deep sigh that made enough noise to inform her mother of her frustration. "Yes, Mom. I'll call if I need anything, but I'm alright."

Robert turned his head toward Belinda and dropped his sunglasses so he looked over the rim, one eyebrow raised. "Yeah, tell her you're at the mercy of a serial killer."

Belinda covered the mic of the phone. "Robert! Behave yourself and watch the road."

"What did he say?"

"Oh nothing, Mom. Someone just yelled an obscenity out the window of their car...Okay. I'll come over on Monday and we can talk more." Abbey popped into Belinda's head.

"Mom, I haven't told Abbey yet. You know how high maintenance she can be. If I needed to change our day to Tuesday, would you mind?"

Dora snickered under her breath. "Tuesday would be fine. Just let me know."

"Great. I'll call when I get back."

"Sweetie, take care of yourself. I love you."

"Love you too. Bye."

Belinda wasted no time confronting Robert. "What was that about? Are you trying to make an enemy out of my mom?"

Robert threw his head back and let out a laugh. "She loved me in our dream and she'll love me now. No sweat."

"I'm glad you're confident. But, until we know for sure, play nice. Okay." She gave him a stern look, wagging a finger. "Do I have your promise?"

He exhaled and like a little boy, muttered, "Okay." She loved that innocent look he gave her. Her irritated mood melted away. If that look continued to have the same effect on her, he would be able to get whatever he wanted from her, not that he didn't already. If he wasn't driving a sports car doing 70 mph down Highway 288, she would have reached over and given her sexy hunk a wet, juicy kiss on those marvelous lips.

"Okay, Abbey, you're next." Belinda shook her phone and pressed Abbey's speed dial number. Glancing at Robert, she saw him watching her with a smile the size of Texas. "Eyes on the road, please." He snapped his head forward, like a good boy, still grinning.

"Hi, Abbey."

"Hey, whatcha up to girlfriend?"

"I'm on my way to the Pendleton company beach house."

Abbey didn't say anything right away. "Is there a company party down there Garrett failed to tell me about?"

"Well, I guess you could say I'm going to a private party for two."

"Didn't Colin already leave for Canada?"

"Yes he did."

Things got very quiet until the screech Abbey sent through the phone nearly deafened Belinda. She held it about six inches from her ear, waiting for the screaming to stop. Abbey started asking rapid-fire questions and wanted all the details of how, why, and when Belinda and Robert came to be. Their conversation lasted the remainder of the trip to the coast. When Robert pulled under the carport and turned off the engine, Belinda said her goodbyes, promising she would meet Abbey for dinner on Monday to continue their talk. Apparently, the last hour of information just didn't seem to be enough. At least she'd have more spicy tidbits for her dear friend after her two night stay with Robert in a romantic setting. But Belinda would never kiss and tell. She would edit the more intimate details.

***

Robert waited on the deck while Belinda went inside to change into her suit. He stretched out on a lounge chair, the only one in the shade, and closed his eyes. He hadn't been getting much sleep since Tuesday, the night he went to see her and anticipated the next two nights wouldn't offer much more rest. He would be going to work dragging on Monday morning, but figured, at some point, sheer exhaustion would smack him in the face, and he'd just play catch-up when it did.

He relaxed, allowing the rhythmic rolling sound of the waves hitting the beach to fill his ears. The caw of a shorebird blurted in every now and then—some close, some in the distance. The heat from the warm July morning embraced him as he drifted off to sleep.

"Robert. Honey." He fluttered his eyes open to an apparition of a woman's image above him—a glowing light encircling her long flowing hair. He felt the warmth of a hand pressing against his face.

"Robert." The angelic voice called to him. "Are you awake?"

He rubbed his eyes and cleared his throat. Adjusting his position, he sat up. "How long did I sleep? What time is it?"

"It's a little after noon. About two hours. You're not in the shade anymore and I didn't want you to burn. Are you hungry? I made some lunch."

"Yeah. That sounds good."

Belinda turned to walk back into the house wearing a sea foam green, two-piece, bandeau swimsuit.

"Hey, that suit looks familiar."

She giggled. "I had it before our dream. I guess I just plugged it in and wore it to the dream pool party." She shrugged. "Come on, let's go eat." She held her hand out for him.

The sun backlit her silhouette. He couldn't make out her distinctive features, but he thought she glowed as the sun formed a halo outlining her. He took it as he stood and tugged her close. "Thank you."

"For what?"

"For loving me." He wrapped his arms around her and pulled her to him. Her warmth against his bare skin filled his heart and enticed a growing need for her.

Belinda smiled at Robert. "Lunch is going to be much later, isn't it?"

Nodding, he bent down and gave her a soft, light kiss. She drifted her hand up the back of his neck, pressing him closer. She parted her lips and he took the invitation to caress her willing mouth with his tongue. Her back arched and she let her head fall back. He sent kisses floating down her neck to her breast. With every tiny touch of his mouth on her velvet skin, she drew him in, taking his soul and mingling it with hers until he felt both wrapping around each other as one. Their breaths quickened and he tightened his grip around her smooth, firm back. He kissed her hard and enjoyed how she responded.

Enthusiastic catcalls and wolf whistles from the beach rang through the air. Robert glanced up and with a thumbs-up, acknowledged the men passing by. He was happy to share his beautiful girlfriend with the world, but he had his limits.

"Angel, we need to go inside before I forget we're on the deck," he whispered in her ear. In one swoop, she filled his arms. His stride long and fast, he wasted no time taking her to the bedroom.

***

Belinda lay on her beach towel on the soft sand, soaking up the sunrays. She flipped onto her stomach. "Put some sunscreen on my back, please." She loosely held the bottle in Robert's direction.

"Do you think that would be a good idea? We might end up back in the sack again."

"Well, it's either you do it or I'll have to ask some poor schmuck walking by to help me out. You do want to get back in the bedroom sometime again on this trip? If I have a sunburn, I'll be off-limits."

He raised one side of his mouth and grabbed the bottle. "Point taken."

She sucked in a deep breath as the cold lotion hit her skin, forming a figure eight on her back. A firm hand pressed and rotated the oily liquid across her shoulders, up her spine, and her lower back. The other one joined in and they moved in harmony, working the lotion into her skin. She felt fingers reach under the back strap of her top and release the clasp. More massaging ensued. Two thumbs pressed every vertebra of her spine as they moved up and down. Skillful splayed fingers kneaded her tense muscles, working their way over her back and then toward her flanks. She moaned. The impromptu massage felt wonderful. The hands settled even with her breasts, followed by the sensation of fingers moving closer in to cup and caress them. She felt the heaviness of his chest cover over her back. He pushed the envelope a little too far for a public beach and it killed her to ask him to stop. "Robert, I think that'll be enough. Please hook the strap."

A puff of air hit her ear as the pressure of his chest lifted. When the strap reconnected, she sat up. "Care for a swim?" She thought the water might help cool down the situation.

He crinkled his brow at her and snatched up a towel, placing it over his mid-section. "Give me a minute."

She sputtered out a muffled giggle and covered her mouth.

He glared up at her, his eyes smoldering. "Belinda, that's not helping."

Her chest tightened trying to suppress her need to laugh. She pursed her lips tight. A giggle erupted out of the sides of her mouth.

He raised a brow. His eyes were like glowing embers burning through hers. The more he tried to be serious, the funnier the situation seemed. Finally, her laughter couldn't be contained and it burst out both sides of her mouth as she clinched her arms around her stomach. Seconds later, uncontrollable tears streamed down her cheeks.

"Okay. Now I've had it." He threw the towel draped across his lap to the side and lunged toward her.

She squealed and jerked out of his reach. Jumping up, she made a beeline for the water. She hit the waves, raising her knees up as high as she could with each stride, attempting to put some distance between her and Robert. She heard splashes not far behind and looked to see him in hot pursuit, his long legs reaching through the waves. The waves crashed against her in the waist-high water slowing her speed. She glanced behind to judge the distance as she felt two arms grab her around the waist and yank her under the water. She turned and pushed against strong shoulders and kicked in an attempt to free herself.

Fighting seemed futile. She went limp and he pulled the two of them to the surface. Laughter rang in the air. Waves hit them as they bobbed, struggling to stay upright. "You can't get away from me that easily." He pulled her up and kissed them.

***

The full moon rose over the water and hung in the sky, illuminating the night. Moonlight reflected on the water, touching the tips of the waves with a hint of silver as they rolled toward the shore. At high tide, the waves rushed in, consuming the beach. The closer to the deck they came, each wave lapping against the shoreline became louder, causing a gentle rhythmic sound.

Robert and Belinda sat curled in each other's arms on a lounge chair listening to the sounds of the beach while they sipped wine.

"Angel. The dress you wore to the cocktail party, did you have it before our dream and just plug it in?"

Belinda rested against Robert's shoulder and swallowed. "No. My mother bought it for me when I was in the hospital."

"Why would she buy you a dress?"

"I found it hanging in her closet when I was getting ready for the New Year's Eve party. I didn't even know she had it until then. She told me she was on the way to the hospital and saw a sale sign in the window of the shop. She could never pass up a sale, so she stopped in. She saw the dress and thought I'd look great in it."

"Belinda, you were in a coma. I don't understand."

Belinda's voice took a more serious tone. "My parents had made the decision to take me off life support. There was a good chance I would die, so as Mom saw it, there were two possibilities. One, I would wake up and live to wear the dress, or two, she would bury me in it."

Robert stopped breathing and tightened his arms around her. He lost her once already and the thought of her being gone for good reignited feelings in him that he hadn't handled well the first time. Then again, he thought he was nuts for being in love with a dream.

He rested his cheek against hers and ever so lightly swayed back and forth. "Angel, I'm glad you got to wear it. You looked as beautiful in it at the company party as you did on our wedding day. I couldn't stop staring at you when I saw you walk across the room to the table."

"Aaah. That explains why you seemed so interested in me at the party. The dress reminded you of our wedding day." She snorted. "I thought that night was very strange. But then, I just thought I was nuts."

Robert laid his mouth next to her ear. "When we got married in our dream, it was the happiest day of my life. Even if it wasn't real. Then seeing you in that dress at the party made me feel like I was back in the dream. Colin had no idea what he was doing to me when he asked me to keep you busy. Us being thrown together that way, the dress, you're favorite song being played when we got up to dance…it all caught up with me."

"You know if you'd given me any indication you would stay with me that night, I would've done anything for you."

"I know, but I'm glad you told me to take a hike. It stopped me from cheating on Karen and lying to my best friend."

Belinda turned to face Robert. "I'm glad we stopped. I couldn't hurt Colin or Karen either, but I hated you because you walked away." Belinda resumed her position resting against Robert's chest. "Besides. It gave us time to get to know each other as friends. I think we both realized neither of us wanted to cross the lines we drew for ourselves and I'm glad we didn't. Things worked out for the best."

"With the exception of Karen. I hurt her."

"I think we both did, Honey. But would it have been better if you married her?"

Robert didn't answer for a few seconds. "No, I knew it had to end."

They sat in silence. Robert wrapped his arms firmly around the woman he loved as he swayed gently from side to side under the moon-filled night.

***

Robert spent Sunday night with Belinda at her patio home and, as he predicted, exhaustion caught up with both of them. They laid wrapped in each other's arms and slept.

CHAPTER 27

ON MONDAY MORNING, the routine of life started with a quick breakfast of their staple, blueberry bagels. Robert picked up his coffee cup and bent over to give Belinda a quick peck on the lips. Her soft expression grabbed him and he placed the cup back on the table. Cupping her face, he engaged her full, soft lips giving her a longer than intended, tender kiss. She reached for his wrist and kissed him back, exciting him. He loved it when she kissed him back. He could feel a slight quiver in that lower lip of hers, which churned his insides with desire. The smallest touch from her sent him soaring. He could never put into words what he felt when she touched him. He had tried to explain it, but his words always seemed to fail.

He would've continued taking the kiss to the next level, but he stopped. He had to leave for work and so did she. He pulled back and savored the sensations her contact brought for a few seconds. "I'll see you later. Don't work too hard. Meet up at my parents for dinner and a ride?"

"I can't. Abbey, remember?"

"Oh yeah." If they met up at his parents, he would at least have a chance of ending up in her bed again. "So, I guess I'll stay at my place tonight?" She stiffened and acted as if she was thinking. One important maneuver his business sense taught him was to keep your mouth shut to give your client time to think. Of course, Belinda wasn't his client, but the same principles applied in love and war. He prayed the next words that came from her would be what he had on his mind.

"Ah. I might not be in until around ten, but I'd like it if you were here when I did come home." She swallowed and then looked at him from under her mile-long lashes. His heart melted. She had a keyless lock, but he had the combination and now an invitation.

He winked at her and a smile slid up the corners of his mouth. "I'll keep the bed warm for you." She giggled. One last peck on the nose persuaded her to release her hold. He picked up the cup, and after putting it in the sink, walked out the door.

As he stepped onto the driveway and took hold of the handle of his car, he hesitated and glanced around. The morning was quiet, the sky big and blue as only the sky in Texas could be. The air smelled fresh and he took in a good lungful. He couldn't remember the last time he actually felt this alive.

From the first time he experienced the dream with Belinda, it set him on a path to a downward spiral. As much as he craved being with her, the dream caused him to become unbalanced. He spent so much time sleeping, trying to live in their dream, that to the outside world he seemed depressed. It took a toll on his family, his work, and his social life. He fought to survive in both worlds, but had no choice in the end. By limiting the time he had slept, he managed to pull back from the dream and their life, to keep his sanity. He started dating Karen, which plunged him back into the real world, but his decision caused him to lose the only woman he loved.

He took one more deep breath and pulled the car door open. Yep, today was a great day to be alive. He had the love of his life and she was real.

***

Belinda punched the code into the pad and opened the front door. She'd had a long workday that led into dinner with Abbey. Although she loved her to death, Abbey's questions exhausted her. The thoughts of a hot bath and her comfortable bed made her sleepy just thinking about them.

The only lights in the house came from the hood over the stove and the master bedroom. They gave the place a warm glow and lit the rooms enough for her to have a clear path down the hall. She rounded the corner of the entry and stepped into the kitchen. Placing her purse on the counter along the wall, she noticed a new red rose with a note attached.

"For my Angel."

Hand-drawn hearts surrounded the words. Belinda traced the lines of the tiny symbols of love on the paper. "He's real," slid softly over her lips. She looked down the hall toward the bedroom. Giving the rose a quick sniff, she placed it in the vase with its older brother and then switched off the light over the stove.

Robert looked up from the magazine article he'd been reading and watched Belinda climb onto the bed. She curled up and snuggled against him as he wrapped an arm around her and pulled her close. Hi, Angel. How's Abbey?"

"Exhausting as ever. That girl just has too much energy. It isn't right for someone to be that way at any time of day." Belinda let out a big sigh.

Robert tightened his hold as she nestled closer. "Angel?"

"Hmmm." Belinda closed her heavy eyelids. Her bed and Robert's radiating heat were just too inviting. Sleep overcame her.

She felt the bed rock from side to side. Her feet were freed from her shoes, followed by a thump sound that annoyed her ears. The zipper slid down and her pants slipped over her hips, then freeing her legs. Fingers unbuttoned her blouse and warm lips placed a kiss on her stomach just before she lifted into a sitting position. Her arms were helped out of the blouse. Fingers unlatched the clasp of her bra as her head rested comfortably against a shoulder. Fingers brushed softly over her left breast but the sensation only lasted a second before her head and arms were guided into a t-shirt. Lastly, Belinda remembered the softness of the pillow under her head as a smooth sheet and comforter floated over her body.

The warmth of Robert wrapping around her made her feel safe. A whispered voice puffed out the words into her ear, "Good night, Angel," as she drifted off into a deep sleep. She would need her rest in order to repeat another workday and night of questions and answers as she ate dinner with her parents on Tuesday.

***

Four months passed and during that time, Robert and Belinda were inseparable. Most nights after work, they had spent time with their horses and listened to music while they worked around the stable. Inevitably, Belinda would make her way into Robert's arms and they would dance on the dirt floor of the barn.

After dinner, the pair retreated to Belinda's patio home. Robert and she felt more comfortable there. They were close enough to both sets of parents, yet far enough away from well-meaning, but possible parental interference.

Slowly Robert's residence, on his parents' estate, became void of his personal belongings. Belinda gladly made room for her boyfriend and lover. She gave him the walk-in closet in the empty third bedroom. The only storage for his folded clothes became the floor of the same room. In the morning, Robert would rummage through the stacks of clothes that lined the walls. The dresser from the guesthouse belonged to that bedroom suit, so moving it was not an option.

Early one Saturday morning, while the couple lay in bed slowly waking up, the doorbell rang. Robert sprang out of bed, rushed to put on some clothes, and then vanished from the bedroom, closing the door behind him. Belinda yawned and fell back to sleep.

Voices and bumping sounds from the hallway forced her to wake up. She listened for a few seconds. She heard Robert but couldn't identify the voice of the second man. She jumped up and scurried around to find something suitable to wear. The grunts and groans seemed louder as she approached the door. "What the hell?" Slowly she opened the door to find Robert and a deliveryman struggling with a six-drawer dresser. Robert had his back to her as she leaned against the doorjamb of the master bedroom. The two men were trying to make the corner into the third bedroom.

"We have to be careful. I don't want to nick the walls or woodwork. My girlfriend will kill me if we do," Robert instructed the deliveryman.

Belinda crossed her arms, and raised a brow, as she glared at the deliveryman. He stopped assisting with the progression of the dresser. Robert held the tilted dresser against his shoulder. Belinda quietly watched. He seemed to realize he carried the brunt of the dresser as he shifted his weight. He peered over the top edge of the beast to find the deliveryman offering little support, his eyes fixed on something. "My girlfriend is behind me, isn't she?" The man just nodded. In a flash, Robert spun his head around sporting his signature smile of perfect teeth. "Hi, Angel. I'm kinda busy right now, but I'll explain after this nice gentleman leaves."

Belinda pursed her lips and, with a flip of her hair, stomped back into the bedroom. Through the walls, she heard a bit more huffing and puffing. Muffled voices came from the hallway, followed by the closing of the front door. She walked toward the kitchen. As she passed the spare bedroom, she glanced at the dresser that now sat in the middle of the floor.

She popped a K-cup into the coffeemaker as Robert appeared around the corner. "So what do you think?"

"What do I think about what?" Belinda rested her butt against the island with her arms crossed in front of her.

"The dresser."

"Why ask me now? You apparently made your decision." She raised her brow.

Robert walked over and placed his hands on her waist. "I guess I should've discussed it with you first."

Belinda huffed. "That might have been your first move."

"Look, I'm sorry. I can call on Monday and have it picked up if you want me to."

She didn't know why he said that...oh yes she did! It was his way of softening her up. She glared at him. "You know damn well that's not going to happen and that dresser is here to stay."

Robert froze for a moment, and then his mouth turned into a smile. "I love you when you lay down the law." He tugged her close and she melted into his embrace, flopping her arms over his shoulders and around his neck. She couldn't stay mad at him no matter how hard she tried.

"Angel, I needed someplace to put my clothes. The piles on the floor are getting old." He put a little distance between them and shrugged.

She just nodded, agreeing the dresser was be a better solution.

***

By the fifth month, Robert had completely moved in and taken over the third bedroom. He had lined one wall with bookshelves from floor to ceiling. A couple of comfortable man-size chairs facing a flat-screen TV also managed to steer their way into the "mini-man cave." Belinda kept the second bedroom as her study and studio. It seemed to be a good compromise.

On Saturday, the day before Christmas Eve, Robert made reservations at upscale restaurant in the Sugar Land Town Center. The steakhouse had an elegant, quiet atmosphere, the type of place where you didn't feel rushed by the waitstaff to finish a meal. The couple could sit and talk all night enjoying their meal and each other's company. It would be the perfect place for him to execute his plan.

Robert finished dressing, and sat in the living room waiting for her. She usually managed to be on time but today it took her longer. He walked to the closed bedroom door and tried to turn the doorknob. It didn't open. He rapped with a knuckle on the door. "Angel, are you almost ready?" Robert couldn't figure out what could take her so long. She had spent the last hour and a-half locked in their bedroom.

"I'm almost ready. I'll be out in a minute. Go back into the living room," he heard through the door. He let out a sigh and had no choice but to go wait. He sat on the couch and felt like a high school kid sitting next to the hovering father of his date, minus the father of course. His nerves started to grate on him. Tonight had to be perfect. He had a lot riding on this evening.

The sound of the click from the lock on the bedroom door caused him to raise his head toward the hall. Belinda floated out into the glowing light of the living room Christmas tree. At first, he couldn't move or say a word. He could only stare.

"Robert, say something. Do I look alright?" She twirled around in a light blue, chiffon dress.

Robert stumbled over his words. "You…you look terrific." He stood and walked toward her. "Is that the same dress you wore on New Year's Eve and to the Spring Formal in our dream?"

"Yep. I had Mom shorten it for me." She swished the skirt from side to side. "I remembered how much you liked it in our dream."

Her hair fell softly over her shoulders but she had it pulled up at the sides. "I wanted to look special for our special night." Her fingers toyed with a single diamond drop at her slender neck.

Robert held Belinda's upper arms. He slid his wanton lips up her shoulder to her ear and felt her quiver as she took in a deep breath. "You know what this dress does to me. I can cancel the reservation and peel it off of you right now," he whispered as he pulled his phone from his jacket pocket and waved it.

He felt her stiffen as she swung her head around until her luscious mouth came within an inch of his. "You put that thing away, take my arm, and walk straight out that door." She nodded in the direction of the foyer.

He smiled. "There's my little lawmaker. Do you think you'll need a coat? It is December."

She tightened her lips. "I forgot about that," she huffed before disappearing into the bedroom. Seconds later, she returned with a black velvet cape draped over her arm.

Robert took it from her and placed it over her, running his hands softly down her shoulders, and then her arms. At the same time, he leaned in close to her back and rubbed his lips against her ear. Her breathing quickened as she molded herself to him. "I can still cancel the reservation," floated out of his mouth.

To his surprise, she didn't move. She stayed pressed against him, as she fastened the cape at her neck. Her breathing shortened and her breasts heaved as she continued to meld against him.

He didn't expect her reaction. She had been so excited about tonight, he didn't think any amount of sexual teasing would deter her. Now he wasn't sure and felt he may have ruined the evening by taking it too far. He held his breath and waited, praying he hadn't derailed his plans.

"Not on your life. I've waited all week for tonight." She stomped the heel of her silver shoe and flipped her hair as she turned to look at him. Belinda raised her arms to encircle his neck. She leaned in close and brushed her lips over his ear. "But after we get back...." He heard her smack her lips. "You can do anything you want with me." She broke away and took a couple of steps, looking back at him. His mouth dropped open. She placed her fingertips under his chin. "Here, let me close that for you."

***

Robert walked behind Belinda and a sense of pride swelled within him as the patrons turned to admire his date. Men and women alike took notice.

The hostess led them to a table in a quiet corner of the restaurant. As soon as they were seated, several waitstaff appeared and offered them water, gave them their menus, took their bar order, and recited the specials for the evening. As quickly as they appeared, they vanished like a swarm of honeybees buzzing on to their next flowering bush.

Their drinks arrived and the waiter took their order. Robert lifted his glass to Belinda. "To a beautiful lady who fills my heart and life." She smiled and her glass met his, making a clinking sound.

"And to a wonderful man who completes me." Another clink followed. Belinda lifted her glass to her lips and then took a sip of her wine, zinfandel of course.

Belinda glanced over her shoulder to a table directly behind them. She turned back and pressed her lips to her glass about to take another sip when the room started to spin—slowly at first. She put her drink down. She stared straight ahead and watched Robert fade away into a blur. Her chest tightened and her breathing shallowed so much she thought she would pass out from the lack of oxygen. The spinning sped up. She reached for Robert's hands and held on, digging her nails into his flesh. A stabbing pain penetrated her brain from temple to temple. She gritted her teeth wishing the spinning would stop. And it did, just as it had so many times before. Like a roulette wheel, the blur around her slowed and chunks of a memory began to fall into place.

When the spinning stopped completely, Robert came back into focus.

His expression was one of horror. "Belinda, are you okay?" His voice sounded shaky.

Belinda forced herself to concentrate. She hadn't had a memory episode in months and this one came on faster than any of the others. She couldn't talk at first. She just put her head down and attempted to fill her lungs with long deep breaths. She never let go of Robert but did ease up on her grip.

Finally, she looked up. "This is where it all started."

Robert knitted his brows. "Are you okay? What started?"

"Us. This is where I first saw you." She raised her pitch and talked quickly as if she wouldn't have enough time to say everything she had floating around in her head. "I was sitting where you are. You were at the table over there." She pointed to the table she had glanced at earlier. "You caught me staring at you, then you started staring at me. You were the most gorgeous guy I had ever seen and I couldn't stop watching you. I tried to hide and let my hair cover my face. I thought you wouldn't notice my glances if I hid, but that didn't stop you. You just kept looking at me." Her words came fast until she dragged a breath and stopped talking.

"Should we leave?" Concern filled his voice.

Belinda remembered—Robert had never witnessed a memory episode. The first one her mother saw almost had Belinda in the car and on her way to the emergency room. "Oh, Robert. I'm sorry. You must be scared to death." She looked at the indentions her nails had made. "Oh my God! Did I hurt you?"

"No. Look you didn't even draw blood." He flipped them over and then rubbed at the marks. "I'm just worried about you. Will you be alright?"

"Yes. I'll be fine." She waved attempting to dismiss how it really felt—confused and elated all at the same time. She smiled to herself. *Very much like sex.*

She ran a finger over a nail indent. "You sure I didn't hurt you?"

"No, I'm fine."

With spread fingers, she gently placed them over Robert's. "Okay. Now let me finish telling you about this memory."

CHAPTER 28

BELINDA SHIFTED IN her seat and bounced forward, leaning over the table toward Robert. She tugged on his hands, which signaled him to do the same. She had recovered from the memory episode and with her adrenaline rush lowered, she calmed down.

"I was home for summer break after completing my sophomore year of college and because I made good grades, my parents decided to treat me to a fancy dinner. The hostess seated my family at this table. Your family was already seated at that one." She tilted her head back toward it. He looked in the direction she indicated.

The expression on his face told Belinda he was trying to remember. He moved his head in small motions from side to side. His eyebrows knitted closely together. "Belinda I'm sorry, but I don't remember."

"That's okay. I wouldn't expect you to. This happened years ago and I wasn't much to look at back then anyway. The dinner took place before I matured physically and my mother forced me out of my cocoon."

Belinda rolled her eyes. "But boy did you make an impression on me." She feigned a swoon covering her heart, patting over it.

"At first I gave you a few fleeting glances, but the more I watched you, the more you drew me in. I was fascinated by the way you moved and the few subtle inflections of your voice I could hear. I found myself just flat out staring, but when you caught me watching, you flashed me that smile of yours and I was in love."

She adjusted herself and drew in a breath, focusing back on Robert. "In that split second...I imagined a life with you. I had us in love, married, raising children, and sitting on a porch in rocking chairs growing old together."

Her eyes moistened. She raised her lids and fanned at her tears. After all, she didn't want mascara running down her cheeks. The memory episode had been enough drama and fortunately, Robert appeared to be the only one in the restaurant who knew anything had happened.

She leaned forward again, this time planting her hands on the table to emphasize her next point. "Now it gets better." She widened her eyes. "I'm over here falling in love with you, when you get distracted by a petite blonde dressed in a perfectly fitted, pink suit, white pumps and matching purse, but the way she was dressed isn't important."

Robert snorted. "Seems to have been if you remembered all that."

Belinda narrowed her brows and then waved him off. "Let me get back to the story." She took a breath. "It was Karen with her father. He called your dad by his full name. All I heard was 'Pen.' I never got the last part."

Robert's mouth opened and he looked dumbfounded.

"Honey, your mouth is open again."

He dropped his head for a second, shook it, and then stared up at her as a sweeping smile crossed his face. "I remember that. It was a Sunday afternoon. She and her dad had just finished lunch and came over to say hello." His smile grew wider. "I remember you now."

His expression became more serious while he recalled the memory. "My parents took me out to eat before my flight back to school for the summer session. I was starting my master's degree. I had just graduated from Brownston University and had been home visiting with them for a few days."

She rested back against her chair and let out a sigh. *He remembered me.*

"And you're right, you weren't much to look at then." He let out a smothered snicker.

"Robert!" She smacked his hand.

"Well, you're the one who said it first."

She made her eyes squint and glared at him to let him know she didn't appreciate his last comment, although she agreed. She knew she had lacked in the attractiveness department, but hearing the words come out of his mouth struck her in the heart a bit too hard.

She let it go and moved on. "You don't get it do you?"

"No...Oh yeah, I think I do. That's how I got plugged into our dream. I remember I took Karen's arm to lead her a little bit away from the table to talk. I glanced over at you and you were watching us. Your face looked sad, almost like you would cry. It threw me a bit because I realized, in some way, I had hurt you."

"My fantasy about you had hit a brick wall. At that moment I knew I wasn't your type and a girl like me would never in a millions years have a chance to date someone like you." She heard the sadness reflect in her voice. Robert must have as well. He reached over and stroked her cheek.

The buzzing around of the waitstaff erupted as their food rolled up on a cart. One waiter cut their meat into slices, and then served it, while another filled the wine glasses. Everything they needed to complete a leisurely meal magically appeared before the waiters retreated. In the background, the soft soothing music of a violin filtered through the dining area.

Robert wasted no time picking up the conversation where they left off as soon as they were alone. "Belinda. You affected me as well. Something about the way you looked at me intrigued me. I remember how graceful and beautiful you were."

Belinda scoffed. "You must've had your glasses off."

"I didn't need glasses. I saw what lay beneath that long, straight hair. I saw your big, blue eyes occasionally peek out at me, and they grabbed me." He made a fist and placed it over his heart.

"Now you're just trying to save your rear. Go ahead. You can take your foot out of your mouth. I'm not stupid."

Robert frowned. "Okay. You believe whatever you want." He tapped his chest with his finger as he leaned in. "I know I'm telling the truth."

Belinda could see his miffed expression, but how could he blame her. Back then, she knew he would've never asked her out even if she were the last female alive.

The conversation had run its course and she decided to change the subject. She cut a piece of her pork chop and took a bite. She sat there chewing and thinking. She washed her food down with a sip of wine. "You know, since I only got part of your last name at the restaurant. I bet that's why I had it wrong in our dream. I just used what I remembered then filled in the blanks."

"What about the magazine article you saw. Our names were in it."

She had just taken another bite of food. She sat and thought about what he said until she swallowed. "I must have just scanned the article or didn't remember. Apparently the pictures and your first names were what caught my attention." She let out a sigh. "What's important is I remembered a big chunk of something I had forgotten." She sat and reviewed her memories, how bits and pieces had returned over the past year. "You know, I think the only mystery left is how you lived my dream with me."

"Yep. That's a mystery we may never solve." He lifted his glass toward her and she did the same until the rims of the glasses touched making a clinking sound. "To our unsolved mystery."

"Our unsolved mystery." She returned the toast.

The rest of the meal chat focused on a wide spectrum of topics. They never came back to the memory the episode stirred up. Belinda figured all that could be discussed had been. During their conversational lapses, she lost track of time.

At one point, she scanned the room and realized they were the only customers left. Several of the waitstaff leaned against walls with their arms folded in front of them.

She opened her mouth about to suggest they leave when the violinist appeared at their table. The violin's tone sang their song, "Forever in My Mind." With every upward and downward motion of the bow, the melody floated on the air in soft notes. She reached over and took hold of Robert's watch. It read five minutes after midnight, Christmas Eve morning. A little twinge of excitement caused a stir in her belly.

Belinda noticed movement from the staff. They walked over and formed a semi-circle around the violinist. Just as they completed their formation, Robert pushed away from the table. Belinda watched him fiddle with something in his pocket. Now that little twinge grew into an erupting volcano. He came around to her side of the table, went down on one knee, and pulled a small, black velvet box from his pocket. Belinda stopped breathing as she concentrated on the man she loved kneeling before her.

Robert opened the box and presented it. "Ms. Belinda Davies, would you do me the honor of becoming my wife?"

Belinda gasped and then held her breath. She reached for the box that held a three-stoned diamond ring. "It looks like the one in our dream," she said as air passed through her words. With a light touch of her finger, she rubbed over the stones and then took the ring from the box and held it up. The halogen lights made the diamonds dance as she rotated it in her fingers. "Is it your mother's?" She glanced up at Robert and saw him nod. Her gaze fell back upon the ring as she continued to admire and play with it. "Your mother got this from her mother, your grandmother?" She glanced back at

Robert. He nodded. She went back to her fixation on the ring. Seconds passed. Robert clearing his throat made her look at the patient man kneeling in front of her.

"Well?"

"Oh!" Belinda inhaled as she realized she hadn't given Robert an answer. A smile swept across her face. "Yes, I'll marry you." A tear rolled from the corner of her eye down her cheek, followed by another and then another as he took the ring and slipped it onto her finger.

"I love you, Ms. Davies."

"And I love you, Mr. Pendleton."

Robert rose, lifted Belinda to her feet, and twirled her around, squeezing her at the waist as he planted a kiss on her willing lips.

She flung her arms around his neck while the violinist continued playing their song in the background. Over the melody, the restaurant staff burst into a clamor of cheers and applause. Belinda wasn't sure if their jubilation was in congratulations for their new engagement or that now they would finally be able to go home.

***

On the car ride home, Belinda held her left hand in front of her and watched the ring sparkle from the dim light of the streetlights. She loved to watch the light jump through the perfectly cut gems. The streaks of color mesmerized her.

Robert asked, "How did you know about the ring in our dream."

"Your mother was wearing it in the picture of the three of you sitting in the family room in the magazine article and I just assumed it was an heirloom."

"Do you remember your promise to me before we left tonight?"

A half-grin slithered across Belinda's mouth. "Oh yes I do."

"Good. I was just checking."

***

Belinda and Robert entered the patio home. She started to walk through the foyer toward the great room fully expecting Robert to release her hand as she continued on, but he didn't. She snapped back on the ball of her foot as he tightened his grip. As she turned toward Robert, his eyes turned lustful and the crystal blue color magically darkened to teal. His facial expression told her how he planned to complete their night.

He tugged her to him and released the clasp on her cape. "Don't move.

Keep your hands to your side." Memories of the fraternity Spring Formal from the dream flowed into her mind and she did as he asked.

He ran his fingertips under the cape until they found the nape of her neck. She swallowed hard while she watched him concentrate on his actions. He moved his fingers softly over her shoulders, causing the black velvet to slip off and puddle at their feet, and then he held her by her upper arms. He never looked at her face, but studied her until his soft mouth brushed against her neck. She felt his warm breath as he ran his lips over her skin. He flicked her with the tip of his tongue mixed with little nibbles, occasionally just brushing his lips against her. Her heart galloped and she bit her lower lip as her back arched, anticipating his next move. He moved slowly to her side and locked her arms behind her as he gripped her wrists. With his other, he explored her body, igniting every nerve in her. She loved it when he touched her. The touch of his fingers sent electric impulses through her, making her want more of him. She leaned back into his hand clasping her wrist. Her breathing became shallow as her head fell back and she moaned.

She remembered her promise to Robert, one that would not be the least bit hard to keep.

CHAPTER 29

BELINDA BENT DOWN and picked up her light blue, strapless, chiffon dress and velvet cape lying in a pile on the foyer floor. Walking back toward the dining area, she straightened the crumpled masses of fabric and shook them out before laying each piece over one of the chairs around the table. The next task on her agenda—make a hot cup of coffee. She turned to walk across the kitchen and saw a vase sitting in the middle of the counter with one single red rose. No card this time, but it made her smile. *When did he do this? I was with him all night.*

She cupped the bud and brushed the soft petals with her fingertips, taking a whiff. Robert had thought of everything and like its predecessors, when dried, this one too would find its way into the box, which held all her dried roses.

She remembered Robert's endearing expression the first time he discovered a drying rose in the laundry room hanging from the cabinet knob. "Wait. Don't tell me. It's for your treasure box. Like I didn't know that already." He let out a grunt. His reaction reminded her why she fell in love with the man.

Steam rose from the cup of hot coffee. The heat radiated through the cup, warming her hands, chilled from the cool morning air, as she settled down on the couch.

Due to their sexual preoccupation with each other, the lights on the Christmas tree remained lit from the night before. Their glow, the only light in the semi-dark room, made the atmosphere warm and cozy. To add to the ambiance and ward off the chill, Belinda lit a fire in the fireplace. She made herself comfortable on the couch nearest the tree and took a sip of coffee. She loved the early mornings. She liked the way the light slowly filled each room as the sun rose higher in the sky. A quiet morning like this gave her a few stolen moments for herself.

She placed the cup on the end table. A flicker of light from her ring finger caught her attention and she held it up in front of her. The diamonds came alive in the dim light, showing off the V-shaped, multi-colored facets.

"I'm going to be Mrs. Robert Pendleton," brushed across her lips.

Although the ring resembled the one in their dream, the real version seemed to be more intense. Everything in her "New Reality" seemed more intense—Robert's touch, how she responded to him, their lovemaking. Even Abbey seemed higher-strung—as if that were possible. She felt a slight smirk come across her face.

Robert's walking out of the hallway disrupted her serenity. He rubbed the back of his neck and yawned out a lazy, "Good morning," before disappearing into the kitchen.

Even in the morning, when his appearance was the most unkempt, she found him sexy as hell. She loved his stubble, his unruly hair, how his t-shirt clung to his chest, and how his flannel pajama bottoms hung on his hips.

Belinda propped her feet on the coffee table and picked up her cup. A muffled shuffle from the kitchen told her Robert would be on his way out to join her.

"What are you doing up? I figured after last night you would've wanted to sleep in." He plopped down beside her, careful not to spill his hot coffee.

She studied him. "Well, I could ask you the same thing."

He snorted. "I rolled over and felt around for you, but the bed was cold and empty. So I came to hunt down the future Mrs. Pendleton." He took a sip of coffee and let out a spurt of air. "Hot. Hot."

"Careful, Honey." She took another sip of her cooling coffee. "I like the quiet of the mornings and I don't get to enjoy too many anymore. Before a certain someone moved into my life, I had lots of them." She elbowed him softly in the ribs.

"Oh. Do I interfere?"

"Of course you do, but I wouldn't have it any other way. If I had a choice between all the time I spent without you and having you with me...well, I think you know which one I'd prefer."

He placed his arm around her shoulders and she snuggled against his chest. They sat sipping coffee in silence, basking in the warmth of the fireplace, waiting for the soft sunlight to fill the rooms.

Eventually they ended up back in bed and asleep. They had nothing to do until their expected arrival at his parents' home for dinner that evening. The gathering would include Belinda's parents.

Since everyone needed to report for work on Tuesday morning, the day after Christmas, the gift exchange would take place on Christmas Eve with dinner served afterward.

***

The minute Robert opened the front door of the Pendleton home, Sandra and Dora hurried into the foyer and hovered around Belinda.

"Let me see it." Sandra lifted Belinda's hand and gently moved it from side to side. She stepped aside so Dora could admire her daughter's new present.

"Oh Honey, it's beautiful. Have you talked about a date yet?"

Belinda panned between the two most important women in her life. "No, I just got it a few hours ago. I…We haven't had time."

Sandra placed an arm around Belinda's waist and Dora did the same as they ushered her sandwiched between them, toward the family room, talking to each other as they tossed ideas of wedding plans back and forth. Belinda looked over her shoulder at Robert and mouthed, *Help me.*

Robert knew this was a battle not worth fighting and offered his bride-to-be no help. He stood there with one hand tucked into his pocket and shrugged. With the other, he feigned a half-wave. "Hi, Mom. Dora."

His greeting to the elder women went unnoticed. He took in Belinda's pitiful expression moving away from him and wished he could do something to save her. He gave her a salute and whispered, "Good luck," just before he turned on his heels and disappeared into the dining room.

Robert ducked through the butler's pantry into the kitchen. Rob and James were standing by the peninsula sipping drinks and watching the captivity of Belinda unfold.

"Hi, Dad. Mr. Davies." He nodded.

James gave a throaty chuckle. "I think you can call me James or Dad, whichever you prefer, now that you're part of the family."

Robert took James' hand and gave a manly shake. "Thanks, Dad."

"Robert, interested in a drink?" Rob asked. "Your usual?"

Robert nodded and glanced into the great room. "She's their prisoner now."

The three men all let out a mixture of snorts, grunts and ah ha's.

Rob offered Robert a glass of scotch on the rocks.

Robert rolled the cubes against the side of the glass before taking a stiff swallow. "Do you think I should step in to save her?"

"Son, let them be. She'll be fine. She knows how to handle her mother. Besides, the more they're preoccupied, the less they bother us. A little something you'll need to learn. Always let them think they're getting their way." James nodded toward Robert. "You'll learn soon enough it makes for a great marriage."

"He's right. I love your mother to death, but sometimes…." Rob looked at Robert. "You know how she gets when she's on a mission."

Robert rolled his eyes and nodded.

Rob nudged his son. "You'll figure it out."

James spoke up. "Rob, you have a fine young man here. You did a good job raising him. You know he came over about a week ago and asked my permission to marry my daughter."

Robert saw his father's half-smile. "Well, thank you. I'm proud of how he turned out and I'm glad you're giving me some of the credit."

The conversation drifted to the latest football victory, losses, and potential playoff scenarios. Eventually it moved on to recent newsworthy topics. Robert positioned himself so he had a clear view of the three women sitting on the couch in the great room. Belinda remained sandwiched between her mother and his. He swore she hadn't said a word or most likely the pair hadn't given her a chance.

It appeared they had planned their attack beforehand. Sandra came armed with a binder loaded with blank pieces of paper. While she and Dora talked, Sandra made notes. Robert knew what that meant. He had seen this side of his mother on numerous occasions. She was in party-planning mode.

"Robert. We're going into the den. I taped the Dallas-Washington game. We're going to kick back, have a drink, and smoke a cigar. Care to join us?"

Robert focused on his father. "I'll meet up with you later. I think I need to get her out of there for a bit." He nodded in Belinda's direction. "Dad, make sure you close those doors and turn on the vent. You don't want Mom—"

Rob interrupted with a half-grin and a wave. "Trust me. I know how to stay on your mother's good side. Besides, she's trained me well." He raised his eyebrows up and down.

Another low laugh erupted as the older men retreated through the butler's pantry to avoid the women in the great room. Robert heard his dad ask James, "Do you play golf?" as they turned into the dining room and made their way across the foyer to the den.

Robert rested against the counter and finished his drink. He put the glass down and walked toward the henpecking session taking place on the couch. His approach went unnoticed and the two older women never skipped a beat as they continued to talk, with Sandra taking a myriad of notes. They only stopped when Robert leaned over Belinda's shoulder and spoke. "Ladies, I'm going to steal my future wife away. There's something I need to show her."

He heard Belinda let out a sigh as if she'd been sitting there holding her breath the entire time. When he touched her, he felt her tension ease. He whispered in her ear, "Come on. Let's get out of here."

In that second she shot to her feet, waving frantically through the air. "You ladies continue this and fill me in later." She turned toward the door and ran for it.

Her speedy departure took Robert off-guard. It took him a few moments to register that she had almost made her way across the room. Taking widened steps, he caught up and reached for the handle to the patio door, opening it.

Belinda didn't wait for him and darted through her escape route. He saw a coat draped across one of the kitchen chairs and grabbed it, and then raced after her. She stepped out from under the covered patio as Robert dove for her shoulder. He pulled her back and she twirled around before she landed in his arms. "Slow down, Angel." He stroked her hair and she buried her face in his chest.

She looked up and he saw the most pitiful puppy-dog expression peering at him. "Can we just elope?"

Robert gave out a huffy, muffled laugh that forced air out of his nose. "Let them have this. If they want to plan, let them. We'll set limits when necessary on the important stuff, like the budget, invitations, the dress, our vows." He lifted her chin and placed a quick kiss on her mouth.

"But you haven't heard half of what they were planning. It'll be a three-ring circus," she said.

"Come on. We're stronger than both of them together. You know how to say 'no'. I know you do. You tell me 'no' all the time."

A faint smile swept across her face.

"We'll sit down and lay out some ground rules for them. Then we'll just have to make sure they stick to them and we have the final say on what we want to control. Okay?"

Belinda smiled and nodded.

"Besides, I think I'd like the biggest wedding we can manage."

Belinda scrunched her nose and pulled her head back.

"Ah. I see you need an explanation."

"An explanation would be nice," she said.

Robert gave Belinda's nose a soft tap. "You missed out on a big wedding the first time and since this is the last time I plan on marrying you…I want to remember it. Is that a good enough explanation?"

"Yes." She pushed the center of his chest with a forceful finger. "But if they get out of line, I pull the plug. Agreed?"

"Agreed."

Robert tilted his head in the direction of the barn. "Come on. I have something to show you."

He helped her slip on the coat, and then held her hand as they walked across the lawn.

The barn door creaked from the strain of the rollers as Robert pushed it aside to gain access to the interior. He ducked inside to flip on the lights and turned to see Belinda squinting from the glare.

"Come on. What I want to show you is over here." He led her to the back stall, the one the family used for tack.

Just before they entered, he turned toward Belinda and blocked the view with his muscular form. "Close your eyes."

Belinda did as he asked.

He held her by the forearms and maneuvered her inside the stall. The smell of new leather filled his nostrils. He saw her head tilt up as her cute nose sniffed at the air. Her graceful, subtle movements were one of the things he loved about her and he wished he could freeze this moment in time.

"What did you want to show me?"

He stood behind her and maneuvered her into the best vantage point. He leaned into her back and whispered, "Open your eyes."

He couldn't see her but could hear her gasp.

"Robert…" She walked forward and stroked the leather of the new English saddle with the big red bow. "It's beautiful."

He stepped closer. "So you like it?"

Belinda spun around and flung her arms around his neck. She showered him with tiny kisses. He tightened his grip around her and found her warm moist lips. Her reaction told him all he needed. *Yeah. She likes it.* He lifted her off her feet and continued the kiss while he carried her back into the corridor of the barn. He steadied her on her feet and released her from the kiss. From his pocket, he pulled out his phone and punched a few buttons until the barn filled with a melodious sound. Stepping away, he bowed. "May I have this dance?"

She giggled, fell back into his arms, and they glided around the dirt floor.

***

Belinda handed Robert the last serving dish to place in the upper cabinet. His extra height gave him an advantage over her in that respect. After dinner, they buried themselves in the kitchen clean up to get away from the Christmas gathering turned wedding planning session. As he closed the door, their parents entered the kitchen.

"Sweetie, we're going to leave. We'll talk more in a few days." Belinda's mother reached over and gave her a kiss on the cheek.

Belinda saw her mother's face light up. In that second, Belinda realized she hadn't seen her this happy in years. The joy she saw convinced her Robert's idea to let the moms plan their hearts out was the right way to go. She leaned into her mother and gave her a kiss back. "In a few days."

Rob and Sandra escorted the Davies' to the front door, and then returned to the kitchen.

"Mom, Dad, I guess we'll get going as well." Robert folded the dishtowel and placed it on the counter.

Belinda felt Robert put his arm around her waist. She noticed Sandra's frown as she entwined her arm around Rob's.

"Is something wrong?" Belinda looked at Sandra and then to Rob.

Rob rubbed his chin. "Ah." He placed his hand over his wife's. "Can you two hang around? Um…we have something we'd like to talk to you about."

Belinda felt uneasy by Rob's request. Robert gave her a tug at her waist. "Is that okay with you," he asked.

"Yeah. I don't mind."

Rob pointed to the kitchen table. "Let's sit in here. Can I get anyone something to drink before we get started?" Everyone placed their order and then nestled around the table. Rob and Sandra sat on one side with Belinda and Robert facing them.

Belinda wrung her hands as her head filled with questions of what could be so serious that her future in-laws needed to talk about it. She reached for her drink, but put it down as Rob started talking.

"Your mother and I have a confession."

Belinda turned toward Robert. Up to this point, Robert didn't act concerned. Now his brows knitted and he sat upright in his chair, staring at his father.

"Robert, Belinda. Sandra and I went out of our way to push you two together."

Robert let out a puff of air.

Belinda let her eyes roll. "We know that. You two didn't hide it very well." She chuckled under her breath.

Rob and Sandra exchanged glances. "Belinda, honey, we manipulated you. But it was for your own good," Sandra chimed in.

"I don't understand." Belinda's mind searched to make sense of her statement. *Manipulated?* "How?"

"Sandra hired you when we knew Robert would be gone for a few weeks, then I talked you into bringing Beau here because we wanted you to feel comfortable being around us before Robert came home."

Belinda bounced her glances from Rob to Sandra. She didn't know just how to react to what they were trying to tell her. "I don't understand why you'd do that."

Sandra spoke first. "Because you two belonged together." She reached over and took Belinda's hands. "From the first time I shook your hand the day I came over to your house, I knew you were going to marry Robert. I felt it in my soul the second I touched you. Rob felt it too, when he shook yours at the cocktail party. After that, we knew we had to do something to move you two along."

Robert started to say something but Sandra cut him off. "We had to do something." She flipped her wrist in Robert's direction. "You were running from her at every opportunity."

Robert just stared at his mother.

Sandra continued. "Belinda, you've noticed how Rob and I just know what the other wants without saying a word. I know you've seen us pass something to each other when we're in the kitchen or when I pick up the phone before it rings and Rob is on the other end."

Belinda nodded.

"Well, in time, you and Robert will start doing the same thing. You have a deep connection to each other. When you touch each other, is the feeling like nothing you've ever experienced?"

Belinda and Robert exchanged a glance. They both nodded as they turned back to Sandra and Rob's anticipating look.

"It's the same connection Rob and I have. The same connection Rob's mother and father had and his grandparents. That's why we pushed. I hope you can understand why we interfered and can forgive us."

Belinda slowly turned toward Robert. He returned her gaze. They both let out a muffled laugh then turned back to his now confused parents.

"Mom, Dad. We have a story for you."

Two hours later Robert and Belinda finished their recounting of her "Old Reality" and their "Dream Reality."

"We haven't been able to figure out why and how I was able to enter her dream. We even talked to her doctor to see if he had any idea, but he couldn't help and his research into the matter has led nowhere."

"Okay, here's a thought," Sandra added. "Belinda, you said the first time you remembered seeing Robert was at the restaurant."

"Yes that's right."

"Did you feel connected to him?" Sandra asked.

"I knew he was the most handsome guy I had ever seen and I couldn't keep my eyes off of him."

"Anything else?"

Belinda searched her memories. "In the span of that meal, I planned a lifetime with him." She reached for Robert's hand. "That is until Karen and her father showed up."

Sandra scoffed. "Even back then she was a problem. Anyway, she's gone now and good riddance." She looked at Belinda. "Don't you see? Your first meeting was the foundation for your 'Dream Reality.' That's what you called it, right?"

"Okay, maybe our first encounter and seeing the pictures of your family in the magazine, the ones now hanging in your office, could explain how I put Robert into my dream, but that still doesn't explain how Robert experienced it?"

Sandra's attention turned toward Robert. "What did you feel when you saw Belinda the first time?"

Robert rubbed his fingers over his mouth. He placed his arm around his fiancée and pulled her closer. "I thought she was cute. She fascinated me and I enjoyed flirting with her. Karen and her dad changed the mood. After that, Belinda and her parents left. So, if we connected, I can't say."

Belinda saw disappointment on Sandra's face, as if she were hoping he'd had a deeper connection with her at the restaurant. A hushed "Oh," escaped Sandra's lips.

Belinda's breaths became short. The room started a slow spin. "Robert!" She grabbed for his hand. His fingers crushed in over hers just as the spinning accelerated. Everything around blurred as she became unaware of her surroundings.

Feeling a hard surface press against her temple, Belinda batted her eyes open. She realized she had passed out briefly. Her head ached. As she sat up, she caught a glimpse of concern on her in-laws' face. "How long was I out?" She rubbed the sides of her head.

"A few seconds. Are you okay?" Robert asked.

"I'll be better once my head stops throbbing." She buried it in her hands. "Did you explain what was happening?"

"I told them."

She lifted her head and peered at Sandra through her hair hanging down. Rob had his arm around Sandra. The expression on her face was sheer shock.

"Are you sure you're okay?" Sandra reached over and patted her arm.

Belinda straightened and sucked air in through her teeth. "Yeah, I'm fine but better yet, I remembered something. I was in your car the night of the accident."

"Angel, we know that's impossible."

"No. You had on a light blue Oxford shirt and your tie was loose around your neck. You were cussing at yourself while you were wiping up a drink you spilled all over the passenger side." She paused. "Am I right?"

Robert's head cocked to the side and nodded.

"You reached over to pick up the cup and I thought you would touch my leg, but your hand went right through it. I realized you didn't know I was there. I remembered you from the restaurant and thought I'd never get the chance to see you again alive. I reached over and just as I was about to touch you, the ambulance drove away and the next thing I knew, I was sitting next to an EMT looking at myself on a stretcher." A tear rolled down her cheek. "I looked out the back window and watched your car fade out of sight."

Sandra jumped in her seat and leaned in closer to them. "You had an out-of-body experience." She pounded her fist on the table. "That's it! That's when you two connected."

"Mom, what do you mean?"

"I'm suggesting her subconscious reached out to you because she was neither dead nor alive. She was someplace in-between. She knew you two were supposed to be together and she found you in her limbo state.

"Then you reached back when you were asleep because sleep is the closest thing to a coma for you. Your subconscious knew she was meant for you. Robert, in other words, when you were sleeping, you had an out-of-body experience as well." Sandra shrugged. "The mind is a strange and fascinating thing, and many times in our conscious state we ignore subtle signs. At the restaurant, you two connected, but because you were both young and into your own stuff, both of you ignored it. Hell, even as adults you almost let it slip by."

"Mom, you really believe this stuff?"

Sandra tilted her head. "And you don't after what was just described? We have an amazing connection." She motioned between her and Rob. "Your grandparents and great grandparents knew each other's needs and wants, but you two..." Sandra held her hand to her cheek. "You two have taken the Pendleton connection to a whole new level." She sat back against Rob's arm, exasperated.

Robert crossed his arms over his chest and leaned back in his chair. "Okay. Let's say your theory is right. That still doesn't explain why I had no control over the dream. Belinda ran everything."

Rob chuckled. "Son, that's just the way it's supposed to be. The woman controls everything."

Sandra gave Rob a quick jab in the ribs with her elbow. "Rob, that's not true."

"Yes it is. It was Belinda's dream so she controlled it. This is your house and I'm your husband so you control me while I'm here. I may not always agree with it, but you have the control, Sandra," he teased.

Sandra's theory made more sense than anything Belinda had heard so far and she couldn't deny it—Robert and she were connected.

"So we're good here?" Rob slapped the table and threw a glance from Belinda to Robert.

Belinda heard a snicker come out of Robert. "We're good here, Dad. We're real good."

CHAPTER 30

HEARING THE FIRST few notes of dum-dum-dah-dum, dum-dum-dah-dum, the Wedding March, I latch onto Dad's arm to steady myself. My heart is racing ninety to nothing, overcome with excitement. I can't believe the day is finally here, that I'm becoming Mrs. Robert Pendleton, IV.

I look down at myself to make sure everything is in place before we start down the aisle. To my horror, my beautiful ivory wedding dress has turned dingy and rumpled. I run my hands down the sides and front to smooth the material, but that doesn't seem to help. And to make matters worse, I discover a long tear down the side of the skirt. I pleat the fabric over it to conceal it. Luckily, it hides the rip. Oh God! What will everyone think of me? What will Robert think?

As we make our way toward the lattice arch of tulle and satin ribbons...oh no! The red and white roses are wilting before my eyes. My stomach squeezes. Today is turning into a total disaster. My eyes shoot over to Robert's face. A big smile is plastered across it as I approach him. Relieved by his expression, I reach for his hand, but I'm met with a cold, stiff one. Smooth skin. It's like he's a mannequin.

To my relief, Robert softens and molds his hand around mine.

A chill races down my spine as a deep, strange voice catches my attention. There before us stands a tall, thin man dressed all in black with skin as pale as a full moon. As he speaks, I swear I see fangs. What happened to the minister we hired?

"Belinda, do you take Robert to be your lawful wedded husband, to have and to hold from this day forward, in sickness and in health, 'til death do you part?"

A glint appears in Robert's eyes and my favorite signature smile spreads across his face as he squeezes my hands, easing my tension. I say, "I do."

"Robert, do you take Belinda to be your lawful wedded wife, to have and to hold from this day forward, in sickness and in health, 'til death do you part?"

Excitement fills me. The words I had longed to hear are about to pass over his lips.

Robert says, "I—"

"No you don't." Robert and I whip around to look down the aisle in the direction of the screeching voice. "You promised to marry me. That bitch stole you away from me," screams Karen running toward us, pointing at me, with a crazed look in her eyes.

***

Belinda shot up in bed and gasped for breath, her heart pounding. She glanced around the bedroom as she rubbed the damp hair and beads of sweat from her face. "Oh. Thank God. It was only a dream," she mumbled. She took a deep breath and exhaled, flopping back on the bed, questioning everything in the nightmare. How disastrous. *A vampire for a minister?* "I need to stop watching those movies."

Flinging her arm over her face, she continued to bombard herself with questions. *How in the world did Karen get in my dream? Why would I put her in it? Steal him? Why did I think that? Please, don't let her show up and ruin my wedding.*

Belinda didn't think she felt guilty for taking what had been hers in the first place. Maybe not in the physical sense, but they had met and fallen in love in her dream even before Karen appeared in the picture. Surely, she wouldn't humiliate herself by barging in on their wedding. They hadn't seen or heard a word from her since the breakup. Belinda rested her head on her laced fingers and lay there for a few minutes thinking. She figured the nightmare must have been from worrying that something would go wrong at the wedding. And probably because last night was the first night she'd spent away from Robert. She missed having him hold her.

Turning her thoughts in a different direction, a more pleasant one entered her mind, causing the corners of her mouth to kick up into a big smile. The day she had long awaited had finally arrived. The day she'd become Mrs. Robert Pendleton, IV, for real. She couldn't wait to experience a lifetime of married bliss with the real Robert. The last few months they'd spent together had been wonderful. Now, hopefully, the wedding would go as planned. *Whatever that is.*

As agreed, her mom and Sandra had taken over the actual planning of the event and excluded her from the decision making process. She wished she had insisted on being included in more of the planning of the whole affair, but they didn't want her to be stressed with the details. Little did they know being left in the dark was just as stressful.

Belinda took the week off before the wedding and was forbidden to go to her future in-laws' home. Sandra and Dora wanted it to be a surprise when she walked down the aisle on the Pendletons' estate.

She repeatedly asked Robert for some details, but he had given their mothers his oath of secrecy. She had only gotten an index finger and thumb slid across his pursed lips, as though they were being zipped shut.

To add to the frustration, Belinda didn't know the full details of the honeymoon. The only hints she was given were "warm and casual." Based on that information, she needed to figure out how to pack. Even Robert didn't know where they were going. Only their parents and the pilot of the corporate jet knew the details.

***

Belinda's nose picked up the aroma of freshly brewed coffee wafting upstairs. Pushing the nightmare aside, she took in another deep breath and realized staying at her parent's house the night before made sense.

Dora had assured her it would make it easier to help her get ready for the big day. But Belinda figured it was to make sure she didn't sneak over to the Pendletons' house to check out things and to see Robert.

Right now, she didn't care. She had coffee on her mind.

Belinda rubbed her eyes and focused on her alarm clock—10:30. She sat up and stretched her arms out wide as a big yawn escaped her mouth, not in any hurry to get out of bed until she sucked in another deep breath. She caught a mouthwatering scent—pancakes. She lifted her nose and took another whiff. The worries over the wedding drifted away as a growl erupted from her stomach. She hastily slid to the edge of the bed and pushed off, bounding her way to the kitchen.

Dora turned and glanced at her. "Good morning, Sweetie. Pancakes okay with you?" About to pour another measuring cupful of batter, she turned back to the stove, and made several perfect circles on a square griddle.

"Yeah."

"I thought the smell would get you out of bed. Did you sleep okay?"

Belinda slipped into a chair at the table. "Not really? I dreamed all kinds of bad things happened at the wedding. Really strange things. My mind seemed to be in overdrive."

"Don't worry. Sandra and I have everything under control. Just enjoy your day." Her mother walked to the table carrying a plate of pancakes and placed it in front of Belinda. "Would you like coffee and orange juice?"

"Coffee. I'll get it. How about you?" Belinda started to get up.

Dora placed a hand on Belinda's shoulder. "No, you stay seated. I'll get it. Your pancakes will get cold." She reached for an upper cabinet and grabbed two mugs. She poured two cups of coffee and returned to the table, setting them down and joining her daughter. "Do you want to talk about your dream?"

"More like a nightmare, but no, not really. It was stupid. I'm just a little stressed not knowing what to expect and I missed Robert last night."

"Well, I assure you everything will be perfect. So, stop worrying." Dora stood and returned to the stove. "Sweetie, I'm going to fix myself some pancakes, do you want any more?"

"Sure. I'll take two more. Thanks."

Dora returned to the table with the pancake order. She and Belinda ate and talked for a while about several topics, one of which was how she met James.

Belinda had heard the story many times before, but she enjoyed hearing it again. She thought how great it was that they had been high school sweethearts, and remained so even though they went to different colleges.

The fork lay on the plate, which held the remnants of her breakfast. Belinda pushed away from the table and helped her mom clean up the kitchen. She wouldn't going to be hungry again anytime soon.

***

At around 2:30, Dora nudged Belinda. "You need to start thinking about getting cleaned up, and your hair washed and dried. The cosmetologist will be arriving at four."

Belinda strolled back upstairs where she took a long relaxing shower, washed her hair, and then put on a robe. After blow-drying her long tresses, she lay on the bed admiring her gorgeous wedding dress hanging on the closet door.

She snickered remembering how Abbey and she ran her mother around town for two days to four bridal shops trying to find the perfect dress. She must've tried on at least two dozen dresses, but none of them seemed to be "the one."

On the second day, Abbey had found a pale blue, taffeta, off-the-shoulder bridesmaid dress. It looked terrific on her, so Abbey ordered it.

That afternoon, her mom mentioned that she really liked the strapless, ball gown at the last shop. So, they went back the next day. Abbey had an appointment and couldn't make it. She told Belinda she appreciated the invitation. "This is something you need to do with just your mom. I can't wait to see it, though," she said brightly before hanging up.

With the help of Dora, she tried on the dress again, but it just didn't wow her. The saleslady recommended a few more dresses. Still nothing.

Giving up, Belinda had started to get dressed to leave when the saleslady knocked on the dressing room door, informing her a new shipment had just arrived. She asked them to wait while she searched through the selection.

She returned with two more for Belinda's consideration. Dora accepted the dresses and hung them up. They studied each one through the plastic covers. The second dress, an ivory strapless, sweetheart-cut bodice of beaded lace that extended down to a cascading tulle skirt, put a smile on Belinda's face. Something about this one spoke to her.

She remembered the feel of the dress when she ran her fingers down the length of the skirt layers to release them from their protective bag. Running her fingers over the bodice had caused the beads to catch the light, turning them into jewels of little stars twinkling in the night under the halogen lights. The stiffness of the cascading tulle held the layers out a bit away from the hips. They lay over a softer, more moveable fabric.

She studied herself in the full-length mirror and her breath hitched. Her reflection caused tears to well. This is "the one"—the perfect one. It even put a huge, admiring smile on her mother's face.

Belinda was glad Abbey decided to forego joining them. She enjoyed holding it over her by not letting her see the dress, despite the pitiful pleas she received. She relished the thought and couldn't wait to see Abbey's surprised look the first time she saw the dress today.

***

Sitting up on the edge of the bed, she stood and walked over to the dress. She ran the pads of her fingers softly over the nubby texture of the beaded lace. Reaching over to her dresser, she picked up a rhinestone and beaded grosgrain ribbon belt. She held it up to the waist of the dress. The sparkle of the rhinestone added a bit more bling to the elegant design.

The chime of the doorbell interrupted her. She heard her mother's muffled voice greeting a woman and the closing of the door. The time had arrived for all the beauty pampering Sandra had arranged.

"Belinda, Ms. Walters, the cosmetologist, is here. Are you ready for her?"

Belinda rushed to the stairway. "Yes, send her up," she shouted and then waited at the top of the stairs.

As Ms. Walters began to ascend the stairs, she turned and addressed them. "Please, my friends all call me Wendy."

"Hi, Wendy." Belinda escorted her to her bedroom, and then seated herself at the vanity. "I'd like my makeup to look natural, and I think I want my hair in an updo, or maybe pulled back and cascading down."

Wendy gathered Belinda's hair back and studied her in the mirror. "Will you being wearing a veil?"

"No, ma'am." Belinda reached over and picked up a rhinestone headband from the vanity. "This."

"Oh, that's lovely. I know exactly what to do. You'll be easy to work with. I'll have you looking amazing. Your future husband won't be able to take his eyes off you. Before I get started, let me paint your fingernails and toenails with this light pink polish." She held out the bottle for her to see. Belinda nodded. "They can be drying while I do your makeup and hair."

***

The final hour arrived. The cosmetologist had fulfilled her promise. Belinda's makeup looked just like she imagined, only better. And her hair. It was beautiful with wistful tendrils around her face, and cascading curls down the back. The sparkling rhinestone headband added the finishing touch.

Dora knocked on Belinda's bedroom door and called out, "May I come in?"

"Sure, Mom."

She entered completely dressed for the evening event in a light blue, brocade, long dress.

"Oh, Mom. You look beautiful. And your hair. Did you do it? It's gorgeous."

"No. I asked Wendy to fix it before she left." Dora reached up and gently fluffed her hair in the back. "She's amazing, and so nice. We have to thank Sandra again for sending her here."

Dora walked over to the wedding dress, still hanging on the door. "This dress is so pretty. You're going to be the most beautiful bride." She turned toward Belinda and smiled. "I can't wait to see Robert's face when he sees you walking down the aisle."

"Me too."

"Are you ready to put it on? I'll help you."

"Yes. I think it's about that time." Belinda carefully removed it from the hanger and handed it to her mom. Slipping the robe from her shoulders, she let it fall to the floor, and then kicked it aside.

"Aren't you going to wear a bra or something?"

"No. I don't need one." *In fact, I'm not going to wear anything under this dress. I can't wait to see Robert's face when he peels it off me.*

She steadied herself with the help of her mother's shoulder and stepped into the wedding gown, pulling it up into place. Dora ran the zipper up the back. Then she collected the embellished belt from the dresser and tied it around Belinda's waist, finishing off the effect with a perfect bow. She then placed the glistening silver shoes on the floor in front of her daughter. Lifting the front of the dress to see the shoes, Belinda slipped them on. They walked over to the full-length mirror.

Her mother splayed her fingers at the base of her neck. "Oh, Sweetie. You look so beautiful."

"Thanks, Mom." Just like the first time she tried on the dress, her breath hitched and tears threatened, but she managed to blink them away to avoid ruining her makeup. She prayed when Robert saw her, it would have a the same effect on him.

Dora walked to the door. "I'm going downstairs to watch for your ride."

"I'm not riding with you and Dad?"

"No. Sandra arranged special transportation for you. We'll meet you there." Dora started out the door, but suddenly stopped and turned back. "Oh. I almost forgot something. I'll be right back."

Belinda decided to take advantage of her mother's absence to remove the last undergarment—her panties. She lifted the left side of her dress and hooked her thumb in the side of the bikini's, pulling them down a little ways.

She shimmied them the rest of the way to the floor, and kicked them under her bed so her mom wouldn't notice.

Adjusting the front of her dress, Belinda wiggled her hips as she shook the layers straight. A mild shudder ran through her as the smooth fabric of the under layer brushed against her backside. The subtle touch of the fabric reminded her of Robert's gentle hands dancing across her skin. She closed her eyes and took in a deep breath that tightened the bodice around her breast, making her very aware of her naked body beneath it.

Belinda let her breath out as Dora opened the door. "You need something new, something old, something borrowed, and something blue. Your dress is new. Your engagement ring is an heirloom—something old. I'd like for you to wear my diamond drop necklace—something borrowed, and Sandra bought this blue garter for you to wear." Dora held up the necklace and garter for Belinda to see.

"Thanks, Mom." She hugged her mother, and kissed her cheek. Turning her back to her, Belinda lifted her hair, and Dora fastened the necklace around her neck. She sat on the bed and lifted the dress just above the knee, careful not to expose herself. Her mom slipped on the garter. Belinda fluffed the layers of the skirt back into place, enjoying the sensation.

Dora stepped back and sighed. "I guess that's all." She used a finger to stop an escaping tear.

"Mom." Belinda took a step toward her.

She raised her hands to stop her daughter. "No. No." Dora tucked her chin down. "We can't touch because we'll both start crying." Raising her head, she peeked through her lashes at Belinda, smiled, and walked to the door. "I'll see you downstairs."

"Okay." Belinda walked to the dresser and picked up Robert's wedding ring. She slid it onto her thumb. It spun with ease, so she clinched her fingers around her thumb to hold the ring in place. She walked to the mirror and stared at herself, fingering the necklace. *It's almost time. Time to become Mrs. Robert Pendleton, IV.* Her dream was finally becoming reality. Butterflies began to flutter around in her stomach. *Please let my wedding day turn out perfect and not like my nightmare.*

"Belinda, your ride is here."

"Okay, Mom. I'm coming." She took a deep breath, and then dashed out of her room.

CHAPTER 31

AFTER TAKING A few steps down the stairs, Belinda stopped, startled by the flash of a camera.

"Don't stop. Keep coming," the photographer said as he continued to snap pictures.

"Oh, my little girl is so beautiful." Dad walked up a few steps and escorted her down the remainder of the way. He kissed her on the forehead. "Robert's a very lucky man."

"Thanks, Dad." She kissed him on the cheek. She raised her head and lids to the ceiling and fanned her eyes with her fingers to control the threatening waterfall. Beside her, she could hear her father suppressing his chuckles.

"James, don't make her cry," Dora scolded.

"Okay." He turned toward Belinda, took hold of her elbow, and escorted her to the opened front door where her mother waited.

"Wow!" Belinda couldn't believe what she saw parked in front of the house—a shiny white limousine. A man in a uniform stood by the side of the car.

Arm in arm on either side of Belinda, Dora and James walked her down the path to the waiting vehicle, where a chauffeur stood at attention by an opened door. The photographer hovered around snapping pictures. Occasionally, he halted their progress to ask them to smile and pose. At their destination, she hugged her parents, and slipped into a seat. She placed her fingers to her lips and blew them a kiss as the door clicked closed.

***

The limo pulled into the circular drive at the Pendleton house and parked with Belinda's door aligned with the walkway to the front entrance. The chauffeur exited, walked to Belinda's door, and opened it. "Miss Davies, Mrs. Pendleton instructed me to let her know when we arrived so she can make sure your fiancé isn't in the house. I'll be right back." He closed the door.

Through the window, Belinda saw her parents make their way toward the limo as the chauffeur conversed with Mrs. Pendleton. Sandra nodded. He turned and quickly stepped down the path to open the limo door.

He smiled and offered his hand. "The coast is clear. Let me assist you."

"Thanks you." She took hold of it and placed one foot on the pavement. The photographer came out of nowhere. He instructed her not to move and told her how to pose as he snapped pictures inches from her, from all angles.

Finally, allowed to stand up, Belinda's mother swooped in and started working with the skirts of her gown, fluffing and smoothing everywhere needed. The photographer continued clicking away. Belinda thought of smacking him the same way one would swat at an annoying bug.

The spontaneous flurry settled down and the chauffeur extended his elbow to escort her toward the front door. Her parents walked ahead of her as the pesky photographer continued his irritating shooting spree.

A big smile formed across Sandra's face as Belinda stepped into the foyer. "You look gorgeous."

"Thank you, and so do you." Belinda admired Mrs. Pendleton's beautiful long dress of gold brocade.

"Wait here. I'll go get your flowers. I'll be right back."

"Oh! My! God!" caught Belinda's attention from the top of the stairway. Holding a nosegay of red roses, Abbey came bouncing down toward her with a huge smile. "You…You…there isn't a word expressive enough. You're right. This dress is 'the one.' It's perfect and worth the wait. Although it *was* mean of you." Abbey took her by the shoulders and touched each of her cheeks to Belinda's. "I'd hug you, but I'm afraid I'll muss you up." She stepped back. "You're going to knock that hunk of yours flat on his ass when he sees you."

Belinda let out a little giggle and held Abbey by the hands. "You look beautiful too, and making you wait…I wanted you to see the complete package, not just bits and piece."

The pressure on Belinda's hand by Abbey's grip reminded her about Robert's ring placed on her thumb for safekeeping. She slipped the wedding band off her thumb and held it out for Abbey. "Here's Robert's ring. Place it on your thumb." She pressed it into Abbey's palm. "Don't lose it." Abbey nodded and slid it onto her's, clasping her fingers around it.

Sandra returned and presented Belinda with a cascading bouquet of red roses, baby's breath, and long, ivory satin ribbons. "I hope you like it."

"It's beautiful." She lifted the roses to her nose and inhaled a deep breath. "They smell wonderful. Did Robert tell you I love roses?"

Dora and Sandra nodded simultaneously.

Sandra glanced at her watch. "It's time to start. All of the guests are seated and we need to head for the back." Sandra gently placed her hand under Belinda's elbow and led her to the back door, where her dad stood waiting for her. Dora followed.

"Come on, Dora. Let's go take our seats." Sandra guided her out the door to where their ushers waited.

Belinda's dad turned toward her. "Well, Sweetie, this is it. Are you ready?"

Her heart began racing and butterflies began bouncing about from side to side in her stomach, making her voice quaver as she spoke. "I think so." Belinda examined her ivory gown, checking its condition. Relief washed over her. It hadn't turned dingy and rumpled like in the nightmare, and thank goodness, it wasn't torn. Now, if she could only make it down the aisle without tripping and falling.

Soft music drifted in through the open door. The tempo changed and Abbey started her procession.

Dad extended his elbow and Belinda latched on. Her knees wobbled and he tightened his grip to steady her. "Come on, Sweetie. You can do this. You've waited a long time for this day. Think of Robert."

She had waited a long time. In fact, sixteen agonizing months had passed since Robert proposed. Waiting was the price Belinda paid for a May wedding. But now the day had arrived and she would be Mrs. Robert Pendleton, IV within the next fifteen minutes, as long as nothing went wrong. Karen flashed through her head. *She'd better not show up!*

Belinda tucked her chin and wiped her mind clean. She let the vision of Robert's charismatic smile chase all other thoughts away. With a deep breath, she straightened and smiled. "I'm ready."

They walked out to the backyard and down the carpeted walkway to the aisle between the guests.

Belinda caught her breath as she glanced around. The decorations were amazing and, in some aspects, reminded her of the dream wedding reception. Tiny white lights twinkled throughout the trees. Floating candles and white pearl-colored balloons drifted over the pool surface. The flickering flames between the bobbing balloons gave them an effervescent appearance and mimicked giant champagne bubbles. It had to have been Robert's contribution. He must've remembered those details from their dream.

Her gaze drifted past the seated guests to the huge, enclosed tent with arched windows. What little she could see through the plastic arches looked like twinkle lights had been strung everywhere and she thought she saw bits of what could be a chandelier. She stretched her neck trying to get a glimpse of the furnishings, but with the doorway flaps closed, it was impossible.

She turned her head as much as she could without appearing to be a fool, attempting to take it all in, and cursed herself for agreeing to be kept in the dark. Sandra and Dora did so much, but what she saw so far, she loved.

As her father led her to the rows and rows of seated guests, her attention shifted to their faces, turned to watch her approach. Mostly strangers—smiling at her. It made her a bit uncomfortable. She found herself scanning the guests, making sure Karen wasn't among them. She felt inwardly relieved Karen didn't seem to be crashing her big day, but the ceremony wasn't over yet. A sick feeling erupted in her throat and she took a spontaneous deep breath, which seemed to help momentarily.

Reaching the back of the aisle, she abandoned acknowledging the seated people. Thoughts of Karen vanished. Her attention shifted to the beautiful lattice arch of tulle, satin ribbons, and perfect—not wilted as in the nightmare—red roses. Under it stood her waiting groom. His eyes glistened and he had a heart-stopping smile, one she'd never seen before. He rocked back on his heels a few times before shifting his weight from one foot to the other. For the first time in their lives together, Robert looked nervous, but she became lost in his expression and it washed away all her fears.

Belinda didn't hear the Wedding March begin or see anything but Robert. Her father gave her a tug to start her down the aisle. Her heart quickened, but her gaze never faltered from Robert. He became her rock who drew her to their *Destiny Reborn*.

Totally focused on her fiancé, everything became a blur until Robert reached for her hands. She fumbled with her bouquet and passed it to Abbey. She placed her hands in Robert's and the minister began, "Repeat after me."

As Robert finished saying, "til death do us part," his face lit up.

The haunting memory of her nightmare crept back. Holding her breath, Belinda glanced over her shoulder down the aisle just to reassure herself Karen wasn't running toward them. She closed her eyes and let out her breath, relieved the devil herself was nowhere in sight.

Belinda refocused her attention on Robert's clear blue eyes. As she repeated her vow, her heart hammered and her breath seized. A tear of joy escaped with her ending words. Robert gave her hands a few quick squeezes and winked.

As the ring ceremony began, she noticed Colin, the best man, for the first time when he handed Robert the ring. Colin winked.

Robert slid a white gold band onto her finger. "With this ring, I thee wed."

The band looked just like the one from their dream. She smiled up at him and he whispered, "Forever."

Abbey handed Belinda his ring. She slid a matching wider band onto his finger. "With this ring, I thee wed."

He smiled and she whispered, "Forever."

"I now pronounce you husband and wife. You may kiss your bride."

Belinda wrapped her arms around his neck and his wound around her waist as their lips crushed together. She felt herself float backways, as Robert dipped her in his strong arms, causing the kiss to last a bit longer than it should have. The minister cleared his throat and snickers erupted from a few guests. The kiss...well, Robert had to peel her off him after they were upright again. It was a kiss he'd never forget, and even better than the one in their dream wedding.

Another song played as Abbey and Colin retreated down the aisle. Robert surprised Belinda, whisking her off her feet and carrying her. She hugged his neck and kissed his cheek. "I love you, Mr. Robert Pendleton.

"I love you too, Mrs. Robert Pendleton.

"I like the way that sounds."

"Me too."

The parents joined the wedding party and greeted the guests as they headed for the tent. With the last welcome complete, the wedding party returned to the lattice arch where the photographer took numerous pictures, finishing just before twilight.

CHAPTER 32

BELINDA AND ROBERT walked through the door of the air-conditioned tent. She touched her fingers to her parted lips and gasped. The sight before her was beyond anything she could've imagined.

"Oooh, Robert. It's gorgeous."

He squeezed her hand and grinned. "I'm glad you like it. I told our moms about our dream wedding reception. They came up with the other decorations."

Twinkle lights ringed the perimeter at the ceiling and crisscrossed the top of the tent several times like the spokes of a wagon wheel. At the peak, hung a beautiful chandelier. Just enough light glowed to set a mystical mood. To the left of the entrance sat a long, rectangular table draped in a floor-length, pale blue tablecloth, piled full with beautifully wrapped white presents. Numerous round tables flanked the dance floor, forming a horseshoe. A floor-length, pale blue linen tablecloth and a smaller white topper adorned each table. In the center of each sat an arrangement of red roses and baby's breath around a clear glass hurricane shade containing a lit white column candle. Place settings included sparkling crystal glasses, and shiny silverware peeking out from rolled napkins of white linen.

A crackle from a microphone followed by a high, ear-busting shrill, caused the guests to turn toward a man standing in the middle of the dance floor. "Honored guests. Allow me to present to you, our newlyweds, Mr. and Mrs. Robert Pendleton, IV."

Robert grabbed Belinda's hand and led her down the aisle between the tables, making their way toward the dance floor. Once in the middle, they turned to face their guests and he thrust their clenched hands in the air above their heads. The room went wild. People stood and applauded. A few shouted, snide remarks from his coworkers sent a ripple of laughter around the room. Robert made a "V" with two of his finger and pointed them from his eyes to the hecklers standing around their tables.

The crowd returned to their seats while Belinda and Robert continued to make their way across the dance floor toward the head table.

She returned to her examination of the decorations. She wanted to take all of it in. She noticed that between each window of the tent stood a tall, thin, white tree with white blossoms and draped with more twinkle lights. Elegant, soft music touched her ears above the chatter from the guests. It drew Belinda's attention to the far left side of the tent. There sat a quartet—a harpist, a violinist, a cellist, and a flutist. She realized they were the ones who played the wedding music. When she and Robert reached their table, Belinda noticed a deejay and several huge speakers on the right side of the tent. She figured he'd probably be playing the popular songs later.

Waiters and waitresses started serving salad on elegant bone china plates.

Belinda glanced all around the tent as she attempted to take in all of her surroundings. There seemed to be so much and she wanted to experience every little aspect of her special day. A touch of warmth encompassed her hand followed by a mild tightening sensation. She turned to meet Robert's eyes and the chaos that roared inside her melted away.

***

As the delicious meal ended, Robert's father stood and made a toast to the couple, followed by her father, and then the matron of honor, Abbey, and finally the best man, Colin. Of course, he had to make a joke about Robert stealing her away from him. "I hope I'll meet someone as sweet and lovely as Belinda, someone who makes me as happy as Belinda makes Robert." He looked toward the couple, raised his glass, and smiled.

The quartet began to play a soft, barely audible tune in the background. "Dear guests, please follow the bride and groom to the stables so they can have their first dance." Colin bent down toward Belinda and Robert. "Come on. Get up." Arm in arm between the couple, he led them into the stable and directed them to stand in the middle.

"Ladies and gentleman, you may think it's strange for the first dance to be held on the dirt floor of a stable. And I agree—it is strange…well, so is the couple standing in front of you, but dancing on this ground is something they have shared and I hope will share for years to come. Ladies and gentlemen, I present to you, Mr. and Mrs. Robert Pendleton, IV, in their first dance as husband and wife." Applause from the guests standing at each opening of the stable filled the space as Colin backed away.

In the background, the quartet music filled the dimly lit barn. Just like in the tent, twinkle lights gave the space a romantic ambiance. The horse stalls displayed light blue and white ribbons.

Robert held Belinda around the waist and positioned them to begin to dance. "Are you ready, Angel? Our audience awaits."

Belinda glanced around at the guests watching them. Robert lifted her chin and his gaze captivated her. "Now follow me." She nodded. He took a step and she followed his lead. He twirled her around and made her feel like a princess dancing with her prince charming, even though her dance floor was made of dirt. She wouldn't have had it any other way.

Returning to the tent, the party went into full swing. The deejay had the room hopping as the drinks flowed. Earlier, Colin caught the garter to the relentless whooping and hollering of his ex-office mates. He wore it on his bicep like a badge of honor while he danced with every single and some not so single females who would say "yes."

Rob's secretary caught the bouquet. Belinda knew very little about her, but she glowed as she emerged from the huddled mass of ladies scrapping over it. She thrust it above her head, holding it like a torch.

Belinda and Robert retreated to the front table to relax. Colin had a "one to many" sway to his walk as he gave Robert a slap on the back. "Your moms sure know how to throw a party." His speech came out slurred.

"Colin, you're in the guest house tonight. Give me your keys." Robert held out his hand, palm up.

"Nope. I'm fine."

Robert gestured with an upward motion of his hand and pointed to it.

Belinda giggled. Colin tsked, but dug in his pocket and relinquished the keys to his beloved car.

"I'll give these to my mother. There's t-shirts and shorts in the dresser. Everything you'll need to clean up with in the morning is in the bathroom. I'm sure Mom will throw in brunch and a swim in the pool for her favorite adopted son."

With a lopsided grin, Colin centered himself between Robert and Belinda, throwing an arm over each. "You know, you two are my favorite people and I love you both."

Robert took a deep breath and rolled his eyes.

Belinda snickered under her breath. "We love you too."

"Hey, I was wondering…did you think about inviting Karen? Now *that* would have made things interesting," Colin slurred out.

Belinda lifted her head. Her back went rigid. She knew the alcohol made Colin's judgement fuzzy, but hearing that name sent chills up her spine.

Robert intervened in an instant. "We didn't think that would be a good idea. Besides, her father told my dad she's moved to Europe. Dad told me she took over her father's holdings over there."

Robert caught Belinda's attention and nodded toward her. He stood up and put his arm around Colin. "Come on, let's go find you someone to dance with." He mouthed, *I'll be right back,* as he led Colin away.

It didn't take too long before Robert returned and placed a kiss on the back of Belinda's neck. He sat and bounced his chair close to her so he could put his arm around her. "I'm sorry about that." He tilted his head until his forehead touched her's. "Are you okay?"

"Yeah, I'm fine. How come you didn't tell me about Karen moving?"

"I didn't think it was important and I didn't want to upset you. I found out months ago."

Belinda shook her head. "I would've loved knowing she was out of the country. I've been worrying myself sick that she would crash our wedding." She placed her thumb and index finger about a half inch apart . "That little piece of information might have calmed my nerves a tiny bit."

Robert stroked her forearm. "Am I forgiven?"

"Of course you are, you goof."

"Good, let's dance!" He picked her up by the waist and led her to the crowded dance floor.

During a slow dance, Belinda laid her head against Robert's shoulder. The sway started to coax her to sleep as the exhaustion from the day started to catch up with her. Robert leaned close to her ear. "Come on. Let's get out of here. You look tired."

She nodded. "But what about our guests?"

Robert let out a laugh that confused her.

"What's so funny?"

He leaned back into her so she could hear him. "You said the same thing in our dream at the Homecoming frat party and my answer is the same as it was then…Who cares?" He held out his hand. She hesitated a moment, took it, and followed him out of the loud, music filled tent.

***

In the upstairs guest bedroom, Robert closed and locked the door behind him. Belinda toed-off her shoes and walked backward toward the bed, waiting for him to turn around. As he did, she beckoned him with her finger, swaying her hips from side to side. He formed a half-grin. "I thought you were tired?"

She reached out and grabbed the lapels of his tux to pull him along. When she felt the mattress against the back of her legs, she sat down and motioned for him to kneel in front of her. He raised a brow but did as she asked. Taking his hand, she guided it up under the hem of her skirt and onto her calf. It didn't take Robert long to figure out her plan. She let go and rested back on her hands, watching him. His eyes never left hers as he maneuvered closer up her thigh, exploring. Her breath became more irregular with every upward movement of his soft touch toward her inner thighs. Her back arched but she refused to break their gaze.

Suddenly Robert stopped. His half-grin grew to a full smile. "You naughty girl! Going commando for our wedding? Tsk. Tsk."

She lunged forward and grabbed his lapels, pulling his lips within an inch of hers. "Nothing but the best for you, Mr. Pendleton."

***

Robert wore a simple shite t-shirt and jeans. He put on his lightweight flight jacket, and then reached for his phone.

"Who are you calling?" Belinda leaned around him to see.

"Karen. We didn't invite her to the wedding, so I thought the least I should do is give her a call." He gave her an impish grin.

She popped him in the arm and then backed away. "That's not funny!"

"I'm just joking. Chalk it up to bad timing." He walked over to show Belinda the screen. "Look, I'm just calling my mom. She wanted me to tell her when we were ready to leave."

He held up his finger toward Belinda while he talked into the phone. "Okay. We have to wait a few minutes."

He pivoted and wrapped his arms around her. "Have I told you lately how much I love you?" He kissed her nose.

"Does your moaning over the last half hour count?"

Robert tilted his head and raised his eyebrow. "Technically you did more moaning than I did, but you can consider my contribution to the noise level as a 'yes'." He gave her a soft kiss on the lips. "Am I forgiven?"

She purposely hesitated before answering. "Hmm. I'll think about it."

He lifted his arm and glanced at his watch. "Okay, you think about it, but we have to leave now. Let's go." He waited for Belinda to put on her jacket and grab her bag, and then escorted her down the stairs.

Sandra waited for them at the front door. As they approached her, she opened it to show off the remaining guests lining the walkway to the limo. As Belinda and Robert rushed toward their ride, tiny bubbles filled the path and floated all around them as the guests cheered them on.

Once inside the limo, Robert pulled Belinda toward him, and wrapped his arms around his new bride, planting a slow, sultry kiss on her full waiting lips. She closed her eyes and reveled in the electrical feeling buzzing up her spine. As the limo pulled onto the street, Belinda raised her eyelids and looked over Robert's shoulder, out the tinted window. What she saw shocked her. A familiar Mini Cooper sat parked alongside the curb. In the driver seat sat a female with short blonde hair—her narrowed eyes shooting daggers as the limo drove by. *What the hell is she doing here?!* Her back straightened, her muscled tensed, and her heart skipped a beat.

Robert rubbed her back. He cradled her in his arms. "What wrong?"

Belinda smiled, not wanting to upset him or ruin the rest of their night. "Nothing. I'm just enjoying being Mrs. Pendleton." She leaned in and placed her mouth over Robert's, brushing Karen out of her mind.

The trip to the Sugar Land Airport took no time at all. They boarded the jet and made themselves comfortable. Jessica, the flight attendant, saw to their needs and brought them drinks.

Before leaving, the captain came out of the cockpit and spoke to them. "Congratulations, Mr. and Mrs. Pendleton." He sat down facing them. "I have been sworn to secrecy by my boss, your father, not to tell you where you're going. What I can tell you is, you'll have approximately twelve hours of travel time. We'll be making one stop to refuel before we touch down at the final airport. There will be a limousine waiting to take you to your final destination about two hours from the airport. Once you arrive, you will receive a binder with all the information needed to complete the first half of your trip. At your next destination, you'll receive another binder with the itinerary for the last half. So for now, relax and enjoy the flight. The bedroom has been made up if you choose to use it."

Belinda saw a slight rise of the captain's brow. She noticed a smirk brush across Robert's face as he stared at the captain. She assumed some guy-speak was taking place.

She looked at the captain. "This all sounds so cloak-and-dragger, but I'm hooked."

"Sorry. I can't give you any more information." He got up and closed the door of the cockpit behind him.

A garbled, "Please fasten your seatbelts," came over the intercom. "Jessica, prepare for takeoff."

The cabin lights dimmed and within minutes, Belinda watched the ground fall away. The lights below blended with the stars in the clear night sky. She lolled her head against the backrest and remembered their first date in a blue Beamer on "Make Out Ridge," from a dream that seemed so long ago. She felt the jet bank to the left, and then level out as it flew east.

"It is now safe to move about the cabin," blared over the intercom.
The attendant approached her only passengers. "Can I get you anything?"

"No. I'm fine."

Robert started to unbuckled his seat belt before he answered. "No. I'm good as well. We'll be in the bedroom. Please wake us two hours before we land. We'd like a light breakfast. Bagels, coffee and orange juice will be fine."

He waited for the attendant to leave and then leaned over to Belinda. "Unbuckle your seatbelt. We're about to become members of the 'Mile High Club'."

***

The jet touched down and rolled to the tarmac. The sign across the hangar doors told her she had just landed in Paris, France. As she stepped out of the fuselage of the jet, she felt refreshed despite their antics that made her an official member of the "Mile High Club." The sun rose in the east and the air was balmy. As soon as she and Robert deplaned, a uniformed chauffeur escorted them to a black limousine parked a few feet from the jet's ramp.

The drive north to their final destination took two hours. Robert and Belinda made a game out of guessing where they were heading, but she figured out they were somewhere in the Champagne region of France.

The limo stopped in front of a magnificent chateau. The chauffeur opened the door and one of the chateau's staff greeted them. "Welcome, Madame and Monsieur. Please follow me."

The trio hopped onto a waiting golf cart that sped off on the path leading to the back of the main house. It stopped outside a quaint cottage and he escorted them in.

"I hope this will be to your liking?"

Belinda couldn't believe the expense and time their parents took to make their honeymoon so extraordinary.

Robert walked around the cottage with his fists on his hips, exuding a sense of confidence as if he did this sort of thing all the time.

The man walked over to the table in the center of the room and picked up a black binder. He then pulled a white envelope from his inside pocket. "I was asked to give both of these to you on your arrival. Please, Monsieur, open the envelope first."

Robert took them and the man stepped back toward the door and waited. Opening the envelope, he let out a chuckle. He pulled what looked like French currency out of it and walked toward the man, handing him a bill. "Thank you. Everything is perfect. I'll call the front desk if we need anything."

The man bowed and relinquished two sets of keys. "Monsieur, the first set is for the golf cart. It is for you to use around the grounds. This set is for the cottage. Your luggage will be delivered shortly." When he finished, he left.

Robert held up the envelope and shook it at Belinda. "They thought of everything." He walked over and picked up the black binder he had laid on the table, and then made his way to the couch and plopped down. He opened it and started to study the contents. He never looked at Belinda, but patted the seat beside him. "Aren't you interested in knowing how our parents have planned our lives for the next week?"

CHAPTER 33

A COOL BREEZE lifted the lace curtain and made it float. The song of a nearby jay filled the air. Belinda stretched, and took in her surroundings. The morning sunlight flooded the room, casting shadows over the walls. She swung her feet over the edge of the overstuffed bed. They had done very little over the last day and a half but eat or sleep. The jet lag had taken its toll.

She walked into the sitting area of their honeymoon cottage to find Robert lounging on the couch, reading a book. He sported a wide grin as she approached him. "Sleep well? I ordered us some breakfast. Coffee is on its way."

"Coffee. I need coffee." She curled up next to him and nestled into his chest. Strong arms encircled her. They gave her a sense of security. She liked that feeling.

"Well what should we do today? We really should get out of the cottage and at least see what this area has to offer. Who knows when we'll get back to France again." Robert tightened his arms around her.

"I'm happy just where I am, but I guess you're right. It would be a shame not to take advantage and do some sightseeing. How about we take a ride in the golf cart to see what the grounds look like. We could go up to the chateau to see if they have any information about what to see close by. Also, let's eat dinner in the main dining room tonight." She patted his chest.

"While you were snoozing, I took the liberty of looking over the information the place supplied in the room. Did you know there is a nine-hole golf course on the grounds? Have you ever played golf?"

"No, but, do you really want to spend time on a golf course? It's our honeymoon."

She adjusted to see him. His pushed out lip and pouty expression gave her the answer she wasn't looking for. "Tsk. I guess I'm going to get some golf lessons."

His expression changed and perked up. He tightened his arms around her. "You'll like it. The course can be very peaceful and it's relaxing."

A knock at the door alerted the pair, breakfast had arrived. Robert climbed over her, nearly tossing her on the floor, but he caught her and made sure she was firmly on the couch before he headed for the door.

The aroma of fresh brewed coffee hit her. After a few cups, she would be ready to take on whatever France had to offer, including golf lessons.

By the end of mid-morning, not much had change. The couple had moved to the side patio, still clad in their pajamas, to have breakfast.

Belinda propped her feet up and sipped at her third cup of coffee while Robert went inside to set up a tee time for her first golf game ever. She closed her eyes to enjoy the quiet and the fresh air. A gentle breeze rustled the leaves as the chirp of birds drifted through the air. From the other room, she heard Robert speaking French into the phone. *French? Robert can speak French?* She listened closer. From what she could tell, he was fluent in the language.

"Well, we have a three o'clock time set up."

She sat staring at him.

"What? Is something wrong with the time? I figured we'll play nine holes and still have plenty of time to come back and get duded up for a nice dinner."

"The time is fine. How come you didn't tell me you speak French?"

Robert rolled his tongue inside his cheek and furrowed his brow. "It never came up." His shoulders briefly lifted. "I took it in high school and then in college. After I started working with my dad, I found it came in handy with some of our French-speaking Canadian clients." He sat next to her. "Maybe that's why we're in France and not some other country?"

"What other little secrets will I learn about you?"

Robert leaned back in his chair and crossed his arms. "I'm sure as much as I'll discover about you."

Golf, it was interesting. Although Belinda didn't have much power in her swing, she did manage to hit the ball straight and keep it on the fairway, unlike Robert, who walloped the ball several hundred yards.

He lost four balls. With each loss, he spent at least fifteen minutes raking his club through the brush attempting to find the lost sphere. The entire time he mumbled under his breath small obscenities of what he would do when he found it.

"Honey, I thought golf was supposed to be relaxing. You seem so stressed looking for those balls."

He gripped the steering wheel of the cart and winked. "It's just part of the game." The cart jolted forward as he made a sharp turn in the direction of the clubhouse. Belinda shifted and would've fallen out if her instincts hadn't caused her to grab onto the cart's roof. She scowled at Robert.

"It's all part of the game." He snickered.

***

Robert scanned Belinda who looked sexy as hell in her black dress. It had long sleeves and the top half was covered in lace. The tone of her smooth skin peeked through over her shoulders and arms while the back plunged in a "V" to her waist. The skirt came mid-thigh and bounced as she moved. Her heels gave her legs a long slender appearance. She wore her hair up, twisted in curls on top of her head, exposing her neck. He could tell she had very little on underneath, and the sheer sight of that little black number draped over her delicate frame, made him want to explore. From what he could tell, one shiny button at her waist was all that kept the dress in place.

Robert watched her lift her fork and take dainty bites of food. *If she keeps eating like that, I'll never get that dress off of her.* A ray of light bounced off that button and teased him. Excitement stirred within him. But, he just smiled, raised his glass to her, and took a sip of champagne, bidding his time.

The dress intrigued him. She obviously wasn't wearing a bra or stockings. He caught a glint from her side. *What would happen if I unfastened that button?*

On their way back to the cottage, they walked down a path lit by ornate dim lamps. He rubbed his fingers over her bare back. She snuggled in closer. He felt a slight quiver rush over her skin as he floated his fingers under the "V" of the dress. Robert reached in under her arm and brushed the underside of her breast. She giggled. He pulled her closer.

As soon as he closed the door of the cottage, he took her in his arms. She rolled her head back and let out a gasp while he kissed the crevices of her neck. He toyed with the button at her side. Next to her ear he whispered, "I've been wondering about this button all night." He nibbled at her earlobe.

"And what would happen if I unbuttoned it." With a slight flick of the finger, the button released and the dress back fell open.

He glided his hands down her bare ass. "Commando again?" He squeezed each cheek and her gasp filled him with desire. He turned her so her back was against his chest and teased her soft flesh as he peeled off the dress.

She melted against him, swaying her head from side to side, and moaned, "Robert, please. I want you." Her breaths came fast and her chest heaved.

He placed his hands on her shoulders to steady her. "Stand here and don't turn around."

As he slid his hand over her backside, she turned slightly toward him. He nibbled at her ear. "I said not to turn around."

She tucked her chin and looked forward.

A few seconds later, he returned. First, he pulled the pins that held her hair in place and let it cascade down around her. He buried his nose in it and inhaled, taking in her scent. Next, he continued his exploration of her body, this time pressing his naked flesh against hers.

She molded to him and cooed. He turned her toward him. Her eyes widened as he stroked his fingers over the side of her face. Placing a hand on either side of her chin, he kissed her hard and backed her up to the edge of the couch.

***

Early Monday morning the limo arrived and whisked them back to Paris. Belinda and Robert still had one week left, but had no idea what lay in store for them.

The sleek, black limousine came to a stop in front of the Ritz, located on the north side of the Seine River. A bellman took charge of their luggage. A concierge greeted them and escorted them to a private elevator, which took them to the penthouse suite.

Belinda gasped when the double doors opened to reveal the two thousand square foot suite of pure luxury. As before, a black binder and an envelope stuffed full of French currency lay on the table in the foyer.

Walking into the living room, Belinda kept her arms tucked close so she could control her urge to touch everything. She took small steps and walked casually around the room, trying not to be too obvious. However, once she and Robert were alone, the story changed.

"Oh my God! Can you believe this place? What the hell were our parents' thinking?" She ran to the French doors leading to the terrace and flung them open. "I'm dreaming....I thought the chateau was magnificent, but this is insane." She stepped onto the terrace to a full view of the Seine River and the Eiffel Tower just beyond. Robert wrapped his arms around her from behind and they stood admiring the view. "This is...I can't describe what this is."

With a quick jerk, she turned. "The bathroom, I have to check it out."

"We have Paris at our fingertips and you want to check out the bathroom?"

Belinda made it halfway into the living room with Robert following. She checked out the door placement and chose the one she deduced would lead to the master bedroom. Her exaggerated hip movements and beckoning finger enticed Robert to continue to follow a few paces behind. Grabbing the handles, she put a bit of drama into opening the doors, making wide arm gestures. "Voila! Success!" After she stepped inside, she focused on the open door leading to the bathroom.

Robert caught up to her, standing, hands on hips, in a bathroom the size of Paris. In the middle, stood what looked like a small swimming pool. "Is that the tub?"

"Yep." She reached for the first button on her blouse. "And I'm getting in it." The blouse fell to the floor. "Care to join me?"

Robert had a hint of a smile. "Fill it up. I'll go get the champagne and chocolate covered strawberries from the dining room table."

"Robert, honey." Belinda stood in her bra and panties pouring bubble bath near the jetting water filling the tub. "Don't forget the 'Do Not Disturb sign.'"

***

According to the itinerary found in the black binder, the first day belonged to Robert and Belinda. After a relaxing bath and nap, the couple ventured out onto the streets of Paris. They strolled alongside the Seine, stopped for a late lunch in a quaint street-side café, and ducked in and out of numerous shops. The day was the perfect description of romantic. After all, they were in the "City of Love."

Belinda flipped through a rack full of dresses in a very chic boutique. She glanced at Robert, who walked around acting as if he was interested in his wife's shopping needs. She knew he was bored stiff. How could she not love this man? With several fast sweeping motions, she completed one rack and moved on to the next, attempting to speed up the process.

A glimpse of a petite blonde walking out of sight caused Belinda to freeze. Was her mind playing tricks on her?

She turned toward Robert who stood at the next rack. She continued to browse through the clothes. "Robert, what country did Karen move to?"

Robert stopped his meandering and knitted his brows. "I don't know. What made you think of that?"

"I was just thinking about it and wondered if you knew."

"No clue."

"Come on, let's get out of here. I don't see anything I can't live without."

She tucked her arm around Robert's and they walked out to the street. She looked in the direction she had seen the blonde walking, but couldn't see anyone who looked like Karen.

The rest of the week was jam-packed with visits to the Louvre, the Eiffel Tower and multiple museums. In mid-week, the couple had a private tour of Bes de Boulogne, which included a picnic alongside one of the lakes in an English garden-like setting. Their evenings also followed a plan, which included dinner while cruising on the Seine and a night at the Moulin Rouge.

Robert and Belinda frequently laughed that they would need another week off to recover from their honeymoon, but neither would have given up the experience, no matter how exhausting.

On Saturday morning, they met the limousine at the front door of the hotel. They were chauffeured to the private terminal where they boarded the corporate plane bound for Texas. As before, the bedroom had been prepared for them. This time the "Mile High Club" folly didn't even enter their minds. Robert wrapped his arms around Belinda and they slept.

"Jessica, prepare for landing." The pilot's voice crackled over the intercom.

A tall woman stood in the aisle next to Robert. "Please fasten your seat belts." She reached for the empty glasses, and then vanished to the rear of the jet.

Belinda rolled her head toward the window. The clear night sky filled with small pinpoints of light blended with the lights below. The jar of the wheels hitting pavement brought a hint of a smile across her face. She settled her hand over Robert's. He curled his fingers around hers. She rolled her head to face him. They sat locked in each other's gaze as she imagined the rest of their life.

Welcome to *The Kismet Collection*

by
PF Karlin

Shattered Fate is a fictional love story about Robert and Belinda who meet under the most unusual circumstances, but are destined to be apart.

Destiny Reborn is the sequel of Belinda and Robert's life, as the two discover the reasons for their attraction

Fulfilling Destiny is an epilogue of Robert and Belinda's journey through their life.

Follow **PF Karlin**
At
PFKARLIN.COM
as more novels are added to the
The Kismet Collection.

Did you Like What you just Read?
Then write a Review

If you read a book that you enjoyed, share your thoughts with others by writing a review. Written reviews help your favorite authors in several ways.

Positive reviews help increase the books rating on major internet book selling sites. The more positive reviews a book receives the more the book is promoted by the site.

Reviews help other readers determine if they will take a chance and read a book.

Letting people know what you think helps promote your favorite authors to other readers.

So don't be afraid to write a review. You don't have to make it sound like you have a degree in English. The review just needs to be from the heart. Then post it on several sites.

Thank you,

PF Karlin

Share your passion!

About the Authors

Now Writing as **PF Karlin**

Karen Pugh was born in Chicago, Illinois and graduated from Amundsen-Mayfair City College with an ADN in Nursing. She has had a long interest in writing, practicing the craft with contributions to local newsletters. She is a member of RWA. Currently she lives in Texas with her husband.

Linda Fagala was born and raised in Texas, and currently resides there with her husband. She graduated from Stephen F. Austin State University as an art teacher. She is a member of RWA.

Join us as our story of Robert and Belinda continues in our new and exciting series called:

The Kismet Collection